$20.00

MYS   Love, Wlliam F.
F   Bishop's revenge
LOV   4/03

BISHOP'S REVENGE

BY

William Love

DONALD I. FINE, INC.
New York

Library of Congress Cataloging-in-Publication Data
Love, William F.
Bishop's revenge / William F. Love.
p. cm.
ISBN 1-55611-351-X
I. Title.
PS3562.0848B55   1993
813'.54–dc20   92–54462
CIP

Manufactured in the United States of America

10 9 8 7 6 5 4 3 2 1

Designed by Irving Perkins Associates

To Dad—
two parts Regan,
one part Kessler,
and just a dash of Blake.

1

GIVE THINE ENEMY BREAD TO EAT *and water to drink; and thou shalt heap coals of fire upon his head.* Thus the Good Book, and thus my boss, Bishop Francis X. Regan. He threw that one at me right in the middle of the Compton case.

The Compton case. The weirdest case Regan and I ever worked on. Also the one we fought over most, at the time. At the time? Hell, to this day we can't agree on something as simple as when the damn thing even started. Regan insists it was a Monday. I say it was the previous Saturday. But just to prove which of us isn't a total egomaniac . . .

It was Monday, April second, and I was taking dictation. Regan was having a hard time finding the right words. Rolling aimlessly around his office, fingering his pectoral cross for inspiration. Every two seconds his damn wheelchair would squeak, and it was driving me nuts. Of course I couldn't say anything. He'd have just come back with, "Whose responsibility is it to keep it oiled, David?" and he'd have had me.

Regan tends to roll around a lot when he's nervous about something or concentrating extra hard. This time I guess he was both. The letter he was composing was to some rabbi and the boss had decided to use the occasion to teach yours truly a little more about my religion. Somewhere down the line he and my mother made a pact: she wouldn't object to my working for a Catholic bishop if he'd try to make an observant Jew out of me. Fat chance.

He'd have probably spent the rest of the day dithering over that letter—and my lesson in Judaism—if Sister Ernestine hadn't interrupted in her own timid way. God knows how long she'd been in the doorway before we spotted her. I'm convinced the first thing all nuns are taught is how to move without making a sound. "I'm sorry, Bishop," she whispered when he happened to turn her way, "but Mr. Baker is here."

Regan looked relieved. "You're excused, David. This letter can

1

wait." I nodded and closed the notebook. Davis Baker's a friend of mine and we occasionally work together, him being a criminal attorney and me a private investigator (when I'm not working for the Bishop). Just the previous Wednesday he'd phoned about a case he wanted help on and I'd turned him down flat. Now he was probably here to see if, face to face, he could get me to change my mind. But—

"No, Bishop," Ernie said, wringing her hands. "He says he wants to talk to *both* of you. Shall I tell him he'll have to make an appointment?"

Regan frowned at me. I frowned back, as puzzled as he was. Then it hit me what Baker was up to. I cursed under my breath. Not far enough under. Regan raised an eyebrow.

"Is that expletive intended for Mr. Baker? Or for me?"

"Not for you. Not this time. Look, you don't want to see the guy, Bishop. I know exactly why he's here. Let me go kick him out. It'll be a pleasure, believe me."

Regan gave me a long look, turned to Ernie. "Ask Mr. Baker to wait, Sister. Tell him Mr. Goldman and I will be with him shortly."

She turned and went, quickly but without a sound. Nuns.

Regan's eyes narrowed at me. "Now what's this all about, David?"

I showed him both palms. "Listen, Bishop. You don't want to know. I'll just—"

He shut me up with a palm of his own. "Let me hazard a guess: Mr. Baker is here about Eddie Goode. At least that's why you *think* he's here."

That startled me. "Since when did a two-twenty I.Q. give a guy the power to read minds? How the hell did you—?"

"No need to read minds, David. I read newspapers. Yesterday's *Times* reported that Davis Baker is representing Mr. Goode in the Compton matter. That, combined with your anger at his coming, gives rise to the conjecture that he had already approached you about assisting."

I threw up my hands. "I don't know why I bother trying to keep anything from you. Well, since you know why he's here, you know why you don't want to talk to him. I'll just go get rid of him." I got up.

"Why so precipitous, David? Shouldn't we hear what he has to say?"

"I know what he has to say. He told me last Wednesday. And I told him in no uncertain terms where he could go." I sat back down and took a breath. "All right, I didn't exactly yell at him. I mean, he had no idea what he was asking—then. But for him to barge in here today, now that he knows what Goode did—"

"Please, David." Regan's voice was settling into his now-David-let's-just-calm-down tone that really irritates me, which of course is exactly why he does it. "Just tell me what Mr. Baker said."

I gave him a long look and decided he meant it. So I told him about the phone call.

Baker had been all excited. He'd been assigned, he told me, a client who was getting shafted by the D.A. Talking a mile a minute, he gave me the scoop: his client was innocent, it was a put-up job, a good investigator (meaning me) could certainly get to the bottom of it. But he hadn't told me the client's name or what the case was. He finally took time out for some oxygen and I jumped in.

"Okay, Davis, okay. Your guy's innocent. Got it. Just out of curiosity, when was the last time you had a client you didn't think was innocent?"

He growled at me, not in anger. He was just being intense. Dave's very intense. "I do not think all my clients are innocent. In fact I generally think they're guilty as hell. But dammit, not this time." He took a breath. "Look, Davey, this guy Goode didn't do it. What I need for you to do is—"

I cut him off. "Whoa! Who did you say?"

"Oh, right. I guess I hadn't mentioned his name, had I? My client. Guy name of Eddie Goode. Oh, he's gone down a couple times, but on this one he's—"

"Wait a minute, wait a minute! You're defending Eddie Goode? In the Compton murder?"

"Oh, you read about it. Great. Let me tell you what I want. I need you to—"

"Nope. Hold it right there, Counselor. You're wasting valuable time—yours and mine."

"But look, Davey—!"

"No, you look. You want to sell somebody on the idea Eddie Goode's a poor innocent soul who's getting the shaft, you came to the wrong address. Maybe he didn't pull the trigger that blew Compton away, but frankly, my dear, I don't give a damn."

Baker didn't answer for a few seconds, probably because he was trying to remember the quote. Lawyers are really cretins when it comes to classic flicks. Finally: "Are you saying you've got something against Eddie Goode?"

"Yeah, Davis, I guess you could say that. Me—and the Bishop."

"The *Bishop*? What does *he* know about Goode?"

"Oh, this and that. I guess you know, don't you, that Regan was shot eight years ago? By a mugger?"

Baker was irritated. "Of course I do. Who do you think you're talking to? I know all about it. What does that have to do with—"

"You obviously *don't* know all about it. For instance, what was the mugger's name?"

"How the hell should I know? I remember you telling me once, the guy beat the rap, but I don't—"

"Yeah, he beat the rap. A guy named *Eddie Goode*. Your client. You're asking me to help the guy that put Regan in that wheel-chair. For life."

2

THE BOSS HADN'T INTERRUPTED to this point. Now, surprised, he cut in. "Mr. Baker hadn't known Eddie Goode's background?"

I shook my head. "Not the part about you. At that point he hadn't even met Goode."

Regan shook his head. 'He's the man's attorney! How could he not? Hadn't he seen his—what do you call it?"

"Rap sheet? How could he? Like I said, he hadn't even talked to the guy yet."

Regan's face was sour. "I take it he knows the situation now."

"Yeah, I'm sure. But he hadn't then. I could tell by the way he reacted."

There had first been a sharp intake of breath. Then silence. Then, in a whole new tone of voice: "Say again?"

"You heard me, Dave."

"*Damn*, Davey! You have got to be *kidding*! Eddie Goode was the shooter who got the Bishop?"

"The same."

Another silence, this one longer. "Naw, it can't be. Dammit, there's nothing about it on his rap sheet! It's got to be a different Eddie G—"

"Hell no, it's not on his rap sheet! The son of a—" I calmed down. "Look, it's the same guy. I can read, you know. I saw Wednesday's paper, about the cops picking Goode up for the Compton killing. Same guy, trust me."

Baker let out air, which seemed appropriate, me having just punctured his balloon. When his voice came again, it had lost most of its zip. "So. He's the guy that did the Bishop. Damn! I don't know what to say."

"Well, I do. How sweet it is! I can't tell you how good it makes me feel to have Eddie Goode, of all the people in the world, come crawling to me for help! And to be able to kick him in the teeth! Sweet, sweet revenge! Give him a message for me, will you, Davis?" I waited for Baker to respond. He finally muttered something.

"Tell him what goes around comes around, baby. Tell him my only regret is we don't have the electric chair in this state. Since we don't, I hope he enjoys spending the rest of his natural life in Sing-Sing."

"Yeah, I guess. Yeah, well . . . " Baker sounded dazed, which isn't like him. "I was sort of hoping maybe you'd poke around and see what really happened at the Compton mansion Sunday. I mean I've got serious questions on this thing. Like, why'd Eddie go there in the first place? And why would he shoot an unarmed guy, when violence hasn't been part of his track record? And—"

"Hey!" I was getting hot again. "Wouldn't shoot an unarmed guy? Violence hasn't been part of his track record? Have you seen Regan doing much tap dancing lately? What do you mean, violence hasn't—"

"Hey, yourself! Let me finish, will you? I'm talking about his *criminal* record, and over the past couple years. The most violent thing I've heard about's an armed robbery, suspended sentence, and that was ten years ago. Since then, he—"

"Since then, my friend, there's been the little matter of his mugging and shooting an unarmed Catholic Bishop, damn near resulting in said Bishop's death. This was followed by a circus show of an arraignment, with a chicken-livered Assistant D.A. allowing your boy to walk, all because one of your high-priced attorney colleagues screamed civil rights violations, of which there were none. If it hadn't—"

"Hey, calm down, Davey. I'm on your side. But geez, I'm having a hard time absorbing this. My God, Eddie Goode?"

Yeah, Eddie Goode. It had been eight years, but the memories were flowing back like it was yesterday. The night it happened had been a turning point in the Bishop's life—and mine. And no way could either of us have ever seen it coming.

3

IT HAD BEEN SPRINGTIME THEN, too, but a little later in the season— early May, when days that make you think summer's right around the corner are followed by nights that remind you that corner's got lots of sharp edges.

Following a warm day, twilight was phasing into night and it was just starting to get cold. I was regretting not having grabbed my mackinaw before heading for the stake-out. The stake-out— watching the apartment of a former friend of a killer who'd just broken out of prison—was down in the Village. I never made it. The guy I was supposed to replace wound up collecting six hours more overtime than he'd figured on.

I was tooling down Ninth, approaching Thirty-ninth, when the squawkbox came on and I was notified, amid all the static, "Shooting on West Thirty-seventh between Tenth and Eleventh. Victim down, possible fatality. Where are you, One-oh-six?" I wasn't 106, but Tenth and Thirty-seventh was only three blocks away. I flipped on the siren, put the red flasher on the roof and went, radioing my destination as I did. I was on the scene in less than a minute.

The small knot of people spilling out into the street moved back for me. The spinning red light gave their faces a ghoulish cast, but these weren't ghouls. Just people fascinated, as they always are, by danger and possible death.

Naturally, this being New York, not one of them had done a damn thing to help the guy that was down. He was sprawled on the sidewalk, face in the gutter. First thing I noticed about him was the mop of unruly white hair and the expensive dark suit. A wealthy, middle-aged businessman who'd been mugged, I guessed. And, by the looks of him, dead. I was about half right. On both guesses.

I yelled at the crowd to back up and give me room. They obeyed—slowly and sullenly. Nobody ever wants to lose their place in the front row. I eased the victim over on his back as carefully as I could, not liking the loose way his head rolled. I saw the Roman collar and realized I had a priest on my hands. The silver chain, dangling loosely around his neck, should have tipped me he was a bishop, but my knowledge of things Catholic wasn't as developed then. I also didn't know—till later—that the crucifix that should have been attached to it had been ripped off. Literally.

And I had a lot more on my mind than the guy's ecclesiastical standing. Mainly I was noticing that he wasn't breathing and his face was losing color. The squawkbox had told me an ambulance wasn't far behind, so I didn't waste time yelling at people to call. Just concentrated on doing what I could to keep him alive till the medics got there. Which meant mouth-to-mouth like I'd been taught in cop school.

The two minutes I tried to breathe for the poor bastard felt like two hours, and didn't do a thing for him—I thought. Finally the ambulance came barrel-assing up, siren making enough noise to wake the dead which, by then, I figured the guy was. I was still glad to hear it.

I didn't stop mouth-to-mouthing till I felt a hand on my shoulder and the quiet, confident voice, "Two more, officer, and I'll take it...One more...Okay!"

I backed away wiping my mouth, glad to breathe normally for a change, and looked around. Three medics: one on the mouth-to-mouth, one loosening the priest's collar, belt and shoes, and one setting up a respirator. Working quickly and smoothly, they soon had him on a stretcher and into the ambulance without ever interrupting the resuscitation process.

They roared away, siren blaring, and I started questioning bystanders. A surprising number were willing to talk—maybe because the victim was a priest—and I picked up a few details about the guy who'd shot him, the guy that later turned out to be Eddie Goode. One woman, name of Jane O'Connor, had seen the shooter running east, heading for Tenth, and gave me an excellent description of Eddie Goode. "A little dark-haired fella, lots of curly hair, dark pants, maybe they were jeans, fancy running shoes. But he almost tripped, running, 'cause his laces were untied, flopping around all over the place. Very sloppy dresser, you ask me. Disgraceful."

Bob Long, another Homicide sergeant, showed up in about ten minutes, along with a rookie named Joe Parker. It's funny: Long's now dead, I'm off the force and Parker's a seasoned veteran, a Homicide sergeant himself, and one of my closest friends. That was the night we met.

"Hey, took you long enough," I said to Bob after a nod to the rookie.

"Hell, the kid and I had to finish our gin game, Davey. I had him blitzed. Couldn't walk away from that, could I?" The rookie blushed and looked away. He obviously wasn't used to his partner's brand of humor. Long surveyed the scene. "Got this sucker solved yet, Davey?"

"Hell, yes! I mean, I been here ten minutes! You think I been standing around with my finger up my nose?" I got serious. "What's the word on the victim?"

Long waggled his fingers. "Not good. Caught it in the spine. Name's Regan. A Catholic Bishop, no less. Lives on this block." Long squinted at the row of brownstones, pointed at the third one to the west of us. "That's gotta be his there—eight ninety."

I looked where he was pointing. Next to the front door of the house, eight steps above the sidewalk, was a brass plate. I didn't bother trying to make out the words on it. I can now recite them by heart: ROMAN CATHOLIC ARCHDIOCESE OF NEW YORK: BISHOP'S RESIDENCE. Who could have known then that I was squinting at my future home?

Parker cleared away the people, taking down names for later interviews. The threat of more conversation with the cops will scare most people away. While Parker did that, Long and I searched the sidewalk and gutter. I finally located the shell casing in a crack in the gutter ten feet from where the victim had been lying. It smelled of cordite, so it hadn't been there long. Tests later proved it matched the slug they pulled out of Regan's spine.

I went by St. Anthony's Hospital later that night to see how the Bishop was doing.

"He's out of surgery and in ICU," said the head floor nurse, a young nun. "Are you the policeman who saved him?"

"I thought that was Jesus," I cracked, and immediately regretted my fast lip. But this nun had a sense of humor. "Jesus saved his soul, all right," she smiled. "But I think you saved his assets."

She sobered. "Seriously, Sergeant Goldman, I want to thank you. The paramedics told us how fast you responded. Dr. Lindsay did the surgery. He says the Bishop will probably have unimpaired brain function—if he pulls through. All because you reacted fast and knew what to do. And did it."

I shrugged. "Glad to do what I could, ma'am—uh, Sister." I turned to go. "Well, glad he's doing okay. I'll stay in touch. I'm going to go see if I can nail the S.O.B. that did it to him."

She gave me an un-nunlike scowl. "I hope you do, Sergeant. I really and truly hope you do."

4

WELL, I GOT HIM. For all the good it did me. In fact, nailing the shooter turned out to be a piece of cake. A couple of things pointed in the direction of Eddie Goode: his criminal record; the fact that he lived in the neighborhood; but mainly that he'd just been tagged the month before for a grocery store robbery not two blocks away from where the Bishop got it.

So I brought the female witness from Thirty-seventh Street—the one who'd seen a guy running east after the shot—down to HQ to look at some mug shots. I shuffled Goode's picture in with a dozen lookalike thugs, half of them police officers. Her nostrils flared and she went straight to Goode's photo like an Irish setter on point. This O'Connor was middle-aged and pretty much of a hag, but at that moment it was all I could do not to plant a wet one right on her mouth.

Next step was to go get the perp. About five the next morning Parker and I drove to where Goode lived, over near the Hudson. First we established, by phoning and buzzing from downstairs, that he wasn't home. Then we went outside and found a parking place halfway down the block and began what turned out to be a very brief stake-out.

We'd been there less than an hour when here he came from the opposite direction, shuffling and jiggling down the sidewalk, shoelaces flopping. He looked just like Jane O'Connor had described him: a real weasel. A thin, malnourished-looking mustache. Dark, greasy hair. And shifty, darting eyes, trying to look in every direction at once. Unfortunately for him, he couldn't see us hunkered down in the front seat of the Toyota behind dew-fogged windows.

Goode was barely in the building before Joe and I were out of the car and moving. I jimmied the lobby door in nothing flat and we were up the two flights of stairs and on both sides of Eddie before he had his key in the apartment door. One of the tricks of the trade: if you don't have a warrant, get the perp to invite you in.

"Hey! Whaddaya want?" Goode whined as we flashed our badges, his head swiveling back and forth.

"Routine, Eddie," I told him. "Let's go inside. We need to have a little talk."

"Aw, come on!" he moaned. "I gotta get some sleep, guys! Gimme a break, okay?"

I grinned at him. "Glad to, Eddie. But we've got to talk. Want to do it out here in the hall or inside?" He looked up at me, then at Joe. We both gave him innocent looks.

"Aw, to hell wit' it," he muttered. "C'mon in and let's get this over wit'." He opened the door and led Parker and me inside. I looked around. It was even a cut or two below mine, which meant it was no candidate for *House Beautiful*. It smelled of garlic and onions and a few other items I'd just as soon not go into. Eddie threw himself down on the moth-eaten couch just inside the door. "Okay, guys. Ask away."

"Mind if I take a look around, Eddie?" I asked him, careful to go through all the legal hoops. "I might want to rent here sometime."

Goode looked up at me, eyes crafty. He came to a decision. "Sure. Take a look. What do I care?"

I studied him for a second. Sounded like he'd already ditched the weapon. Or had it hidden someplace outside his apartment. But I had nothing to lose by trying. "Get his statement, Joe," I said, "while I take a look around."

Parker glanced at me, back at Eddie. "Okay, Eddie. Something went down last Wednesday night. Mind tellin' me where you were that night? Say between eight and eleven?"

I'm not bad at searches. But fifteen minutes tossing the little apartment got me nowhere. I looked in all the standard places and most of the nonstandard, and found nothing: under the mattress, back of the top shelf of the closet, his bureau drawer beneath the underwear, the well of the toilet. I'd have probably never found it at all if Eddie hadn't gotten a little too cocky when I came back in the living room. My discouraged look must have showed.

"Come on, guys," he whined. "I tolja, I need some shut-eye!

Gimme a break! I didn't do nothin'!" He threw both arms along
the back of the couch and shot me a challenging look. Somehow
his eyes and his posture didn't go with his words. And when I
held his gaze a few seconds he started to get twitchy. I had an
idea.

"Up off the couch, Eddie," I snapped. The sudden flicker of
fear behind his eyes told me I'd guessed right.

He tried to stay put. "Hey, come on, guys, I'm just startin' to
get comf't'ble. I said you could look around but I didn't—"

That was as far as he got. His head flew back as I grabbed a
fistful of lapel and got him upright. Resisting the temptation to
give him a whack with my free hand, I tossed him toward Parker.
If I'd known the way things were going to go down, I'd have
given him a couple.

I had the couch upside down in two seconds, the rattle inside
telling me I'd guessed right. "Come on," Eddie moaned. "This
is illegal, guys! You can't do that! Come on!" I wondered if he
thought his nasal voice was attractive. If so, he was just as wrong
about that as he'd been to think his weapon was in a safe place.

When the gun plopped onto the floor, I gave it a look: Smith
& Wesson .38—exactly what we were looking for. I grabbed it
with a hanky. "Give me that bag," I muttered. Parker didn't let
go of Goode as he reached into his pocket for a plastic bag. I
deposited the gun in it and taped it shut. I put the date and my
initials on it, had Parker initial it, and slipped it into my jacket
pocket. "Let's go, Eddie," I said. "Your nap's going to have to
wait."

His face grew venomous. "*You* wait, asshole! You'll see how
far this gets you. You can't go around breakin' into private homes
without you get a warrant."

"Wrong, Eddie," I told him, trying to smother a feeling I had.
"You invited us in, remember? Bring him along, Joe."

Half an hour later in the interrogation room, Goode was even
more nervous. His eyes refused to look at me or Joe, and his
hands were in constant motion.

"You can't do this to me," he kept saying. "I gotta right to a
phone call."

"Don't be in such a rush," I said wearily. "We'll get to that.

First I just want to know: why'd you do it, Eddie?"

"I didn't do nothin'! I never shot him. I never even went near there!"

"Shot who? Near where?"

"Wherever whatever you're lookin' for went down! I didn't do nothin'!"

"Did you know the guy was a *Bishop*, Eddie? A *Catholic* Bishop? You're a Catholic, aren't you, Eddie?"

Goode's eyes were wild. "Shit, *I* didn't know who the hell he was! I didn't even see the cross till—" His mouth snapped shut. His eyes got wise.

"Hey, I've said everything I'm gonna say, asshole. Either lemme out of here or let me call a lawyer. I got rights, you know. I'm a citizen of the U.S. of A., and you can't hold me this long without I get a phone call."

"Fine, Eddie," I said, getting up. "Call anyone you like. I'd call my landlord if I were you. You're not going to be needing that apartment anymore."

Shows how much I knew. Just like Eddie, I'd let myself get a little too cocky.

5

OH, IT SEEMED LIKE a pretty good day's work at the time. I'd nabbed Eddie Goode, I'd impounded what I was pretty sure (and what Ballistics later proved) was the gun that had shot Regan. To put the icing on the cake, in a manner of speaking, it also happened to be my twenty-seventh birthday. Lousiest birthday of my life. Because that was the day I met Cabot Crowe.

I'd got Goode printed, booked and into a nice warm cell and was back at my desk, typing up the report, when the phone rang. The front desk: my pal, Molly, known to her nearest and dearest as Sergeant Folsom. She didn't start out with an insult, which should have clued me that something was off-kilter. "Davey, uh, there's a Mr. Crowe here to see you. He's with the District Attorney's office."

I was harried and out of sorts. And it was the first time I'd ever heard Crowe's name. "Crowe? Don't know him. He an A.D.A.?" I continued typing as I talked.

"That's right, Davey. He wants to see you." I stopped typing and frowned. What was with Molly? Normally she's a fun-time gal, full of jokes and jive. Why so serious? Furthermore, why hadn't she told the guy to just come on back? "What's the problem?" I barked. "He got a broken leg or something? Send him on back."

Her voice was prim. "He'll wait for you here, Davey." She hung up.

"What the hell is this?" I grumbled, getting to my feet with a last look at the report rolled into the typewriter. Shaking my head disgustedly, I hurried to the front desk.

Molly looked relieved to see me. Standing in front of her, feet apart, expensive attaché case gripped in both hands, was an officious-looking, smooth-faced guy about my age, height and weight. His hair was Ivy League, short and neat; shirt a white buttondown; suit expensively tailored. Everything about him reeked of prep school.

He extended a manicured hand and looked down his patrician nose at me. "Sergeant Goldman?" I admitted it. "We have to talk. I've been appointed to represent the people in the matter of Edward Goode."

I'm serious, those were his exact words. He obviously needed taking down a peg or two, and I figured I was just the guy to do it. I poked him in the chest. "About damn time you got here! *I'm* people, and I was getting pretty damn tired of being unrepresented. Where the hell you been?"

The lawyer gave me a long, slow look, and then a smile as narrow as his nose. "I think we'll do better, Sergeant, without the humor. Is there some place we can talk? I'm here to take your statement."

That was the inauspicious start of my short, unhappy relationship with Cabot Crowe, one of the two biggest jerks it's ever been my displeasure to know. The other's a guy named Charlie

Blake, who's a cop—a lieutenant, in fact. Charlie started out with me as a rookie fourteen years ago, and we failed to hit it off from day one. Crowe's the only other guy I've ever known who could even come close to Blake in overall jerkiness. He had a way of— well, let me just tell you what happened.

I found us a conference room, then had to wait while Crowe used his handkerchief to dust every surface he or anything he owned might come into contact with. That done, he sat, placed a spotless white legal pad on the part of the table he'd dusted, shot his cuffs and pulled out a gold pen. "Now. Tell me everything you witnessed, Sergeant. From the beginning."

I couldn't resist. "From the beginning. Okay. Of course there was the doctor. And a couple of nurses. It's funny, I can't remember seeing my mother, though I must've, because—"

Crowe, writing furiously, raised his left hand to cut me off. He stopped, frowned at what he'd written, then at me. "Your mother? What are you talking about?" Crowe's voice and face were in a battle over which was more irritated.

"When I was born, of course. Next thing I saw was the little crib they put me in. Well, it wasn't exactly a crib. I think it was one of those—"

"Sergeant!" Crowe's smooth face was pink with anger. "I'm sure you get plenty of laughs around the station. But when you're giving a statement to me, I'll thank you to remember you're a professional. *If* you don't mind." He ran his thumbnail along the perforated top of the sheet he'd been writing on, pulled it from the pad, placed it aside and gave me a long look. "Now. If you'll start again, Sergeant. I'm interested in the incident of last night. What happened?"

I shrugged. "Well, you said from the beginning."

Crowe took a breath. "Yes. I'm well aware of your reputation, Sergeant, as the station clown. I am not amused. And I haven't got all day."

"You don't? Then you're going to have to tighten up your questioning technique, aren't you? Okay, last night. The dispatcher's call came through at eight fifty-one. I immediately proceeded to . . ."

That's the way things started off between me and this self-important jackass the D.A. had seen fit to inflict on me. From that scintillating start things went downhill fast. I'd never cared that much for Harrington anyway, and his assigning Crowe to the Regan case didn't improve my opinion of him any. I'm no lawyer, but like most cops I always had feelings about any prosecutor I got assigned to work with. Cabot Crowe was not only obnoxious, he had to be one of the worst lawyers I ever met. And when Aaron Lovitz signed on to represent Goode, Crowe really went to pieces.

I saw that the first day he and I went over the evidence we— meaning I—had managed to collect. I was conscientiously twiddling my thumbs while Crowe reviewed the statement I'd taken from the old gal, Jane O'Connor. When he finished he flipped it back to me. "Your phraseology could use some work, Sergeant. But in this instance it doesn't matter. That testimony's unusable."

I stared at him. "Say what?"

Crowe patted a yawn. "No can use, Sergeant. She's just not credible."

Images flashed through my mind: the way Jane O'Connor's hands had trembled when she picked Goode out of the line-up; how her eyes had come alive when I'd assured her he'd be put away, thanks to her; the way Crowe's throat was going to feel when I got my hands around it.

My voice returned. "Not credible? Not credible? What're you talking about? Goddamn, she not only saw the guy running from the scene and gave a positive I.D., she picked him out of a lineup. What the hell do you want? An egg in your beer?"

Crowe smiled in his superior way and stood up. "Mr. Lovitz would tear her to pieces." He sounded like a teacher trying to explain geography to a first-grader. "He would point out that she was excited, she was confused, she didn't see the actual shooting. Mr. Lovitz would have a field day. What we have, Sergeant, is a tenuous case—tenuous at best. If you'll excuse me?" Apparently the meeting was over.

He strode from the room, wingtips flashing. I sat awhile, fuming. After I calmed down, I decided I needed to dig up more evidence.

So I got Judge McKinnick to issue a search warrant. I grabbed

Bob Long—a good reliable witness in case we found anything—
and went back to Goode's apartment.

We hadn't been there ten minutes when I got lucky. At the
bottom of a cigar box on top of Eddie's dresser lay a silver crucifix.
In the jumble of cheap cufflinks and various assorted gewgaws,
it stood out like a nun in a whorehouse.

"Hey, Bob!" Long was at my side in three seconds. I nodded
at the box. "Look at this."

Long gingerly pushed some of the jumble aside to see the cross
better. "Geez, I didn't know Eddie was so religious."

"Yeah, impressive, isn't it? Be funny, wouldn't it, if this turned
out to be the—what do you call it?—pectoral cross Regan's
missing?"

Long pulled out a baggie. We copped the cross and took it to
the lab. Once they were through with it I wasted no time taking
it to Regan's bedside. He still looked lousy, hooked up to a bunch
of tubes. His green eyes were red-rimmed and drowsy.

"Sorry to bother you, Bishop, but I need to know something.
Is this yours?" I showed him the cross.

His eyes closed as he took it. "Yes," he sighed. "This is my
pectoral cross. It was a gift from my—no matter." His eyes opened
again and found me. His voice was slurred. "The criminal's been
apprehended?"

"Well," I hedged, "we have a suspect..." Regan smiled
weakly. "Okay, Bishop. Yeah, it's the guy." I told Regan about
how I'd nabbed Eddie Goode, and how I'd found the cross. He
sighed and closed his eyes.

"Thank you, Sergeant. I only wish I could identify him."

"Oh, you'll get your chance, don't worry. When you're better
we'll have you down to the station to look at a line-up."

He gave a slight shake of the head. "No point, Sergeant. I have
no memory of that evening."

"Sure, I know. But maybe seeing the guy will trigger something."

No such luck. He tried, but seeing Goode didn't trigger a thing.
The only guy in the line-up he had even a slight suspicion of
was Officer Mike Hanley, and Mike's alibi was airtight.

Also not helping the case, at least according to Cabot Crowe, was the way I had gone about collecting the evidence. He was in daily contact with Aaron Lovitz. It's hard for me to believe even now, but thanks to the combination of a feisty defense lawyer and a gutless prosecutor, our case was about to go up in smoke.

6

CROWE CALLED ME OVER to his office to give me the bad news the day after Regan viewed the line-up. Seems I hadn't dotted all the I's and crossed all the T's. At least not enough to satisfy the lawyers.

Crowe took a blustering tone. "Your search warrant specified 'weapons or other paraphernalia involved in a crime.' But you picked up a cross. That's neither a weapon nor is it paraphernalia, Sergeant. So how can you say it's covered under the search warrant?"

I looked at the attorney. "What are you saying? That I should've got a warrant for this particular cross? I didn't know this particular cross was there! That's why I said *paraphernalia*."

Crowe was getting a little red. "A cross is not *paraphernalia*. You had no right to carry it out of there."

I shook my head in disgust. "That's so much horse crap, Crowe, and you know it. Why don't you let Lovitz represent Goode? You're supposed to be representing the people."

Crowe was embarrassed. And mad. "It is wonderful, Sergeant, how completely justified you feel in telling me what I'm supposed to be doing. It's too bad I bothered to go to the trouble of getting a law degree when apparently you know my profession without any training at all."

I took a breath and tried to control my temper. "Look. I'm not trying to practice law. I'm telling you I was in that apartment legally. And I had every reason to suspect that cross was stolen property. Which it was."

Crowe shook his head. "Your warrant didn't authorize you to

search for stolen property." He sighed. "It gave you the right to search for weapons or paraphernalia that might be *used* in a robbery. Mr. Lovitz is extremely unhappy and has every right to be. He'll make sure no jury will ever see that cross. Or the gun, for that matter."

I blew up. I probably do that oftener than I should. "The gun? What's the matter with the gun? Are you nuts?"

Crowe cleared his throat. "I'm not satisfied with the way you found it. Goode claims you forced your way into his apartment. You had no warrant. You had—"

"We asked his permission! Both Parker and I are in agreement on that. We asked permission to come in, and we asked permission to search. And he gave it."

Crowe tried to look me in the eye. It didn't quite come off. "He says you used force to get him to agree. Did you?"

"No. And you can talk to Parker, too."

"Parker's a rookie and Goode's lawyer thinks you're intimidating him into backing your story and that you did use force on Goode. And I'm inclined to agree with him." Crowe turned away. "So the gun's tainted evidence." He looked out the window. "We can't get it before the court."

I couldn't believe this. My voice went up a half-octave. "You're throwing out the gun *too?*"

Crowe looked away. "Lovitz says you—"

"The hell with what Lovitz says! What do *you* say?"

Crowe's answer was almost inaudible. "I don't think we can use it. Frankly, I don't think the jury will believe your story."

I gave him a long look. "I guess that means you don't. Right?"

He shrugged. "What I believe or don't believe doesn't matter. I have to look at what will appear credible to a jury. And I just don't think—"

"What you don't think is that you're any match for Lovitz. And you know what? You're right. What you're doing is lying down and letting him roll all over you." Crowe reddened. I took a breath. "So. Where does this leave us?"

Still avoiding my eye, Crowe got to his feet and picked up his briefcase. "It leaves us nowhere, Sergeant. We've decided not to pursue the case. The District Attorney has instructed me to drop it."

That took a second to sink in. When I finally spoke I was surprised at how quiet I was. "Say that again."

The lawyer shifted weight, passed the attaché case from right hand to left. He looked away. "I said . . . " His voice gained confidence and volume as he spoke. " . . . we've decided not to pursue the case. I've thought long and hard about it. The evidence isn't in credible form. The victim's unable to make an identification. And we're open to all sorts of charges of wrongfully obtained evidence and witnesses. Oh, and the old woman, that Mrs. O'Brien—"

"O'Connor!"

"Whatever. She's not credible, Sergeant, regardless of what you or I might like to believe. No jury's going to accept her identification." Crowe took a breath. "So what do we have? No gun—thanks to your poor judgment. No eyewitness, no circumstantial. Leaving us with nothing."

"Nothing." I shook my head. "So what happens to Eddie Goode? He walks?"

Crowe nodded. "He walks. What we'll try to do is—Sergeant! Where are you going?"

I didn't bother to turn around or raise my voice. I don't even know if he heard me. "I'm walking," I said. "If Eddie Goode can walk, so can I."

It would have ended there, with Cabot Crowe high up on my enemies list but no ill effects for either of us, if he'd just left it alone. But of course he hadn't.

Our next—and final—meeting was the very next day, in the basement cafeteria at Headquarters. I was carrying my tray to the back where I'd seen a couple of buddies. And at a table I had to pass were Crowe, and a couple of other A.D.A.'s I knew slightly, and a very attractive young lady I didn't know. Fran Wilson and I later became very good friends, but I didn't know her then. She'd just graduated from NYU Law School and was brand-new to the D.A.'s office. Fran's presence, I guess, inspired Crowe to show off. With disastrous results—for us both.

"Behold the eager beaver," he proclaimed to his cohort, making sure I could hear him. I stopped and looked down at him. He smiled up at me in his superior way, then glanced around the table.

"Object lesson in what we're talking about, people: how a policeman is *not* to behave." He smiled up at me. "Sergeant Goldman believes in prancing around and digging up dirt on those he likes to call 'offenders'—excuse me, I guess it's 'perps,' isn't it, Sergeant?—regardless of any and all constitutional rights said 'perps' might have. Right, Sergeant?" He smiled innocently.

I could feel my blood pressure rising. After a struggle, I decided not to say anything I'd regret later. I started to move on. I should have stayed with that notion. But of course I didn't.

"Oh, don't leave, Sergeant," Crowe called after me. "I have a question for you." I gritted my teeth and turned to face him. His smile widened even as his eyes got meaner. "Have I been able to teach you anything about the proper way to collect evidence?"

His sideward glance at the pretty woman on his left made it clear who he was grandstanding for. And I have to admit, what I did next may also have had something to do with her too. Not the dumbest move I've made in fourteen years of law enforcement, but right up there.

I set my tray on the table, turned deliberately and leaned over to get my face about two inches from Crowe's. Several conversations at nearby tables died down. I spoke loud enough so no one had to strain.

"Well, Cab, I don't know about evidence, but yeah, you've taught me a few things. You've taught me what a little effin' chicken you are. You've taught me you'd rather let a criminal walk than use good evidence to try to convict him—if you can find a way to lay your shortcomings off on the police officer who's trying to help. And you've taught me that you're a big blowhard with no real guts."

Crowe reddened. "You can't talk to me that way! Back off!" He shoved me away and stood up. I didn't much care for the shove but let it pass. I'm afraid that gave Crowe the wrong idea. So he shoved me again. "Look buster, you're a lousy cop. You botched this case and you—"

I slapped him. Dumb move. Maybe it was the shoves, maybe it was the jerk telling me I didn't know my job, maybe it was the "buster." Whatever, it was dumb. The back of my hand caught him flush on the cheek with a crack that resounded around the room. I regretted it as soon as I did it.

For a second I didn't move, hoping he'd hit me back—for a couple of reasons. First, simple justice: I had it coming. Better reason: if he hit me back—harder than I'd hit him—and I let it go, I could claim it was just a little dust-up. Disgraceful, maybe, but nothing permanently damaging. But as usual, Crowe didn't do what he should have. He just glared at me, his face equal parts fear and anger. "You hit me!"

"Hey, I'm sorry, man. Look..." I tried to smooth his lapels "...I got a little carried away. Just let me—"

Crowe pushed my hands away. "I'm bringing you up on charges, Sergeant! I'm going to have your badge!" He turned and left with all the dignity he could muster.

I'd gone too far and I knew it. Crowe was bound to report it— in some sanitized version—to the D.A. And Harrington wasn't the type to let something like this slide. The atmosphere around Headquarters changed instantly. People avoiding me. Eyes averted when I walked down the hall. My career as a cop had entered its final hours.

Of course, Molly, the desk sergeant, would kid the Devil himself if he ever got within earshot of her. "Hey, Davey! Hear you nailed Little Lord Fauntleroy pretty good yesterday. Sorry I missed it." She got serious. "But you're out on thin ice, fella. Fact, word is you're outta here."

I shrugged. "Maybe so, sweetheart, but it was worth it. I'd had about all of Cabot Crowe I could take."

She grinned. "Amen to that."

Noon, two days later, Kessler called me in. The office was filled with pipe smoke and he was stroking his beard like a maniac. You can measure his nervousness by how fast he strokes that goatee of his. Or puffs his pipe. So I made it easy for him. Maintaining to the end my image as the office clown, I pretended to search under his desk. "What're you doing?" he growled.

"Just looking for the ax, Inspector. I don't think you called me in just to discuss last night's Mets debacle out at Shea." I grinned at him. "This *is* an axing, isn't it?"

Kessler quit worrying the goatee, put his pipe down and sighed.

"It is if the scuttlebutt's accurate about what you did to Assistant District Attorney Crowe."

I chuckled. "Would the grapevine lie?" Kessler didn't smile, so I got serious. "Yeah, I told the S.O.B. off. And, tell you the truth, sir, I'd do it again—in a minute. I've never seen a guy ask for it so long or so hard."

Kessler shook his head. "Davey, Davey." He gave me a long look. "Let me tell you the facts of life, okay? You may not know it, but I've gone out on a few limbs for you. Not that I minded. You're a good cop and I've liked having you with me."

He sighed. "But your procedures! God knows, I've talked to you about it. About the right and the wrong way of doing things. But I could never get through to you. Shortcuts, shortcuts. Your way of avoiding search warrants, the way you lie to prisoners. You want things slick and fast and easy, don't you, Davey?"

"You want me to answer that, sir?"

"Not really. Thing is, I've always put up with it because you're a damn good cop, and I wanted you on the force. I took some heat for you on the Kessenich thing, and I even went to see the Commissioner when the Mayor asked for your head in the Kalafut affair." He shook his head again and looked at the ceiling. "But this time you've gone too far, Davey."

I nodded and shrugged. He raised his hands in a gesture of helplessness. "You went over the line, Davey. You know the rules. Harrington's turf is sacred. And he's really on the warpath this time."

The Inspector leaned forward and lowered his voice. "Between you and me, he doesn't like Crowe much more than you do. Guy's pissed off half the judges in the city, and the other A.D.A.'s don't like him. He's a total jerk. But this! There's no way Harrington can overlook it! Too many people saw and heard that incident in the cafeteria. That was dumb, Davey, real dumb. I'm sorry—resign now or Harrington'll bring charges."

And that was it. Kessler's not the most decisive boss I've ever had, but take him over the edge and you're history.

That night, some of the guys took me across the street to Ace's, and I got satisfactorily smashed, as did most of the others. Next morning, I got out of bed with a hangover and nowhere to go.

After a few days' unpaid vacation I jumped into detective work. Probably not the brightest career move I ever made, but what else did I know? I'd gone into the force right out of junior college six years before and never even considered anything else. A good golfing buddy, Dennis Kelley, was—and is—a private eye. He invited me to join his agency. Nice of him, but I told him I didn't want to work for somebody else, even if the somebody else was a friend.

"Hell, I've got plenty of work, Davey," he argued. "More than I can handle." Kelley'd already given me a commission schedule he'd worked out for me, based on how much business I brought in, success rates on cases taken, referrals followed up on. Sounded like everything depended on finding clients.

"I don't get it, Dennis," I complained. "When does a guy get around to doing some actual investigating? Frankly, all this business crap bores me to death."

Dennis's wide Irish face lit up in a grin. "Name of the game, Davey. Hell, I don't need guys working on cases, I need guys who can bring in the business. And hey—with all the contacts you've made in six years on the force, you'd be perfect!"

I took a pass. It was depressing to think of myself as a salesman. ("And this month only, we're offering a special on tailing wives. Just present this coupon...")

So I told Kelley nothing doing, and went out and opened up my own office. Found a little cubbyhole for under five hundred a month, down on Avenue D, just a couple of blocks from where I grew up. And began a new lifestyle: starvation.

7

I'D BEEN A PRIVATE INVESTIGATOR about five months when I got the phone call that would change my life. It was Bob Long with his usual "How's it goin', pal?"

I glanced around the office with its dilapidated secondhand

furniture, the paint peeling from the walls and the window so dirty I could barely make out the equally dirty window in the next building twenty feet away.

"Great, Robert! Couldn't be better! What's new with you, buddy?"

"You lucky bastard!" Long sounded wistful. "You pull that asshole's chain, get your ass fired and wind up smellin' like a damn rose. You were just effin' born lucky!"

"Aw hell, Robert, you know, one of these days you're going to wake up and smell the coffee, quit like I did and start giving me some competition. Till then I got it made." My last job had been for a guy looking for his wife who'd walked out on him. Finding her had cost me triple the retainer, but I'd done it. In the three weeks since, my only business activity had consisted of chasing the bozo for the rest of my fee.

That day's crop of mail was two items: my own letter to my so-called client, returned and marked, MOVED, LEFT NO FORWARD- ING ADDRESS; and a letter from the collection agency my landlord had sicced on me. The latter ignored my generous offer to do some skip-tracing for them at very reasonable rates, and told me my furniture was going to be impounded if the entire rent wasn't brought current within seventy-two hours. Some threat. I put the fair market value of all the furniture in my office at $2.98. Unless you wanted to deduct what I owed on it, in which case we're talking heavy negative.

Bob got to the point. "Anyway, Davey, I'm calling to tell you an old friend of yours is looking for you. Wants you to give him a call. Bishop Regan."

I frowned, then remembered. Oh yeah, the guy Eddie Goode had shot. I'd lost track of him after he'd gone home from the hospital. Word was he'd never walk again.

"How's he doing, Bob? In a wheelchair?"

"No idea, Davey. Hell, call him. I hear he thinks you did him a favor. Probably wants to bless your circumcision."

I wasn't about to let Bob get away with that, and the conver- sation degenerated into a round of mutual insults. Which is too bad because it's the last time I ever talked to Bob. Two months later, on what was supposed to be a routine drug bust, something went wrong, bullets started flying and he caught one in the eye;

he never even made it to the hospital. Shit happens.

Despite having matters of grave importance to attend to—such things as making an accurate count of all the cracks in the office ceiling before my eviction—I worked a call to the Bishop into my busy schedule.

"Mr. Goldman," Regan said, after I identified myself. His voice sounded crisper than I remembered it. "Thank you for returning my call. I understand that you've resigned from the police force."

"Yeah. Decided to go it on my own. What can I do for you, Bishop?"

When Regan's voice came again it sounded uncomfortable. "Frankly, Mr. Goldman, I want to thank you. Putting it bluntly, I owe you my life."

"You don't owe me a thing, Bishop. Part of the job. If I hadn't been there, somebody else would've—"

"Nonsense. You *were* there and performed admirably by all accounts. I do owe you my life. Along with considerable gratitude." I gave up. Why argue with someone that stubborn? He continued, "I'd like you to join me for lunch the next day you're free. To thank you in person."

I gave him the standard, "Hey, you don't have to do that, besides, I'm real busy," blah, blah. But he kept insisting, so what the hell. Guy wants to thank you, what are you going to do? The following Tuesday I was at his door at one o'clock sharp.

And got my first view of the interior of 890 West Thirty-seventh. And of Sister Ernestine Regnery, O.S.F. Little knowing I was going to be seeing a lot more of both.

Ernestine let me in. (It was months before I started calling her "Ernie.") In her modified nun's habit—black veil, calf-length skirt, black hose, sturdy black shoes—she was a forbidding sight at first. Then she smiled and I saw the twinkle in her clear blue eyes. "Mr. Goldman! Welcome!" She pumped my hand. Nothing wrong with her grip, either. "I'm so grateful for what you did for the Bishop." The blue eyes misted.

I mumbled something and she led me down the hall to the Bishop's office. I scoped the room. In one incisive glance I absorbed every detail: the crucifix and the Van Gogh prints on the walls, the big oak desk in the center of the colorful Karastan rug, the two south windows with their view of the back of Sally

Mueller's brownstone across the courtway. Not to mention the computer on the right-hand wall flanked by the antique chessboard and the big fat Webster's Unabridged on its pivoted stand. And finally, the fact that the room measured exactly thirty-nine by twenty-four feet. Amazing the powers of observation you develop during six years of police work.

You're not buying? Okay, okay, so I didn't get it all that first day. So it did take several months of living and working on the premises.

Truth is, at that moment I was too busy checking out the Bishop in his wheelchair to notice much else. His purple clerical robe was hiked halfway to his knees to avoid getting it caught in the wheels, revealing the black pants covering the useless legs and the shiny black shoes with their pristine soles.

The new silver crucifix that dangled from the chain around his neck, I later learned, had come to him from the Pope just the week before, along with a personal handwritten note about the accident. Years later Regan would show me the note, his pleasure in it obvious despite his grumbling that it was "probably penned by some sycophantic Vatican underling."

Regan's handsome face was impassive as he studied me, purple skullcap perched on his mop of silvery hair. I later learned he uses the same kind of pin to anchor it as I use on my *yarmulke* on those infrequent occasions I wear it.

"So you're the redoubtable Mr. Goldman," he said, pushing himself toward me with outstretched hand, green eyes steady, no smile in evidence. As I later learned, he's not much of a smiler. "You visited my hospital room several times, didn't you? My memory of those days is deficient, but I vaguely remember your face."

"Yeah, that's me," I said, shaking his hand, surprised at the strength of his grip. His hand was as big as mine and at least as muscular. "I guess I dropped in once or twice. No big deal."

He spun away and headed for the windows, raising his voice. "Life is not made up of 'big deals,' Mr. Goldman. I am deeply grateful for your kindness." At the window he turned the chair to face me, shadowed by the light behind him. "You saved my life, sir. But you did more: you visited me. You are Jewish, Mr. Goldman?"

The change of subject threw me, but I managed a "Yeah." Before I knew it we were into a discussion of the history of Judaism, something I'd gotten plenty of in Hebrew school, though not enough to keep up with the Bishop. I found myself enjoying him, even if his interests were a little dry. I mean, who really gives a damn whether the Book of Judith is part of the Bible or not? Or whether the Babylonian Talmud is closer to ancient Jewish tradition than the Palestinian? Or why? Still, it was kind of fun to talk with a guy who obviously knew so much about so many different things. And he seemed to enjoy instructing me.

The lunch was up to the standard of the conversation, with Ernie's fricasseed chicken and rice winning a lot of favorable comments from both of us. Ernie has, I have since learned, her blind spots as a cook, but some things she does superbly, and she was in top form that day. I guess she figured nothing was too good for the guy who'd saved her boss's life.

Back in the office after lunch, the Bishop made his pitch. I could see *something* was on his mind by the way he couldn't keep his wheelchair still.

"What are you doing to keep busy these days?" He put his empty coffee cup on his desk.

I shrugged. "Working for myself. Best thing I ever did." Right.

He gave his chair a powerful push to his left. "I see. Doing what?"

"Investigating. Private investigations. I have a license from the State of New York. You ought to try me sometime. What did you say you were? Head of Personnel for the Catholic Church in New York? You ought to hire me to tail some of your clergy. Might be surprised what you'd learn."

Regan moved back to his right, a ghost of a smile on his lips. "I doubt it. But thanks for the offer." He suddenly stopped and turned the chair in my direction. He gave me the most direct look he'd shown me so far. "What would you think of coming to work for me?"

I stared at him.

8

TALK ABOUT GETTING BLINDSIDED "Work for you? Is this some kind of joke?"

"Not at all." Regan sure looked serious.

I shook my head. "Doing what?"

He shrugged and met my gaze. "A wide variety of tasks. You've mentioned that you have some proficiency in shorthand. And that you type eighty words a minute. Your mode of speech suggests your intelligence is above average. All of which prompts the conjecture that you would make a very adequate assistant.

"What the job requires, Mr. Goldman, is a man with stenographic as well as—other abilities. Strength, frankly, is a *sine qua non*. Despite my disability I am still fairly capable. But there are certain—problems."

He sighed. "For instance, this house. Though the archdiocesan real estate manual, with characteristic pomposity, calls it an 'episcopal mansion,' it is, in fact, a multi-story brownstone. With all the attendant difficulties for one without the use of his legs. I have considered moving."

He gave a helpless shrug. "But in the six years I have lived here I have grown accustomed to it. It suits me. So I had an elevator installed instead. Utilizing the original dumbwaiter shaft, long since fallen into desuetude, I managed to have it put in without excessive expense. Of course that means the terminus on this floor is the kitchen, hardly what I've had chosen, *ceteris paribus*. But it suffices."

Regan grimaced. "Nonetheless, remaining here means that I require some rather muscular and dextrous assistance from time to time. Assistance which, by the looks of you, would present no great problem." I was embarrassed and probably showed it.

If I did, he ignored it. "You should understand, Mr. Goldman, my assistants up to now have all been priests. Unfortunately, since my—disability, no priest has proved adequate." His face reddened. "I'll grant that the problem may lie with me. Frankly, Mr. Goldman, I am not necessarily the most engaging administrator in the archdiocese. My fellow clergy—some of them—regard me as irascible and overdemanding; that judgment may not be entirely without merit. You stand warned." I shrugged.

"Well," he went on, "you see the problem. I am without an assistant, an untenable state of affairs for both Sister and myself. Having a layman in the post would be, umm, unusual, but not unprecedented. Of course, you would have to live here, but you're single and shouldn't find that burdensome. The accommodations, while not palatial—despite the appellation—are certainly adequate."

Regan spun his chair and headed for the windows. I've since learned that's his way of giving listeners some room to ponder what he's said, not a bad idea considering all the three-dollar words. I even threw a glance at the big dictionary and wondered how he'd react if I went to it and started looking up *appellation* and *desuetude* and *palatial* and a few others. I decided against it.

Because I'd got the gist and was already seriously considering it. On the one hand, playing nursemaid to a guy in a wheelchair wasn't the job I'd always dreamed of. On the other, it had its points.

For one thing, I liked the Bishop. His vocabulary was a little intimidating, but he was obviously just doing what came naturally, not trying to show off. Also, he liked hearing me talk about my experiences as a cop. And his mind seemed to work the way a cop's does. A very brainy cop.

But the two best reasons for accepting his offer were my landlords. The company that rented me my office was about to take it back, and I'd just received the first eviction notice from my apartment landlord. And I had other, lesser worries: New York Telephone, Con Ed, VISA—all were sending me hate mail. Unless I could come up with a quick five grand, I was soon going to be in bankruptcy court. And the prospects for a quick—or even a slow—five grand were close to nil.

Oh, I had a place to lay my head if it came to that, but what guy wants to move back in with his mother? The Bishop's offer, if that's what it was, was an answer to a prayer, if I prayed, which

I don't. I was tempted. But I didn't want to seem easy.

"Geez, I don't know." Regan, now at the south windows, spun to face me. I cleared my throat. "Wouldn't you get a lot of flak from the Pope or someone? I'm not Christian. In fact, to tell you the truth, I don't even believe in God."

Regan's cheek twitched. "That might be a breath of fresh air." He waved it away. "Not a problem, Mr. Goldman—unless it is for you. At least not insurmountable. The Cardinal is being quite, umm, accommodating with me at the moment."

I nodded. The hour and a half I'd just spent with him had told me Regan didn't worry too much about flak. I'd said it mainly to eliminate any misunderstanding. And to give him an out if he wanted one. But I had another problem and this one was real. I looked away.

"Even so, I guess not, Bishop. That is, unless..." I met his eyes. "...I could do it on a part-time basis. So I could keep working as a P.I. on my own time."

Regan gave me a long look. I'm convinced that was the moment he realized that having a private investigator under his roof would give him the opportunity to involve himself in criminal investigations. (He denies that, of course.) "Well," he finally said. "I'd prefer a full-time commitment, certainly. But to be honest, the priests who have held this position have themselves not been free of other duties—be they pastoral or scholarly. So—why not?"

I nodded, relieved. "So how much time would you need from me?"

Regan squinted at the ceiling and pulled in some air. "Well, let's see. I suppose I could get by with a thirty-hour-a-week employee. Satisfactory?" I nodded.

Regan pivoted and rolled over to the computer. Stared at it as if a secret message were printed on its screen. Maybe it was, because when he turned back to me his eyes showed no more doubt.

"So we're agreed?"

I grinned. This was getting out of hand. "Whoa! Aren't we getting a little ahead of ourselves?"

"Not at all. You have agreed to give me thirty hours a week, and I find that acceptable. How soon can you start?"

"That may depend on what you're willing to pay."

I laughed contemptuously at his first offer but all my cajoling couldn't hike it more than another fifty cents an hour. Well, every little four bits helps when you're starving.

The following week I moved in. And have been there ever since.

Well, I'm not there *all* the time. Lots of evenings I don't get home till three or four A.M., depending on how Sally Castle and I are feeling about each other at the moment. And I think Regan has come to realize, over the years, that he doesn't need me nearly as much as he once thought he did. But we're comfortable around each other—most of the time. When we're not . . . well, that's when it gets interesting around the old mansion.

Then, or when we're working on a case. I said a minute ago that Regan eventually started elbowing in on my cases. It happened gradually and without much foresight, at least on my part. Started with him just listening. Then he went on to make some suggestions. Then I started taking his suggestions seriously. Then—

Well, he became what you might call my consulting partner the day Father Willie Fuller woke up in the same apartment with a murdered woman and came running to Regan for aid, support and counsel. The Bishop enlisted me to help solve the thing before the cops learned about the priest's peccadillo (which was *not* Regan's word for what Willie had done). I worked the case, but Regan solved it. Solved it? Hell, not only did he dope it out just in time to keep the cops off Willie's back, he damn near bought the farm himself.

Then some poor schmuck from out of town, an Okie named Jerry Fanning, got arrested for a series of murders. Since Regan couldn't believe a born-again type like Jerry would go around offing prostitutes, he jumped in again with both feet.

Most recently there'd been the Carney case. The cops had it doped one way; Regan another. And Regan turned out to be right.

Davis Baker had been involved in all three of those cases—mostly as the defense attorney for the guy we were trying to help. So he'd seen firsthand how Regan's mind operated. And that's why he'd come, I was sure: he was looking for Regan's help for his client, Eddie Goode.

Well, it wasn't going to do him any, you'll pardon the expression, good. Over the years I've come to know Regan pretty well, and how he thinks. I knew that the only way my boss'd take on a case having anything to do with Eddie Goode would be if it promised to send him straight to Sing-Sing.

Which just goes to show: you don't always know people and their motivations half as well as you think you do.

9

I COULDN'T BELIEVE IT: Davis Baker was really and truly embarrassed. The Bishop was about a hundred times politer than the lawyer deserved, but Dave was still having a hard time meeting his eye. You'd have thought it was him, not his client, who'd been accused of killing Laddie Compton.

"I apologize for this, Bishop. And to you too, Davey." He reddened. "Only thing is, I'm at my wit's end. I'm trying to get a case together and—" He stopped and got my eye. Took a while because I wasn't feeling very friendly toward him right then, but he waited.

"Remember the Penniston case, Davey?" He went from me to Regan. "I know you do, Bishop." He waited a second; decided neither of us was going to answer. "Well, I was convinced that that Okie Fanning killed those four women. But I wasn't discouraged, because guilty or not, I had a *case*. Even if the guy was guilty—and I thought he was guilty as sin—I had a real shot at getting him off. Of course, thanks to you two, it never came to trial. Where'd Fanning go, by the way? Back home?"

Regan nodded. "Prison ministry. McAlester, Oklahoma. I just had a letter from him."

Baker nodded politely. "Good for him, I guess. At least he's not there as an inmate. But this case! Dammit, Bishop, I *know* Goode didn't do it! Now, Jerry Fanning—I didn't believe him, but I still could have gotten him off. At least I think so. But with Goode—who I'm convinced is innocent—I've got no case at all. He's going down.''

Baker raised a triumphant finger. " 'Hah!' you say. 'You don't *need* a case! The man's innocent till proven guilty!' Right?'' He shook his head. ''Wrong. With what the D.A.'s got, I'm dog meat. Rather, Goode is. And with his track record, he'll be in prison the rest of his life, no hope of parole—and all for something he didn't do!''

He looked from the Bishop to me. ''All due respect to you, Davey, I wouldn't be bothering you with this if it weren't for the Bishop.'' Back to the Bishop, blushing. ''Frankly, Bishop, on this one I need a genius. I'll never know how you managed to unravel that whole thing that pointed straight at Jerry Fanning, but you did. I don't think anyone else alive could've. Hell, *everybody* thought he was guilty! Everybody but you. And you saw through the whole mess and got him off.''

Regan opened his mouth but Baker stopped him. ''I know what you're going to say, Bishop. Why should you bother to help this guy, Goode, after what he did to you?'' He shrugged. ''Well, I know I can't really ask it of you. All I can tell you is you're the only guy I know who *can* help him. And if you'd be willing to let bygones be bygones and take a hand, I'd be deeply grateful.'' He sat back, eyes on Regan's face.

I'd been watching the Bish while Baker talked. The frosty look I'd expected to see was there. Regan's a handsome guy—or would be if it weren't for the lines of pain in his forehead and around his eyes and mouth. I've seen pictures of him before the shooting, and he probably aged ten years during the six weeks he was in the hospital. So I wasn't feeling any too charitable toward Baker. I wanted him to butt out and would have told him so if it had been my place. So Regan took care of it for me. At least he tried.

''I'm sorry, Mr. Baker,'' he said in a tone that said he wasn't. ''The answer will have to be no. This man Goode is obviously well represented with you as his counsel. I'm afraid you're going to have to face the jury unassisted—at least by me. This will leave you your own considerable legal talent. That will have to do him. Frankly, I think he deserves far less.''

Baker cleared his throat and looked at the floor. ''Well, uh,

Bishop—" He cleared his throat again. "Before I go, there is one other thing."

"What is it?" Regan's tone suggested Baker was overstaying his welcome.

The lawyer flushed. He cleared his throat again. "Well, uh..." He finally looked Regan in the eye. "It's a little complicated. May I background you? It'll help you understand."

Regan shook his head no, but his mouth had a mind of its own. "Well, all right. If you feel you must."

Baker gave a quick nod. "Right. Okay." More clearing of throat. "See, I need to tell you about this tape. I had the guy hypnotized and videotaped."

I stared at Baker. "You had Eddie Goode hypnotized? Why?"

Baker nodded. "Well, as you've probably seen in the papers, the cops found a Smith & Wesson .38 next to the body. That's how they found Goode."

"His weapon of choice," I nodded, interested in spite of myself. "They traced it to him by the registration?"

"Nope. It wasn't Goode's gun—at least not provably. The registration took the police nowhere except to a guy who'd had it ripped off while visiting here from out of town four years ago." He paused. "Naw, they found Goode because three of his fingerprints were on the gun."

I stared. "You mean they—"

Baker nodded. "Yeah. And they're Goode's, no doubt about it. I've been over them with Parker. It's his bust. I'd have hired a fingerprint expert to look at them, but why bother? I've got eyes, and I've seen the points of resemblance. One of the prints you could argue about—there's only five points. But the other two, forget it. They're Goode's left middle finger and his right thumb. No doubt about it."

"So why are you convinced Mr. Goode is innocent?" Regan murmured, his eyes lit up like a Christmas tree. I cursed under my breath. Regan loves this kind of stuff.

I tried to cut it off at the pass. "Come on! It really doesn't matter, does it? Maybe he's guilty, maybe he's not. Who cares? Like you said, Bishop, we're not involved." I jumped up. "Let's go, Dave. Meeting's over."

"Mr. Goldman!" Regan's voice was sharp. "Your job descrip-

tion does not include shielding me from any and all unpleas-
antness. If you cannot keep your peace, please leave." I shrugged
and sat back down. I couldn't believe it: Regan was seriously
considering jumping in.

Dave winced at the interchange and threw me a glance. "I'm
really sorry about this. But believe me, when I tie it together,
you'll both see why."

He looked at me. "May I give you the technical details, Davey?"
I nodded. I didn't like it but was damned if I was going to let
him snow Regan with technical stuff. Baker continued, "With
those fingerprints, one thing I can't claim is that Eddie Goode
never touched the gun. There's still no way to transfer fingerprints onto a hard metallic surface without the person touching
it. Can't be done. So it's clear Eddie touched the gun.

"Now, this part hasn't been in the papers yet. Eddie's story is
kind of strange. It's so strange, in fact, that I'm convinced it's got
to be the truth. He says—well, before I get into that, let me ask
both of you: how much do you already know?"

Regan rubbed his chin. "Some. Your client was picked up last
Tuesday, March twenty-seventh, for the murder of T. R. Ladd
Compton, son of T. Randolph Compton. Compton Senior is the
owner of Midas Touch Autocare, a far-flung car washing enter-
prise. The son, also an officer in the company, had been found
by his parents two nights before, dead from a gunshot wound in
the back of his head. Umm, that would have been Sunday, March
twenty-fifth.

"Mr. Compton's body was in his parents' bedroom in their
home on East Eighty-seventh, lying on the floor beneath a wall
safe. The safe had been ransacked and some valuable jewelry
taken. The murderer had apparently forced Mr. Compton to open
the safe, then shot and killed him in cold blood." Regan frowned.
"As I recall, Mr. and Mrs. Compton found the body around ten
P.M. when they returned from a charity function: a black-tie affair
at the Beauchamp, if I recall correctly."

Regan took a breath and went on. "The case received front
page attention from the New York *Times*, probably because the
Comptons are well-connected socially. Inspector Kessler was
quoted as promising a full-scale investigation, and lived up to
his word with the arrest of your client less than forty-eight hours

after the discovery of the body. The Inspector proclaimed that he had—I believe his expression was 'good and plenty'—to take to the grand jury to bind Mr. Goode over for trial. Bail was set at five hundred thousand dollars and as far as I know has not been met." Regan turned inquiring eyes on Baker. "Is that right? Your client is still in jail?"

Baker was staring at him. "Yeah, and will be. He doesn't have anything like that kind of bread." He raised his eyebrows. "I must say, you're pretty current on the case. Do you follow *all* murders that closely?"

Regan blushed. "I read the papers, Mr. Baker, and my memory is passable. I'll admit I paid special attention when I saw the name Eddie Goode." He grimaced. "Now I have told you all I know. You have answered one question I had by telling us about the fingerprints on the weapon. I had marveled at the extreme celerity with which Mr. Kessler was able to get his man. Can you tell us more?"

Baker nodded. "Plenty. Let me tell you the cockamamiest story—by the way, is that a word, Bishop?"

Regan smiled. "*Cockamamiest?* I doubt it. I don't believe *cockamamie* has a superlative. But your meaning is clear. Proceed."

Baker grinned. "Well, if the word exists, this is the place to use it. As you'll see."

He took a breath. "Two weeks ago—according to Eddie, now—this guy Compton came to see him."

Regan stared. "Which Compton? The victim?" Baker nodded. "Came to see Mr. Goode?"

Baker nodded. "Yeah, that's right. But—"

I couldn't resist butting in. "Where is this meeting supposed to have taken place?"

"In Eddie's apartment in Soho," Baker shrugged. "I know, I know, seems crazy." I started to cut in again, but Baker raised a hand. "And you're wondering: how did Compton find Goode?" I nodded. Baker'd read my mind. He grinned. "Goode doesn't know. He says he asked the guy how he found him and Compton wouldn't say.

"But that's just for openers. It gets crazier. Eddie says Compton wanted him—that is, wanted Eddie—to pull off a heist. Says Compton wanted him to go to his parents' house. Gave him the key. Eddie says Laddie told him they—the Comptons—had some valuable jewelry that was heavily insured. He wanted Eddie to go there and steal it. He told Eddie he could keep the jewelry; all the Comptons wanted was the insurance money."

Regan frowned. "Has Goode told this to the police?"

Baker nodded. "When he told me this last Thursday, I called Billy Weaver, who's handling the case for the D.A.'s office, and told him we were ready to make a statement. And Eddie gave the same spiel to Weaver. He listened to it and was nice enough not to laugh in our faces. See, trouble is, there's that damn gun with his prints all over it. That's what I keep running up against."

Baker looked at Regan. "What's crazy, Bishop, is that I *believe* him! I do! Oh, I laughed at him at first, told him he was nuts to think I'd buy it, much less a jury, but he insists it's the truth. And wait: there's more."

I rolled my eyes. Baker winced and raised his palms. "I know, Davey, I know. Just listen, okay?" He took a breath.

"So Eddie told Compton he'd pull the heist. Compton gives him the combo to the safe, combo to the security alarm system, everything. Eddie writes everything down. Which is another reason to believe him, by the way: how else could he have got those combinations?" I snorted and Baker blushed. "Okay, okay, an ex-cop like you could think of a way. Still, it does back up his story—a little.

"Anyway. He agrees to do it, and Compton slips him a quick thou. Which he's still got—Eddie does. He's got ten crisp new C-notes. Well, now the cops have them—they impounded those C-notes along with the Comptons' jewelry when they searched Eddie's apartment."

Baker looked grim. "They dusted the hundreds—they were nice and crisp—and found the victim's prints on them. This backs up Eddie's story. Trouble is, it also backs up the police theory. Which is that Eddie forced Compton to open the safe, then blew him away. The cops figure the hundreds were there in the safe along with the jewels. Victim's parents can't remember whether there was any money in there or not."

"So," murmured Regan. "Mr. Goode acknowledges that he went to the Comptons' on the night in question. And from what you say, I gather he also acknowledges stealing the jewelry?''

Baker nodded. "According to Eddie, he went there and the house was empty—well, let me take that back. He says Laddie warned him there was a servant in the basement, but said he—Laddie—would keep the guy occupied. He warned Eddie not to go down to the basement; told him to go straight to the master bedroom on the second floor, steal the jewels and beat it out of there.

"And according to Eddie, that's what he did. That's *all* he did. He's got no idea how Compton got killed.''

I shook my head. "I don't believe this, Davis. The guy admits being there, he admits stealing the jewels—but he denies not only that he shot anyone but that he touched any gun. And the gun's got his prints all over it. If that doesn't tell you something, Counselor, nothing ever will.''

Baker, unsmiling, met my gaze. "Okay, I agree with one thing. There's no doubt he touched the gun. But I still believe him. To see if I was completely crazy, I had a polygraph administered.'' He looked at me.

I gestured impatiently. "And?''

"And he passed with flying colors. Far as the polygraph operator's concerned, the guy's telling the truth.''

I made a rude noise. "Yeah, and half the guys in Sing-Sing can do the same thing. I can't believe you—''

Baker raised a hand. "I know, I know. I wasn't satisfied either. So I hired a hypnotist.''

"Yeah, so you said. Why in the hell—''

Regan spoke up. "To permit Mr. Goode's unconscious to come forth in the hope that he might recall something about the weapon. Bringing back memories is one of the useful functions of hypnosis. Perhaps the only one.''

"Exactly, Bishop,'' Baker said, nodding at him. "And I videotaped the session. Of course it's inadmissible for trial purposes, and the hypnotist is immunized—can't testify on either side. Just like the polygraph guy. But since Eddie had no memory whatsoever of ever having touched the gun, I wanted to see if he'd remember it under hypnosis. And maybe even recall killing the guy. I mean, crazier things have happened. Despite your experience with him, Bishop, Goode isn't a hardened killer. It seemed to me just possible he might have been so horrified at what he'd done, he'd blocked it out of his memory.

"But whatever the explanation, his fingerprints were on that gun, and that had to be explained. I warned him that he was running the risk that if he did kill the guy, he'd say so under hypnosis. He didn't even hesitate—wanted to go ahead."

Regan nodded. "And he did; you videotaped it, and you have the tape with you."

"Exactly," Baker said. "And that tape—well, it partly concerns you, Bishop." The lawyer quickly opened his attaché case and pulled out a videotape box. "I'd like to play this for you—if you don't mind. It's only thirty minutes long, and I don't have to run all of it. The last part's what I really want you to see."

The Bishop stared at Baker. "It concerns me? What do you mean, it concerns me?"

Baker colored. "I'd rather have you see it," he gulped. "Then you'll know what I'm driving at. It's a little hard to explain." He got up to hand me the tape. "Could you just stick this in the VCR, Davey?"

I grinned at him. "What VCR?"

Baker's head swiveled from me to the Bishop back to me. "No VCR?"

I shook my head.

"I must get one sometime," Regan semi-apologized. "Yours is the fourth or fifth offer I've had in the past several months to watch something either entertaining, educational or engrossing. I am sorry I can't—"

Baker raised a hand in appeal. "Please, Bishop. There's a pawn-shop around the corner on Eleventh. Let me just run over there and—"

I cut him off. "Do you really want to see it, Bishop?"

Regan glanced at Baker, then nodded slowly. "Since Mr. Baker is so insistent, yes, I suppose I should. Why?"

"Then there's no need for Dave to run out and get himself ripped off by Sammy, the Sultan of Swap." I hauled myself to my feet. "Be right back," I told them. "With my VCR." I headed for the stairs.

10

BAKER RENEWED HIS EARLIER OFFER to fast-forward the tape to the good part.

Regan glanced at his watch. "No. Let us begin at the beginning, Mr. Baker. I may decide to ask you to move it ahead." I glanced at my own watch. It was 11:40.

I pushed Play. The tape started abruptly with a close-up of a guy who proclaimed himself to be a hypnotist, giving his name as Dr. Maurice Highland. Sitting behind a desk, reading from notes, he gave a few facts about hypnotism, claimed it wasn't mumbo-jumbo, it was scientific, intended to free the subject from his or her inhibitions, permitting him or her to retrieve otherwise unretrievable information from his or her subconscious. Sounded like he'd once been traumatized by some he- or she- type feminist.

The scene shifted. Same guy, different room. The picture was fuzzier. I guessed it was taken from behind a one-way glass. The sound quality was poorer, though you could hear it okay if you listened hard.

A typical doctor's office: standard decor, window with drapes, pictures on the wall, a desk and couch; and two men. The one in the foreground was Highland. At first I didn't recognize the other one, sitting on the couch in jail-issue yellow coveralls. Then I did. Sometime in the past eight years Eddie Goode had dropped the mustache and about half his hair. The slicked-back look was gone. In its place was shorter, grayer, sparser growth. I didn't remember his nose being that smashed; maybe it'd taken a few more shots since I'd last seen him. But his weasel eyes hadn't changed.

Highland was talking directly into the camera while Eddie, behind him, looked bored. Highland said that yes, the camera was out of sight behind a mirror, but no attempt was being made to "fool" the subject, a Mr. Edward L. Goode. Goode looked up and grinned at the elaborate form of his name.

41

Then the hypnosis began. No dangling watch or mirror on a chain. Highland just had Goode lie back on the couch and close his eyes. The hypnotist began talking in a low, confident tone, telling Goode he should just rest and everything would be okay. (I doubted it.) Then he led him up to and through the night of the murder. Eddie told about his entry into the house, his going up the stairs.

"You were alone in the house, Eddie?"

"Naw. Guy warned me somebody else might be there. Down in the basement. But no one anywhere where I was."

"So you never saw anyone the entire time you were in the house?"

"Naw. I never seen anyone."

Soon Eddie was talking about the bedroom and the safe. Once Eddie was in the bedroom, the doctor wanted more details. So, to my surprise, did I.

"All right, Eddie," Highland said in that low, confident voice. "Set the scene in your mind. You're now in the Comptons' bedroom."

"Yeah. Uh—" Goode looked drugged, eyes half open.

"Eddie, I don't want you to do anything right now but focus on the appearance of the bedroom. What does it look like, Eddie?"

Goode frowned. "Uh, nice wallpaper, flowered. Expensive bedspread. Flowers, I think. A desk. Two chairs. No, four. Gawd, it's big! I never seen a bedroom this size! Big as a whole house. Bed's huge. Nice place."

"Is anyone else there, Eddie?" Highland pressed. Goode shook his head, his eyes half open.

"All right, Eddie, tell me about the safe."

"What's to tell? I work the combo the guy gave me, open it, clean it out, sayonara. That's it. That's all."

"But there was a man killed there that night, Eddie. Did you know that, Eddie?" Goode's eyes widened in terror.

"What is it, Eddie? What else do you see?" The hypnotist's voice increased in volume but stayed calm. No echo of the fear and excitement now in Eddie's. Eddie gulped hard, his eyes darting from side to side. *Now,* I thought, *now we're getting to it.*

"Go ahead, Eddie," Highland persisted. "What's wrong? Tell me. Tell me, Eddie!"

"It's—"

"Go ahead, Eddie. It's nothing that can hurt you now. It's all in the past, Eddie. Tell me what you see."

"Don't wanna be here! Don't wanna be here! Cops say somebody got killed here! Was it him again? Was it that bishop? I won't—" Goode's eyes were like saucers. He tried to burrow into the couch.

"Eddie!" Highland snapped. "Listen to me, Eddie! What bishop? What bishop are you talking about?"

I glanced at Regan. His face was drawn, intent on the screen. He blinked a couple of times.

Eddie finally answered, his voice choked. "The guy I shot, goddammit! Don't you understand? The guy I shot! But goddammit, I didn't shoot anyone *this* time! I didn't!" Goode's eyes were wild. "Jesus, I never meant to *shoot* the priest—I didn't! He scared me, you unnerstand? He swung around and I thought he was goin' wit' a karate kick and the goddamn gun went off! Goddammit, why won't anyone *believe* it was a freakin' accident? I didn't mean to shoot the guy! I didn't! The freakin' gun went off! I didn't—"

"Eddie!" Highland's voice cut in. "Eddie, listen to me! There's no bishop here! No bishop in this room. But is there a dead man? What do you see, Eddie?"

Eddie, panting, shook his head. "Naw, not now. No dead man. No bishop."

Highland watched the patient closely and didn't go on till his patient's face cleared and his breathing became normal again.

"Did you rob the safe, Eddie?"

Goode smiled happily. "Yeah. Piece a cake. Had the combo. Nothin' to it."

"Who was with you, Eddie?"

Still calm. "No one. I came alone."

"Did you bring a gun with you, Eddie?"

"Naw, no more gun. No gun since that bishop. Won't touch one."

The hypnotist delayed a minute. "Eddie." Goode tried to focus on him. "Eddie, how'd your fingerprints get on that gun? You say you won't touch a gun. How'd your prints get on the gun, Eddie?"

Goode frowned. "Dunno. I maybe—dunno."

Highland had a few more questions but nothing new came out of Eddie's answers. Finally, the hypnotist was ready to close it out.

"All right, Eddie. We're done here. The next time I say the word *sunshine*, you'll wake up feeling fine. You'll think you just had a good nap and you'll feel . . . " I tuned out until the hypnotist said the magic word, when Goode woke up and the video ended.

I walked over to the machine, turned down the volume and pushed Rewind. Regan sighed. Baker studied him.

"That's what I wanted you to see, Bishop. You see, it throws light on a couple of things. It—"

"Yes, yes," Regan muttered. "I need to think for a moment."

Baker shut up. He threw a glance at me; I put a finger to my lips. Regan spun his wheelchair around and gave both of us his back. Silence for about thirty seconds. Finally Regan spoke, without turning. "What are Dr. Highland's credentials, Mr. Baker?"

Baker shrugged. "He's a licensed hypnotist."

"Degreed?"

"Oh, sure."

"From what university?"

Baker shrugged again. "I don't know. Is that important?"

Regan gave his own version of a shrug. "I suppose not, if you're satisfied. What was his opinion?"

Baker glanced at me, eyebrows raised. I shook my head. "What do you mean, Bishop?" Dave said.

Regan sounded irritable. "About the patient's frankness. Was he really under?"

Baker nodded. "I see. That's important, all right. Well, Highland's opinion is that Eddie wasn't faking. He's telling it like it is. Or at least like he sees it."

"*As* he sees it," Regan murmured, turning around to face us. He gave a glance at Baker, who gave him a little nod of acknowledgement. "And you," Regan said, "agree with him."

Baker nodded again. "Highland's convinced that Eddie never

saw or touched any gun. I mean, that night. That's his expert opinion. So he and the polygraph expert are in agreement."

Regan closed his eyes and rubbed his face. Baker started to say something, but I waved him down. Baker nodded and waited. Another thirty seconds went by—then forty.

"Mr. Baker," the Bishop said. Baker grunted. "Why do you believe Goode?"

Baker shrugged. "Hey, you saw him. What do you think?"

"Just that? Just this interview?"

"Umm, no," Baker acknowledged. "I've had several talks with him. Look, I'll be the first to admit, the guy's an inveterate liar. Prison makes a guy good at that, and Goode's spent lots of time in prison. But on this he's not lying—I'm sure of it. I mean, just think about it. The dumbest of jail rats would come up with a better story than what he's telling. In a second."

Regan sat, staring at nothing for another minute. Normally that means he's thinking, but there was nothing to think about. Maybe he was praying. Finally he looked at Baker. "How soon can we see Mr. Goode?"

I jumped to my feet. "No way! You want to go see Goode, go ahead. But you'll go without me."

Regan opened his mouth. Closed it. He turned to Baker. "Wait in Mr. Goldman's office, will you, Mr. Baker? We'll just be a moment."

Blushing and uncomfortable, Baker got up and went. Regan watched him go, then looked at me. "Your problem, David?"

"Look, Bishop. Count me out. I'm never sure what motivates you. But whatever it is you're doing here, I don't want any part of it. As far as Eddie Goode's concerned, all I want's revenge."

Regan smiled. "Oh, make no mistake, David, revenge is very much on my mind as well."

I stared at him. What was he saying?

He met my eyes. "Do you ever read your Bible, David?"

"What's that got to do with anything? No, I don't look at it much. Maybe twice in the past year." I still have the Bible Mom got me for my bar mitzvah. I didn't tell Regan that twice in the past year was when I dusted it.

"From your early lessons in the Bible in Hebrew school, do you recall what it has to say about revenge?"

Regan seemed to want an answer so I thought about it. "An eye for an eye? That kind of thing?"

Regan nodded. "Very good. The Yahwist interpretation of God's will. And very influential in the jurisprudential history of western civilization. Fortunately or unfortunately, Jesus seems to have rejected that approach to settling with one's enemies. His ideas have been equally influential and have in fact mitigated the earlier teaching.

"But within the ancient Hebrew canon, in what is called its wisdom literature, a different approach than the eye-for-an-eye can be found, one that found favor in early Christianity. I became acutely aware of this when I went searching for such wisdom after I was paralyzed. I'm afraid I'll have to direct you to it, if you're to understand why I'm opting to assist Mr. Goode."

I shook my head. "You know, I don't have the foggiest idea what you're talking about."

"Well, look up Proverbs twenty-five, verses twenty-one and twenty-two." Regan pulled a worn leather-bound Bible from his desk drawer and handed it to me. "In here. One exposure to a Christian Bible won't contaminate you, David. Here: look it up."

I took it. "Proverbs, what?" He gave me the chapter and verses again. I found the passage and read it aloud. *If thine enemy be hungry, give him bread to eat; and if he be thirsty, give him water to drink: For thou shalt heap coals of fire upon his head, and the Lord shall reward thee.*

I read it again silently, then looked at Regan. "What in the world is that? *Coals of fire upon his head?* Is that what we're going to do to Goode?"

"Precisely."

"How?"

"That will become clear as we go along." Regan's eyes narrowed. "I don't think Mr. Goode killed that man. I'd like to help Mr. Baker prove it. But I'll need your assistance."

I stared at him. "Mind sharing your reasoning with me? Why are you so sure Goode didn't do it?"

Regan snorted. "Not because of Maurice Highland, you may be sure."

"You don't think—"

The Bishop waved it away. "But to answer your question di-

rectly: Mr. Baker's logic is cogent, David. The utter outrageous-
ness of Goode's story is proof enough of its veracity. It's ridiculous. I refuse to believe a criminal as adroit as Mr. Goode would
be foolhardy enough to tell it were it not true."

I thought about it. "Okay. I don't know if I buy your reasoning
all the way. And I sure don't understand that piece of Scripture.
But for the chance to pour a few burning coals on Eddie Goode—
count me in."

The Bishop nodded. "Good. Please ask Mr. Baker to return and
we can be about the business of establishing Mr. Goode's innocence. Innocence! Hah!"

11

BAKER WAS DELIGHTED with the news. "Hey, this is great!" He
jumped to his feet. "Use your phone? I want to give Eddie the
good news."

"A moment, Mr. Baker," Regan said. "Have a seat, please.
Before you talk to your client I have a question or two."

"Ask away."

"What was the value of the stolen jewelry?"

"Two hundred and fifty thousand—according to the insurance
adjuster. That's one helpful piece of information the cops had
for me. They had that even before they arrested Eddie."

"And the jewels have now been returned to the Comptons?"

Baker frowned. "Don't know. The cops were holding onto
them, last I heard. I imagine they've still got them. Those jewels
are vital to the state's case."

Regan nodded. He thought for a minute, then asked, "And Mr.
Goode's *modus operandi*: was he in the habit of wearing gloves
while...at his work?"

Baker's eyebrows went up. "Good point. He sure was. That's
a point I'll hit hard in court. How can they explain Eddie's fingerprints on the gun when he was wearing gloves? The D.A.'s

not sweating it, for which I can't blame him. I mean, the prints *are* Eddie's. But I'm sure he'd like to know—preferably from Eddie—what made him take the gloves off. If he *did* take them off."

Regan looked satisfied. "And speaking of fingerprints, were the victim's found on the safe?"

Baker raised his eyebrows again. "You know, you're in the wrong profession, Bishop. You should have been a cop. Uh—I mean that as a compliment."

"So taken," Regan murmured.

"I mean, that's a *great* question. And very important. Yeah, Ladd Compton's fingerprints were on the safe, along with some of his blood and hair." Regan winced.

Dave apologized. "Sorry about that, Bishop. I mention it because it shows he was standing directly in front of the safe when he was killed. The bottom of the safe is five feet above the floor of the Comptons' bedroom; the top is six feet, four inches. Laddie was five-ten. The bullet went all the way through the victim's head and was later found by the cops, lying at the back of the safe."

Baker glanced at me. "I can tell you the cops' theory. Eddie somehow got inside knowledge of the Comptons' household routine. He managed to get into the house, intending to force whoever was there to let him into the safe. Laddie was the lucky guy. Then, after Laddie opened the safe, Goode shot and killed him. To shut him up."

"I see. But what was Mr. Compton doing in the mansion in the first place? According to the *Times* he lived elsewhere."

Baker shrugged. "You're right. Had an apartment over on the West Side. No one seems to know what he was doing at his parents' that night. Or when he got there. Or even *how* he got there. The cops struck out with all the cab companies."

I had a thought. "Maybe Goode brought him. Picked him up somewhere else and forced him at gunpoint to come with him to the Comptons'."

Baker grinned. "Whose side you on, anyway? The cops'd love that theory." He shook his head. "But it won't wash. A neighbor saw Goode enter the house—alone."

"At what time?" Regan snapped.

"Nine-oh-five. And saw him leave at nine-fifteen. Nailed down tight. Another nail in Goode's coffin."

Regan thought about it. "How does the police theory account for Mr. Goode's having the combination to the safe on that slip of paper they impounded? If he already had the combination, why the need for Mr. Compton to open it?"

Baker nodded. "Another good point, Bishop. But their theory is he got the combination only after he was in the house, probably from Laddie. But he still wanted Laddie to open it for him. Then he killed Laddie to keep him from talking."

"So," Regan mused, "the Comptons were greeted with the sight of their son's dead body when they walked into their bedroom that night?"

"Afraid so. Must have been horrible for them. They arrived home just after ten. Went up to their bedroom to find their son's body there."

The Bishop frowned at the floor. "One is drawn," he murmured, "to one of two conclusions. Either Mr. Goode is lying through his teeth, or someone persuaded the victim to enter the bedroom and dispatched him between the time Goode left and the time the police arrived. Please sit down, Mr. Baker. And you as well, David."

He spun the chair and headed for the south windows. He sat awhile, looking out. Davis glanced at me and I nodded back. For the first time I was starting to feel okay about helping. In spite of myself Baker's problem was beginning to intrigue me.

When Regan finally broke the silence, his back was to us and his voice so low that both Baker and I had to lean forward to hear it. "So we have two questions to answer at the outset, assuming we believe Mr. Goode. First of all, where was the victim— or, for that matter, the murderer—while Mr. Goode was pilfering the jewels? Second, how did Mr. Goode's fingerprints find their way onto the weapon?"

He spun the chair to face us. "I see no way at the moment to deal with the first question, though it will have to be addressed. As to the second, fortunately, we have virtually unlimited access to the best source."

Baker stared at him. "What do you mean?"

"Your client, of course."

"But he claims he doesn't know—"

"Of course he knows. Or do you believe someone pressed his fingertips to the gun while he was sleeping?" Baker frowned.

"No, Mr. Baker. Somewhere in your client's brain is the knowledge. All we need do is bring it out." Baker shook his head.

"That's what the hypnotist tried to do."

"Perhaps your good Dr. Highland is not as expert as you thought." Regan threw a quick, ironic glance at Baker but the lawyer didn't notice. "Or perhaps Mr. Goode was not yet educable. As you know as well as I, Mr. Baker, the etymology of *educate*, is to 'lead forth.' Let us see if we can lead Mr. Goode's memory forth. I'd like to question him as soon as possible."

Baker was excited. "Name the day, Bishop!"

Regan shrugged. "What's wrong with right now?"

12

So I HAD ANOTHER REASON to resent Eddie Goode: I had to tell Ernie to hold lunch. And I was already hungry. We normally eat at 12:30; it was almost that by the time the Bishop decided he wanted to talk to Goode. So while Regan changed and Baker called the jail to set it up, I walked over to Fred's garage where Regan keeps his Seville. Baker got the honor of bumping the Bishop down the eight steps to the sidewalk. I wasn't able to critique his style, since they were already waiting for me by the time I drove up. But Regan wasn't bleeding, at least that I could see, so Dave must have handled it fairly well.

It had been a year and a half since Regan had been to the jail— that time to see Jerry Fanning. "A new shade of green," he muttered as he pushed his way into the waiting room. I looked around and nodded. It *was* freshly painted. (And the bleeding hearts try to tell you we taxpayers don't spend enough on our prisoners.)

But the visitors' room probably hadn't been painted since the turn of the century. Don't ask me which century. It was still gray

and just as ill-lit, gloomy and cheerless as ever. Also more filled
with people than I'd ever seen it. All the carrels but one—ours—
were taken when we walked in. If you ever want to see a bunch
of gloomy Gusses, go to the visitors' room of Rikers Island when
there's lots of visitors around. I saw tears on three faces—all
belonging to women, and all on the visitors' side of the glass.

The carrel they'd saved for us had a double phone set-up on
the visitors' side so two of us could hear what Eddie had to say.
No good: all three of us wanted to listen in. The beefy desk
sergeant didn't much like the idea of making special arrangements, but Dave was firm.

"Look, Sergeant—Macy, is it?" he smiled. "Sergeant Macy.
These two gentlemen are consulting with me on the case. Now
I'd be happy to talk to Inspector Callahan if you like, but I'm
sure you—"

Macy reacted to the name Callahan like Bela Lugosi to a crucifix. "Naw, naw," he said, more animation in his face than I'd
have thought possible. "Uh, tell you what, Counselor. I think
one a those carrels has a third jack. Lemme see if I can't dig up
another phone for youse." He swung around and bellowed, "Sawyer!" A uniformed guard came on the double. "Give these gem-
men number six 'n' get 'em an extra phone. They're here to see
Goode."

Sawyer mumbled something to the effect that the other prisoners weren't going to like it. Bad move. Macy upped the volume
into the hundred-decibel range. "I don't give a rat's ass *what* the
others like or don't like! Give these folks number *six. Now!*"
Sawyer left on the double, still mumbling, but not so Macy could
hear him.

The sergeant swung back to us and gave Baker what he probably thought was a pleasant grin. "You're all set, Counselor."

It was a bit crowded on our side of the bulletproof glass, the
carrel having been intended for two fairly small bodies and neither of them in a wheelchair. But we managed to squeeze in. I
got to sit closest to the glass at the counter so I could take notes.
Baker took the rear chair, but he could still see the prisoner and
hear him, thanks to a longer phone cord.

Having already seen Eddie on the video, I wasn't surprised at
the changes eight years had made in him. His hair was even

grayer than it had looked on TV. And he had a fairly sizable bald spot on top. His face was lined, with bags under his eyes and a fairly severe case of prison pallor. Of course, he'd never been a guy with a lot of color in his face anyway. His watery gray eyes flicked over the three of us, jumping away from Regan quickest. He finally settled on looking somewhere just over our heads.

Baker opened the proceedings. "Eddie, this is Bishop Regan and David Goldman. I told you I was going to try to get them to help, remember? They haven't agreed to yet, but they're willing to talk about it. Eddie . . . Eddie!"

Dave waited till Goode brought his eyes down from the wall. "Eddie, I told them your story and showed them the tape of your interview with the hypnotist." Goode colored a little and shot a glance my way. "I also told them I believe you, don't ask me why." Goode's lip twitched in a half-smile. "But there's some information I don't have, and they think they know how to get it." Baker nodded at Regan.

"Mr. Goode," Regan said, leaning forward. Eddie looked down at his feet. Regan waited until Eddie looked at him. He had to wait even longer than Baker had. "We have a mystery to explore." Goode looked away. "Mr. Goode!" The Bishop's voice crackled through the phone line. Eddie winced and gave Regan his eye.

The Bishop was blunt. "Mr. Goode, you have no reason to avoid looking at me. However, I know how you feel. Believe me, our positions could easily be reversed. Under a different set of circumstances, I could be facing you through safety glass from over there. That I am not is due to God's grace, nothing else. So please do me the courtesy of meeting my eyes."

Goode started to answer and his voice cracked. He cleared his throat. "Yeah, okay. I'm . . . I'm really sorry for what happened, man. I didn't . . . "

Regan showed him a palm. "Apology accepted, Mr. Goode. Now let's discuss your current predicament." Eddie heaved a sigh of relief. So did Baker, who told me later, "That's the first time I was sure Regan was going to take the case."

"The predicament," Regan said, "is this. The police have positively identified your fingerprints on the murder weapon. That weapon, Mr. Goode, is the most curious part of this whole affair. What do you know about it?"

"Nothin'. I never seen it." I nodded to myself. Goode's face and hair may have changed but his grammar hadn't improved and the whine was still fluent.

"Never?" Regan stared at him hard.

Goode matched his look. "Not. Ever."

"Wrong," Regan murmured and raised a hand to cut off Eddie's objections. "I'm not saying you're lying, Mr. Goode. I agree with your attorney: many other lies would have served you far better. But it is manifestly untrue that you have never seen that gun. Your fingerprints were on it; therefore, you have seen it—or at least touched it. Our purpose now is to discover when and where that was, and in whose company. Once we know that, we'll be well down the road to discovering the identity of the person who murdered Mr. Compton."

"But—" Eddie stopped, glanced at Baker.

"Yes?" Regan prompted.

"But me and Mr. Baker been all over this. I ain't touched a gun in eight years!"

Regan glanced at me. His acknowledgment that fingerprints— and guns—are my domain. I tapped on the glass to get Eddie's attention. His bitter look told me he'd neither forgotten nor forgiven the way I'd bounced him around his apartment eight years before.

"Bullshit, Eddie!" I barked into the phone. He opened his mouth to respond, but I didn't give him a chance. "Look. Let me tell you something about fingerprints, Eddie. They don't last eight years; if they do, cops know right away they're not fresh. The prints on that gun were fresh. So don't tell me you haven't touched a gun in eight years. Because that gun had your prints on it."

"Oh yeah?" Goode was hot, which was partly what I was after. "Well, let me tell you something, wise guy. That gun was a plant. I know I don't have to tell you about plants!"

I was opening my mouth to answer that, but Regan cut in. "Oh, it was a plant all right, Mr. Goode. Someone else put it there, be he the killer or someone else. But knowing it was a plant doesn't solve our problem. Which is: how did your fingerprints find their way onto it? Even if the police planted the gun there with malign intent, how were they able to obtain one with your fingerprints?"

Eddie was sullen. "They *put* them on it."

Regan glanced at me. I shook my head. "No can do, Eddie. Believe it, when I was a cop there were plenty of times I'd have loved to do just that. But it can't be done."

Eddie looked away sullenly. Regan continued, "So sometime within the past—" He raised eyebrows inquiringly at me.

"Couple of months," I prompted. "Three, max."

Regan nodded and turned back to Goode. "Sometime within the past three months, probably more recently, you had your hands on that gun. When?"

Eddie shook his head stubbornly. "You're wastin' your time, man," he muttered. But Regan was unperturbed. He stayed with the questions, the prisoner getting more and more stubborn with each question asked. Finally he exploded.

"Look! The last time I ever *touched* a gun was when I shot— when I was with you that time. That really . . . " He took a breath and spoke more softly. "I just never felt like usin' a gun after that. Or even touchin' one. And I haven't."

Regan looked impressed. "All right. I suppose I can respect that. But you violated that pledge, sir, sometime within the past ninety days. Of this there can be no doubt." Regan was studying the prisoner's eyes as much as I was, and I doubt he saw anything other than what I saw—total confusion. But the Bishop just kept probing.

"Let's try this, sir." Eddie glowered at him. "You had a pistol in your hand for some other purpose than its normal use." Regan frowned, thinking. "Someone showed you a gun. A friend, per- haps? An associate? For some purpose for which a gun would not normally serve. At some point you handled a Smith & Wesson thirty-eight caliber automatic. Surely you—yes?"

Regan had picked up the same flash in Eddie's eyes that I had. We waited while Eddie, eyes closed, concentrated. When his eyes opened again they were wide. "Oh my God!" he nearly shouted. "Ruthie!"

"Ruthie?" Regan asked.

Goode took a breath. "Sorry, man. You said I must've handled a gun. I did. See, I've got a—friend. Ruthie Benedict." He frowned. "But she wouldn't of—"

"Wouldn't have what, Mr. Goode?"

Goode looked anguished. "She wouldn't of—set me up like that. Not Ruthie." He shook his head.

"She managed to get you to leave your fingerprints on a gun?"

Goode looked Regan in the eye. "I guess she did." He looked down. "She called me about a month ago and I went over. She was going to kill herself. I took the gun away from her." Goode smiled bitterly. "And it was an S&W thirty-eight."

13

REGAN WAS AS INTENT as I'd ever seen him. "This woman was threatening to kill herself?"

"Yeah." Eddie's nasal voice was whinier than ever. "And she really *was*, man! She was climbing the walls. Had this .38 and swore she was gonna do it. Scared me! Jesus, I thought for a minute she might do *both* of us. I tried to talk calm to her, you know? Musta spent five or ten minutes just talkin' to her, calmin' her down.

"She finally started cryin' and gave me the gun. Man, I'll tell you, I didn't waste any time breakin' it and takin' the ammo. Had a full clip—nothin' in the chamber, thank sweet Jesus, or she mighta blown both our heads off while she was wavin' it around."

"Who is this Ms. Benedict, and where can we find her?" I doubt if either Eddie or Dave picked up the excitement in Regan's voice. They don't know him like I do.

"She's got an apartment in Soho," Eddie said. "Not far from mine. Walking distance. It was the first time I'd seen her in months. She and I once had a—" Goode blushed and stopped.

"Go ahead," Regan said. "We want to hear about her. Can you give us her address?"

"Sure," Eddie shrugged, and reeled off an address on Vandam. "She's been a friend of mine since—"

"Hold it!" Baker held up a hand. "You say her name's Benedict?" I swung around and gave him a contemptuous look. We'd only mentioned the name about five times in the past three minutes. But Baker was too excited to notice my look.

"Yeah," said Goode.

"Of the Benedict crime family?" That took the sneer off my face. I should have recognized the name myself. The Benedicts were among the leading mobsters in the city, into prostitution, drugs, numbers, you name it.

I looked at Eddie. He was blushing. "Yeah. Well, she married into it. She's not really part of it, though."

Baker stayed with it. "She the high school kid who married Joe Junior, a few years back?" Eddie nodded sullenly.

Under my breath, I cursed myself. Half a step behind Baker again. Now I remembered. Junior Benedict had been married briefly. Junior was a definite baddy. Son of Joe Benedict, a guy with a reputation of being a man of honor—for a gangster. Junior's reputation was otherwise. He was probably one of the top five or six crack distributors in greater New York City. I hadn't met him, but he'd had his picture in the paper a number of times. Never with his wife. I had a vague recollection of a loud and messy divorce.

Junior was about thirty—tall, dark and handsome, as they say, and absolutely vicious. If you believed the street talk, he was especially adept with a knife.

Eddie must not have liked the looks on our faces. "Hey! Ruthie married the guy before she was old enough to know better. She's wasn't no more'n sixteen or seventeen. By the time she hit twenty, they was history."

Eddie's weasel face softened into a smile. "I met her right after she got rid of him. She ditched him in prison. She was just out when I met her. We was on the same work release program five years ago.

"She'd been nailed for fencing hot jewels, me for some damn thing or other—usin', I guess. We were doing time on parole, had the same parole officer. We had kind of a thing there for a while, but it didn't last. She mighta made up wit' her family, I don't know. Somethin'. Anyways, didn't last." Eddie sniffed and wiped a hand across his nose.

"Well, I'd run into her in Mulligan's every once in a while—that's a bar. It's not far from my place, and not far from hers. She was never with anyone—I mean, *with* anyone in that way, y'know? But I could never get anything started with her again. She finally told me once, she likes 'em bigger." Eddie blushed. "I mean *taller*, know what I mean?"

He took a breath. "So it came outa the blue, her callin' me like that last month. I—"

"When was that exactly?" the Bishop asked. "Can you remember?"

Goode thought about it, finally shook his head. "Naw. Two, three weeks ago, I don't know. Early in March. Said her boyfriend ditched her, she didn' wanna go on livin'. She was goin' ape. I could barely unnerstan' her. I tole her to cool it for just five minutes and I'd be there. And I was.

"I got over there and I about freaked out, her wavin' that gun around. But I talked to her nice 'n' easy, kept tellin' her everything was gonna be jake. Her eyes finally eased up and she let me have the gun, like I said, so's I could unload it."

"What did you do with it?" Regan's eyes were intent.

"Wit' the gun?" Eddie frowned. "Let's see. I, uh, put it some place up high, on a bookshelf maybe. And I took the clip wit' me, I remember that. No way I was leavin' Ruthie wit' the means to load up that gun again." He smiled. "Course, she mighta had another clip around to load it wit'. But I did what I could. That's one little girl I don't want dead."

The Bishop tried to get more information about the woman but without much success. Eddie thought she'd been married only once and was now about twenty-five. He didn't know where she grew up, who her family was or who she was running around with these days.

He seemed strangely ignorant about a woman he was obviously in love with. "Hey, she didn't wanna talk about her backgroun' none, know what I mean? And I never felt like pushin' it."

Regan didn't leave it at that. He kept probing, wanting to know all the other guns Eddie might have left prints on, till Goode exploded again. "Look, man! Get off my back! I tole you, I never *touched* a freakin' gun since that thing with you. Well, except for with Ruthie that night. But that was different."

Regan was patient. "Mr. Goode. Twenty minutes ago you assured me you had *never* touched a firearm in the past eight years.

Your denial was unqualified and categorical. Five minutes later you were recounting the incident with Ms. Benedict. Now that we know about it, I want to know if we should concentrate all our efforts on her, or whether there are other guns on which you've left your fingerprints. From your description of Ms. Benedict, I should think you'd be enthusiastic about looking elsewhere for the person who—set you up."

The last three words hung in the air. Goode sat, glaring at Regan, thinking about it. Then his eyes drooped. He nodded. "Yeah. I would. And you're right, man. Someone is setting me up for a fall, ain't they? Okay. Keep askin'."

But Regan was just about asked out. He stayed with it another ten minutes but got nowhere.

Baker wanted to chat after we left Eddie. He had Macy, the most cooperative cop you've ever seen now that he thought Baker was a buddy of Callahan's, find us a spare office in which to confer. Baker grabbed the chair behind the large desk; I copped the other one; Regan steered his wheelchair just inside the door. It was going on 1:30 and I was trying to ignore my rumbling stomach.

"Do you think that's the gun, Bishop?" Baker blurted as soon as the three of us sat down.

Regan shrugged. "How could I know? But it is interesting. An interview with this Ms. Benedict is certainly in order. If she can produce the gun to which Mr. Goode alluded, that may be sufficient proof that she's not involved. The murder weapon is indubitably in the hands of the police. On the other hand, if she cannot—well, we'll see. One thing is certain: she must be seen. I will put the intrepid Mr. Goldman on her trail."

Baker stuck around when we left; he had more things to talk over with Eddie. "I'll grab a cab," he muttered in the doorway. "Thanks a lot, Bishop. You've already learned more than I was able to pick up in three different tries with the guy. I don't know how you do it."

Regan shrugged but his eyes showed he appreciated the compliment. He was in a good mood on the drive home.

"Maybe you should background yourself on this Ms. Benedict, David. Perhaps you can find something through your contacts at

Headquarters. Or ... " His lip curled. " ... through your friend, Mr. Rozanski, the *former* journalist."

I grinned. Chet Rozanski's one of my golfing buddies; he's also the crime reporter for Channel 54. Chet knows everything about everybody in the underworld, or at least so it seems. Regan, who used to like Chet, despises TV, especially TV news shows. So he'd been disgusted when Chet made the jump from the Manhattan *Dispatch* into TV-land. He'd said, "Television journalism is an oxymoron," forcing me once again to the dictionary. But whether Regan admitted it or not, Chet was a helpful guy to know.

"Good idea," I said. "Sounds like this Benedict broad—excuse me, I mean this Benedict *lady*—has a rap sheet, so I should be able to find out something. And even *former* journalists sometimes know things. I'll call Rozanski."

Regan grunted a contented grunt. He's never happier than when he's got his teeth sunk deep into one of my cases.

14

WHILE REGAN WENT UP to his room to change back into his purple robe, I notified Ernie that we'd have lunch in ten minutes and called Rozanski. Ernie wasn't pleased at our slipshod attitude regarding lunch; neither was my stomach.

Rozanski acted like my call was the most important thing that'd happened to him all day. What a change from the days on the *Dispatch*. Then it was rush, rush, rush; never a spare second. Now he sounded bored to tears. I imagined him tilted back in his chair, feet on desk, cigar tilted up at the ceiling, the fluorescent lighting of his modernistic office glinting off his bald dome.

"Hey, Davey! Tomorrow's supposed to be gorgeous. How about a quick eighteen at Albemarle? You name the time."

I snorted. "You desperate for cash or something? Look, you're that bad off, just tell me. I'll send you a check. At least I'd avoid humiliating myself in front of all those other golfers."

Rozanski chuckled. "You may be wiser than you know. Guess what I shot yesterday . . . "

I cut him off. A little of Chet's bragging goes a long way. "Hey, Chet, I'm already convinced you're a helluva golfer. What I need you to do is prove you know something about what Channel Fifty-four pays you for. Who's Ruthie Benedict?"

He sighed. "I'd rather talk about golf. Who'd you say? Ruthie Benedict?" He started mumbling. "Ruthie Benedict, Ruthie Benedict. Hmmm. Obviously part of the Benedict crime syndicate, or you wouldn't be asking. One of 'em just died; Dom, Big Joe's older brother. But Ruthie?" He whistled tunelessly for a few seconds. Then, "Hey! I got it! The one that married Junior, right?"

I grunted admiringly. "Chet, you're amazing. Give me the skinny on her."

He laughed. "Sorry, pal. I've just told you everything I know. But not to worry. I'm sure I can dig up some dirt if you'll tell me a little bit more about her. Why do you want to know?"

I told him she might have some connection to the Compton murder case. Of course he wanted to know why I was looking into that; I told him I was doing a little work for Davis Baker. But when I told him about Ruthie's run-ins with the cops, Chet said, "Ah! That gives me something to go on. Let me get Jodi on the line."

Jodi Nakamura is Chet's producer—a fancy word for gofer, a strange occupation for someone as bright as she is. She puts up with it for two reasons: (a) she likes Chet, and (b) it's a way to learn the business. In a couple of years she'll have her own gofer, mark my words. Her eyes are beautiful but they're hard as ball bearings.

She got on the line and Chet gave her instructions. "Give Davey whatever he wants on Ruthie Benedict or anything else. He's just given me my scoop for tonight's six o'clock news: 'New development in Compton case! Davey Goldman now working for Eddie Goode!' " He hung up.

Jodi took over. She must have been sitting in front of a computer terminal, because she was a fountain of information. "Okay,

Davey," she chirped. "Get your pencil out and write fast. I'm only going through this once. Ready?

"Lady you're asking about's full name is Mrs. Joseph D. Benedict, Jr., Eight twenty-three Vandam. Twenty-four years old, married only once, seven years ago; uh, divorced two years later. Ex-hubbie's got no convictions, but everyone says he's the next *capo di tutti capi* of the Benedict syndicate. No kids.

"Lady's maiden name: Mary Ruth Healy. Grew up in Queens— 1033 Broadyke. Goes by Ruthie, always has. Mother: Maribeth O'Connor Healy—deceased. Father: Jeremiah Healy—we've got nothing on him but the name. Apparently still alive, but no current address showing.

"Background on Ruthie shows three arrests but only one conviction. That was six years ago, when she was barely old enough to be tried as an adult. Did six months of a scheduled sixteen. Let off for good behavior. Charge was 'Possession of stolen property in excess of two thousand dollars.' What's the word for that?"

"Fencing," I muttered.

"Oh, right. Charges in the other busts read the same but were dismissed before they ever came to trial. Ummm. Seems like the lady's kept her nose clean for the past five years, Davey. Nothing new on her sheet."

Five minutes later I greeted Regan coming off the elevator with an announcement calculated to irritate both Ernie and my stomach lining. Even more than they already were.

"Just spoke to Mrs. Benedict," I told him with a glance at Ernie. "Took the liberty of inviting her to lunch. She's expecting her ex-hubby for some kind of business chat and says she'd be delighted to come if I wouldn't mind picking her up. It'll give her an excuse to ditch him. It's a quarter to two now—I think I can get down there and be back before two-fifteen. What do you think?"

Regan's eyes lighted up. "Yes, by all means. Does she know what we want to talk about?"

"Nope. She's so anxious to get away from hubby, she's ready to go anywhere. I told her we were representing Goode."

Regan nodded. "Bring her."

I turned to Ernie. "Two-fifteen, Ernie?"

She sighed and shook her head. "Just don't blame me if the casserole's as dry as day-old bread."

Regan rolled his eyes and headed for his office. I headed for the door, happy I'd left the Caddy in front instead of returning it to Fred.

It was 2:00 straight up when I parked and got out of the car. Eight twenty-three Vandam was a medium-rise brick apartment building just like a thousand others in the city. What wasn't just like the thousand others was that the front door was standing open. As I approached I saw why. The foyer was in use—as a temporary conference room.

The guy in the electric blue suit and Italian tassel loafers doing the conferring was tall and broad-shouldered with long dark hair tied back in a ponytail. He looked vaguely familiar. I could see only the legs of the woman he was conferring with. The legs were fine but she wasn't. She was cowering in the far corner of the foyer, obviously afraid. I'm not a huge fan of guys that use size and muscle to intimidate people smaller than them. I decided to join the conference.

As I got to the doorway I heard him growl, "Why don't you use your goddamn head and sign it, Ruthie?" I realized the conference Ruthie had told me she was going to have with her ex was going on right in front of me in the vestibule.

Over the ex-husband's shoulder a pair of beautiful brown eyes threw me a message of appeal. Suddenly—shockingly—he nailed her right across the face with an open palm. Like a rifle shot. Her head flew to the side and a sheet of paper she'd been holding fluttered to the floor. That was enough for me. I moved in.

Something—maybe her eyes, maybe a sixth sense—alerted him. He crouched, spun around and flicked open a switchblade, all in one fluid motion.

In situations like this I watch the eyes. His were dark and hostile, set deep in his angular face. And determined. I put up both hands in a gesture of friendliness and gave him a smile. He didn't smile back.

"Just move it, pal." His voice was strained. "This don't concern you."

I raised my hands higher. "Hey, no problem, fella. I'm just on my way upstairs." I glanced at Ruthie. She met my eyes with a look of appeal. I refocused on Junior, widening the smile. "Gotta hassle with the little lady?"

Benedict looked me over, decided I was no threat, and grinned. "Naw. No hassle. Go on by. Gotcher key?" For all the smile and friendly words, his eyes stayed watchful and the knife steady, pointed straight at my crotch.

"Key? Sure." I took my eyes off him and, pretending to search my pockets, started to edge past.

The next move would be crucial. Of the various outcomes I was imagining, several involved large quantities of blood—mine—all over the floor. The way Junior handled his blade told me he'd probably gotten his reputation as a knife man the old-fashioned way: he'd earned it.

In fact, I don't know what I'd have done if Ruthie hadn't moved. But it doesn't matter; she did. With Junior's eyes on me, she grabbed her chance and broke for the door to the street. He turned and lunged at her with the knife. The direction the blade was headed—right for her kidneys—must have given me an adrenaline rush. Before the knife could get to her, my stiffened hand came down on his forearm with everything I had. His arm went limp and the knife clattered to the floor. End of fight, right?

Wrong. As pain swept over his face and Ruthie burst through the door, he shifted his weight and sent a vicious kick right for my gonads. Damn near got them, too. With or without the knife, the guy was cat-quick. But something—instinct, training or adrenaline—made me a little quicker. I deflected the foot with my hip, grabbed it and tugged. His other foot lost purchase, and I flipped him. Hard. His skull made a satisfying *thunk* as it hit the floor.

I didn't start relaxing yet. Not with this guy. Before he could move I trapped his arm under my foot. He stifled a shriek and I realized my hand chop had broken his arm. Just as well. Even with a broken arm, he was no cupcake. Ruthie had done me a real favor when she diverted his attention. She was now out on the sidewalk watching us, her face a little less worried.

I looked down at Junior. "Ready to call it a day, pal?" He bared his teeth—I guess partly from the pain, partly in anger. I rolled his arm with my foot; he gasped. "Okay, okay," he groaned. "Leggo, dammit! You broke my goddamn arm."

"I came to talk to your ex-wife," I told him, laying on a little more weight. He moaned. "I'm going to let you go, but first I want to know what the fight was about."

"About this," came a breathy, female voice behind me. I swiveled my head. It was Ruthie; I hadn't heard her come back in. She picked up the paper she'd dropped and handed it to me. High up on her left cheek Junior's hand print was visible. Next to it the eye looked puffy: she was going to have a shiner.

"He wanted me to sign it," she said. "And I didn't wanna." I looked at the paper: a page of printed text under the title POWER OF ATTORNEY. It contained several blanks to be filled in but none of them had been; two big black X's at the bottom indicated the blanks labeled EXECUTED BY and DATED.

I looked down at Junior. His color was pasty but his dark eyes, still fixed on me, glowed with hatred.

"I'm Mrs. Benedict's attorney, Junior," I told him, rolling his arm again. The *attorney* brought a noise from Ruthie, but Junior didn't notice. "I'll just take this with me," I went on, "and advise her on whether or not she should sign it. Trust me, I'll be fair."

I took a step back and scooped up the knife. "I'll keep this as a memento. You'd better go before I advise Mrs. Benedict to call a cop."

He struggled to his feet, holding his arm, face drawn in pain. "I'll see you again, asshole." He turned the glare on Ruthie. "This ain't over, Ruthie." She gave a glare right back.

"Anytime, Junior," I said. "But if I were you I'd get that arm fixed before I started talking about a rematch."

He had to have the last word. "Wanna tell me your name, asshole?" I waved him away. He gave Ruthie and me a final menacing look before he went out the door holding his arm.

I folded the razor-sharp blade back into its handle and pocketed it. Ruthie smiled at me, eyes bright. Very pretty even with the blotch on her face. "You were wonderful!" she breathed. "Thanks."

I grinned at her. "Hey, no problem." I tried to breathe normally.

She thought of something and her dark eyes narrowed. "You never told me what you wanted."

"Simple. Got a guy wants to talk with you. He's a Catholic

bishop, so you don't have to worry. He just wants to hear your confession."

It took a little persuasion and a bit of explanation, including further mention of Eddie Goode, but she finally agreed to come, primarily because she was grateful for the rescue. Within five minutes we were in the Caddy, heading for Thirty-seventh Street.

15

MY GUESS THAT RUTHIE'D have a shiner didn't prove out: by the time we got to the mansion, the mark on her cheek was starting to fade and the swelling was almost gone. I was able to understand how she'd made conquests of Junior Benedict and Eddie Goode and who knew how many others. Somehow the shadows under her dark eyes made them that much more mysterious. Her lips had that pouty, vulnerable look men love. And her soft and curvy body didn't hurt either. As for her sometimes ungrammatical way of talking, it might have bothered some people, but the breathy way it came out struck me as intriguing.

My attempts to find out why she and Junior had been battling over that power of attorney wasn't wildly successful.

I tried to ease into it. "What's with you and the ex?"

She wrinkled her nose. "He wants me to do sumpn' I don't want to do, that's all." And that was as far as I could get. I decided to let Regan have a crack at it if he wanted to.

I let us in the front door and led her into the dining room. "Hungry?" I asked.

"Starving!"

"Good. Me too. I'll challenge you to see who can eat the most. The Bishop—"

Ernie came rushing in from the kitchen. "He's talking to the Cardinal," she whispered. Don't ask me why, but she can't say the word *Cardinal* in anything but a whisper.

"Oh. Well, should we—"

"He said you and your guest should go ahead and eat. I took a tray in to him. He said he'd eat in the office; you two should just join him when you're done." She smiled at Ruthie. "Hello, dear. You must be Mrs. Benedict."

I apologized for not introducing them and invited Ruthie to sit down. When Ernie brought in the casserole I had an idea.

"Why don't you join us, Sister? Since the Bishop's not going to."

She blushed and mumbled something, but I insisted and so did Ruthie. Ernie finally pulled up a chair and dished herself a plateful. There was method to my madness; the two women seemed to hit it off and I thought Ruthie might loosen up. She sure had no trouble eating. She liked Ernie's cooking and said so.

"Sister," she beamed, "I didn't eat like this since Mama died."

"Well, you're just as sweet as you can be, dear, to say that. You make Davey bring you around more often, you hear? By the way, are you Catholic, dear? You look Irish."

Ruthie grinned, her mouth full. "As Paddy's pig!" That came embarrassingly close to describing the way she ate. I decided she was going to have to do something about her table manners before she added me to her list of conquests. Holding Ernie's eye, she finally got the bite down and jerked a thumb at her curvy chest. "Mary Ruth Healy's my maiden name."

"Mary Ruth! What a lovely Catholic name. Do you ever use the Mary, dear?"

Ruthie hoisted another forkful. My challenge about who was hungriest had been answered in spades. In fact, just watching the way she ate was making me less hungry by the second.

"My daddy," Ruthie said between chews, "is the only one that calls me Mary Ruth. Everybody else calls me Ruthie."

"Well, I'll just call you Mary Ruth too, dear. Were you brought up in the faith?" I smiled to myself. Ernie was helping without even knowing it.

"Brought up, yes," the woman admitted. "But I got away from it a little."

Ernie gave her a tsk, tsk and was about to start a pitch to get her back to the Church when she noticed her plate was empty.

"Have some more, dear, please. Oh, I do love a body with a good appetite!" Ruthie obeyed.

After seconds, Ruthie talked Ernie into giving her the recipe. The nun handed her a notepad and dictated, Ruthie scribbling laboriously. Her handwriting, I noticed, was slow but elegant: exaggerated Palmer method with lots of swoops and swirls. Her spelling was a little less successful. She spelled *chile* 'chilly,' and *spoonfuls* "spunefulls."

They went from recipes into Catholicism, and my mind turned elsewhere. I excused myself, went down the hall and stuck my head in Regan's office. He was on the phone, listening. He rolled his eyes at me, held up one finger and shrugged. Then pointed at the little silver bell on the desk. He'd ring when the Cardinal finally shut up. "Yes, Your Eminence," I heard him murmur as I shut the door and returned to the dining room.

The conversation was still on Catholicism. Ruthie, I quickly gathered, was telling a shocked Ernie what she thought of the Second Vatican Council.

That surprised me: not Ruthie's opposition to it, but that she gave a damn. She struck me as both too young and too uninvolved in the Church to have even heard of it, much less be arguing about it.

Ernie's defending it didn't surprise me. I've heard her talk about the Council before. About once a year she'll get into an argument with Regan about some churchly affair, and more often than not, her parting shot will be, "That's not what the Council said." That irritates Regan so much I wish I could work it into one of our arguments, but I haven't figured out yet how to do it.

It soon came out where Ruthie's interest in, and opinion about, the Vatican Council came from. They were arguing about Latin in the Mass—Ernie was against it, and Ruthie for it. By this time they were both getting a little red in the face.

"I don't see," Ruthie declaimed, "what's so bad about Latin. If it was good enough for Jesus, it's good enough for us."

"But Mary Ruth! Have you ever attended a Mass in Latin?"

"Plenty a' times! It's so holy and pure—"

"Balderdash!" (Ernie's harshest curse. She was obviously losing control.) "You sound like one of those St. Titus fanatics!"

Ruthie got redder yet. "You mean the Knights of St. Titus?

What's so wrong with that? My daddy's a member." I groaned inwardly.

As it happened, I knew something about the Knights of St. Titus, due to some dust-ups Regan'd had with the bunch over such burning issues as the use of whole-wheat wafers at Mass instead of the standard white ones, or whether the people in the pews should be allowed to drink the wine. Crucial, heart-pounding issues like that.

Regan had been forced into the battle by the Cardinal, who for some reason, a couple of years before, had appointed him arch-diocesan liaison to the Knighthood. Regan had stuck it out about six months before he got so burned out by the constant kvetching, he wrote a long letter of resignation. One of the few letters I can ever recall him completely rewriting after I'd typed it. He decided his description ("totalitarian zealots") of the group was perhaps a tad stronger than diplomacy would allow.

So Ruthie's dad was one of those. When the argument sim-mered down, I asked her, "You and your daddy agree on most things?"

Ruthie blushed. "I don't see him that much anymore. We been sorta on the outs ever since I married Junior."

The three of us were still at the kitchen table sipping coffee, the argument forgotten, when Regan's bell tinkled. I jumped to my feet, even beating Ernie. "I'll go see if he's ready for us," I told Ruthie, pouring a cup of coffee to take him. "Back in a sec."

Regan raised his eyebrows when I came in alone. I put his coffee on his desk. "Before you hear what Lady Benedict has to say, I should fill you in on what happened at her place a little while ago. It'll help you understand how I got her here. And maybe tell you something about her."

I managed to brief him in about four minutes flat. Three min-utes and fifty-nine seconds longer than I'd promised Ruthie, but still not bad. Regan listened, with no questions or comments. That's unless you count his shudder when I mentioned breaking Junior's arm. When I showed him the power-of-attorney form he told me to leave it. He was scanning it when I went to get Ruthie.

I brought her in, and she settled into the chair in front of Regan's desk. He pulled up tight to his side of the desk, set his brake (something he always seems to do when a pretty woman's in view) and studied her. "I have some rather personal questions to ask you, Mrs. Benedict. If you—"

"Please, Bishop," she interrupted in that fantastic semi-whisper. "Call me Ruthie."

Regan blushed. "Thank you, I'd prefer not. I'd like to ask you: what was going on between you and Mr. Benedict? Mr. Goldman has described the incident to me."

She shrugged. "What I told Davey. Junior wants me to do sump'n I don't wanna do."

"And that is?"

Ruthie looked stubborn and clamped her jaw. Regan waited her out. "Okay," she conceded. "You look friendly. No reason I shouldn't tell you, I guess." She took a breath.

"They're openin' his uncle's will next Monday. I might be in it. Junior wants to be my attorney." She pointed at the sheet on Regan's desk. "That's it on your desk, isn't it? Think I shoulda signed it?"

Regan gave a small shrug. "I don't know, Madame. Probably not. Why *didn't* you?"

"Someone tole me not to."

"A lawyer?"

"Someone."

"Does this someone understand the situation?" Ruthie nodded. Regan studied her. "Then he or she is probably giving you good advice. Here is your document." He handed it to her. "We're trying to assist in the defense of your friend, Mr. Edward Goode, on a charge of murder. I trust I am not misspeaking in calling him your friend?"

Ruthie smiled and looked confused. "Mis-what? You mean, is Eddie Goode my friend? I don't know as I'd go that far, but—"

"You're aware of his incarceration?" Ruthie stared at him. Regan saw she wasn't following and cleaned up his language. "Excuse me. You know he's in jail?"

She shrugged. "Naw. But he's been in there a lot. I'm not surprised."

"But you hadn't heard of his latest incarcer—jailing?"

"Naw."

"Does the name Compton mean anything to you? Specifically, Laddie Compton?"

I was watching her face. She showed not a flicker of expression at the name and shook her head no. I cursed Goode under my breath. Had he led us down the primrose path?

"When did you last see Mr. Goode?" Regan continued.

She frowned. "It's been a while. A year. Maybe more."

"Or maybe considerably less." Regan's voice toughened. "Say about a month ago? Or less?"

Ruthie's eyes widened. "A month ago? Lemme think." She closed her eyes and wrinkled her brow. I was puzzled. She seemed to be telling the truth. "Naw." She looked at Regan unblinking, then at me. "Naw, I haven't seen Eddie in—oh, a year or more."

I suddenly realized how completely I'd bought Eddie's story. For the first time since I'd seen him on the video I was growing suspicious of him. I looked at Regan; he seemed to be having the same doubts.

My mind was now working. How easy for Eddie to pick on someone he'd met once, maybe was attracted to, and tell us that cock-and-bull story about an attempted suicide. And we'd bought it, hook, line and sinker.

Regan pinned Ruthie with his eyes. "Your notebook, please, David." He waited, eyes on her, while I pulled it out. "What was the name of the bar in Soho where Mr. Goode said he occasionally met Mrs. Benedict?"

I found it. Ruthie was maintaining eye contact with no difficulty. "Mulligan's," I said.

Regan eyed her. "Have you ever been in Mulligan's, Mrs. Benedict?"

She stared at him and frowned. "Yeah, I used to. I haven't been there in a while." Her face brightened. "I think that's the last place I saw Eddie!"

"And when was that?"

Ruthie shook her head. "God, I dunno. Lemme think. Oh, maybe last summer—wait! I remember, the game was on, in the bar! The Mets were playin' the Pirates and Gooden was pitchin'. It was Labor Day weekend, I remember! Eddie wanted me to go out with 'im, but I said no."

Regan's eyes gave her no relief. "It won't do, Madame. I know—and so does Mr. Goldman—about your purported suicide attempt three or four weeks ago. You'd better tell us the truth."

"My what?" Ruthie's eyes were wide. She threw a frightened glance my way. "What would I do that for? Hey, I don't know what you're talkin' about!" She got up. "I'm gettin' outa here!"

"Sit down!" Regan snapped. "We're going to get to the bottom of this." She sat back down, scowling at both of us, but Regan's confidence was crumbling. So was mine. It was beginning to look like Eddie Goode had got us again. And neither one of us was very happy about it.

Ruthie didn't budge an inch, despite Regan's best efforts. At least some of what Eddie'd told us was the truth. He and Ruthie had been in a work-release program together for just under a year. They had seen each other occasionally in Mulligan's. But, according to Ruthie, that was it.

"I've never even owned a gun!" she insisted. "God! If I was gonna kill myself, I wouldn't use a gun! I think Eddie's sellin' youse a bill a goods."

I was beginning to agree with that, but with a nodded okay from Regan gave it a try of my own. "Look, Ruthie. Are we being nice to you?" She nodded, unsmiling. "You better believe we are. A helluva lot nicer than several guys down at Headquarters I could mention, a few of whom you probably know. So give us a break. Or better yet, the truth."

Ruthie looked about to cry. She shook her head at me. "I'm tellin' youse the truth, I swear! Look!" I looked. She raised her hand and looked straight into my eyes. Hers were dark pools, hard to face, but I did. "On my mother's grave, I never had a gun, I never said I'd kill myself; and I haven't seen Eddie since last Labor Day." She turned to the Bishop. "And that's the truth, Bishop, on my mother's grave."

Regan's face was a thundercloud. "Madame," he said severely. "I take it you understand the seriousness of the oath you have just taken."

She didn't back off. "I know, Bishop. I know the seriousness, and I mean it. On my mother's grave."

Regan broke eye contact and nodded. "All right. At the moment, I can't say whether I believe you or not. But I'm inclined to." He turned his green eyes back on her dark ones. "But if I find you're lying—"

She gave him a small smile and dropped her eyes. "You can send me straight to the deepest part of Hell, Bishop, and you'd be right to. I wouldn't swear on my mother's grave and lie." She looked up at him. "And I think you know that."

He nodded. "Well. Thank you for coming."

She bounced up. "Thanks for the lunch." She waved Ernie's notepaper in the air. "And I even got the recipe!"

After calling her a cab and letting her out—with a ten-spot for the cab ride home—I returned to the office. Regan was glowering.

"Someone is lying to me and I don't like it. I think it's Eddie Goode." He took a breath. "David. Get Mr. Baker. This changes my whole attitude toward his request. Unless he can—yes, Sister?"

Ernie was in the doorway. "Telephone for you, David. Ms. Nakamura."

I turned to Regan, who gave me a dismissive wave. "I'll be right back," I said, and headed for my office. I grabbed the phone. "Yeah, Jodi. Got something for me?"

"Yeah. Something you probably ought to know before you go tracking down this Benedict babe."

"Too late, Jodi," I said, feeling a sinking feeling in the pit of my stomach. "She's already come and gone. What is it?"

"This. Were you aware she's a former next-door neighbor of the guy who was murdered? Laddie Compton?"

I stared at the Van Gogh on the opposite wall. It's called *Sunrise at Arles*, which I've never understood. Not a trace of sun in it anywhere.

"Say that again, Jodi."

"You heard me, Davey. As I told you this morning, the Healys lived for years at 1033 Broadyke, Queens. That's where they were living when Ruthie married Junior Benedict. Well, until they went upscale two years ago, the Comptons lived at 1035 Broadyke. So what do you think about that, buddy? Ruth Benedict and the late, lamented Laddie Compton grew up together. Next-door neighbors."

16

I TRIED TO GATHER my wits, but it wasn't easy. Ruthie'd sworn on her mother's grave. I shook my head and gritted my teeth.

"How'd you come up with this, Jodi?"

"Just talent," she laughed. I didn't join in. "What's wrong, Davey? You sound—funny."

"I've think I've just been lied to by a champ. And the Bishop has just has his nose twisted good. He's not going to be happy about this." Something hit me. "Hey! How'd you come up with it?"

"Brains, guts and raw talent." She laughed. "No, I got lucky. Strange things sometime stick in my mind. Somehow, when I gave you that address for Ruthie Benedict, I remembered I'd seen that street name before. I guess because it had kind of an MCP sound to it."

I blinked. "Say what?"

"Come on, Davey! Broad? And dyke? Two words for women only a male chauvinist pig would use."

"What?" Then I got it. "Oh. Geez, you've got a very twisted mind, Nakamura. Which isn't to say I'm not grateful. You got any other little tidbits? Like, say a videotape of the Compton killing in living color?"

She laughed. "Nope, that'll have to do you. Hope it's not too late for you to use."

"Oh, don't worry about that, Jodi. We'll use it. And thanks."

I sat awhile thinking before heading back to the Bishop. He looked up at me and his eyes narrowed. "David? Is something wrong?"

"You tell me. I just learned something interesting. Our friend, Mrs. Benedict, is not only beautiful, she's also a helluva liar. She said she'd never heard of anyone named Laddie Compton? She must have been a slow learner as a child. She grew up next door to him." Regan's expression didn't change.

"Oh she did, did she? I take it you have this on good authority?" His voice seemed to come from somewhere north of Alaska. I told him about Jodi and what she'd said.

Regan closed his eyes tight and rubbed his forehead. "I am an arrogant, self-deluded idiot," he muttered. "Led by the nose by a hoyden." He opened his eyes and looked at me. "She made a fool of me." He sighed, spun his chair away from the desk and began his version of pacing, rolling aimlessly around the office.

"Never heard of Laddie Compton. No, of course not. On her mother's grave!" Regan stopped and looked at me. "Will she have arrived home by now?"

I glanced at my watch: 3:12. I nodded. "Probably, if she went straight home. But since she told me that's where she was going, she's probably someplace else."

"No doubt. See if you can get her on the phone. I want to speak to her."

My luck went from rotten to rank. I went to my office, called and got a busy signal. Tried every thirty seconds for eight minutes: same thing. Then, at 3:22, I finally got through. The phone rang. And rang. And rang. After eighteen rings I hung up. Went back to Regan's office to report.

He was at his desk working on a personnel file. I told him of my scintillating success in getting hold of Ruthie. He just nodded. He'd calmed down.

"It may be just as well. I am considering a call to Inspector Kessler." He frowned at the ceiling. "But I don't know if it would do any good at this stage." Back to me. "I think what we need to do is first prove that Mrs. Benedict is lying. Then we might have something to take to the inspector." His rage broke through again. "The little hoyden! I shouldn't be surprised to learn that she's the murderer herself. A very clever woman. And dangerous."

He sighed. "Well. If we're to trap Mrs. Benedict in her lie, how are we to proceed?"

I grinned. "You're asking me? You kidding? That's what I pay you for!"

Regan didn't smile back. "I'm serious, David. I have an idea, but it's not particularly brilliant. I'm not feeling particularly brilliant right now. Give me your ideas."

I shook my head but gave it some thought. Regan waited patiently. "Go back to Eddie?" I finally said. "I don't know. Maybe he could add some more details about the time she pretended to commit suicide."

Regan nodded and frowned. "Perhaps. But we'd still have little or no leverage. Any other ideas?"

I rolled my eyes. "I've shot my wad. Come on, give! Don't let that little liar get you down."

He shut his eyes. "Her father. From what you said, she feels close to him. Furthermore, he is a former next-door neighbor, and perhaps a friend, of the Comptons. I'd think that, using a bit of subtlety, you could discover something from him that might give us some leverage. Try it." He went back to the file. I was dismissed.

I nodded, a waste of energy with him not looking, and returned to my office. Actually, I liked the idea—I wished I'd thought of it. He was right: it wasn't that brilliant. Or maybe it was. Part of brilliance, maybe, is seeing things that are right there but that nobody else can see. Thought for the day.

Problem was, his brilliance had handed me two problems, neither of which he could help with: how to locate Jeremiah Healy, and how to get him into the frame of mind to tell me what I needed to know.

I sat in my office with my feet up on the desk—my best thinking position. Came up with no brilliant ideas. Finally pulled the Queens phone directory from my bottom drawer. No J. *Healy* at 1033 Broadyke. I scratched my head.

Got an idea. Not brilliant. In fact it was the kind of roundabout scheme I normally try to avoid, but it was the best I could do at the moment. I put the Queens directory away and pulled out the Manhattan. Looked up *Midas Touch Autocare* in the business section. The address was One East Fifty-ninth.

When the young lady informed me I'd reached Midas Touch, I asked for Mr. Compton's secretary and was informed her name was Ms. Arnold.

That lady's nasal voice sounded awesomely efficient. And no-nonsense. So I went to my deep Southern drawl.

"Howdy, ma'am. Hey, don't bother Mr. Compton with this, but I'm jes' tryna reach my ole buddy, Jerry Healy. Jerry usta live right next door to Dolph 'n' me, back when me 'n' the missus lived in Queens. I been gone a few years, 'n' I'm back in town fer the day 'n' sorta wanted to get in touch with ole Jerry. You happen to have his number there on your Rolodex? That's 'Healy.' Jeremiah's his first name, if you need that."

Silence. Then, "You don't sound as though you come from Queens, Mr., ah . . . "

"Beauregard. Freddy Beauregard. No 'm, I'm from Tennessee, born 'n' bred. But I settled in Queens a few years ago. Then moved back home. Been in Tennessee over four years now. Waal, I'm back in town on a trip and—"

"Excuse me, Mr., er, Beauregard, then you aren't aware that Mr. Healy is now, er, working for Mr. Compton?"

The surprise that came through in my voice was no act. "Naw! You're kiddin'! There at the comp'ny?"

"Well, no. Mr. Healy works at Mr. Compton's residence. He— takes care of anything around the household that needs taking care of. He chauffeurs Mr. Compton occasionally."

"Well, now, ain't that sumpn'? So I could reach ole Jerry at Dolph's house?"

"Yes. Would you like to speak to Mr. Compton? He's rather busy, but an old friend like you—"

"Oh, no'm. Actually, I wasn't never as close to him as I was to Jerry. Don't you bother him none, ma'am. If I could jes' have that number?" She gave it to me. I thanked the charming lady and was about to tell her goodbye when I thought of something.

"Oh, ma'am, one more thang?" She murmured something. "Uh, I wonder if I oughta bother Jerry right now. I mean, wouldn't Mr. Compton have him on call?"

The woman's voice warmed. "Well, that's very thoughtful of you, Mr. Beauregard. But don't worry. Mr. Compton is working late tonight. I'm sure he won't need Mr. Healy till after eight. And Mrs. Compton is out of the office all day, so she won't need him at all."

I thanked her and hung up, rolling my eyes. How did Ruthie think she was going to get away with it? Saying she didn't know Laddie, when her dad worked for his dad? I thought about how much I was going to enjoy my next meeting with Mrs. Ruthie Benedict.

Well, I'd solved the first challenge: found Healy. Now I needed entry. I thought over what Ruthie'd said about him. One aspect looked promising (assuming she hadn't been lying about that, too.) Back when Regan had had dealings with the Knights of St. Titus, he'd had me keep a file on them. After he resigned he told me to get rid of it. Fortunately I seldom keep up with my file work; I still hadn't got around to purging it. I pulled it out and found what I needed. I called the number Ms. Arnold had given me.

" 'Lo." Deep, gravelly, male voice.

"Mr. Healy?"

Silence for several seconds. Then, suspiciously, "Yeah. Who's this."

"My name is Goldman, Mr. Healy. But I need to be sure I'm speaking to the correct Mr. Healy. Are you the Mr. Healy who's a Knight of St. Titus?"

Long pause. "And supposin' I am?"

"Well, Mr. Healy, some questions have arisen that may make it mandatory for the Knights to reconsider your membership."

Another long pause. "Say your name again."

"My name? David Goldman."

"Goldman. That's what I thought you said. Isn't that kind of a Jew name for a Catholic organization?"

That had occurred to me too; I had an answer ready. I darkened my tone. "Mr. Healy. May I say that not one person in the Knights of St. Titus—not one—has ever questioned my parentage. My forebears came from Germany, and I can assure you, sir, my bloodline is quite as pure as yours. Quite." I spoke even more distinctly. "In particular, Mr. O'Halloran has never voiced the slightest concern about me or my lineage. Not once."

J. Michael O'Halloran was the founder and still the Grand High Exalted Knight—that is, the top dog—of the Knights of St. Titus. I'd met him once at a function the Bishop was attending, and what I'd told Healy was the plain truth: O'Halloran had voiced no concern about my name or background.

My use of his name had the desired effect. "Naw, naw, hey. I'm not sayin' anything against you, unnerstand. It's just I knew a guy once named Goldman, he was a Jew, that's all. I was just askin', know what I mean?"

"Well, I'm glad that's settled. May I come and ask you some questions about your membership?"

"Yeah, but geez, what about? I been a good Knight for twenty years."

"That's true, Mr. Healy, very true. However, a crime has recently occurred in your place of employment, giving rise to some question about your fitness for membership. I'm sure I can clear it up, if you're willing to answer a few questions, honestly and completely."

"Yeah, well, sure. But you gotta know, I didn't have nothin' to do with Laddie's—with the crime that happened here."

"I'm sure that's true, Mr. Healy. Nonetheless, questions do arise when something like this takes place. It would be better to clear it up right away. Don't you agree?"

"Uh, well, sure. When?"

"Well...what about today? Say in fifteen minutes? I'd be happy to come there."

That part was true.

17

I TOLD ERNIE I might be late for dinner. The news didn't make her happy, but that was okay: I was happy enough for both of us. In a few minutes I was going to be talking to Ruthie's father inside the house where the murder took place. This had possibilities.

I decided on a dark suit with a white shirt and somber tie. The Knights were a very serious bunch. I smoothed down my hair as I checked myself in the mirror. I concluded that St. Titus would be proud to have me represent his organization. My alligator-skin attaché case with the Knighthood file inside completed the total ensemble.

As I discovered as soon as I parked and got out of the Seville,

589 East Eighty-seventh was very impressive. Three-story, brick, probably late-nineteenth-century, well kept up, and about a hundred times more entitled to be called a mansion than the Bishop's. It looked to have been tuck-pointed not more than two or three years before.

A waist-high wrought-iron fence protected the tiny rose garden from would-be tramplers. The fence had two gates, neither one locked. The gate in the middle led to the front door. The other, forty feet to the east, opened to a sidewalk that ran around to the rear through a ten-foot gap between the Comptons' and the equally affluent-looking house next door.

I pushed through the middle gate, walked up the five steps to the stoop and rang the bell. In about thirty seconds the massive front door opened and a lantern-jawed, white-haired guy, puffing a bit, looked me over. Nearly my height and a good fifty pounds heavier, he wore a black blazer, white shirt and tie.

"Yeah?" He looked and sounded belligerent. His bulbous nose was interlaced with fiery-looking veins.

"Mr. Healy?"

"That's me. Whadda ya want?"

"What do I want?" I smiled. "I'm David Goldman, the gentleman who just called. About your membership in the Knights of St. Titus?"

Healy's face changed. "Aw, I'm sorry! I expected you to come around to the side door—that's where I live. But I guess I didn't tell you that, did I? C'mon in."

He held the door for me and I slid by him. Some people will tell you that a house where a murder's been committed gives off a definite aura. Well, I've been in a few and I've never been able to detect it. Nor could I this time.

I was standing in a huge two-story hallway with marble floors and walls, sunlight sparkling off a crystal chandelier. I didn't stand long: Healy didn't give me the chance. As soon as he closed the door behind us, he moved. He led me from the entranceway into a wide hall, made a sharp right turn down a narrow flight of stairs into a much narrower hall—obviously the servants' quarters. At the far end of that hall were three doors. The windowed one led outside. The one on the left was open, revealing a large kitchen about a hundred years newer than the house. My fleeting impression was of gleaming white tiles and plenty of modern appliances.

"In here," Healy said, opening the third door, the one to the right. "Where I live."

I walked in. It was a small sitting room connecting to a spartan bedroom. Healy waved at a club chair. "Sit!"

I sat. Healy threw himself on the couch, glanced at the blank TV screen of the set on the wall opposite and looked at me. "Getcha anything? Soda? Coffee?"

I shook my head, trying to read his face. I'd picked up a few things already. Not well educated, uncomfortable in his job as butler/chauffeur, a boozer.

I tried the gentle approach. "I'm pleased you're willing to answer my questions, Mr. Healy." I opened the attaché case in my lap, pulled out some official Knighthood stationery I'd pulled from the file, and got my pen ready.

"I'd like your response to some questions which have arisen." I looked at him. "The organization is not fond of publicity. Especially negative publicity."

Healy's eyes widened. "What do you mean? You mean, like about the murder?"

"First things first, Mr. Healy. We've come into some information about your daughter, sir. The family life of our members is vitally important to us. I'm sure you'll agree that it should be. Don't you, Mr. Healy?"

"Uh, yes, I understand you wanting to know about members' families, I guess." He swallowed. "I'm a widower. Guess you know that. What else do ya wanna know?"

I looked away from Healy as if embarrassed. "Well, I hesitate to mention it, but—" I looked at him. "Some information has come to our attention about your daughter. Tell me about her, Mr. Healy." I pretended to rack my brain. "Mary Ruth, I believe?"

Healy got redder. "Whaddaya wanna know? She's my only child. My only family anymore." He shrugged helplessly. "Tell me what you wanna know."

"Do you see her regularly, Mr. Healy?"

He shrugged. "Oh, once in a while. What difference does that make?"

I gave him a long look. "Everything about our Knights is important to us, Mr. Healy. I believe your daughter is divorced, is she not?"

"Right," he muttered. "Yeah, she's divorced. S'pose you think that's awful."

"Oh, no," I smiled. "If we held every member responsible for everything done by everyone in their family, we'd have few members left." I tittered and he smiled. "No, no, Mr. Healy. We just want to know about her." I got serious. "The more serious matter is the known connection of her husband—ex-husband, excuse me—with organized crime." I raised my eyebrows. "The Benedict crime syndicate, you know?"

Healy reddened. "I don't know how you know that but, yeah, you're right. There was just nothin' Mrs. Healy or me could do about it at the time, that's the God's truth, Mr. Goldman." Healy appealed to me with his hands. "We didn't encourage the weddin', we tried to forbid it, we had her talk to Father Doherty at the parish. I don't know what else we coulda done, and that's the God's truth. Course, you know, they run off and was married by a J.P. The Benedicts had it fixed up later, had a priest say the words over 'em and all. But we never approved."

"And then she was divorced a few years later?"

"Two years later. Maribeth—that's my wife—and I begged her to go for an annulment, but she wasn't interested. Broke Maribeth's heart. She died the next year."

"And how do you and your daughter get along now?"

"Well..." Healy's eyes, studying my face, took on a sneaky look. "...I don't see her very much. I didn't feel like she grieved over her mother as much she ought to've. I guess I'd have to say, we don't talk much."

He was lying. Wherever his daughter had picked up her technique, it didn't seem to be from him. Was it his fear that I'd disapprove of his being close to a divorced daughter? Or did he have some deeper reason?

I decided to try a different tack. "Let's talk about something else," I said briskly. "The Knights are interested in the fact that a murder took place in this house just last week. What can you tell me about that?"

"It was godawful. The son of the family I work for got himself murdered Sunday before last."

I nodded, jotting on the pad. "That was Ladd Compton?" Healy nodded, staring at the floor. "He and your daughter grew up together, isn't that right?"

Healy's eyes narrowed at me. "You sure know an awful lot. Where'd you get all this stuff?"

I smiled at him. "We do our homework, Mr. Healy. We can't be too careful, don't you agree? The Knights of St. Titus have enemies, you know."

Healy nodded. "Well, that's true. Yeah, they grew up together."

"And were they—romantically involved at any time?"

Healy blinked. "No," he said slowly, then seemed to get the implication for the first time. He glared at me. "Hell no, they weren't involved!"

Regan's got a saying he got somewhere: "Methinks the lady doth protest too much." I had a feeling I was getting somewhere.

"No?" I said skeptically. "That isn't what our sources say."

Healy tried to bluster. "Dammit, where do you get all this stuff? I tell you, they never—" A glance into my skeptical eyes stopped him. He seemed to wilt.

"Awright, awright. Yeah, I think they had something going. I don't know, mighta been just before he died."

Healy took a breath. "I'll admit, I was pretty mad about it. Laddie was—well, he was rich and all, but he wasn't the right one for my Mary Ruth. And I told him that!"

"You told him, Mr. Healy? When was that?"

"Night he died. He was sittin' right where you are, half an hour before he died. I told him to leave my Mary Ruth alone! And by God, I meant it! If whoever done it to him that night didn't, I mighta done it myself."

18

I STUDIED HEALY'S red face. "When was this, Mr. Healy?"

He glared at me. "Like I said: the night he died."

"So you saw Laddie Compton the night he died?"

Healy shrugged. "Yeah. He was here. He was talkin' fast and hard. For all the good it did him."

"About what?"

Healy's eyes suddenly got suspicious. "What difference does that make to you? You're questionin' whether I deserve to stay in the Knights, right? So why all these questions about Laddie?"

He had a point. "You have a point, Mr. Healy." I met his look. "But the problem is, the Knights have enemies." Healy gave a reluctant nod. "Well, we can't afford to have the slightest suspicion about any of our Knights. So if someone asks me about Jerry Healy, I want to have an answer. See what I mean?"

His eyes gave up the fight. "Yeah, okay, I guess I can see that. Go ahead and ask."

I nodded. "So what were you and the young man talking about? The night he died."

Healy's eyes looked everywhere but at me. "Oh, uh, just things." He thought of something and gave me a direct look. "See, he wanted to see me. He asked to come talk to me. So I said okay. He wanted to talk about him and my daughter."

My head was starting to spin from information overload. "When and where was this exactly?"

"Right here. He was sittin' right where you are now."

"When was that?"

"Hell, right before he died, I guess. He called me that day, said he wanted to see me. He knew how mad I was. First I told him I didn't wanna see him. Then—"

"Excuse me, Mr. Healy. Why were you angry at him?"

Healy shrugged, eyes on the floor. "Just the way he treated my

83

daughter. Uh, couldn't make up his mind if he wanted to marry her or not."

I wanted to probe, but the stubborn look on Healy's face told me I was on thin ice. So I shifted ground. "Did anyone else— any of the other Comptons—know you were angry at Laddie?"

"Naw. I didn't wanna mess up what I got here. This is a pretty good job. Anyway—"

"Excuse all the interruptions, Mr. Healy, but did anyone else know Laddie was coming to talk with you?"

Healy shook his head. "Naw. Not unless Laddie told someone, and I don't think he did. Anyway, when Laddie called me sayin' he wanted to come talk, I finally gave in and said, okay, come over, we'll talk. It's funny, he had a special time he said he wanted to talk. Wanted to come by right at ten to nine that Sunday night. Guess he wanted it when his mom and pop'd be gone. They had some kind of a deal they were goin' to that night." He thought a minute. "Diane, too, I guess. That's his sister."

"Was he right on time at eight-fifty?" Healy nodded. "And how long did you talk?"

Healy scratched his head. "Lessee. Damn phone kept ringin'. Laddie got a couple of phone calls—said he'd left my number with a friend. And the phone rang one other time but stopped before I got to it.

"Laddie's were real short calls. Last one was about nine-fifteen. That's when he laughed and said since his buddy wouldn't leave 'im alone, maybe we ought to go across the street to the Red Lion 'n' have a drink. Less interruptions. It's a bar back of us, over on Eighty-eighth. Laddie said he had to run upstairs and get somethin', but for me to go across and save us a booth, he'd be right along."

Healy shook his head while I scribbled furiously. "Hell, I thought it was a good idea. It was my night off, so I didn't hafta stay here. But he never came. I wish to hell now I'd come back. But how was I to know?"

Healy took a breath, avoiding my eye. "Anyway, he never came to the Lion. I ran into a coupla buddies and we started shootin' the breeze. Next thing I knew, it was after eleven. I came home to find cops all over the place."

His tone sounded pleading. "I just couldn't tell 'em I saw Laddie that evening. Dolph was all upset, you know, still in his tuxedo, tie loose. So I jus' told him and the cops I'd been at the bar. That part was true. I didn't lie any—just didn't tell 'em I had that talk with Laddie."

I cleared my throat. I tried to make the next words come out normal. "Then you didn't tell the police anything about that conversation you had with Laddie?" Jeremiah shook his head. "Or that he stood you up at the Red Lion?" Another head shake.

I mentally shook my own head. Healy didn't seem to realize what a hole he'd dug for himself. He was probably the last person who'd seen Laddie alive. Except for the murderer, of course. Assuming that wasn't Healy.

I tried to nail it down. "So *no* one, none of the Comptons, the police, no one knows you had that conversation with Laddie?"

Healy looked at me. "Nope. Nobody but you and me. I don't think—" The phone rang. He reached behind him, pulled the phone into his lap, punched the button with the blinking light. "Yeah, Healy."

He listened for a few seconds, his eyes widening. "No, listen!" He glanced at me, still listening. He got to his feet and turned his back to me. "Listen!" he said again; said it a third time. Then, "Don't do a thing! I'll be right there!"

Healy hung up and turned around. He was pale. "It's, uh, it's Mr. Compton. He . . ." Healy began moving toward the door, hand out to move me along with him. " . . . needs me to pick 'im up right away. Uh, an emergency. Maybe we can talk later."

"Sure, Mr. Healy." I was being herded into the hall and toward the outside door. He was breathing hard, car keys already in his hand. Healy was either very afraid of his boss or something strange was going on. In another three seconds we were outside. I grabbed the door to keep it from closing. I'd had a thought. I clapped a hand to my forehead. "Oh, no!"

Healy tried to shut the door but I held it. "What's the matter?" he asked irritably. "I got to go!"

"I'm sorry," I apologized. "I left my briefcase." I pulled the door open. "You go ahead—I'll grab it and let myself out."

Healy looked suspicious, glanced at his watch, back at me. I gave him my open, honest look. "Okay," he growled, turned and broke into a panicky-looking jog toward Eighty-eighth. He didn't look back.

19

I WENT BACK in the house and closed the door. I checked my Timex: 4:31. I was now, as far as I knew, the only human being in the house where Laddie Compton was murdered. And I figured to have a good half hour to look around before Healy got back with Compton—if that was really where he was going.

Wait a minute! I suddenly remembered what Compton's secretary had said to me on the phone: Compton was working late, Healy's services wouldn't be needed till late in the evening, if at all. Why would Healy lie to me about where he was going? But apparently he had.

But I didn't have time to ponder that. I was in the murder house and wanted to investigate it. I grabbed my briefcase from Healy's sitting room and retraced my steps back to the entrance hall.

Which, now that I had time to look it over, was even more impressive than I'd thought. Smaller than the Capitol rotunda in Washington, but for the entrance hall of somebody's home, not bad. I stood in the center of it and gawked.

The vaulted ceiling with four square skylights was more than thirty feet above me; the marble floor I was standing on was a circle about fifty feet in diameter. To the south were the big front double doors; to the north, a wide curving stairway. The late afternoon sun shining through the skylights and second-floor windows made crazy patterns on the shiny marble floor. At least a dozen large paintings cluttered the lower walls, and on a mahogany table in the corner stood foot-high statues of Cupid and Venus (I think), and a dozen smaller figurines.

Ten or twelve feet above me, a balcony ran from the top of the stairway all the way around the room. Still more paintings hung on the wall along it. That balcony looked like a good place to start my exploration.

I was halfway up the curving stairway when I heard a sound that stopped me in my tracks. The distant sound of a vacuum cleaner being turned on. My assumption that I was alone in the house was being severely challenged.

I followed the sound up the stairs, down a corridor and through an open door. I was now in a room I recognized from Goode's description: the master bedroom, a.k.a. the murder room. It was as big a bedroom as I'd ever seen. A king-sized bed and accompanying furniture occupied most of one end. The other half was cluttered with furniture: a round oak table and four padded oak chairs surrounding it; a couple of easy chairs; a desk and chair; and a huge dressing table with mirror. Vacuuming under the round table, her back to me, was a young black woman in sweatshirt and blue jeans.

"Excuse me!" I shouted over the noise. The vacuumer jumped like she'd been shot and spun around, eyes wide. She flicked off the machine.

"My God! Where'd you come from? You like to scared me half to death." She clapped her hand to her breast humorously, to show me how close she'd come to a heart attack.

"Sorry," I smiled. "I guess I sneaked up on you." My mind was working fast—and not the way you're thinking. Oh, she was pretty enough to provoke those kinds of thoughts; but I'm a professional. My mind was on what she might know about the murder, and how to get it out of her. I flashed the license.

"I'm investigator David Goldman, ma'am. Looking into the death of Mr. Compton. I was just discussing it with Mr. Healy downstairs. I decided to take a look around."

Her eyes were suspicious. "He said that was okay?"

"He didn't say it wasn't. What is your name, please?"

She gave me a glare but I waited. She caved in. "Gwen Jackson. I work here."

I looked around. "This the room it happened in?"

She nodded. "Right over there. She pointed in the direction

of a picture on the wall next to the bed. "That's right where he was found."

I moved to the picture. "And the safe's behind it?" I didn't wait for her answer. I lifted the painting off the wall and saw the safe. I studied it. I'd seen it in the police photos in the paper, but there's no substitute for an up-close look. Gwen made a sound of disapproval, and I decided not to push my luck. I replaced the picture carefully and straightened it. I'd seen enough: the Comptons had a Tinker, the Cadillac of safes. I turned to Gwen. "Mind answering a few questions?"

She grimaced. "I got to get this room finished. I got to get out of here by five-thirty to get home in time to fix dinner."

I glanced at my watch: 4:49. "No problem, Ms. Jackson. I'll only take a minute. Were you in the house the night of the incident?"

She leaned on the handle of the machine and shook her head. "I'm off Sundays. Thursday afternoons and all day Sundays."

"Mr. Healy was off too, but he says he was on the premises that day, at least part of it. What about you, Gwen? Were you in the house at all that day? Or that evening?"

She shook her head. "No. See, Mr. Healy lives here; I don't. I live in Harlem."

I thought of something. "Do you know Mr. Healy's daughter? Mrs. Mary Ruth Benedict?"

Her eyes narrowed. "What's she got to do with this?"

I met her look. "Her name's come up in a couple of connections. Do you know her?"

Gwen nodded. "I've met her. She stops in from time to time to see her daddy. They're very close."

"Stops in from time to time," I repeated, getting it into my notebook. "Very close to her daddy." I looked up. "Did she know Laddie Compton?"

"Oh, sure." Gwen gave a small smile. "They was very good friends, you know? She knows the whole family. She and Di used to be close, too, but that's sorta cooled lately."

I mentally shook my head. That damn Ruthie. She'd looked Regan and me in the eye and said she didn't know Laddie from a hole in the wall. Not much she didn't. I was now seriously wondering if she might be the murderer.

20

I PUT AWAY the notebook. Gwen looked relieved. "Anything else you need?" she asked, toe poised on the power switch of the cleaner. "I don't think I ought to allow you to wander around up here."

"I agree with you, Gwen. You've been extremely cooperative. I'm leaving." Only one false statement out of three: not bad.

And even the false one wasn't all false. I mean, I did go all the way down the stairs. At the bottom I looked at the front door and had a thought. The vacuum was going strong. As long as I could hear it, I was safe. I decided a chance to explore the murder house shouldn't be wasted.

I spent eight or ten minutes going through the rooms on the first floor, but aside from discovering they were all on the scale of the master bedroom—extremely large—it didn't tell me much. Back in the hallway, the vacuum still going, I turned and went back up the stairs.

I walked around the balcony thinking about the night of the murder. Eddie had come in the front door at 9:05. And the murderer had been waiting—waiting for Eddie to come and go—before killing Laddie in a way that'd stick Eddie with the blame. I tried to visualize Ruthie doing that. Couldn't. Too pretty.

I thought about the times involved. At 9:05, Laddie must have still been alive. (Unless the murderer had killed him elsewhere, then moved the body later, but that didn't make sense.) So during the time Goode was in the house, at least two other people must have been there also: Laddie and the murderer. Jeremiah's story was that Laddie'd been with him downstairs from 8:50 to 9:15. Was Jeremiah the murderer?

I followed the balcony around to the front of the house till I was directly over the front door. At this point a bay window jutted out over the stoop, forming a little alcove. It was partitioned off from the rest of the balcony by a tall secretary bookcase.

89

I squeezed past the secretary into the alcove, wondering why the tiny room had been made so inaccessible. A very fat person or a person in a wheelchair—like the Bishop—wouldn't have been able to get into it at all.

The only other furniture in the alcove was a desk chair. The secretary desk was bare except for a white telephone, but the three-shelf bookcase was completely filled with books. The alcove was, in effect, a tiny, very secluded office. Secluded, that is, from the rest of the house. The absence of blinds on the bay window made it a fishbowl to the outside world.

I turned to the window and studied that outside world: a deserted Eighty-seventh Street. I was scoping it when some sixth sense told me I was being watched. I spun around and peered around the bookcase into the interior of the house, half expecting to see Gwen Jackson and Jeremiah Healy advancing on me, accompanied by twenty cops. Nope. No one in view, and the vacuum still purring nicely. I turned back to the window. And saw my watcher.

She was in the house directly across the street in the corresponding second-story bay window. She was sitting at a desk similar to the one behind me, in an alcove like the one I was in, talking on the phone. She had turned her own chair to view the street—and me.

I guessed her to be about the same age as Ernie. Like Ernie, she was dressed in black. Unlike Ernie, her face showed no spark of good humor. She was glaring at me as she talked a blue streak into the phone. Nor was she the least bit embarrassed by my noticing her. Just went on glaring at me and talking. Her body language told me she was telling whoever was at the other end all about me.

Her house, I saw, was a mirror image of the Comptons'. Or would have been, if it'd been as well kept up. Its paint wasn't as new as the Comptons', the mortar between the bricks wasn't as white, the cornices and molding weren't as clean. And up above a couple of shingles were missing.

I tried a tiny wave but that only made the woman madder. I checked my watch: 5:15. Time to beat it. As I made the decision, a nondescript car pulled up below and into the spot marked RESERVED FOR RESIDENT: TOW-AWAY ZONE. Before I could get my wits together and edge away from the window, I'd been spotted.

By a tall, good-looking guy with wavy blond hair getting out from behind the wheel. As he was walking around the car to open the door for his companion, something made him look up. When he spotted me his eyes widened. He took his eyes off me only long enough to open the passenger door. His companion emerged, a small, expensively dressed woman, blond like him but not as good-looking. The man flicked a finger in my direction and said something. She looked where he pointed, saw me, and her mouth opened. Talking rapidly, glancing repeatedly up at me, they pushed through the gate and headed for the stoop, she leading the way.

Odds were, this was Diane, Laddie's younger sister. So who was the guy? A boyfriend? I tried to remember if I'd heard the name of any boyfriend in what I'd learned about the case so far. I didn't think so; but I had too much on my mind to be thinking very clearly. I wanted to run, but it was too late. Way too late. I was trapped.

21

IN SITUATIONS LIKE THIS, nonchalance is everything. So I walked casually around the balcony to the top of the stairs, putting on a smile. Thus proving I was a 'friendly' when they came through the door. But if my body was showing ease, my mind was racing. What kind of a friendly was I? What was my story? Who was I? What was I doing here?

Friend of Healy's? But if so, where was he? Friend of Gwen's? Not likely. Or—how about friend of the senior Comptons? But how long could I carry that off? Or, hey!—how about doing Davey Goldman, Private Eye?

Nope, they'd never buy it.

They came through the door just as I reached the head of the stairs, still not knowing what I was going to say. I gave them a bright smile. "Hello. You're probably wondering who I am and what I'm doing." They stared. The woman's eyes were bright blue. Her companion's eyelashes were longer than hers. Must be a boyfriend, I figured.

Meanwhile, I had the floor. Let's see, where was I? Oh, yeah, telling them they must be wondering who I was. Inspiration hit: I now had a plan, thank God.

I focused on the woman. I wiped away the smile, hoping to hell I hadn't started out too friendly. "I have just a few more questions. If you don't mind, ma'am."

The boyfriend started to say something but she cut him off. "How'd you get in here?" she demanded.

I gave her a long look. "And what might your name be, ma'am?"

She didn't answer right away because the boyfriend was involved in a paroxysm of coughing, bent over, covering his mouth with a handkerchief. He finally cleared his throat, straightened up and spoke to the woman, who looked annoyed. "I'm sorry, dear." He turned to me. "Excuse me. I'm just getting over a virus. This is Ms. Diane Compton and I'm Larry Vosburg. I'm Ms. Compton's fiancé." He coughed again, a rasping cough deep from the lungs.

His fiancée rolled her eyes and waited till he finished. She looked at me. "I think," she said firmly, "the family's answered all the questions we're going to for a while, *if* you don't mind. And what's *your* name, by the way?"

"David Goldman." I gave her a hard look and started down the stairs. "Ms. Compton. I have some questions I need to have answered. I've already interviewed Mr. Healy and Ms. Jackson. And I've been waiting for you. For some time. I'm sorry, but I am going to need just fifteen minutes of your time. We can do it here or—if you'd prefer—downtown." I gave them both a menacing smile, leaving it to their imaginations what *downtown* meant. Diane glared at me, obviously considering refusing, then just as obviously changing her mind.

The fiancé started to say something, but she cut him off again. "We'll go in the library," she snapped. "And it had better not take more than fifteen minutes. Should Larry join us?"

"That would be fine," I said. "I might have a question or two for him."

"Fine. Come along, Larry." She gave us her back and, circling the stairs, headed down the main hallway, clearly assuming—rightly—that we'd tag along.

As we followed her, the boyfriend muffled another cough with his handkerchief and gave me a quizzical look. "You said your name was Goldman?"

I met his eye. (Another anti-Semite?) "You got it. Have we met?"

Vosburg smiled. "Never."

I glanced at my watch. Five-seventeen. I wondered when Healy would be back. And the parents.

The library was as impressive as the rest of the house. Three walls were floor-to-ceiling bookshelves. Most were bound in leather. Overstuffed chairs were scattered around, and a solid-looking mahogany card table with upholstered chairs around it sat in front of a floor-to-ceiling stained-glass window.

"No, over here, Larry," Diane commanded, seeing him start toward an overstuffed chair by the door. She pointed at the card table. He snapped to attention and went to the indicated chair.

She also designated mine. I obeyed. If her future husband wasn't going to argue, I certainly wasn't. "Should I bring us something to drink?" Larry asked.

Diane shot that down with an imperiously raised eyebrow. I was getting some clear indications as to who was going to be wearing the pants in their family.

I pulled out my notebook. "I'll try to make this quick, Ms. Compton. I'd just like to go over the evening your brother died."

Larry was overcome by a prolonged coughing spell that temporarily ruled out any conversation. When he finished with a muttered apology, I asked Diane, "Tell me about the evening your brother died, if you will."

Diane shrugged. "Where should I start?"

I shrugged back. "Why not start with dinner?"

Her eyes widened. "But that's where it *did* start—with dinner. At the Beauchamp, the Easter Seals Banquet."

I nodded. "That's what I meant. Tell me about the banquet. When did you arrive there?"

She looked accusingly at the boyfriend. "I was alone. Larry

didn't even—" She sniffed. "I was alone." I jotted in my note-book, "What's w/ Vosb. & Di?"

"I got there early—at seven-thirty. I was the first one at our table. I came alone . . . " Another glower at Vosburg, who blushed. (I underlined my previous note.) " . . . and didn't know anyone, so I had to wait. But Mom and Dad weren't far behind—they were there by a quarter to eight."

Diane's face flushed as she went on. "Daddy'd bought a table for ten, but we were already down to eight. Larry was sick—he said! I—"

Vosburg had had enough. "Oh now, come on, Di, could you be just a little more unfair? You know damn well I was sick. The doctor said I—" He yanked out a fresh handkerchief and went into another long coughing fit. By the time it ended, Diane and I were both laughing.

I raised an eyebrow at her. "I don't think you can prove he wasn't sick, ma'am. Seems to me he's got a pretty airtight alibi."

Smiling, she shook her head. "You're right. He *was* sick. Quite sick. And I knew that, even then. It's just that I was so darned disappointed that he wasn't able to make the party. It meant a lot to me."

"Why don't we get back to that party," I prompted her.

"Yes. Well, there were supposed to be ten: Mom and Dad, Larry and I, Laddie and Janine, and our four guests. I'd arranged for them. You see, my job with Midas Touch is to find locations for new units. I'd gone to California, to arrange for one in—well, not *in*, but near Beverly Hills. We're a very upscale company, Mr. Goldman, *very* upscale. Our carwashes are all where the de-mographics are the highest. This will be our first operation west of the Mississippi. I'd done all the spadework, gone out there three times, found an absolutely perfect location, six blocks from Rodeo Drive—absolutely the nearest we could get to the *heart* of Beverly without the zoning board coming totally down our throats. And . . . "

I took a surreptitious glance at the Timex. The minute hand was racing toward 5:30 and Di wasn't getting a damn bit closer to telling me about the murder and where she was when it hap-pened. Was she crazy like a fox? Vosburg flashed me a knowing smile. That bothered me. I wasn't as smooth as I thought I was.

I started watching and waiting for Diane to take a breath so I could leap in. While I did that she was working her way back to the fatal evening.

"... so I had the California developer and the local agent and their wives join us for the banquet. They—"

"Excuse me, Ms. Compton." I smiled apologetically and pointed at the notebook. "I'm having trouble keeping up." I jotted a couple of notes. "What did you say these peoples' names were? Your guests at the banquet?"

She was irritated. "Well you *must* have that. Mom and Dad gave them to you, I've given them to you, we've—"

"Oh, I've got them, all right, but I forget." I smiled apologetically.

Diane sighed. "John and Louise Wellington from Beverly Hills. Joel and Grace Steinborn from Great Neck. Joel's the one who put me in touch with John. They—"

"You're giving me a little more than I really need, Ms. Compton," I said with another smile. "They arrived with your parents?"

She turned away, miffed. "Yes."

So she was going to be curt. Excellent. "Who came next?"

"Janine."

"Janine—"

"Mason." Di had obviously decided to punish me for my rudeness by holding her replies to single words.

Larry, looking uncomfortable, decided to fill in. "Uh, Janine was Laddie's girlfriend. The latest—the last, I guess."

I jotted notes and asked, "So she's the one who told you Laddie wasn't coming?"

After a pause, Di spoke up, sounding a little less miffed. "Well, he'd called her that afternoon, told her he'd be late, might not even make it at all. I'm afraid I acted badly. Of course, you know all about that." Her voice caught.

I looked up. "No, I really *don't* know all about that, Ms. Compton. Please tell me."

She was happy to. "Well, it was just like Laddie! Here it was: my evening, my triumph. I'd gotten us into a new market in an absolutely super location. It was my night. And then Laddie wouldn't even make the effort to show up!

"So Larry couldn't come to the dinner, and Laddie wasn't there either. So I said the hell with it, I'm not staying around for this. And I left."

I stared at her. "You left. What time?"

She smiled. "I've answered that question so many times, I know the answer by heart. Eight-twenty-four. That's the consensus, the result of a million questions by you guys, and answers given by everyone from my parents to every employee of the Beauchamp.

"And now you want to know where I went, right?" She *was* right, so I nodded. "Well, here's the same answer I gave before and I've got a feeling you're not going to like it any better this time around. I jumped in my car and went to see Larry."

I glanced at him. He smiled and raised a cautionary hand.

"Oh, I never got there," Di said. "And that bothered the other cops greatly."

"I wish you had, sweetest," Vosburg said. "Both for the obvious *and* the not-so-obvious reasons." He coughed.

"It doesn't matter," she said, looking me in the eye. "I did *not* kill my brother, regardless of what you might think. We fought like cats and dogs, always did, but we loved each other. And even if we didn't, I'd never kill someone just for not showing up for my party." She glared at Vosburg. "Otherwise old Larry here would have been history years ago." He looked abashed.

"What Miss Compton is referring to, Officer, is a little hitch in our wedding plans. All my fault."

Di sniffed. "I was good and mad for a while." She turned to me. "He wanted to postpone our wedding. I was mad. The whole thing was off. But ... " She patted him on the cheek, harder than necessary. " ... he saw the error of his ways. And I'm not mad anymore." She took a breath and got serious.

"Getting back to the party. What happened is, I headed for Union Grove, to pour out my troubles on Larry's shoulder. And—"

"Union Grove?" I asked. That was a new one.

"It's right next to Bronxville," Vosburg smiled. "It's just a few apartment buildings, a couple hundred homes and the Williamsport Country Club. I'm one of the pros at the club, and I live in Union Grove."

I looked at him with new respect. Bronxville's a very posh suburb, and the Williamsport G&CC is supposed to be one of the finest courses in the greater New York area. I'd never played it, nor will I ever. Jews aren't welcome.

"You're a golf pro?" My tone must have shown my admiration. Vosburg smiled and nodded.

Diane gave him a calculating look and resumed. "Well, I got halfway there and turned around. I suddenly realized how childish I was being. Especially with Larry being sick." She looked at him. "And he really was. Terrible bronchitis. Though I didn't realize how sick till later that night."

"When you both learned Laddie was dead," I guessed. They looked at me. I met Vosburg's eyes. "When you heard about Larry, you came straight here?" He nodded. "Tell me about it. Wait. First of all, did you come straight here, Miss Compton? I mean, once you decided not to press on to Union Grove?"

"No." She sighed. "I needed a workout. I went to the East Side Racquet Club, where I'm a member, and went for a run. Didn't get home till nearly eleven. The police were already here. Lots of them. They—" Her voice caught.

"She called me right away," Vosburg filled in for her. "I'd just gone to bed. I came straight here as fast as I could. I—" He stopped to cough. Or maybe he'd developed the same catch in the throat as his fiancée had.

"You have to understand, Officer Goldman," she went on, "Larry was really closer to Laddie than I was. Laddie and I fought a lot; Larry and Laddie, never. They grew up togeth—"

"Now, I have to defend myself on that one, Diane." Larry had regained his composure and gave us both a smile. "We fought plenty. I can remember once, in fifth grade—"

She smiled back. "Yeah, when you were kids. But you were such close friends."

I raised a hand and looked at Larry. "You grew up together? On Broadyke in Queens?"

He nodded, serious again. "Yeah. Next-door neighbors. What Diane is trying to say, Officer, is that I came to get comfort, the night Laddie died, not to bring it. Once I knew Laddie was dead, I had to come."

Diane gave him a perfunctory smile and turned to me. "Have

we answered enough questions, Officer? You said fifteen minutes, and according to my watch you're on overtime."

I didn't fight it. I thanked them and folded up the notebook.
I'd gotten what I came for and then some: spoken to four people
and three of them potential suspects.

I'd gotten interesting alibis: Jeremiah in the Red Lion Pub;
Vosburg at home in bed, miles from Manhattan; Diane in a car
between Manhattan and the 'burbs, and then at her athletic club.
Looked like some alibi-checking was going to be next on my
agenda.

22

I WAS BACK in my office by 6:10. Through the interconnecting
door I could hear Regan pecking away on the computer. He
doesn't like to be interrupted between three and six—that's when
he does his writing. Today he was putting in overtime. His writing's not *quite* as sacrosanct as the praying he does every morning
up in the chapel from six to eleven, so he'll tolerate interruptions
for high-level emergencies. But what I had to tell him, while
interesting and important, did not reach the status of a high-level
emergency. So I decided to make a personal call. I thought awhile
about what I was going to say, then pulled the phone to me across
the desk.

Sally Castle and I go back ten years. Interesting relationship.
Lots of loving, fighting, laughing, playing, fighting, dancing, con-
certgoing and fighting. And—let's see, did I mention fighting? At
the moment our relationship was somewhere in never-never
land. How it got there's a story in itself.

The previous summer Sally and I'd had a little falling out over
a gal named Dinker Galloway. Okay, a *big* falling out. When I'd
gotten over Dinker, I tried to resume with Sally, but...

"Davey," she said, "I hate to be the one to have to tell you
this, but we just aren't going anywhere. Oh, I won't deny we've

had some good times. But you're going to have to get your head together and decide what you want. Till you do, I'd just as soon not see you. Okay?"

It wasn't, but what was I going to do? The days when you could grab your woman by the hair and haul her off to the old cave for a heart-to-heart are long gone, unfortunately. I'd made a few abortive attempts to get things going, but nothing really panned out. We got together once—Valentine's Day. Seemed like a good idea at the time, but it didn't turn out that way. The date started out cold and ended hot—unfortunately not the kind of heat I'd been hoping for. Since then, nothing.

Sally's secretary sounded vaguely hostile. Ten minutes later Sally returned the call. "I'm between patients, Davey. What do you want?"

"Well," I joshed, "aren't you a regular bundle of laughs!" Silence. I sobered up. "Okay. Won't keep you, Sal. Just wanted to pick your brain about a case I'm working on. It involves hypnosis."

"Yeah, okay, hypnosis. So what about it?"

"Well, I've got some questions. Like, can a person tell a lie when they're in a hypnotic trance?"

She sounded irritated. "Of course they can, Davey. You have enough experience to know that."

I crossed my fingers. "Look, I'd like to tell you about it. Could I have just a couple of hours of your time? Like, say, over dinner sometime this week?"

Her laugh sounded genuinely amused. "You never quit, do you, Davey?" The laugh faded. "Davey. Call me sometime when you have something to say. Okay?"

"Well, geez, I don't know what you . . . " Wasted. She'd hung up. Looked like I was going to have to look elsewhere for psychiatric advice this time around.

The Bishop kept banging away at the word processor till Ernie called us at 6:30. Once in the dining room he immediately fell into a discussion with Ernie about some legal problem involving her convent over on Staten Island. He mumbled that he wanted to hear about my afternoon's activities but that it'd have to wait.

Dinner was meat loaf, mashed potatoes and green beans. Not as dull as it sounds. Ernie's meat loaf is about ten times spicier than the meat loaf you'll get in any restaurant in the city that's not Thai or Vietnamese. She uses jalapeño peppers. Liberally. Regan and I have an undeclared war over who can stand the hottest food, a war Ernie observes with keen interest.

But that night's contest ended early. I'd just helped myself to a second big slab of meat loaf and was blowing my nose—jalapenos affect me that way—when Ernie gave me a high sign from behind the kitchen door. Unfortunately, Regan, ever alert, saw her before I did, which was precisely what she was trying to avoid.

"Yes," he said, irritated. "What *is* it, Sister?"

"Telephone for Davey," she said, embarrassed. "Mr. Rozanski says he has to talk to him. I told him you were at dinner, but he says it won't wait."

Regan opened his mouth to reprimand her, then closed it, knowing she hates interruptions even more than he does. "Go ahead, David," he growled. "Deference must be paid, I suppose, to a celebrity. This *can't* be that important."

I took the call in my office. Chet's voice sounded strange. Partly because he was on a speakerphone, partly because his voice was about half an octave higher than normal.

"Davey? Have you heard the news?"

"What news? You and I are playing golf tomorrow?"

As soon as I said it I wished I hadn't. My mouth had outrun my brain—again. "Sorry, Chet. Never mind me. What've you got?"

"Then you haven't heard what happened to Ruth Benedict?"

I felt the blood run out of my face. "Ruth Benedict? No! What?"

"Run over by a car an hour ago. Hit-and-run. Got taken to St. Anthony's. Dead on arrival."

23

I STILL CAN'T BELIEVE what I said next. A surefire winner in the All-Time Stupidest and Most Inappropriate Comment in Response to Tragedy contest, if and when they ever get around to holding it.

"Why are you using the speakerphone, Chet?"

It didn't throw him. He'd heard enough dumb questions from me not to be surprised. "Because Jodi's with me. She just brought me the news."

"Oh. Hi, Jodi." But I wasn't thinking of Jodi. I was thinking of Ruthie. Beautiful Ruthie. My face felt numb. I finally managed to say something that made some sense. "Any leads on the driver?"

Muffled conversation. Then Jodi's soprano chirp: "Not according to what I've got here, Davey."

I couldn't think of anything else to say. But Chet could. "It's a brutal thing to ask, Davey, at a time like this. But any comment on the fact that she got it right after you called me to get some info on her? And Jodi tells me you met with her. Today."

I was scratching my head over that one when here came the next one. "Think her death's tied in with the Compton case? I mean, she *was* the guy's next-door neighbor. Once."

I still didn't answer. So Chet made an observation. "Broadyke doesn't seem to be a very safe street to have once lived on, does it?"

He'd finally given me something I could answer. "Yeah, I was just thinking the same thing. About your questions. If you don't mind, I'm going to pass. We'll talk later."

"But if you—" I cut him off with a goodbye he probably didn't hear, and hung up.

Sat awhile, elbows on desk, head in my hands. Breaking the news to Regan and Ernie was going to be hard. Especially Ernie. In that short time at lunch they'd become friends—my God, could it have been only four hours ago! I groaned. Why me, Lord?

Putting it off wouldn't help. I sat upright, took a deep breath and headed for the kitchen. Ernie started a smile, saw my face and cut it off. "Davey! What's the—"

I raised a finger. She closed her mouth. I beckoned her to follow me to the dining room.

Regan was still peeved. "So. Was it indeed nothing?" He looked up at me. "I don't suppose you—what in heaven's name's the matter?" Again I raised my finger. It shut him up too.

"Sit down, Ernie." I waved at a chair. "I've got some bad news." Eyes fixed on my face, Ernie sat. I stayed on my feet.

Regan turned pale. "No! Don't tell me Mrs. Bened—" His mouth snapped shut. He didn't look at Ernie but she was why he'd stopped: he'd already guessed. His mouth turned downward in self-disgust. A fleeting thought crossed my mind: *I hope this isn't going to tip him over into a depression.* Regan's always far too ready to blame himself for any and everything that goes wrong in this lousy world.

Since Regan already knew, I concentrated on Ernie. (How did he know? Don't ask me. If I knew, I'd be as brilliant as him and we'd never be able to work together.) Ernie was pale, wide eyes fixed on me. "What, Davey? What is it?"

I sat next to her and took her hand. "I'm sorry, Ernie. It's Ruthie—Mary Ruth. Benedict. She's—she got hit by a car. Just a while ago. I think she—well, she didn't make it." Ernie's eyes searched mine, and a tear started its way down a wrinkled cheek.

"Oh no, Davey. Oh no." She gulped, pulled her hand away and stood up. "Thank you for telling me." She started for the kitchen.

"I'm sorry," Regan said gruffly. "Sister, if you'd like to—"

"I'm fine," Ernie replied, back to us, voice muffled. "I'll be fine." She turned, both eyes wet. "Maybe you'd like to wait for dessert? Apple pie à la—" Her voice broke.

Regan nodded soberly, his eyes as tender as I'd ever seen them. "Later will be fine, Sister. We'll let you know. For the moment, just leave the dishes." He turned to me. "My office, David?"

Ernie stayed true to form. "Coffee, Bishop? Davey?"

We told her no, Regan mumbling something nonsensical about waiting to have it with our pie. I started to follow her into the kitchen, then decided there was nothing I could do for her. Not at the moment, anyway.

By the time I reached the office, Regan was staring out the window. I could barely hear his question. "Should we have anticipated this, David?"

"Probably. I don't know. You're pretty sure she was murdered?"

He swung to me, anguish in his green eyes. "For heaven's sake, what do you think? Have you the slightest doubt?" He had me. All I could do was shrug.

He shook his head. "We urgently need to learn what she did when she left here. And with whom she communicated."

"Yeah. But before we do that, I spent some time with her dad today and met a few other people who know something about the killing—Laddie's, I mean. You might be able to figure something out from it. Want to hear it?"

He did. I took the next hour and a half, consulting my notebook often to give him the complete rundown—words, expressions, everything—on my visit to the Compton mansion. I wasn't always sure he was listening: he sat slumped in the chair, eyes closed, head resting on his hand. But every time I thought I'd lost him, he'd come at me with a sharp question. Such as when I was telling him about the Comptons' alcove over the front door.

"This alcove has a telephone, you say? Any means of concealment there?"

"Yes and no. Not from the street; there's no blinds on that bay window. But from the inside of the house, yes. The bookcase would give almost total concealment."

He nodded, eyes closed, and gestured for me to continue. And he got it all, as he later proved—to me, the police and the murderer. Of course at the time, it didn't help much. When I finished, he had only one comment. "This is more than I can absorb at the moment. I must think. And pray." He started his wheelchair toward the door.

"Hold it!" He stopped rolling but didn't turn around. "Look," I said. "I don't want to get pushy. But before you go, I need some advice."

Regan still didn't turn. "What advice?" he muttered.

"I'm going to call Joe Parker at Headquarters. Maybe he can

tell me something useful about the hit-and-run. What else should I ask him? Any ideas?"

He spun his chair and looked at me, his face sagging with fatigue.

He sighed. "As a matter of fact, yes." He rubbed his eyes. "When Mrs. Benedict left here this morning, she apparently went straight home. When you tried to reach her, her line was busy. It would be of interest to know with whom she spoke. Perhaps you could persuade the sergeant to obtain records from the telephone company."

I stared at him. "Yeah, that should be obtainable. Not a bad idea."

He didn't bask in my praise. "I'm going to the chapel," he muttered, once again in motion. "I don't want to be disturbed. We'll talk tomorrow."

I watched him down the hall to the kitchen. He looked as weary as I'd ever seen him. Suddenly I felt the same way.

24

BUT MY WEARINESS wasn't going to bring Ruthie back. Nor would it avenge her death. I took a couple of deep breaths, went into my office and called Parker.

I said before, Joe Parker and I supply each other with information. What I didn't say was, we keep a running total of who owes who. The debt had been running heavily in Joe's favor ever since two summers before when he'd given me a crucial (and, for him, career-jeopardizing) tip on the McClain case. Making matters worse, he was still pissed over the way I, well, stretched the truth on him in the Carney thing the next summer. So my chances of getting anything from my buddy weren't great. He had absolutely no reason to tell me a thing. Except our friendship. I was going to have to put my feelings about Ruthie aside and play him like a fine violin.

He picked up after the first ring. I took the breezy approach. "Hey, Giusepp'! How's it hangin', babe?"

"Whaddaya want, Davey? I'm busy." The fiddle apparently needed some tuning.

"Hey, come on! Who says I have to want something?"

"Because you always do."

"Come on!" (I winced at the sound of my voice. I was starting to talk like Eddie Goode.) "How about friendship, Joe?"

"Yeah, how about it?" His tone got even wearier. "Whaddaya want, Davey? Spit it out."

"Well, I *will* admit, I'm curious. Know about this hit-and-run thing?"

"*What* hit-and-run? Goddamn, we only get about ten a those an hour!"

"Yeah, yeah. But most of 'em aren't like this one. There's a dead woman, probably on her way to the morgue right now, name of Mary Ruth Benedict. She was killed about an hour ago."

"What hospital?"

"St. Anthony's. A D.O.A."

"Okay, Davey. Same old question. Why ya askin'?"

I tried to think fast. And brilliant. "I had a little tiff with her husband just this morning. Guy named Junior Benedict."

Joe found himself interested in spite of himself. "Junior Benedict," he mused, "Junior Benedict." His voice shot up an octave. "Junior *Benedict! The* Junior Benedict? Of the Benedict family?"

"The same."

"How's your kidneys?" Joe sounded serious. "Junior's pretty handy with a knife. Least that's his reputation."

"The kidneys are fine, thanks for asking. And Junior's not at all bad with a blade. I had to break his arm to get him off my case."

Joe's tone was respectful. "Not bad, Davey. I don't know how Junior's daddy's gonna take it, but—good goin', sport!" He thought a minute. "But hey, wait a minute! I didn't think Junior was married."

"You haven't lost your good memory," I said admiringly. "Yeah, I misspoke. I should have said ex-husband. He and this gal, Ruthie, had a brief, unhappy try at matrimony a few years ago. That's why she carries—make that *carried*—his name. He was beating up on her this morning, which is when I got involved."

"Involved? You're lucky you didn't wind up with your fanny in Junior's back pocket."

"Point is, Joe, that's who just got killed by some hit-and-runner, Junior's ex. I'm looking for details."

"Ya still ain't told me what your interest is."

This time I was ready. "Tell you what, Joe. You get me something on it and I'll tell you."

He didn't like it but decided to lump it. He said he'd call me back " . . . *if* I find out anything. And you get nothin' without you tell me *why* you wanna know."

While waiting for the callback I mourned Ruthie in my own way: sitting back, feet on desk, thinking about her breathy voice, and hating that I'd never hear it again. Parker allowed me ten minutes for that before calling back.

"Okay, Davey, I got the dope on the hit-and-run. But first, gimme what you got."

I told him everything. Well, everything that wouldn't get me in hot water. I left out only my visit to the Compton mansion, including my semi-impersonation of a cop with Diane and Vosburg. It took a while to tell, but that was his fault: he kept interrupting. His first interruption came only twelve seconds into my recitation. "Hold it right there, Davey! You're sayin' Baker came to you—and the *Bishop*—to help get Eddie Goode off?"

"Hey, don't yell at me. I think it's just as stupid as you do. *I* can't control what Baker does."

"Yeah, but you can control *you*, can'tcha? You're not tellin' me you're *really* gonna help that creep, Goode. After what he did to the Bishop? I can't believe you!"

"Hey, it's not my idea, man. Regan thinks we ought—"

"I don't give a goddamn *what* Regan thinks. Goode *shot* Compton! Just as sure as he shot Regan! Man, I've never understood that Bishop, but I thought *you* had some sense. You got any idea of the kind of evidence we got on the guy?"

"Hey, I'm all ears!" I whipped out my notebook. Parker proceeded to tell me some very interesting things.

First of all, Joe got the case assigned to him because of his having been involved with Goode a couple of times before, back when he was just a wet-behind-the-ears rookie. Now he was talking about the Compton business.

"And Davey me boy, on this one we got everything we need for a conviction: the gun; three usable prints off it—when was the last time you ever saw *that* happen?—a *strong* witness: a little lady, honest as hell, that lives with her sister across the street from the Comptons'. She saw him go in and saw him come out fifteen minutes later. She noticed 'cause he looked suspicious as hell."

I hated to cut Joe off when he was rolling, but I was curious. "This old lady, Joe. That's the house directly across Eighty-seventh Street? The one that's a twin of the Comptons'?"

"Oh, you know the neighborhood? Yeah. Straight across the street. It's got a bay window on the second floor that overlooks the street. She had a perfect view, and she picked him out of the line-up. The Comptons got lights outside their house that light it up like it's daytime. So this old gal was able to give an absolutely positive I.D.!"

"Okay, Joe. Sounds impressive. What else you got?"

"Plenty. More'n we need. The M.E.'s got the time of death narrowed down to within an hour of when Goode was there.

"We got the jewels—and they're the Comptons', no doubt about it.

"We got a piece of paper from Eddie's apartment—picked up legally, *with* a search warrant. And that paper's got the address of the Compton place, the combo to the security system, and the combo to the safe; in Eddie's handwritin', sure as you're sittin' there, certified by two handwritin' experts.

"Last but not least, we got ten crisp C-notes, and three of them have Laddie Compton's fingerprints. These we also picked up in Goode's apartment."

Parker took a well-deserved breath. "Gotta tell ya, Davey, the guy's goin' down. This is as open-and-shut as any case I ever worked on. What I *can't* believe is that you—or the Bishop—are tryin' to *help* the creep. After what he did to the Bish! I mean, I heard of Christian forgiveness 'n' everything, but this is gettin' outa hand. What the hell you guys doin'?"

I chuckled. "You make a damn good case, Joe. But let me tell you what we've found out, then tell me if we're spinning our

wheels. A minute ago you asked me why Regan and me are
involved with Ruthie Benedict. Now you want to know why we
want to help Eddie Goode. Well, you've heard Eddie's statement,
right?"

"His statement! Don't tell me you're buyin' *that*, for God's sake!
He doesn't have a single corroboratin' witness that he ever *had*
the conversation wit' Compton. An' even if he did, what does
that prove? He still coulda killed him."

"Joe, he passed a lie-detector test. Plus, under hypnosis he
denied knowing anything about any killing. All he ever did was
waltz in there and rip off a few diamonds."

"Gimme a freakin' *break*, Davey, f'cryin' out loud! I can shoot
holes in all that and I'm not even a lawyer. First of all, what's
the first thing any jailbird learns their first week in jail? How to
burn a polygraph, right? And far as hypnosis goes, guys lie under
hypnosis. Oh, sure they do, Davey. Happens all the time."

"Okay, Joe, off the record, let me tell you something." I told
him all about Ruthie Benedict, Eddie's description of her feigned
suicide attempt, the way she'd got him to touch the gun, Ruthie's
out-and-out lies to Regan and me.

Joe listened, but his final comment was a loud snort. "Hell,
Davey, what's happened is this guy's come up wit' a story to
throw the blame on this Benedict babe—and you guys buy it."
He sighed. "You haven't told me a thing worth a damn, Davey.
Goode's guilty as hell."

"Yeah," I said sarcastically. "And to be sure his old girlfriend
wouldn't shoot holes in his story, he drives a car out of his jail
cell and runs her down. No problem there."

"Is that what you think, Davey?" Parker said. "That the broad
was murdered? The hit-and-run wasn't no accident?"

"The Bishop's convinced of it, Joe. And he's no dummy. Which
brings us back to the point of this whole conversation. What have
you got on it? The hit-and-run, I mean. We got a little sidetracked
there."

"Yeah, I gotta admit, you did what you said you'd do—opened
the bag." He sighed. "Okay, here we go. It happened down in
the Village. On King Street, just west of Seventh. Nobody saw it
happen, far as we know. A wino came across the body on the

sidewalk a little after five, called it in, so it happened before five. And we know it happened after four-thirty."

"How do you know that, Joe? M.E. give it to you?"

"Naw, he says she coulda been dead up to an hour. But we got the vehicle."

"You mean the car that hit her?"

"Yeah, only it wasn't a car, it was a panel truck. Paint on victim's clothes match the paint of the truck; and the front right fender of the truck's got the woman's blood on it."

"So you got the perp?"

"Naw. Truck belongs to a florist in the Village, couple kids were makin' a delivery two blocks from where the accident happened. They had a delivery to make, went in together, left the motor running. They didn't think they'd be gone more'n a minute. Turned out to be more like twenty. Couldn't find the right apartment, then hadda wait. When they came back their truck was gone.

"They went in at four-thirty-five or a minute or so after, and didn't get back till four-fifty-six. They both agree on the time. Furthermore they rushed back into the apartment they'd just delivered to and used the phone to call nine-one-one. Nine-one-one records the call comin' in at four-fifty-eight. The kids in the truck are off the hook. Not only do they alibi each other, they were seen by several of the tenants while they were tryin' to find their customer. So they're clean. The truck was found at five-thirty, dented and blood on the fender, four blocks north—just two blocks from where it was stolen. So the accident happened between four-thirty-five and five."

I held a short time-and-place seminar with myself. King and Seventh was a block and a half from Ruthie's apartment. She'd apparently been there between three-twelve and three-twenty when I was getting the busy signal. Then she'd either left the apartment like a bat out of hell or decided she wasn't taking any more phone calls. And sometime between four-thirty and five she was killed a block and a half away.

Parker was continuing. "The Benedict woman suffered all kinds of internal injuries, but the worst was to the head. M.E. says she died almost instantaneous."

"She was murdered, Joe."

"Wait a minute! You can't have it both ways, Davey. First, you tell me Compton's murderer pulled off some fantastic scheme to lay it all on Goode. Then you say he just randomly steals a truck and runs Ruthie down. Which is he: a clever conniver or an impetuous killer who got lucky?"

"I agree he was lucky. But here's what I think, Joe. The guy knew he had to fact fast. He'd learned Ruthie talked to us. He had to silence her quick. He was on his way to do just that, saw the truck with the motor running, and seized his opportunity."

Yeah, well, that's your opinion, Davey. But even if true, it don't prove nuthin' 'bout Eddie Goode. You were just sayin', this Benedict babe 'n' her old man—her ex-old man—were havin' a tiff this mornin'. And as you noticed, Junior Benedict's no one to mess wit'. Guy's a killer."

"You going to pick him up?"

"Tell you what, Davey. You come in and give a statement on what happened this mornin', and yeah, maybe we will. You wanna do that?" I could almost see the grin on Parker's face. He knows how much I like going down to Headquarters.

"I'll let you know, Joe. But it wouldn't hurt for you to check—"

"—to check Junior's whereabouts between four-thirty and five, yeah, yeah, Davey. I'll do that. But back to the main point: Goode's still guilty as hell."

"Maybe. But I've got another hole in your theory, Joe."

"Oh, yeah? Name it."

"Okay. How many of Eddie's fingerprints did you find in the house?"

"None, but—"

"None? Didn't you follow procedures? Didn't you dust every possible hard and semi-hard surface in the house for latents?"

"Yeah, but—"

"And came up with zip. For any of Eddie's. Right?"

"Awright, you made your point!" Joe was irritated. "But that proves nothin'. We already thought about that, wise guy. See, Eddie's a pro. He always wears gloves. So we didn't expect any prints."

"So what about the prints on the gun?"

"I'm comin' to that. We were surprised he was even carryin'. His M.O.'s not to carry a gun—least not any more. Been shy of 'em ever since you and I rousted him that night in his apartment and found the one he used on the Bishop.

"But he's known to of shot people before, Davey, as your boss should know better'n anyone. What we think is, he decided just for this one to carry along a gun. When Compton surprised him in his parents' bedroom, he panicked and killed 'im. So—"

"Yeah. With a shot in the back of the head while Compton was opening the safe. Some surprise."

"Okay, okay. So Goode flipped out. He forced Compton to give 'im the combo, then decided he wanted Compton to open it for 'im. Soon as he had it open he shot him. Remember: Compton was a witness. Goode woulda got hit with a long, long sentence, four-time loser like him. Plus he's got an established M.O. as a back-shooter. Don't forget what he did to Regan."

"I'm not forgetting. Neither Regan nor I are about to forget that."

"Oh? You coulda fooled me. Anyhow, I'll tell you how it happened, if you wanna hear it—I mean, why Eddie only left prints on the gun, nowhere else." I grunted.

"Okay. See, like I said, he was wearin' gloves. Now, for some reason, he brings a gun wit' him—forgettin' he'd made prints on it earlier. Did you know the prints are on the barrel of the gun, not the butt or the trigger? So when he squeezed that round off into Compton's head, he didn't leave any prints—he was wearin' gloves. His bad luck he'd already handled the gun at home, loadin' it—which is the way the prints look like they got there: loadin' it."

"Or unloading it," I muttered.

"What?"

"Never mind." I sighed. "So why'd he leave the gun behind, Joe?"

"Why'd he leave the gun? I don't know. Somethin' happened, is my guess. A noise; who knows? So he dropped the gun and skedaddled. Like I said, the neighbors saw 'im.

"So my guesstimate is, when whatever it was that scared him happened, he dropped the gun and ran. Without it we'd still have a case. With it, the guy's goin' down, Davey. An' the way he did it, cold-blooded, he ain't comin' out for a long, long time.

Probably never. Which, I'd think, would make you and Regan pretty damn happy. Instead of which, you're tryin' to get 'im off. What's wit' you guys, anyway?"

I sighed. "I don't know, Joe. I don't know. But do me one more favor, would you?"

Parker gave a sigh deeper than mine. "What is it this time?"

"How about using your official clout and get the phone company's records of Mrs. Benedict's phone calls? I'm specifically thinking of today's." I gave him the number.

Parker breathed a minute. "I s'pose," he finally said. "Any special reason for askin'?"

"Yeah. She walked out of here this morning, lying up a storm. When we figured out that she was lying, I tried to call her, but her line was busy. For at least eight minutes. Be interesting to know who she was talking to, don't you think? When you consider what happened to her?"

Parker's tone showed he was still unimpressed. "Yeah, I'll take a run at it, Davey. But this don't change a thing. Goode's still guilty as hell."

25

ERNIE AND I were a pair of sad campers next morning. I sat sipping coffee and rereading the tiny story on the hit-and-run on page 37 of the *Times.* Didn't tell me much. The only item that added anything to my store of knowledge was the last sentence: "Inspector I. M. Kessler of Homicide, who has been placed in charge of the case, declined comment."

That got me thinking. Protocol at the police department is for hit-and-run cases to go to the Department of Traffic and Public Safety—unless deliberate murder is suspected. Then they go to Homicide. And they'd given this one to Kessler. Did they suspect premeditation? And had my phone call to Parker had anything to do with the assignment?

Ernie put the omelette in front of me with a sigh. "What else can I get you, Davey? Before I go upstairs." I responded to her tone rather than her words.

"Tough, isn't it, Sister?"

"Oh, Davey!" She put a hand on my shoulder and bowed her head. Her voice was choked. "That poor little thing. I keep thinking how happy she was. How much she enjoyed her food. She ate with such—gusto!"

Normally a remark like that would have brought a grin or a wisecrack. She's like Mom: people enjoying her food's important to her. But I didn't feel much like grinning. Or cracking wise. "Yeah, she loved your cooking, Ernie. But not as much as I do."

She sniffed a couple of times, straightened up and went to the elevator. She tried to force a smile. "*No one* likes their food like you do, Davey!" The door rattled open and she climbed aboard. Time for chapel.

I finished breakfast—every bite—and refilled my cup and carried it into my office. I sat awhile, sipping coffee and wondering what to do next.

Regan wouldn't be available for consultation till eleven, and I didn't feel like waiting two hours to do something. But do what? I'd staked a lot, and I suspected the Bishop had too, on getting Ruthie to change her mind and tell us the truth. Now that help from her was out of the question, I was lost... or was I?

I began turning over an idea in my mind. Regan had wanted to look at Ruthie's phone records. Fine. With luck, Parker'd come through for us—maybe even with something we could use. In the meantime, what if Ruthie'd left something in her apartment? Maybe...

I went to the file cabinet. Out of the always-locked, deep bottom drawer I pulled a couple of all-purpose jimmies and a few skeleton keys. I dashed off a note to Ernie, tacked it to the bulletin board in the kitchen. Before leaving, I stopped to think. Anything else I needed? Something came to mind.

Whoever'd done Compton and Benedict was no one to take lightly. I went back into my office, unlocked a different file drawer and pulled out the .38 automatic with its armpit holster. I loaded it, adjusted the holster under my arm, and slipped the gun into it. *Now* I was ready.

The day was beautiful: spring warmth in the air, trees beginning to bud. I was tempted to walk. But only tempted. It's a long way from Thirty-seventh Street to the Village. I decided on the subway.

The subway's a lot like New York: you can't live with it and you can't live without it. In fact, the way the gangs have taken it over, you're lucky if you just *live*. Life's an adventure down there.

As I boarded the downtown train and grabbed a seat, four homeboys eyed me from the other end of the car. Early teens, but big for their age. T-shirts and designer jeans. And of course the mandatory high-topped sneakers. They and I were the only people in the car. Apparently the other, more experienced riders had spotted them and chosen to sit elsewhere.

I caught a couple of them eying me. "How you doin'?" I asked them, using my friendliest tone.

They turned away. But a third, the biggest of the bunch, turned and met my look head-on. "We doin' fine. You okay?"

"Yeah, great. No school today?"

A couple of startled looks. The leader's grin widened. "Shee-it. Don' need no stinkin' *school*, man."

I grinned back at him. "Sure you do. If you want to—"

"If we wanna im-*prove* ourselves, we *gots* to go to *school*! That right, my man?" He grinned at me.

I saw his grin and raised it. "Improvement's got nothing to do with it, friend. I'm talking about not being taken for a punk."

His grin froze and his eyes got hard. He gave his followers a nod and moved in on me. His pack followed, not eagerly. As they clumped around me I lounged back on the seat, studying the four faces, happy I had my piece. They were older than I'd thought, probably fifteen or sixteen, fully grown except in girth. They'd acquire the weight eventually—those that lived long enough. The leader's eyes showed plenty of bravado and a little fear. The followers' showed plenty of fear and a little bravado. I was probably bigger than most of the people they'd done this to.

The leader got close enough so I could feel the toes of his Air Jordans against my shoes. Smiling time was over. "Don't call me 'friend,' boy. And I'm no punk. Guess you owe me an apology, huh?"

I grinned up at him. "Sorry about that. I can see you're not a punk." I looked at each face and raised my eyebrows. "You fellas looking for something?"

None of the other three pairs of eyes met mine. The leader's became grim. "Damn right I ain't no punk, *boy!* You bein' insultin'. Jes' f' that, you goin' have t' gimme some of yo' money."

The train was pulling up to a station. All four swayed and grabbed straps.

I shook my head. "Well now, I'm sorry I took you guys for punks. I must have misjudged you. Trouble is, see, you don't want to be treated like punks, you got to quit *acting* like punks. That's the way it works, see?" I shifted my body. The coat opened and gave them a glimpse of the gun. I got to my feet, chest to chest with the leader. I had a couple of inches on him. He realized he'd miscalculated. His eyes wavered. I grinned at him and held his eye.

"You gentlemen settle down, okay? And quit rousting people. The subways are for people to use, not for gangbanging. And do yourselves a favor: go to school."

Three furtive glances at the leader, the man on the spot. He decided it was time to cut his losses. "You all right, man!" he said suddenly, slapping me on the shoulder. He looked around at his companions. "Le's go t' school, 'kay, *boys?*"

That broke the tension. They giggled, chortled, gave each other high fives, low fives, medium fives.

"Shee-it!"

"Damn right!"

"School it is, bro!"

With final challenging grins at me, and a muttered "See you in school, sucker," they moved away, shuffling and swaggering in their hightops, moving on to find a more pliant victim. I shook my head. Subways. Gangs.

The lock on the outer door of 823 Vandam was rusted and loose. Just a little nudge from the slim jim, and I was in. I hadn't had time or inclination to study the inside of the foyer in my brief scuffle with Junior the day before. Not that there was much to study. Twelve mailboxes. *M. R. Benedict* was 3A. I glanced around and, seeing no one, wasted no time jimmying the inner door. A little tougher than the outer, but no real problem. Took about twenty seconds.

The door of the apartment itself was a different matter. A deadbolt and a good one. I was ready to give up and reconsider my options, when one last try did it. The bolt slipped back with a satisfying ka-chunk; I slipped inside and locked the door behind me.

The apartment couldn't have been more different from its late tenant. Ruthie'd been beautiful and alive; the apartment was drab and dead-looking. And not very clean. The odors of long-ago onions and garlic and something ominously like sewage tainted the air.

A one-roomer. Murphy bed on the far wall. The wallpaper in the kitchenette was peeling and covered with old grease stains. The couch was shabby, the cushions askew. The rug was faded, and dustballs bounced along the floor when I walked. An old, scarred wooden desk, flush against the right-hand wall, struck me as a good place to start the search. I wasn't sure what I was after. I just hoped I'd know it when and if I saw it.

I hit paydirt the very first place I looked: the top drawer of the desk. Two items, in fact. First, something I didn't expect: a Yale key, amid a clutter of rubber bands and paper clips. Probably a duplicate of her apartment key. I pocketed it.

I pulled the drawer out further to reveal a jumble of papers, mostly bills. Ruthie'd been as sloppy in her bill paying as in her apartment cleaning. I riffled through them. Phone, electric, Mastercard. Then one that deserved closer study.

An invoice, dated March 27, from a Dr. Charles A. Morris, M.D. at an address in Queens. Amount: $1,877.75. Breakdown: $1,850.00: Pregnancy Testing and Surgical Proc. Feb. 27; and $27.75: Finance Charge (1 Mo. @ 1½%/Mo.)

That got my attention. What got it even more was the word *Laddie* scribbled across it in Ruthie's handwriting. That started so many different trains of thought I decided I'd better not I think about it at all till I got home and could discuss it with the boss.

A letter, also dated March 27, accompanied the invoice:

Dear Ms. Benedict,

Please find enclosed a revised invoice for services rendered.
I must tell you, I am personally distressed at having to write this
letter. At your last visit you both assured me the matter would be
taken care of within a few days. It was this assurance I relied on
when I went forward with the procedure.
That was February 27, a full month ago. Since you have not seen
fit to return my phone calls, I have no choice but to charge you for
a month's interest.
I am not, however, unsympathetic to your subsequent feelings
about the procedure. Accordingly, if you settle the amount owing
on or before April 15, I will happily rescind the finance charge.

> Sincerely,
> Charles A. Morris, M.D.

A battle over what was the proper and ethical thing to do broke
out and raged inside my soul for a good two or three seconds. I
won. Result: letter, bill and envelope shot into the side pocket
of my jacket. The spoils of victory.

It was another half hour before I found anything else useful.
Partly because I was looking in all the wrong places, partly because of the interruption. The interruption came first.

I was headed for the kitchenette when I heard movement in
the hallway. I froze. Someone muttered something. Then I heard
the unmistakable sound of a jimmy in the lock.

I had a feeling who it was. As I saw it I had two alternatives:
let them in and take them on inside the apartment; or surprise
them right away. I chose the second. If they had as much trouble
with the lock as I had they might get frustrated and smash down
the door. And I'm opposed to wanton destruction of property.

I tiptoed to the door and listened. I'd guessed right: one of the
mutterers was Junior Benedict.

"She told me she signed it," I heard. "So it's gotta be here."

"Don't worry, boss," came a higher-pitched whisper. "If it's
here we'll find it."

The rattling got louder and the mumbling more profane. They
were having even more trouble with the lock than I'd had.

I came up with a plan. The trouble was, with the gun, the deadbolt and the doorknob, I needed three hands to do it right. I decided I'd try my best with two.

I released the safety catch on the .38 and loosened the gun in its holster. Then I silently gripped the doorknob with one hand, the deadbolt knob with the other. I took a deep breath. I turned both knobs simultaneously and pushed. Hard. I followed with my body, shouldering through the door, simultaneously unholstering the gun.

The door crunched into something, jarring my shoulder. I burst into the hallway, gun at the ready, and scoped the scene. On his back on the floor, the guy who'd been jimmying the lock was cursing and holding his bleeding face.

That left Junior, startled but uninjured. I leveled my gun at him. His eyes widened in recognition. And hatred.

"Damn you!" shouted the guy on the floor. "You broke my friggin' nose!"

I took my eye off Junior long enough for a quick, confirming glance. "Yeah," I said sympathetically. "I'm afraid you're right. Damn! I'm really keeping the Benedict doctors hopping lately, aren't I?"

26

I GAVE MY ATTENTION back to Junior. His right forearm was in a sling and his eyes were as dark and mean as I remembered them. He called me by name. "You son of a—"

"C'mon, Junior, have a little respect. I came to take care of some final arrangements for your ex-wife." I turned to the goon on the floor. He was feeling his nose to see if it was broken. "Sorry about your nose, friend. Next time, make sure it stays out of other people's business." Back to Junior. "Now clear out before I call the cops."

"Oh no you don't, asshole! We're—"

"Oh yes I do. I'm an asshole with a gun. Out!"

Junior's eyes were wild. "You're dead, numbnuts! You've bought it now! You're dead."

I waved the gun. "Out!" I waited till the goon got to his feet and gave me a glare of his own, and the two headed for the elevator. Then I went back in and locked the door. Damn interruptions. Shaking my head, I got back to the search.

The kitchenette also yielded nothing, unless you call a couple of overripe bananas, two boxes of dry cereal and a quart of sour milk something.

I checked the dresser. That yielded nothing but the knowledge that Ruthie'd been as sloppy about folding her underwear as in paying her bills.

For some stupid reason, I pulled down the Murphy bed and searched it before trying the nightstand. Nothing.

So the nightstand was the last place I looked, which will tell you something about how the years can erode your investigative abilities. The dusty lamp on it was a cracked Tiffany-type. Both it and a box of tissues left sharp imprints in the dust when I moved them. Then I opened the drawer. And found the item that easily paid for the subway token I'd spent on the trip.

The drawer contained only one object: a blank envelope. In the envelope were three items.

First, another Yale key. Though shinier than the one I'd found in the desk, the teeth looked the same. Another dupe to the apartment, I figured. I slipped it back in the envelope, making a mental note to try both keys before I left.

Second, something I'd seen before: the power of attorney form that had got Ruthie into such hot water with Junior. Except it was no longer just a form: it had been written on, in Kelly green ink. The blank at the top, after the words "do designate, select and appoint" was filled in, in Ruthie's exaggerated Palmer-method longhand: "Biship Reegen or Dave Goldmon." And at the bottom, in the proper blanks, also Kelly green in Ruthie's handwriting, were the words, "Mary Ruth Healy Benedict," and yesterday's date: April 2.

I couldn't help grinning. So Mary Ruth had given the Bishop and me power of attorneys. And I'd thought I was just joking when I told Junior the day before that I was Ruthie's attorney. The grin grew as I imagined what Junior's face would look like if he ever saw this thing: Ruthie naming me her attorney. The grin faded. I realized I'd better watch my back from now on, whether Junior ever saw this or not.

That filled-out power of attorney was an eye-popper; but the third and final item topped even it. A letter—well, the start of a letter—scribbled in the same awful green ink in Ruthie's same distinctive longhand. It wasn't dated, but it didn't have to be— the contents made it clear it had to have been written the day before.

Deer Biship.

You were darn nice to me & I lied to you & I want to apolagize. I was wrong not to trust you & I shouldn't of lied like that. Specially talking about my mothers grave. If Id of had the least idea that gun was the one that killed Laddie Id of never gone along with it. Im thru lying now

That was it. I read it a second time more carefully, turned it over to be sure the other side was blank (it was) and pondered. Why hadn't she finished it? And why didn't it mention the power of attorney? The only answer I could come up with was, she went to meet her someone, intending to finish the letter after their conversation. Turned out there was to be no conversation. Her someone had seen to it that Ruthie's conversation days were over.

A ballpoint pen was also in the drawer. I tested it: Kelly green ink. I pocketed it. Who knew when it might come in handy? Like for my party invitations next St. Paddy's Day.

I continued to ransack the place but had apparently found all I was going to find. Not that I was complaining.

I was looking for hidey holes I might have missed, convinced there weren't any, when I heard more voices in the corridor. They got closer. Two men. Junior again? Nope. These guys were making no attempt to keep their voices down. I recognized one and let out a curse. Parker. What was he doing here? And furthermore, what did people think this was, Grand Central Station?

One of the apartment's two windows led to a fire escape. Go for it? That impulse lasted less than a second. The window'd be a bitch to open. And I could already hear a key rattling in the door. Hide? That thought didn't last long either: hide where?

Better wait and brazen it out. I was trapped like a rat. This seemed to be happening to me a lot lately. Was I getting too old for this line of work?

A cracked, crusty-sounding voice said, "...awful damn irregular, you ask me, Officer..." and the door swung open. The talker—an old geezer in overalls—appeared, then Parker right behind him. Joe saw me, instinctively went for his holster, recognized me. His startled look relaxed into a grin. "Well, well, well, Davey. Breaking and entering, hmm? Want me to read you your rights?" The grin was friendly but the eyes were dead serious.

27

I SCOWLED AT PARKER. "About damn time you got here! I was getting tired of bouncing this place by myself!"

My attempt at humor only succeeded in driving the smile off Parker's face. He turned to the super, who was still gawking at me. "You can go, sir. I'll handle it."

The geezer wasn't so sure. "Well, I don't know 'bout that. This feller's in here 'thout permission. With Miss Benedict dead and all—"

"It's all right, sir!" Joe's voice took on some bite, and the super backed away. Mumbling something about "goldarn strange goings-on," he backed out into the hall. Parker pushed the door closed without taking his eyes off me. No smile whatsoever.

"Dammit, Davey, that's it! I'm runnin' you in. I've put up with your shenanigans up to now, but this time you stepped over the line."

I grinned at him. An idea was beginning to grow. Maybe I wasn't trapped. "Aren't you making some unwarranted assumptions, Joe?"

"What assumptions? Breakin' and enterin' is fairly obvious stuff, Davey. You—what're you doin'? What's this?"

The idea had reached fruition. I handed him Ruthie's envelope. He pulled out the two sheets, unfolded them and tried to divide attention between reading them and watching me. "That, Joe," I told him, "is what's going to make you apologize for your unwarranted assumption and your ill-founded accusations."

I flicked one of the papers with a fingertip. "Never mind that unfinished letter to the Bishop. Check out the power of attorney."

Parker scowled at me and began reading.

"Read it and weep, Joe," I said when I saw him glance at Ruthie's signature. "As you can plainly see, it gives me the right to be here. In fact, if you and I weren't such good friends I'd demand an explanation for you breaking and entering."

Joe ignored that. His eyes flicked from me to the paper. "What the hell *is* this, Davey?"

I looked him in the eye. "What it says. Ruth Benedict gave the Bishop and me her power of attorney. She was afraid Junior'd try to—"

"When?"

"The date's right on it, Joe. Yesterday."

"Why didn't you tell me about this when you told me you thought we ought to look into her death?" Joe was mad. Mad and confused. He studied the paper again.

"Hell, I couldn't tell you *everything*, Joe! See, she wanted me to take care of some things for her . . ."

While I was talking, Joe was reading Ruthie's unfinished letter to the Bishop. Then he took out the key and studied it. Gave me a hard look. "You broke in, didn't you, Davey? And found this envelope here?"

I met his eyes. "There's just one thing wrong with that, Joe. The key's in the envelope. How'd I get in if the key was already here?"

Parker flared up. "How'd you get *in*? Hey, Davey, it's *me* you're talkin' to, not some green rookie. I've seen you get in dozens of places without a key. Don't gimme that How'd-I-get-in crap!"

"I'm sticking to it that I used the key, Joe."

"Like hell. This envelope is blank. No postage or nothin'. She never sent you this. You *broke* in here, Davey, then found the envelope. I don't give a damn *what* papers you got, you picked the lock, and that's called breakin' and enterin'. So you're under arrest."

"Like hell! The key I used is right in your own damn hand."

"You found that key *here*! *After* you broke in!"

"You can't prove that, Joe, but suppose I did?" I was thinking fast. "Is it breaking and entering if you're trying to get in to where your key is?"

"Damn right. If it's not your apartment."

I shook my head. "You're wrong, Joe. But it doesn't matter because I used that key to get in. And you'll have trouble trying to prove otherwise."

Parker glared at me, at the key, at the power of attorney. Then he grinned—one of his meaner grins. "Tell ya what, Davey. If this key works the door, you're off the hook. Otherwise, I'm runnin' you in."

I nodded, confident the key would work. Parker gave me a long look, strode to the door and tried it. It went in easily but wouldn't turn. He pulled it out and upped the grin. "Don't work. Sorry, Davey, you're comin' with me."

I shook my head and sighed. "God, Parker, do I have to do everything? Give me the damn key."

"I'm not givin' you—"

"Gimme the *key*, Joe! You obviously don't know how to use it."

Parker scowled but gave it to me. "You're under arrest, Davey."

I ignored him and pulled the door open. "Come on, Joe." He stared at me, finally followed me into the hall. I closed the door and inserted the key. Again it went in easily but wouldn't turn. I tried again: nothing. Not a budge. Wrong damn key. I turned on him, trying to show honest anger. That wasn't easy because what I was feeling was surprised. Why would Ruthie have put a different key than hers in that envelope?

Parker, on the other hand, was having very little trouble showing his anger. "Goddammit, Davey! Now we're locked out. You stupid—!"

"Hey, don't yell at *me*! It worked before!" Suddenly I got a thought. What about the *other* key, the one from the desk? After all, it had been only a guess that the two were identical. Maybe . . .

"Uh, wait a minute, Joe." I searched my pocket, careful not to clank the jimmies. "Maybe that was the wrong key." I pulled out the other one.

Joe glowered. "What's that?"

"What does it look like? *This* is the right key. I must have got 'em mixed up somehow." Mentally crossing my fingers, I inserted it in the lock and applied pressure. The lock didn't budge and my heart stopped. I jiggled it and used a little force. Suddenly it turned. I pulled the door open and started breathing again. Parker grabbed the key before I could get it out of the lock, put it in the envelope and the envelope in his pocket. Meanwhile I was unobtrusively slipping the key that had failed—the one originally in the envelope—into my left-hand pocket. "After you, Sergeant!" I said, snapping off a salute with my right hand.

Parker didn't go right in. He gave me his favorite gimlet-eyed stare. I met it with my favorite angelic look. He finally re-entered the room, muttering to himself. I followed and closed the door.

He spun to face me. "Siddown, Davey. We're gonna have a little talk." He waved a hand at the couch.

"Glad to." I plopped. "Want to continue our conversation about whether Ruthie's death was really an accident, Sergeant?"

Parker paced, not looking at me. "All right, I got my doubts, I admit it. I'd love to nail Junior Benedict. He—"

"He didn't do it, Joe." Parker stopped pacing and faced me. "The guy that did it is the guy that killed Laddie Compton. And much as I'd love to nail that slimeball Eddie Goode, he's in jail, so he couldn't have done it. This proves Goode's innocent of Laddie's death, Joe, if nothing else does." It sounded good, but I wasn't as sure as I sounded. Seemed to me it might have been Junior. He'd sure been mad enough.

Parker threw himself in a chair and gave me a gloomy look. "All right, never mind Junior and never mind Goode. Like I started to say, Davey, we gotta talk. You're gonna tell me how you *really* got this envelope."

I looked away, thinking. Parker waited, eyes steady. "Okay," I gave in. "I found it in the nightstand drawer. But the important thing is, she signed it *yesterday.*"

"Did you know it was there?"

"On or off the record?"

Parker grinned. "Hell, *off.* I'm not mad anymore."

I grinned back at him. "I had no idea. But if it comes up, I'm going to swear Ruthie called me and told me to come get it."

Parker nodded. "Did you Parkerize the place?" His word for a complete and thorough search.

"Yeah. There's nothing else here."

He got up. "Then let's get goin'."

"Uh, before we do, Joe . . . " Parker looked at me. He continued to study my face as I told him about my second meeting with Junior Benedict, conducted not more than twenty minutes before Parker's arrival.

"He's probably waiting for me outside, Joe. I just wanted you to be aware of the risks you're running by being in my company." Parker snorted.

Outside, we saw no signs of Junior or any henchmen. I couldn't decide whether that was good news or bad. I knew one thing: I wasn't building up much of a reservoir of good will with Junior Benedict.

Parker headed for his car, but I blocked him. "I don't guess you're planning to give me back that envelope, Joe? And the contents?"

He smiled that mean smile. "Whadda you think?"

I didn't smile back. "Well, I'm not going to start a fight with a police officer. And I suppose it's my own fault. I mean, I'm the one got you all interested in Ruthie's death being a murder. But it is my property—and the Bishop's . . . " Joe scowled and opened his mouth. I stopped him. "Oh, I'm not going to get technical with you, Joe. But I do want a copy of both pages."

Joe shrugged. "No sweat. Drop by Headquarters whenever you—"

"Oh no you don't! Right *now*, Joe."

"Fine. C'mon down to Headquar—"

"Nope." I pointed over his shoulder. "Look." He did, and saw the sign over the small print shop at the corner.

COPIES: 8 CENTS A PAGE

I grinned. "I'll even pop for the sixteen cents."

Five minutes later he drove away in his unmarked police car

and I flagged a cab. But I didn't go straight home. I had the cabbie stop at a lock shop on the way and got a copy of the key I'd pocketed.

My foresight paid off in a hurry. As I got out of the cab in front of the mansion, Parker was waiting for me on the sidewalk.

"Ya get lost, Davey? I was beginnin' to think you must be fleein' the jurisdiction."

"I would've, but the damn cabbie refused to take me to Canada." I got serious. "Actually, it took a while to find a cab. But you're the one that's lost. Or is Kessler moving Headquarters up here?"

Parker didn't answer. Just stuck out a big paw. I raised an eyebrow. "The *key*, Davey; don't play dumb. The other one. One was in the envelope, the other was in your pocket. You switched 'em on me. I knew somethin' was botherin' me. It finally hit me on the way to Headquarters. So gimme."

I shrugged, thanking whatever gods that'd inspired me to stop and make a copy. I pulled the original from the right-hand pocket, giving a little pat to the left-hand pocket that held the dupe.

"What about the key to Ruthie's, Joe?" I said. "It's mine. You going to give it back?"

He took the key I handed him and grinned. "Whadda *you* think, Davey?"

"Guess not."

"You guess right." He headed for his double-parked Corvair. "Oh!" He stopped and swung around, reaching into his pocket. He pulled out a slip of paper. "I almost forgot. Here's that phone log you wanted. Maybe this'll make up for the key. I got no use for it. So be my guest."

The paper itself was no prize. A five-by-seven slip of wrinkled paper ripped from a pad—probably Joe's desk pad. And the writing on it was no prize either: Joe's hasty scribbling. The prize was what it contained, lousy penmanship or not.

At the top Joe'd written, "M. R. BENEDICT PHONE LOG: APRIL 2." Below that were scribbled three lines of writing:

914/338–5522　3:10 P.M.　11 minutes　$1.62
212/771–1003　4:19 P.M.　1 minute　.32
212/246–4119　4:28 P.M.　2 minutes　.58

I looked at Parker, who nodded. "Got it from the phone company over the phone. Yeah. Just the three phone calls all day. We're gonna check 'em out."

I thanked him, trying to remember where the 914 area code might be. "Got the owners of those numbers, Joe?"

"Yeah. Nothin' special. The two shorter calls are to her near and dear: the one at four-nineteen was to Junior. The four-twenty-eight's to her daddy—name's Jeremiah Healy. We'll check those two out. But the first one—the eleven-minute one—I guess the lady must've been planning some kind of a golf game. That's the number of the Williamsport Golf & Country Club."

28

WHEN REGAN CAME DOWN from the chapel at eleven, I was waiting for him in his office. On his desk I'd placed the photocopies of the power of attorney and Ruthie's letter. I was holding back the doctor's letter and bill. And the key. And the fact that Ruthie had talked on the phone for eleven minutes with someone at the Williamsport Golf & Country Club.

"Those," I told him as he glanced at the two items I'd put on his desk, "are copies of what I found an hour ago in the late Miss Benedict's apartment. Any ideas?"

He frowned, bent over and studied both sheets. He looked up. "These are photocopies."

I rolled my eyes. "That's what I just got finished telling you."

"Where are the originals?"

"Parker dropped in while I was there and wanted them. And you know how he pouts when you don't give him what he wants." I grinned. "Seriously, I'm just as happy he has them. They're evidence—of something. Agreed?"

He nodded and went back to studying the papers. I reached in my pocket. "Oh—check this. The Xerox gives you an accurate picture of what she wrote—except for the godawful color of the ink." I flipped Ruthie's ballpoint onto the desk. "So you'll know how awful, there's the pen she used."

Regan picked it up and made a mark with it on his scratch pad. "Kelly green," he muttered. "Your adjective is appropriate." He slipped it into his desk drawer and stared at nothing for several seconds.

"Mrs. Benedict obviously learned something," he said at last, "after she left here." He shook his head. "Perhaps we can find out what it was. Tell me what else you learned." He rolled to the south windows while I described my morning.

When I told him about the keys he listened intently. "You say the one in the envelope *didn't* fit the door of her apartment, but the one in the desk did?" I nodded. "I see. And the provenance of the other is unknown?" I shrugged, not ready to admit I didn't know what the word meant. He didn't push it. He extended his hand. "Let me see it."

"Thought you'd never ask." I put the dupe in his palm. "The original of that was in the envelope, and Parker's got it now. Like I say, it does *not* work the door in Ruthie's apartment. God knows what it *does* work. God also knows what it was doing in that envelope." I jerked a thumb heavenward. "Maybe you ought to ask Him."

Regan ignored me and examined the key. He finally shrugged and gave it back to me. He sat and thought. Finally he said, "I see no way to utilize it for the moment, David. Keep it in a safe place."

When I told him about the doctor bill and the doctor's letter, of course he wanted to see both. He studied them for a solid two minutes. He finally pushed them aside. "So. She had an abortion."

I shrugged. "Looks like it."

"And that word *Laddie* on the bill is definitely her handwriting." He frowned. "Was she implying he was the father? Or the impetus for the abortion? Or both? Or neither?" Regan shook his head and tapped the letter. "This abortionist could perhaps tell us who the father was. If he would."

Regan pulled off his beanie and began kneading it. "But we may able to get it a different way. What about the telephone company records? Have you asked about them?"

"Hah! Is the Pope Catholic?" I jumped to my feet, whipped out the paper Parker had given me, and put it on his desk.

He looked at it, then up at me. "Explain."

I did. "Ruthie made three phone calls between the time she left here and the time she died. The second one's to her ex, Junior Benedict; the third's to Jeremiah. The first one—the long one, the eleven-minute one—Parker tells me that number is for the Williamsport Country Club." I didn't elaborate. Time for the genius to prove he really was one.

If genius equals quickness, Regan flunked. He looked back and forth from me to the paper a couple of times before he got it. Must've taken him all of four or five seconds. But when he did get it his eyes widened. "Ah! Mr. Vosburg's place of employment! How interesting!"

"Yeah, isn't it? Think he's it?"

Regan shrugged. "I make no judgment. I have no idea what motive he may have had. But I find it extremely provocative that Mrs. Benedict saw fit to call him immediately upon leaving us. It must be looked into. I leave that to you." He spun away. "I believe it's time for lunch. Ah! Yes, Sister! I was just expecting you. David will join us, but first he has a telephone call to make. Don't you, David?"

I glared at him. "What phone call?" Before he could jump down my throat I took it back. "Okay, okay," I muttered. "I'll call Vosburg and see when he can see me."

29

I CALLED THE NUMBER from Ruthie's phone log and verified, as if I needed to, that Parker hadn't been wrong when he told me it was the Williamsport Golf & Country Club: the guy who answered the phone used exactly those five words, followed by "May I help you?" I asked for Larry Vosburg and in about three seconds had him on the line.

"Pro shop," he said.

I identified myself and he had no trouble remembering me. "Yes, sir. What can I do for you?"

"This, Mr. Vosburg. I had a thought—"

"Please, it's Larry. My *students* are Mister. *I'm* Larry. Or Lare."

"Okay, Larry. I guess you know about Ruthie Benedict's death last night."

Vosburg's voice changed immediately. "Oh God, yes. God-damn. I once dated Ruthie, a long time ago. I was just—" He broke off. When he resumed, his voice was steadier. "Di called and told me. She'd heard it from Ruthie's dad. He's the Comptons' butler, you know. God, it hit me like a ton of bricks. Two tragedies in two weeks! I offered to go be with Di, but she said— we decided not. I just feel terrible about it. Ruthie was—" His voice broke.

I gave him a minute to compose himself. During the silence an idea came to me. Why not see just how good a pro Vosburg was? That ought to tell me something. Besides, it would kill two birds with one stone. Plus, giving me a lesson might relax him. And it would probably be the only way I'd ever get to see the Williamsport Golf & Country Club.

I thought about how to ask it. "I know it's not a very good time, Larry, but I have just a couple more routine questions. And I was thinking: maybe we could combine your business with mine." I paused. "I mean, I could use some help with my golf swing. Along with that, maybe you'd answer my questions. Of course, with the tragedy and all, I'd certainly understand if you ... "

"No, no!" he said. "It's okay. I think it'll do me good to talk to someone."

We agreed to meet at three o'clock in the clubhouse. "I'll even buy you a beer," he offered, "as long as it's understood I'm not bribing a police officer."

"Never happen," I told him truthfully.

I rushed through lunch, much to Ernie's displeasure. I had to get on my golf togs and grab my clubs. And I had a couple of errands to run on the way.

Not so much errands, actually, as research. I drove first to the Comptons', then got on the FDR on Ninety-sixth, took the Bruck-ner and then the Bronx River. From the Comptons' to Bronxville,

doing pretty close to the speed limit, took me thirty-two minutes.
I didn't know what that proved, but I noted it. I also noted the
mileage: 15.7 miles. Vosburg's directions to the Williamsport
G&CC were perfect. I arrived at 2:42.

The course itself was as beautiful as advertised. Rolling hills,
lush fairways bordered by towering elms. Very few golfers using
it—too early in the season.

The clubhouse itself was nearly deserted. The first face I saw
as I cut through the pro shop was Vosburg's.

"Dave Goldman, All-American!" He grinned and gave me a
crushing handshake. "Got your golf shoes? Good! Right down
those stairs to the locker room. Johnny'll take care of you; just
tell him who you are. Get your shoes on, come back, and we'll
get to work curing what ails you."

Johnny was black, about ninety years old, with a small white
goatee and a big smile. He whisked my street shoes away from
me almost before I had them off. "I'll get these dusted up for you
good, Mr. Goldman! Lemme see them golf shoes, too. Oooee! You
been playin' in too many swamps, Mr. Goldman. Gimme those
too!" He took a second look at the soles and shook his head.
"Any spikes under all this dirt? Oooee!" Leaving me in my socks,
he hurried off.

He was back in two minutes with the golf shoes. "Judas Priest!"
I was shocked. "These didn't look this good when they were
new! Thanks a million!" He grinned and headed back to his lair.
I studied his handiwork. How had he done it? Even the cleats
were shining. I made a note to myself to drop a fiver on him
when I came back in. It's not often you get a pair of new golf
shoes that cheap.

"You're going to have to watch that Johnny," I warned Larry,
as we strode toward the practice tee. "He's got my spikes looking
better than they did the day I bought them."

He grinned. "Johnny's a fixture around here. He'll be here
forever. And as long as he is, all of us will be spoiled. They broke
the mold after they turned him out."

Larry dumped the bucket of range balls he'd brought and had
me hit a couple with my five-iron. He was nice enough not to
wince at my swing, at least not visibly. He stopped me before I
could tee up the third.

"Hold it, Dave, hold it. Okay, now. What do you play to? About a twenty?"

I smiled. "Very diplomatic, Larry. Make it a twenty-eight. Headed for forty."

"No way! Headed for *twelve!*" I laughed. "Don't laugh, Dave, you'll get there. You've got a good swing. But your grip! Who told you to wedge it way up in your palms that way? Get it out on your fingers! Here, like this."

Half an hour later he had me hitting drives two-twenty or so. And straight. "Unbelievable!" I said. "You've unleashed a monster!"

"Damn right," he chuckled. "Nope. Just given you a couple of obvious tips. No big deal. I'm surprised your buddies haven't already told you about it."

"Hah! Buddies? You don't know these guys! Their whole thing is *wrecking* my game, not helping! We play for blood! *And* money."

"Well, forget blood. But keep swinging the way you do, and use that grip I showed you, I've got a feeling you're going to be picking up a lot more cash than you have been."

My tassel loafers, when I picked them up from Johnny, were, if anything, even shinier than the golf shoes had been. And of course Johnny insisted on repolishing the golf shoes. He tried to convince me five was too big a tip but I wasn't having any of that.

Vosburg suggested I follow him to his apartment in my car. "I can give you directions from there to get back on the Bronx River. We can talk at the apartment. And I can offer you a beer."

Since seeing where he lived was part of my plan, I readily agreed. I'd seen his five-year-old Monte Carlo the day before from my perch in the alcove. Of course, I'd had other things on my mind at the time. But my original impression of nondescript was still accurate. "Not the most exciting car in the world," he grinned. "But it gets me where I want to go. Just follow me, Dave. I'll drive slow so you can keep up without needing your siren."

His apartment building was only five minutes away. It was three stories, probably ten years old. A sign in front said GROVE APARTMENTS. The large parking lot was nearly empty; it looked like it would hold about fifty cars. We found two spots in front of the building, side by side.

I followed him to apartment 2H. A large, comfortable two-bedroom. A dozen or more golf trophies stood on a mantel over a fake fireplace. The walls held three or four framed pictures—artists' renderings of imaginary golf holes in impossible locations, such as the bottom of the Grand Canyon or on the side of the Sphinx.

"Sit down, Dave," he said. "I want to change. How about a beer?" I declined and he headed for the bedroom.

As soon as he left I got up and walked around the living room, checking it out. Comfortable couch, TV in front of the fake fireplace so it could be watched from the couch, remote control device lying on the couch. TV on top of the VCR, minicam on top of that. In the corner a big stereo system, including a CD player and a tape-to-tape. All the comforts of home.

Atop the stereo were two or three pictures of Larry and Diane, taken at various ages. In the oldest one, they were almost certainly in high school, he with his hair so long it could have used a ponytail, she showing some baby fat. She'd been more attractive then. I noticed a group picture, picked it up and studied it. Five smiling young people, three women, two men, in swimsuits by a pool. I was pretty sure the building in the background was the clubhouse of the Williamsport Golf & Country Club.

I recognized three of the five right away: Diane, Larry, Laddie. Then I recognized a fourth: the late Mary Ruth Healy Benedict.

I was still holding it when Larry came back in, looking spiffy in a different sweater and slacks. He raised his eyebrows at it. "What've you got, Dave?"

I showed it to him. He winced visibly. "Yeah," he said, shaking his head. "Better days."

"When was it?"

Vosburg opened his mouth, closed it. He gave me a long look. "Uh, sit down, will you, Dave? We've got to talk."

I frowned at him without moving. "Please, Dave," he repeated, putting a hand on my arm. "Sit down. I know you're here to ask me questions. But I've got a couple to ask you first. Okay?"

I didn't like the way it was going. What was he up to? But I

sat down. He grabbed an upright chair, spun it around, sat with
his chin resting on the back of it, his eyes steady on me.

"My question's this, Dave. Are you the same Dave Goldman
Ruthie told me about yesterday? She called me at the club, worried as hell. Said a Dave Goldman and some Bishop had been
talking to her—about Laddie's murder. It never even occurred to
me while you were talking to me and Di yesterday. But last night,
after Di called to say Ruthie'd been killed, I started thinking about
what she'd said on the phone and I remembered the Goldman.
So I'd like to know: are you a cop or not? And do you know more
about Ruthie's death than you're saying?"

30

THAT STUNNED ME. And upset the apple cart. I'd been thinking
about how I was going to spring that eleven-minute phone call
on Larry for maximum surprise factor. I'd been ninety percent
sure he'd try to deny it. I'd visualized myself interviewing every
fellow pro, locker-room boy and member of the Williamsport
G&CC for information. (I knew damn well that Ruthie hadn't
spent eleven minutes trying to arrange a golfing party at the club.)
In short, I'd been planning to knock the wind right out of Vosburg's sails. Instead, he'd knocked it right out of mine.

Meanwhile, he was waiting for an answer: who was I and what
was I doing? I did an abbreviated song-and-dance about Eddie
Goode, the Bishop and Dave Baker, without going into why we
thought Goode innocent. Vosburg seemed to understand, if not
approve.

"Okay, Dave," he said, after thinking it over. "I can see it. And
you never actually told Di and me you were a cop; you just let
us assume it." He laughed. "God, you scared the hell out of us
with your threat to take us downtown!"

Then he got serious. "So you and this Bishop are trying to
show that Eddie Goode didn't kill Laddie?"

I shook my head. "Well, we're trying to see if we can't figure out who *did*."

Vosburg frowned. "I see. I guess."

"So now that you know, would you be willing to help?"

"Sure. How?"

"Like this. For openers, I'd like to know what Ruthie said to you when she called you yesterday. Where were you, by the way? And how long did you talk?"

Vosburg looked at me. "I was in the pro shop. But as soon as she started talking, I could see how upset she was. So I put her on hold and went in Marty's office where I'd have some privacy. That's Marty Littooy, the head pro. He was off yesterday."

He scratched his head. "How long did we talk? Geez, I don't know—a while. Maybe ten minutes."

"Did she say anything that might have any bearing on her death?"

Vosburg stared at me. "You think—" He stopped, gulped. "You think she jumped in front of that car? Geez! Is that possible?"

I shook my head. "No, that's not what I meant at all. I'm thinking something else." I casually rubbed the back of my hand, keeping an eye on the pro out of the corner of an eye. "No, I think she was run over. Deliberately."

Larry gasped, his eyes widening. If he was acting, it was an ace performance. "What the hell for? You think whoever killed Laddie might've killed her?"

"Now why would I think that?"

Larry shrugged. "Hey, you're looking into Laddie's death, right? And now you're looking into Ruthie's. I don't figure you're doing that for your health."

I nodded. "Okay. Anyway, yeah, I'm pretty sure Ruthie was bumped off by Laddie's killer. The last time I saw her yesterday she'd just learned something important. Something having to do with Laddie's death. She lied about what she knew—said she didn't even know Laddie. Since you're probably one of the last people she ever talked to, it'd be interesting to know what she said."

"Yeah, right." Larry closed his eyes tight and thought. Suddenly his eyes popped open. "Holy shit! You think *I* did it! Don't you?"

I lifted both hands. "Don't jump to conclusions, Larry. I'm just trying to collect all the facts. But just in case you did, I ought to warn you: better not talk to me. Better get yourself the best lawyer you can find, tell him the whole story, and do exactly what he tells you."

Vosburg smiled. "Damn good advice. But being innocent, I'm not going to take it." He got serious. "If you think there's a chance Goode didn't do it, I damn sure want to help find out who did. So I'll be glad to tell you everything I can remember about that phone conversation."

I got out the notebook and Larry gave me the story—or what he said was the story. I was keeping an open mind. According to him, she'd been very upset. She'd just come from us—the Bishop and me—and was worried stiff. She'd poured out her soul to Larry: admitted that she and Laddie had had an affair, that Laddie had talked her into having an abortion, and it'd torn her up emotionally. She hadn't told another soul, she told Larry, including me and the Bishop, but now she needed Larry's help. Did he think the Bishop would curse her?

"Curse her?" I said, looking up. "What'd she mean by that?"

Vosburg shook his head. "You have to understand something, Davey. Ruthie was really a superstitious gal. Her mom and dad had a peculiar brand of religion—her dad still does. Her mom and dad were Irish, and they must've had every superstition the Irish ever dreamed of. I swear they had a whole backyard full of upside-down statues when Ruthie and I were growing up. Ruthie inherited that. She thought your bishop was going to put the evil eye on her if he found out about that abortion. She was terrified."

I shook my head.

"Anyway," Vosburg went on, "I told her she shouldn't worry about it. Then she started talking about Laddie. She didn't quite say it, but I gathered she was afraid her old man might've knocked him off."

I stared. "She thought Jeremiah might've killed Laddie?"

Larry nodded. "She said her daddy wormed it out of her about the abortion and made her tell him who she'd been with. She was afraid he might've done it."

"Did she say she was going to call him?"

Larry frowned. "Yeah. No." He rubbed his forehead. "Uh, I think she said she was going to go see him."

I noted it. "She said she was going to go see Jeremiah. Did she say when?"

Larry was still frowning. "Let me see . . . nope, she didn't—not that I can remember. I think her words were, 'I've got to go see Daddy.' That's about all I can remember."

I asked a few more questions, but Larry'd apparently told me everything he could. So I went on to questions about Laddie: without giving the jewel-scam away I probed how Laddie might've gotten in touch with Goode, why he might have wanted the jewels stolen. Vosburg didn't have a clue.

"Laddie was a worrier. But I don't think he'd ever do anything like that. I honestly don't know if the company's solid or not; it isn't important to me, except as it makes Di happy. I'm planning to stay out of the company, so that if it ever should have problems, Di'll have me to fall back on."

I changed gears. "Okay, let's go on to something a little less pleasant. How about alibis?"

Vosburg frowned. "Alibis?"

"Yeah. Yours. I hate to do this to the guy who just knocked twelve strokes off my golf game—"

"Fifteen."

I grinned. "Sorry. But I'd like your alibi for the night Laddie died, and for yesterday when Ruthie died."

"Fair enough," he said. "Let's see. Yesterday's easy. When Ruthie called, I was at the club. I left at four, drove straight to Di's office, picked her up there at five, drove her home. That was when we met you. After that we went out to dinner. When was Ruthie killed?"

"Between four-thirty and five."

Vosburg pursed his lips. "Well, during that time I was on the Cross Bronx and the FDR, but there's no way to prove it. Traffic was horrendous. I didn't make it to the GM building till a couple minutes after five. At that I had to wait: Di came driving up in a cab at five after."

I shook my head. "She came in a cab? But that's—"

He grinned. "I know, I know. She'd tried to reach me, but I'd already left Union Grove. She'd decided to go work out at her club. She wanted to tell me to meet her at the mansion; she'd just take a cab from the club. But when she couldn't reach me, she had to have the cab bring her back to the GM building. Otherwise I'd have waited for her there all night." He frowned. "Anyway, it's not much of an alibi. Just sitting in my car in traffic."

I didn't say anything, but I agreed. My view of Vosburg was darkening by the minute. I tried not to let it show. "So what about the other time: a week ago Sunday night. I gathered from what you said yesterday you were in bed the whole time? Right here in this apartment?"

Larry nodded. "Yeah, till Diane called at eleven."

I thought about it. "So the phone rang, and you went."

"Right. Fastest I ever made it there. Left my apartment at eleven-oh-seven; got to Di's at eleven-twenty-eight."

"Had you been out earlier?"

Vosburg shook his head. "Naw. I'd felt rotten all weekend. Spent most of it in bed."

I nodded. "So how about witnesses?" Vosburg looked puzzled. "For your alibi. Anyone stop by that day? Especially that evening? Anyone that can testify you were here?"

He concentrated, brows knit. "Gee," he said slowly, "I just can't remember. I was in my room all day. Didn't leave. I was really sick. I vaguely recall watching some TV or something. God, all I remember clearly is Di calling to tell me about Laddie!" He shook his head. "No, I guess I can't help you."

"Yeah, well I can understand that. Just no one?"

Larry shook his head again and shrugged. "Sorry."

"Well, okay, if you can't, you can't. Mind if I ask around?

Vosburg frowned. "What do you mean?"

"Ask around the apartment building here. See if anyone else remembers anything." I grinned. "In case you were so sick you went out and don't remember doing it."

He grinned back at me. "Ask all you want." He looked at his watch. "I've got to run. Got some things to talk to Marty about. If you don't have any more questions."

I didn't. I walked down to the lobby with him. "Here's all the

folks," he said, pointing at the mail boxes and buzzers on the
wall. "Start buzzing. And good luck."

I looked at him. "Would you mind if I introduce myself to the
neighbors by telling them I'm doing this at your request? That
I'm a friend of yours?"

Vosburg shrugged. "Why should I mind? You are, aren't you?
My friend, I mean."

I nodded, thinking, *Yeah, I guess. Unless you're the murderer.*

31

I MANAGED TO SEE tenants of six apartments but only two of the
visits—three people seen in all—yielded anything helpful. But
those three were extremely helpful. At least to Vosburg. They
cleared him as effectively as I've ever seen three witnesses clear
anyone.

It took about fourteen conversations over the intercom to get
eight to agree to see me, of which I wound up visiting with six.
The others didn't want to talk or said they couldn't help. When
I told them I'd be the judge of whether or not they could help
they mostly hung up on me.

Once I had eight people willing to let me come up, I started
with Larry's floor—the second. The first two people I talked to
were a couple named Dinkins—no relation to the Mayor, they
were quick to tell me. They knew Larry—golf pros seemed to be
respected around this building—but they'd been gone the weekend in question, so couldn't tell me a thing.

The next was a woman, Mrs. Browning. Also couldn't tell me
a thing. Two more know-nothings followed in quick succession.
I was beginning to feel discouraged and decided to try to change
my luck by going upstairs. A Keith Price on the third-floor had
sounded the most encouraging on this intercom.

I'd given him my standard "I'm a friend of Mr. Vosburg in
2-H, and wonder if you'd take two minutes to talk to me." For

the rest of them, that was all it took—the ones that agreed to see me. They'd just invited me up. Keith had been different.

"What's this all about, son?" Deep-throated Texas accent.

"I'm a detective trying to establish Larry's whereabouts on the night of Sunday, March Twenty-fifth."

His voice was suspicious. "And you say you're a friend a' his'n?"

"Yes sir. I was with him just now in his apartment. You can call the club and check with him. He's in Mr. Littooy's office right now."

Price had chuckled "You got all the names and places right, anyways. Hail, come on up. I'll give you a cold one."

After striking out with my first four in a row on the second floor, I needed a break. Even if Price couldn't help, getting "a cold one" out of the visit didn't sound half-bad. I assumed 3H was the apartment right over Vosburg's. It was.

I tapped on the door. It was promptly opened by a stout, middle-aged man in dyed hair, tinted glasses. T-shirt, blue jeans and loafers. He gave me a big smile. "Dave Goldman?" When I nodded he grabbed my hand and pumped it. "Keith Price! Any friend a' Larry's 'n' all that. C'mon in!" He was from Texas all right.

"Set yourse'f," he said, closing the door. "How about a cold one? I was jes' fixin' to git one fer m'se'f." His head swiveled and he shouted through an open door. "Hey, Evvie!"

"Cold Pearl?" I said, remembering from past experiences that Pearl Beer tends to be big with Texans.

Price roared and slapped his thigh. "You all right, son!" he assured me. "Where the hell'd you larn about Pearl Beer?"

In a second we were joined by a plump woman in her fifties with a full head (or wig) of peroxided bouffant.

"This here's Evelyn, the little woman," Price boasted, throwing a big arm around her shoulders. "Meet Dave Goldman, Evvie. I think he's good folks. Friend of L.V.'s."

"Well," she grinned up at him. "If ol' L.V. likes 'im, he cain't be all bad." She transferred the grin to me. "What can I gitcha, Dave?"

"Brang up a coupla cold ones, squaw," Price told her with a

squeeze on the shoulder. "And no damn back talk neither!"

She struck like a cobra and gave his nose a twist. "You jes be careful what you call me, Mr. Squaw Man. One more nasty word outa you and your beer's goin' out the window. And you with it." She flashed me a grin and headed for the kitchen, jumping away from a slap aimed at her rump.

"Goddamn, if she's not a pistol!" he said, rubbing his nose and throwing me a smile.

I nodded. "What part of Texas you from, Keith?"

He gave me a sharp look. "You shore enough a detective, son." Evvie arrived with two frosty cans of Bud. Keith had to apologize. "Sorry not to have the Pearl. Up here in the boonies, they ain't heard of real beer. Thanks, hon." He took a long swig. "You ast about where in Texas. I'm from Midland; Evvie here's from Shreveport, so she's not even a Texan. Close, though. Close enough." He looked up at his wife and they both looked at me, serious for a change.

"Want Evvie should stay, Dave?" he asked for both of them.

"Sure. The more the merrier. You understand why I want to talk to you, right?"

Price glanced up at his wife. "Siddown, hon." She did, looking worried. Keith's eyes stayed on me. "You're a private eye, lookin' to see whether ole Lare coulda done it, right? To his good friend and buddy, that Compton guy?"

I nodded. Keith looked at me challengingly. "Then I guess you're not up to speed, son. Don't you know they got the guy that did it?"

I grinned back at him with a side glance at Evvie. She gave me a little smile. "Well, yeah, they got him, Keith, but they're also considering other possibilities. Main thing is, Lare'd feel better if he could get this monkey off his back."

The good neighbor took a swig, looked at the can and back at me. "Sure, glad to help the guy."

"Good. So tell me about his alibi, Keith. Or you, Evvie. We're talking about the evening of Sunday, March twenty-fifth. Between, say, nine and ten o'clock. Lare was at home?"

Price took a sip. "Better believe he was at home. Ast me to wake 'im up at—what was it, hon?—nine o'clock, I guess. Wanted to watch that Shelley Long movie on HBO. So I did—"

"Hmmph," allowed Evelyn. "You'd a never remembered if I hadn't a set the timer."

Price shrugged. "Prolly not. But you did. And I did. Anyhow, Lare got me so hyped up, talkin' 'bout that damn movie, wound up watchin' it m'se'f. But goddam! He wouldn't let me! Kep' callin' me!"

I was jotting notes. "Remember the times?"

"Purty close." Price swigged beer and frowned. "First time musta been 'bout fifteen minutes into the damn thing, what the hell was that all about?"

His wife smiled. "He said his set was actin' up." She looked at me. "You'd never guess it to look at 'im, but Keith's purty durn good with electrical thangs 'n' all. So he—"

"Yeah," said the husband. "And Lare's no good atall, tell you that right now. Boy's as he'pless as a puppy in a hog trough." Keith shook his head. "But I tole 'im what to do 'n' that satisfied 'im for a while. Somethin' about the damn color, I don't recall what exactly."

Price shook his head. "Then he called agin! Said his color still wan't no good, could I please come down 'n' fix it fer 'im." Price sighed, reliving the moment. "Guy can be a real pain in the whattzit, know what I mean? Well, the movie wan't all that great anyway, so I went down there and fixed it fer him. When I was done with it, I told 'im to keep his cotton-pickin' fingers off the set, 'cause I wasn't comin' no more."

"What time was that?"

Price scratched his head. "Lessee. When was it, hon?"

Evelyn frowned. "Oh, I don't know, maybe round nine-thirty or so."

Price nodded, then shook his head. "Naw, it was a little later'n that." He glanced at his watch. "It musta been, oh, a quarter to ten, cause I looked at m' watch when I got back up here, now I remember. I'd decided to skip the rest of the movie, catch the ten o'clock news on channel sixteen and go to bed. It was ten to ten when I got back here."

This was looking bleaker and bleaker for Regan and me if we wanted to nail Vosburg. "So you talked to him on the phone at nine and nine-fifteen, and saw him in his apartment at a quarter to ten?" Price nodded and crumpled the now empty can in his beefy paw.

"Yep. Nex' mornin' he come up 'n' apologized for bein' such a pest. And told me what happened to his friend, Laddie. 'Bout how he hadda go tearin' off in the middle of the night. Damn! I was glad I hadn't bitched at him for buggin' me. Poor guy. His best friend and all."

I gave Price and his wife a long look. This was almost too good. "How about it, Evvie? You agree with all this? Anything to add?"

She looked me right in the eye. "It's all true, mister. And there's one more thang Keith didn't say."

She waited for me to answer, so I nodded and said, "What's that, Evvie?"

"Larry's car. Remember, hon?"

Price slapped his thigh. "Oh, hail, honey! Hail yes!" He looked at me. "Yeah, we both noticed Larry's car a couple a times that night. Our parkin' slots are side by side down there..." He pointed at a window. "...and Evvie and I just naturally look at our car. Got it stole once, and that makes you skittish. Well, his car was there all right—least till we went to bed."

I folded up the notebook. "Well, you are two great witnesses," I said. You've got the guy alibied every way from Sunday. You promise you're not putting me on?" I smiled but their faces told me they got the point. And their denials struck me as being as honest as the rest of their story. I got up to go.

"Guess I'm going to have to look for my murderer somewhere else."

Price grinned back at me. "There y' go."

32

I STOPPED IN THE LOBBY of the apartment building and used the pay phone to call Regan. He sounded grumpy when he picked up. He hates to be interrupted at the word processor.

"Hey, don't growl at me," I said. "Save it for when you've got a good reason. Like now, when I tell you Vosburg's off the hook."

"What do you mean?"

"Just what I said. I've checked his alibis. For Ruthie it's not worth a damn. But I don't think that matters, does it? Aren't we agreed that whoever killed Laddie also killed Ruthie?"

"Until we have reason to think otherwise."

"Then Larry's off the hook. I've just talked to his upstairs neighbor, and he never left his apartment."

I told him about Evvie and the Keithster, and their many phone calls to and one sighting of Vosburg that night, and his car not moving.

"Phones can be manipulated," he muttered. "And there's more than one automobile in the world. Tell me more about the actual sighting."

I groaned inwardly but gave him the rundown. He listened but managed to quibble. "At about nine-forty-five, then? And that's the only time Mr. Price saw him in the flesh?"

I sighed. "Yeah. That's what I've been saying. But there were the phone calls and—"

"I'm not satisfied, David. See if you can find other witnesses. And find out if he owns a second car." He heard the sound I made, and upped the volume. "David. That woman left here at two-fifty. She called Mr. Vosburg at three-ten and talked eleven minutes. An hour and a half later she was dead. If you don't find that suggestive, something's wrong with you. We even have Mr. Vosburg's admission that he spoke to her. I—"

"Correction: it wasn't an admission, he brought it up before I did. And that surprised me. I was expecting to trap him into lying about it. I thought I'd blow his mind by telling him I knew she'd called him. Instead—"

"Yes, yes," Regan interrupted. "He anticipated you. Which could have been a clever stratagem. I'm not satisfied with his description of that phone call, for a whole variety of reasons. Probe more deeply and see what you can discover."

"Okay," I sighed. "But my heart won't be in it."

"Just so your mind is." He rang off.

I was as unexcited as I'd told him. On the other hand, it wasn't all that tough a job. I'd already talked to a woman in the apartment immediately next to Larry's—2J. She'd been another who wasn't content just to either hang up on me or tell me to come up.

Her voice had been harsh, strident, unpleasant. "Yeah, what!"

I'd said, "Name's Goldman, Ma'am. Detective. Friend of Mr. Vosburg. I'm just talking to residents here about a crime I'm investigating."

Long pause. "You're a detective?"

"Yes, Ma'am. Only take a second of your time. If you don't mind."

There'd been a pause. Then, "Mr. Vosburg isn't my favorite person. But if you want to talk, I'll talk."

Regan wanted me to see more people. She was probably as good as any. I went up to 2J and tapped. She opened the door, leaving the chain on, and gave me the eye. She looked liked she sounded. Tall, horse-faced, shrewd eyes; the look of someone with a dyspeptic disposition. She studied the license carefully, but didn't invite me in right away.

"So you're a private investigator." I nodded. "What are you investigating?"

"Like I said before, ma'am, your neighbor, Mr. Vosburg. I'm just doing a routine check-up on his whereabouts the night a crime was committed in Manhattan. Were you here at home the evening of Sunday, March twenty-five?"

Her eyes showed she was titillated by this juicy stuff. "Heard all about it. That guy, supposed to be a friend of his, murdered in his parents' home. Wealthy guy. C'mon in. My name's Deborah Porterfield." She backed away and held the door wider.

She invited me to sit, but that was all. None of the open-heartedness of the Texans upstairs, offering me everything from a cold one to plenty of laughs. I decided "Ms. Porterfield" would do better than "Debbie." Somehow she didn't strike me as a Debbie.

"Yeah, I was here," she said. "What do you want to know?"

I pulled out a pen and opened the notebook. "Any indication that Mr. Vosburg left his apartment that night?"

"Yes, he did, thank God." Her tone was severe. "He was keeping me awake all evening with his everlasting coughing. Unnecessary coughing! You don't need to do all that hacking and spitting! Just cough, clear your lungs, and you're done. He was doing it deliberately! Just to annoy me! Course, these thin walls don't help any; they're a disgrace, too! I'm just about at my wit's end, I can tell you that, Detective."

I tsk-tsked and shook my head sympathetically. "You say he went out. Do you know what time that was?"

"Yes, I do. It was a few minutes after eleven: eleven-oh-nine by my alarm clock when he finally went out the door. I know because I heard him knocking around in there. Why can't a body get up and go somewhere without making enough noise to wake the dead? *I* can. You don't hear *me* sounding like a herd of elephants if I have to go somewhere in the middle of the night."

She sighed the sigh of someone who'd endured more than any human being should be asked to. "But at least he left. That infernal coughing was driving me insane. And whenever he came back, at least he didn't come slam-banging in the way he went out."

"So how do you know he came back?"

"Oh, he came back all right. I saw his car when I went to seven o'clock Mass next morning."

I jotted it down. "Now, about that coughing. Was it going on all evening till you went to bed?"

She frowned. "Well, let's see. I was watching 'Murder She Wrote,' I never miss that, I adore Angela Lansbury. That's from eight to nine. And . . . " Her brow knit. "I don't think he was coughing then. No . . . but . . . "

Her face brightened. "*That's* when it started! At nine o'clock! I turned off my TV to read; I've been reading the new one from Anne Tyler. Didn't you just love *The Accidental Tourist?*" I nodded enthusiastically without the slightest notion what she was talking about. I did vaguely recall a William Hurt movie named something like that. I'd found it as fascinating as watching a barber give haircuts.

"Well, I'm halfway through her latest, so I made myself some tea and curled up with the book. Well! How can a body concentrate on her reading when the TV's coming through the wall loud and clear, and so's the coughing. I finally called him and it didn't ring!"

I stared at her. "What do you mean, it didn't ring?"

Deborah Porterfield was enjoying her outrage. "Well! He'd had the gall to turn off the ringer! Oh, I could hear it ringing in my receiver—but not through the wall! So he'd turned off the ringer! So the coughing just went on! And the TV! Outrageous! I tried again, a few minutes later. This time he answered right away."

I was jotting. "When were these calls?"

She rubbed one hand with the other and knit her brow. "Oh, dear. The first time must've been, oh, nine-thirty. Maybe a little before. The next one was maybe nine-forty-five. I wasn't paying much attention to the clock."

"I understand. But you say he did answer the second time?"

She nodded. "Yes, and he was just sweet as pie. Said he'd turned off the phone because he was watching TV. Then he realized that was rude—what if someone needed him for something? And he apologized. And he turned down the TV."

"Since your walls are so thin, could you hear another gentleman with him about that time?"

"Yes! I'd forgot! That loudmouthed jackass, Keith Price, from upstairs. I don't know which is worse, that barking cough of Larry Vosburg's, or that bray of Keith Price's! Thank God he didn't stay long!"

I closed the notebook. "So you're sure Mr. Vosburg was in his apartment from nine to eleven."

A slow nod turned rapid. "Lands, yes! I was so relieved when he finally got up and went out and I could get some sleep. I thought he'd decided to go see the doctor. I only learned next day that his best friend had died. Poor thing." Her tone didn't convey great sympathy.

Downstairs in the car, before putting it in gear, I opened the notebook and drew a heavy line through Vosburg's name. I looked at the names remaining: three Comptons, Jeremiah Healy, Janine Mason and Gwen Jackson. I wondered if Regan and I should start spreading our nets a little wider. This same kind of experience with the rest and we'd soon be down to none.

33

REGAN WAS HALFWAY THROUGH DINNER by the time I made it home through the late rush-hour traffic. He waved me to my seat without looking up from his chicken and dumplings. Ernie came rushing in from the kitchen. "Don't say it, Ernie," I warned her as she ladled soup into my bowl. "Sorry I'm late."

Regan let me get the first spoonful in my mouth before starting to grill me. "So is Mr. Vosburg guilty or innocent? How find you?"

I swallowed soup. "I'm afraid we're going to have to tag someone else." I put down the spoon and briefed him on my conversation with Ms. Porterfield. He wasn't happy. I didn't expect him to be. It was disappointing that our juicy morsel of information— that Ruthie had run right home and phoned Vosburg—hadn't panned out.

"Of course," I told him, "if you want me to spend the rest of my life on it, I can probably prove that all three of those neighbors were paid off by Vosburg. Or better yet, that they're in it with him. But I wouldn't want to bet money on it. Of course, if you—"

Regan raised both hands in surrender. "Desist, David. I accept defeat. Besides, I have another idea."

I was working on the lentil soup again, but I raised an eyebrow to show him I was interested. "What idea?" I demanded. He ducked the question. Ernie brought him coffee and offered me more soup, which I accepted.

Regan took a couple of sips of coffee and eyed me. "Your next assignment, David, is to talk with Mr. and Mrs. Compton. The same kind of alibi-checking in which you engaged with Mr. Vosburg, as well as looking for motives. A likely one has surfaced, by the way. Though it could point in more than one direction."

I ate soup and huddled with myself about the assignment. How was I going to approach the Comptons? Like everyone else in the case, they weren't going to be happy to talk to the guy that was trying to help the accused murderer of their son. Of course, if either of them was the murderer, he—or she—was going to be even less inclined to talk.

I had no intention of using the same approach I'd used with their daughter and her boyfriend. As a spur-of-the-moment inspiration it had worked out—for the short time required. But aside from whether it'd work on the parents, which I doubted, cops have a thing about being impersonated. I could show I'd never identified myself as a cop, but I was still playing with fire. I needed a new ploy.

The way Regan and I usually operate is, I collect the information and he figures out how to use it. I don't go to him for advice in how to do the collecting. But as I thought about the situation, I knew I needed help.

Ernie had taken away the soup bowl and I was helping myself to some chicken and dumplings. Regan was starting his second cup of coffee. I blurted it out. "So what's my approach? I mean, with the Comptons." He put down his spoon and frowned at me.

"Look," I explained. "They're not going to want to talk to someone who's helping Eddie Goode, the man they think killed their son. So how I am going to get in to see them? I can't see any way."

Regan frowned and put his cup down. He gave me a long look. "As you know, David, I often disapprove of the methods you employ in approaching witnesses. In fact, it seems to me you often use subterfuge in instances in which, I could argue, the unadorned truth would serve as well, if not better. However..." His frown deepened. "... in this instance, you're probably right. It's highly unlikely that Mr. or Mrs. Compton would have anything to do with you if they knew whom you're representing.

"Which puts me in a quandary—a moral quandary. On the one hand, for justice and truth to be served, we need to explore this murder. I am convinced—and I think you are too—that Mr. Goode was not the perp. I mean perpetrator." I smiled and he blushed.

"So," he went on quickly, "it behooves me to assist you in gaining entree to the Comptons. On the other hand: every plan I can imagine involves mendacity of one kind or another. So I'm afraid you're on your own."

I stared at him. "You've got ideas but you won't tell me because they'd involve a lie? You have *got* to be kidding!"

He sipped coffee and avoided my eye. "Not in the least."

"Aw, come on. Aren't we on the same team?"

"Hardly. Not when it comes to morality."

"You're saying I'm immoral?"

Regan put down his cup and looked me in the eye. "By no means. I'm saying that your standards of morality are not the ones I follow."

"So you won't help." I was too mad to eat and pushed my plate away.

Regan tapped his empty cup with a fingertip. He finally muttered, "Well, I can do this much. Look at Saturday's New York *Times*. That's as far as I'll go. Which is probably too far." He pushed himself away from the table and rolled for the door.

I called after him, "Which part?"

Regan stopped in the doorway. "Which part of what?"

I rolled my eyes. "Which part of the *Times* will show me this fantastic approach to the Comptons?"

Regan had his back to me so I couldn't see his smirk. But I heard it in his voice. "David. Should I also stir your coffee? And perhaps drink it for you?" He rolled out of sight down the hall. I thought about shouting a smart-ass comeback after him, but decided it'd be counterproductive. Fortunately the Saturday *Times* is the lightest issue of the week. I thanked my lucky stars he hadn't said Sunday's.

I went up to my room. I hadn't read the Saturday *Times* but I still had it. I keep all three papers—the *Times*, the *Post* and the *Dispatch*—several weeks, for just such emergencies, in a wooden cabinet up in my bedroom.

It took me twice through to find it. The only excuse I can give for that is the last place I expected to find it was the Business section. I sure couldn't claim the story was hidden. It was the lead article on the front page of that section, with a photograph, under the headline VICTIM'S FATHER HAS MIDAS TOUCH. It was bylined Janet Ryan Grasso and was mainly about the senior Compton's fantastic success with his company, Midas Touch Autocare. I read it carefully, trying to figure it through Regan's eyes.

After a couple of paragraphs telling how devastated T. Randolph "Dolph" Compton and his wife, Hilarie Ladd Compton, were, at the brutal slaying of their son, it went on to tell how successful they'd been:

The Comptons launched Midas Touch five years ago, following the death of Mrs. Compton's father, Rodney Ladd, an early and successful pioneer in the computer industry (Ladd Electronics Corp). Hilarie Compton poured the greater part of her inheritance into her husband's fledgling car wash business (its prosaic name at the time: Compton Car Wash), leading to the company's transformation into a behemoth extending northward into New England and southward all the way into North Carolina.

In so doing they revamped and updated its mom-and-pop image, changing more than just its name. From the three locations they started with they have twenty-seven at last count, with six more "on the drawing board," according to the company's press release.

The Comptons' new approach was a blatant appeal to upscale car owners. The strategy has been to stress this approach through advertising, locations and overall marketing strategy. This strategy has included such things as special promotions at Lexus and Porsche dealerships, country clubs and exclusive boutiques in wealthy suburbs. The motto "Everything we touch turns to gold" has been featured in countless TV and radio commercials and in print advertising.

Industry rumors about "trouble in paradise" are dismissed by Mr. Compton. "There are always jealous people out there," he says, "ready to take potshots at their more successful brethren, but I accept that. I don't worry about them." When asked about rumors that Midas Touch, with its phenomenal growth, is short of cash to make the balloon payment scheduled on its five-year term loan with a consortium of suburban banks, Mr. Compton snapped, "Absolutely untrue. We have plenty of sources of off-balance-sheet financing if needed."

Ironically, the death of young Ladd Compton, tragic though it is for Mr. and Mrs. Compton personally, could be a possible source of this off-balance-sheet funding: the company holds "key man" life insurance policies on the entire Compton family, including their children, Ladd and Diane. So Ladd's death will bring the company an unspecified amount of cash. "I don't know how much it is," said an inside source, "but I'll tell you this: they need every dollar they can get their hands on just to survive."

I read the article twice. Very interesting. It certainly pointed up a motive or two I hadn't known about. But what had Regan seen in it to help me gain entry to the Comptons? That I couldn't see. Was it something to do with the so-called balloon payment? I looked up the phrase in Regan's big dictionary, but it wasn't there. *Balloon* and *payment*, yes, but no *balloon payment*.

So the following morning, right after breakfast, I settled back in my chair in my thinking posture, feet on the desk, and gave it some thought. A clue came to me. Regan had said his idea involved "mendacity," which is his way of saying it's a lie. What lie could I use on the Comptons, based on this newspaper article? Tell them I own a car wash and offer to sell it to them? I scratched my head and read the story again.

This time, I got it. Okay, so I'm a slow learner. I pondered it, looked at it from three different angles, and liked it. I wasn't absolutely sure it was what the Bishop'd had in mind, but it would do. I was tempted to go tell him the plan, then decided not. If he was morally repulsed by lying, why rub his nose in it? Poor guy was probably feeling guilty enough as it was.

I went up to my bedroom and changed into a dark suit and dignified tie. I pulled my alligator-skin attaché case out of the closet.

I needed one more prop and went back to my office to get it. When I first started out in the P.I. business, some printing huckster managed to con me into buying a hundred fancy embossed business cards, at $125.00 a hundred. He even talked me into reversing my name for the card, so that it read, "J. David Goldman." When I found out later that you can get a thousand cards at any print shop for twenty-five bucks, I went looking for the guy. Luckily for him, I cooled off before I ever found him, and finally quit looking.

I went to my office, pulled out the fancy box, and marked it to show I'd taken one. According to the marks, this was the seventh one I'd used. Leaving ninety-three. When you're handing out a buck and a quarter every time you give someone a card you tend to be selective. On this job it was definitely worth it. I had certain financial incentives to offer the Comptons; but presenting the image of a successful, prosperous private eye couldn't hurt either. Especially when dealing with people as rich as they were.

I remembered the number for Midas Touch Autocare, Corporate Offices from the day before and called. I got the same nasal-speaking female I'd talked to then, but avoided the Tennessee accent. Using my most cultured voice, I managed to get her to put me through to Mr. Compton without even much of an argument. I used my own name: well, J. David, which is close enough.

"Yes?" The deep male voice was abrupt.

"Mr. Compton, this is J. David Goldman." I waited.

"Yes?" Compton finally said. He sounded irritated.

"Oh. The company hasn't notified you about me?"

Pause. "What company?"

"Mid-Atlantic Mutual Life. They haven't called?"

"What's this about?" Compton's voice was suspicious.

"Your tragic loss, Mr. Compton. Your key-man policy."

"Oh." The tone turned respectful, but still puzzled. "But I've always dealt with my agent, Fred Sauers."

"Yes," I said quickly. "And you'll continue to. I take it you've discussed with him the timing on the disposition of the proceeds of your son's policy?"

"Well, not in any detail. We talked at the wake, but just in general. He said he'd be in touch."

"Yes. Well, Mr. Compton, insurance companies often retain outside investigators in cases of sudden, violent or unexpected death. I'd like to come talk with you. Just a formality, really. It's apparent that the police have the murderer in custody."

Silence. Then, "Oh. You're an investigator."

"Yes I am, Mr. Compton."

"Working for Mid-Atlantic Mutual?"

That was the question I couldn't answer. The problem was, a truthful answer would never get me in to see Dolph Compton; but a lie could get me in trouble. Fortunately I'd already decided how to handle it in case he asked. Namely, the old politician's trick: if you don't like the question they ask, change the subject.

"So when could I stop by, Mr. Compton? It's totally at your discretion. Though for the sake of expediting the disbursement of funds I'd recommend the sooner the better." I held my breath.

"Oh . . . might as well get it over with. What about right away?"

"Fine!" I let out air. "I'll be there in twenty minutes."

34

THE COMPTONS' OFFICES were in the GM building on fifty-ninth and Fifth, on the fifty-second floor. The receptionist, a middle-aged type with frosted hair and designer glasses, sized me up. She had the pinched face and mean expression of Miss Kabulsky, my teacher in third grade, leading me to think she was the staff sergeant I'd talked to on the phone. But I realized I was wrong as soon as she opened her mouth. Different voice: harsh but not nasal. Her look gave me the feeling my shirt was dirty, my tie crooked, and my expensive business card covered with deadly microbes. She glanced at it distastefully, picked up the phone and ordered me to have a seat. I obeyed.

From the looks of the anteroom, Midas Touch lived up to its name. No actual gold in evidence, but plenty laid out for the decorations. The carpet was thick, the furniture ornate, the walls were covered with some kind of heavy fabric. As to the artwork—well, I'm no connoisseur of fine art, but I've seen enough to know that the stuff they had hanging from that fabric hadn't come cheap.

I didn't have long to wait. A leggy blond appeared within thirty seconds and invited me to follow her. In a nasal voice. So *this* was the nasal Ms. Arnold—not exactly what I'd visualized. She led me down a wide corridor to a large office. "Right in here, Mr. Goldman," she said through her beautiful nose.

I slid past her into the office, enjoying her perfume. A bulky, bald man was coming around his desk to greet me. He grabbed my hand and crushed it.

"Dolph Compton, Mr. Goldman. Let's sit over here." He waved at four chairs clumped around a table in the corner and gave me a big smile and a clap on the back to get me moving. His gold-rimmed specs seemed to divide his big head in half: the prize-fighter's chin, mouth and nose below, and a huge expanse of scalp above.

He waited for me to sit, then grabbed a chair across the table from me and asked, "How's about if Mrs. Compton joins us?" The direction of his eyes drew mine to the doorway: the leggy blond had lingered. My eyes widened. (*This* was Mrs. Compton?)

I was enthusiastic. "Fine! I'd have suggested it myself if I'd known she'd be here."

"Good. Get Mrs. Compton, would you, Michele?" The blond nodded and left. (Oh well.)

He turned back to me. "Oh, yes indeed, Mr. Goldman, my wife is at least full-time. We run Midas Touch together, she and I. She's vice-chair, secretary and treasurer. The heart and soul of the company. And I'm not just saying that to be polite. Good, here she is."

I got up and met the eyes of a small middle-aged woman with pinched features and piercing blue eyes behind horn-rimmed glasses. I could see the family resemblance between her and Di. She nodded abruptly and gave me a man's handshake, only slightly less crushing than her husband's. I guessed her dress was a Dior or something. I also guessed she was responsible for the office decor. And a lot more.

Next to her, Compton seemed like a farmer disguised as a businessman. Well-disguised. His striped tie and white-on-white shirt together, I guessed, had set him back a couple of hundred, the diamond cufflinks a lot more. I was ready to bet he'd been outfitted by the little woman.

But farmer or not, he took charge. Possibly to show who wore the pants in the family—as opposed to who picked them out.

"Mr. Goldman is just doing a brief investigation of Laddie's death, honey," he told his wife after she sat down between us. "For the insurance company. Just a formality, he says. Right, Mr. Goldman?"

I was brisk. "That's right. Just a few questions and I'll get out of your hair." Dolph's blush made me regret my choice of words.

As they waited for me to go on, I looked at both of them and did a little fast thinking. I knew the question I *wanted* to ask: how big was the policy on your son's life? But since I was purporting to be a guy the insurance company had hired to investigate, I couldn't. No company would send out an investigator without first briefing him on every detail of the policy.

So I came on aggressive. "Let me say at the outset, I'm going to be frank. I think that'll be the most effective in the long run. And the best for all concerned."

Compton shrugged. Hilarie started to say something but changed her mind.

"So," I said, "let's get to it, shall we?" I focused on hubby. "It was the two of you who found your son's body, is that right?"

Mrs. Compton's eyes filled. Dolph threw her a quick, concerned glance. "That's right."

I pulled the rich-looking notebook from my richer-looking attaché case and got ready to write. "Please, just tell me about it. From the top, if you will."

Dolph's eyes were cold. "Okay. We'd been at a function that evening. The banquet for Easter Seals at the Beauchamp. They were honoring several people, including the mayor." His eyes flashed to his wife. Some silent signal passed between them before he resumed. "We left early and came home. It was a Sunday so both Jeremiah and Gwen were off. That's our live-in houseman and maid. Sundays they're off. I guess the thief knew that. At least that's the police theory." Dolph looked at me. "I suppose you've seen the police report?"

I shook my head. "No, I haven't seen it yet. Of course, I'll have to look at it before I file my own report. But the way I work is to develop my own line of reasoning first. Then see if it agrees with the police version. It usually does. Go on, please, Mr. Compton." I glanced at his wife. She looked worried.

"Yes." Compton cleared his throat. "So we left the party early and went home. It was the third one of these benefits that weekend, and we were tired. We got home and—"

"We knew something was wrong right away," Hilarie said.

"There was something wrong in the house. I knew it."

Dolph looked at her. "Well no, hon, that's not quite right. We didn't know something was ... *wrong*, exactly." He turned to me, his broad face the picture of honesty. "Our daughter, Diane, wasn't feeling well, and we expected her to be home. But she wasn't. We looked in her room first. I think that's what alerted us—I mean, made us feel something was wrong."

"Wasn't feeling well"? *Okay*, I was thinking. *That's one way of putting it.* I guess it sounded better than saying she was in a snit.

Hilarie nodded agreement, still looking nervous. She turned to me and for the first time looked straight at me. I was surprised how beautiful her eyes were behind the horn-rims. Piercing *and* beautiful. "Have you ever had the feeling, Mr. Goldman, that something's wrong but you don't know what?" I nodded, mesmerized. She nodded back. "Well, that's just the way I felt."

Compton reached across the table and patted her hand. She covered his with her other hand and gave him a smile. The smile lit up her face. I wondered why I'd thought her features were pinched. I was now guessing her to be at least ten years younger than her husband. Maybe within ten or fifteen years of me. Not so old.

"I know, dear," he said. "You're a lot more sensitive to these things than I am." Dolph faced me, still holding his wife's hand. "Anyway, when we saw Diane wasn't in her room, we called out for her. I was surprised Jeremiah wasn't home. He'd said he wasn't going anywhere. But no. The house was empty. That's—"

"That's when we started getting worried," Hilarie said, releasing his hand.

"Yes," Compton said, frowning. "Thinking back, I don't know why we should have been so nervous. Heck, Diane's often away in the evening. This time, as a matter of fact, she was at the racquet club. And we didn't have any reason to think Laddie'd be home. See, he had his own apartment on the West Side. But— we both just had a feeling."

Hilarie's eyes filled. Dolph reached for her hand again but this time she pulled it back.

He cleared his throat uncomfortably. "I was just saying something like 'where do you think Diane went?' when we walked in the bedroom. And—" He stopped. I waited, pencil poised, sympathetic look on my face.

Dolph took a breath. "Sorry. That's when we saw Lad—Laddie. He was on the floor by the bed, lying—"

I raised a hand. "I know how difficult this is, sir. You don't need to describe it for me." Both of them gave sighs of relief.

I decided it was time to get into what I'd come for. This was the moment of truth. "Before we go on, Mr. and Mrs. Compton, I should apologize for what I'm about to say." Their eyes widened and homed in on me. I tried to show them an honest face. To hoodwink people without actually telling a lie requires, in addition to a careful choice of words, an honest, open face.

"Let me explain the situation. The police have apprehended the murderer." I glanced at both faces. "By the way, I assume neither of you has any reason whatever to doubt that Eddie Goode is the murderer."

I watched their eyes. His seemed to flick nervously to her. Hers never wavered. She spoke. "No, not in the least, Mr. Goldman. The police certainly have no doubts."

I turned to Dolph. "You too, Mr. Compton?"

He looked down. "Sure. Why shouldn't I? I mean, why should I suspect anyone but that—fiend?" I nodded.

"Well, neither does Mid-Atlantic Mutual Life. However, the laws governing disbursement of proceeds of a life policy in the case of murder are somewhat . . . complicated." I paused.

Compton flushed. "Just what are you getting at? Are you trying to weasel out?"

I raised both hands. "Anything but, Mr. Compton. Anything but. But here's the thing: the company does have to obey the law. To the letter. Let me explain how it works." I glanced at both of them, hoping neither of them had any legal training. From the looks on their faces, I didn't think so. Fortunately. Half of what I was saying was stuff I'd learned in the little bit of insurance investigating I'd done. The other half was sheer imagination. I knew they'd consult a lawyer about it and he'd tell them they'd been bamboozled. That was okay. By then I'd have my information.

"The law requires," I went on, "that the company pay out *only* after a judicial finding. There's an exception to that, however. That's where I come in."

I looked at both of them. They were hanging on every syllable. "The reason the law normally insists on a judicial finding is to ensure that death benefits are never paid to reward the commission of a crime."

I waited. Dolph was beginning to look worried. "You mean, you won't pay till Goode is found guilty?"

"*Can't*, Mr. Compton. *Can't* pay. That's the law."

"But that could take years!"

I winced. "Unfortunately, yes. It can happen. It *has* happened. Which is why the company—"

"But we need the—" Compton's mouth snapped shut. He threw me a quick glance, but my head was buried in the notebook and I pretended not to see. "I mean, you surely can't hold the funds *that* long, can you? Besides, what if the murderer got off? On a technicality or something?" His flush deepened. "Dammit! You've just *got* to—"

I raised a hand. "Yes. You certainly have logic on your side, Mr. Compton. And there is a way to accommodate that logic. That's where I come in."

I definitely had his attention. "As I said, there *are* exceptions. Companies pay out early all the time, even in cases like this. As I'm sure Mid-Atlantic will for you. But it depends on your cooperation."

"Cooperation?"

"Yes. You see, the company can pay out and still stay in compliance, *if* the company can show that it has reason in good faith to *believe* the beneficiary to be innocent of any crime. That's why companies employ investigators to assist. So that they can pay out prior to trial. By independently satisfying themselves that the beneficiary is innocent."

"So that's why you're here?"

"Well, you could put it that way. *If* I could satisfy myself that no beneficiary is guilty, I'd then be justified in asking Mid-Atlantic Life to pay out on your policy. Whether Goode is ever found guilty or not."

Compton was following every word. "So how do you do that?"

I nodded. "That's what I'm coming to. In order to satisfy myself,

I'm going to have to ask you some, well, some very blunt questions. Bordering on the discourteous. In effect, I'm going to have
to ask all three of you family members to alibi yourselves. To
prove to me that you *didn't* kill Laddie. That's insulting. And
for that I apologize in advance."

Compton snorted. "Apologize? Hell, go ahead and insult us! I
can guarantee you, *we* certainly don't have any objections. Right,
dear?"

He reached to pat his wife's hand, but she pulled it out of
reach. "All right," she murmured. But her eyes were worried.

35

"OKAY," I SAID. "Let's begin. But before we start discussing your
alibis, I need your help. I'd like to contact the lady across the
street from you. The one who saw the suspect enter and leave.
What's her name?"

Dolph grinned, and Hilarie gave a little smile. "Ruth Lake,"
he said. "She and her sister live alone in that big old house. Been
there for years. Nice people and good neighbors. But strange."
He sobered. "But we're sure glad she was keeping a lookout. It
was thanks to her that they got Laddie's murderer."

I nodded. "I'd like to talk to her. That could help your case.
If you know her, maybe you could tell her I'm coming to see her
in the next couple of days?"

Dolph pulled a leather pocket secretary from his pocket and
opened it. "Know her well," he said, jotting a note to himself.
"But you better call her first, or you won't get in. Here's her
unlisted number." He read it off to me.

I noted it. "Thanks. Okay, to the alibis. We'll start with the
worst first. Tell me where you were that evening between, say,
seven and ten P.M. You first, if you don't mind, Mr. Compton."

Dolph shook his head and smiled at me. "Even the police were
more subtle." His smile widened. "But of course they don't have

a million dollars as an incentive, do they?" I nodded, hoping my face didn't show my elation. Compton had just given a vital piece of information: the size of the policy on Laddie. With luck I'd eventually know as much as I should have known when I first walked through the door.

Dolph saw I wasn't smiling and got serious. "Well, as we said before, we were at that Easter Seals dinner."

I nodded. "Right. Were you with friends the entire time?"

They looked at each other. That gave me a new idea. "Well, were the two of *you* together all the time?"

A signal seemed to pass between them. Dolph looked at me. "No, we weren't, Mr. Goldman. Maybe I'd better take it from the top."

"Fine." I turned to a blank page in the notebook.

He cleared his throat. "I—we'd bought a table at the banquet. It was two grand, all for charity, of course. Di—our daughter, who also works in the company—was thinking of it as *her* affair." He glanced at his wife. She took over.

"Diane and Laddie both came into the company right out of college, Mr. Goldman. When Laddie . . . " She smiled at me. Again I saw the surprising transformation of her face with the smile. "If I seem to be digressing, Mr. Goldman, it's for a purpose. I don't think you can understand what went on that evening without it."

She cleared her throat. "When Laddie got out of college, he came straight into the business. That was five years ago. We were just making the changeover. As I'm sure you know, Mr. Goldman, we changed our name and our image. You know about my inheritance?" I nodded at her but she didn't seem satisfied. "Did you see the article in the *Wall Street Journal*?"

I shook my head. "No, I saw Saturday's article in the *Times*."

She looked contemptuous. "Very superficial. Very. The *Journal* got it right. I'll get you a copy. In fact, since you mentioned the *Times*, I should tell you, it was not only superficial, it was very misleading. Gave the impression I inherited *millions*." She shook her head. "It was very modest: something under eight hundred thousand after taxes. So—"

Compton interrupted. "I don't know if I'd call that a modest amount, dear. And don't forget, it enabled us to—"

"*You* enabled us to." She gave me another of those glowing smiles. Her eyes crinkled. "My husband and I differ on many things, Mr. Goldman, most notably in our opinions of his abilities." She reached across and patted his hand. "He doesn't think he's capable of anything. Whereas I..." They smiled at each other.

"Well," he said, breaking the spell. "Thanks for the vote of confidence, hon, but without the dough, my abilities would have left us in Queens the rest of our lives. Whereas *with* it—"

"Staying in Queens," she snapped, "wouldn't have been the end of the world either. At least we'd still have our son."

He reddened. His voice came out gruff. "Yeah. We might still have Laddie." He took a breath and glanced uneasily at me. "Well. Let's get back to that evening, shall we?"

I raised a hand. "Before we do, let's talk about this million dollars you'll be collecting on the policy." They both flushed. "I know, it's unpleasant, but I'd be derelict in my own obligations if I didn't ask you about it. How about these accusations that Midas Touch needs the cash on your son's life in order to survive?"

They both looked at me like I'd just spit up on the carpet. I didn't care, and told them so by the tilt of my eyebrows. I waited for an answer.

Dolph started to explode. "That's the most outrageous damn—" He took a breath and sighed. "Okay, Mr. Goldman. You did warn us. And, okay, you're just doing your job. Okay." Hilarie put her hand on his. He gave it a pat.

He looked at me, his color getting back to normal. "Okay, let's talk about money. I don't know how much you know about finance, but our company has a slight solvency problem." He glanced at his wife. "Okay, a *big* solvency problem. We need cash. And yes..." He looked apologetically again at Hilarie. "...the insurance money will be a great boon."

He held my eye. "But." The word was a rifle shot. "We are a solid company underneath, in absolutely no danger of bankruptcy."

Dolph pulled his hands away from his wife to give me his full attention. "Look. We've expanded too fast for our cash flow, it's as simple as that. We're profitable, and we generate huge amounts of cash. But we've been pouring the cash into the carwashes—buying new ones and refurbishing the old. Advertising. Promotion. We offer a first-class product to first-class customers. We're not going to get—or keep—those customers unless we convey a first-class image. And that's expensive." He took a breath, and Hilarie jumped in.

"We have a high net worth, Mr. Goldman. Compared to it, our bank loans are tiny. Our banker agrees, and he's going to give us an extension. Of course we don't agree with everything he—"

"He wants to slow down our growth," Dolph cut in. "He's getting a little nervous about our expansion." He grinned. "He calls it our Edifice complex. Of course Di's opposed to that. She wants us to keep on growing."

"Di's a freewheeler," Hilarie smiled. "A damn-the-torpedoes-full-speed-ahead kind of girl." The smile faded. "Laddie was just the opposite. They used to fight constantly. She called him names; we used to laugh about it. It doesn't seem so funny now."

Silence. I finally broke it. "Should I ask what those names were?"

She managed a smile. "Sure. Di called him our nervous Nellie. Or, her favorite, Laddie Go-Slow. It didn't make him mad. He said—"

"He said," Dolph put in, "if we didn't have someone like him around, the rest of us would grow the company right into bankruptcy. He called her High-Fly Di. It was all in fun." The parents smiled at each other, tears in their eyes.

"Who was right?" I said.

Dolph frowned. "What do you mean?"

"Who was right? Laddie or Di? Is the company growing too fast?"

Hilarie was decisive. "No. Di was right. Laddie was a nervous Nellie. Why, he even wanted me to sell my jewels!" She smiled, but there was iron in the smile.

Dolph chuckled nervously. "Yeah, there was no need for that. Sometimes Ladd could get a little paranoid. He figured since the jewels were worth a quarter of a million, we ought to sell them and put the money in the business."

"What he failed to consider," Hilarie sniffed, "is that we'd have never gotten fair market for them. We'd have been lucky to get half their value. And it was so unnecessary."

I got back to the subject. "I'm afraid I sidetracked us a little, talking about the money. You were giving me your alibis."

Hilarie cleared her throat. She resumed in a softer voice, and looked out the window at the cheerless April day. "Alibis, yes. Well, what happened the night Laddie died, Mr. Goldman, had a lot to do with the way he and Di got along, or didn't get along. It's why the party turned into such a disaster."

She sighed. "You see, Laddie helped us right from the start. While Diane was away at Cornell, enjoying her sorority parties, Laddie was working sixteen- and twenty-hour days in the company. So we made him executive vice-president two years ago. By that time Di was also in the company. And she resented that title. She resented Laddie. We tried—"

"Well." Dolph raised his hands. "Let's not go *too* far. I mean, we wouldn't want to give Mr. Goldman..." He smiled at me. "...the wrong impression."

"No, no!" Hilarie was shocked. "Oh, dear God, I don't want to give you the idea that—!" She laughed uncomfortably. "No, I just want you to understand what happened that evening. It turned into a total *contretemps*." Regan had once told me what that meant, so I wrote "disaster."

"You see, we'd made Di vice-president of Development, meaning she had responsibility for our expansion. And I have to admit, she's done an absolutely fabulous job. We're about to make her vice-president of Marketing, too. She just has a natural head for our business. And getting us into California will—"

Dolph burst in. "We're just real proud of her, Mr. Goldman." He raised a finger. "But. She's a very moody girl. I mean..." He glanced at his wife. "...young woman. *Very* moody. And that Sunday night she was really in a rotten mood."

He glanced at his wife (accusingly?) and went on. "We should have been more conscious of what was going on, I suppose. Neither of us even noticed, when we arrived, that she was already mad. She'd brought these other two couples with her and she was miffed at us for being late. We *weren't* late, but that's Diane. We were later than she was so she thought we were being discourteous to her—and our guests. We didn't even notice she was getting down in the mouth."

"That sure changed when Janine arrived." Hilarie was grim.

"Janine?" I asked, as if I didn't know.

Dolph cleared his throat. "Uh, Janine Mason. Friend of Laddie's. Well, Di blew up. Janine may not have put it as gracefully as she might have." He smiled, blushing a little. "Some people find Janine a little—*irritating* I guess is the right word." He seemed unable to look at his wife.

"An earthier word occurs to me," Hilarie sniffed.

Dolph grinned briefly. "Yeah. Anyway, Janine told us Laddie was going to be late. Of course she had to add her two cents' worth about how she didn't blame him, or something. Her idea being that this charity affair was pretty boring. Rude of her, but—"

"Par for the course for Janine," Hilarie muttered.

"Yeah. Anyway, Di exploded. Laid it all on *me*! Said—"

"What do you mean, all on you?" Hilarie's eyes flashed. "*I* was under the impression *I* got skewered pretty well, too!"

Dolph winced. "Probably. But I was too busy dodging bullets to notice who else was getting shot at. Di busted my chops pretty good about how I'd always favored Laddie and this was her big occasion and I didn't care diddly squat about her, and so on."

"She finally walked out," Hilarie said, shaking her head. "So what started out as an attack on *our* rudeness to our guests became an act of unspeakable rudeness on *her* part—to those very guests. Thanks to Janine and her tactless way of putting things."

Dolph shook his head. "Well, it was no different than that thing with Larry. Ready to break up an engagement over a slight change of plans."

Hilarie raised her voice. "Oh, Dolph! It was totally different and you know it! Larry was acting irresponsibly! We had the church, the caterer, the flowers—"

"Yeah, yeah." Compton sounded bored. "I've heard all this before, dear. But you can't blame the man for just wanting to take a little more time. He—"

"Not when the wedding's set and the date's less than two months away! I don't blame Di a bit!"

Compton looked at me. "Sorry for washing our dirty laundry. We were planning a big wedding for early May. Then our daughter's fiancé decides he wants to wait till God knows when. So

Di broke it off. They only patched things up last week. Now it's set for October."

I tried not to show my boredom. "Well, if we could get back to the party. You say Diane walked out. What did your guests do?"

Dolph chuckled dryly. "Poor folks didn't know what to do anymore than we did. We sort of stood there, trying to think of something to say."

Hilarie scowled. "And Janine, oblivious to the whole thing, just prattled on about her tennis game. I don't think she ever realized what she'd done."

Dolph shook his head. "Oh, she knew. She apologized to Di later."

He cleared his throat again and reached for his wife's hand. She took it. But her expression was strange.

"Well." Dolph shook his head. "We're supposed to be talking about alibis, not family skeletons, I guess."

He shrugged. "Anyway, that was the end of the party—at least for our table. Oh, the guests were as nice as they could be. They stayed awhile, then gave some excuse and begged off. Very politely. Said something about thanks for the invitation but things were awkward and they understood, et cetera. Did it nicely."

Hilarie nodded. "They left, leaving the two of us with Janine. And God bless Janine, she finally caught on that something was up. She mumbled something about having to play tennis with Laddie the next day." Hilarie shook her head. "Tennis with Laddie: that's one date I wish he'd been able to keep, even with Janine." Her eyes were moist. Dolph looked uncomfortable.

I looked up. "Can you give me times on all this?"

Dolph looked startled, then nodded. "Yeah. We went over it with the cops some, so we've got it fairly well down. Di walked out within a minute or two of eight-twenty-five, the Wellingtons left at eight-forty and we left right after that."

"But you only got home at ten. And the Beauchamp's got to be—what?—three or four blocks from your house? Where were you between eight-forty-five and ten?"

Both Comptons colored. They looked at each other. For once, neither seemed anxious to talk. It finally came to the wife. "Uh, yes. Dolph had to go to the office, so I told him I'd just go home.

But I—" Her voice caught. She took a breath and lowered her voice to a near-whisper. "I changed my mind. Decided to wait for Dolph. I wish I hadn't done that. Maybe I could have done something for Laddie ..."

Dolph was brusque. "Don't be ridiculous, sweetheart. If you'd gone home then, we'd have had *two* bodies in that bedroom instead of one."

"I'd have preferred that," she sniffled into her hanky.

"Well ..." He looked away.

She wiped her eyes and faced me. "The fact is, Mr. Goldman, I didn't. For some reason I didn't feel like going home to that empty house. So I waited in the lobby, trying to call Dolph to tell him to pick me up on his way home."

I looked at Dolph. "You had the car?"

"No," he said. "When Jeremiah's not around to drive us, we use cabs mainly. But—"

Hilarie interrupted with a smile. "But not that night. I started calling the office about nine o'clock and kept calling. Nobody. I finally decided I'd make my last try at nine-forty, then just go on home alone. And of course that's the time he answered."

I looked at him. His color had increased. "Uh, yeah. I *did* switch gears a little. It was a nice night and I decided to walk."

I did some quick calculations. "Quite a hike, right? The Beauchamp's at the corner of First and Ninety-first. You walked all the way here?"

He shrugged. "I walk here from home all the time—takes twenty minutes or so. And the Beauchamp's just a little further."

"But that night it took you—what? Forty-five minutes?"

Dolph shook his head. "Half an hour. I ran into Charlie Stratford out on the sidewalk—he was leaving early, too—and we talked a few minutes."

I looked up from my notebook. "Charlie Stratford?"

"Stratford Tool and Die." Dolph glanced quickly at Hilarie for no apparent reason. "Charlie's a friend of mine. Anyway, that slowed me down. It was nine-oh-five by the time I started trekking. I walked in here at nine-thirty-five."

"You're sure about that time?"

Dolph glanced at his watch. "Yeah. I always check the time. Anyway, Hilarie called, asked me to pick her up, so I grabbed the one thing I came for—a demographic survey of southern California. Course, I'd planned to do some other things, but when Hilarie called and said she didn't feel like going home alone, I left right away, picked her up in the cab, and we both went home."

"Getting there when?"

"Ten o'clock."

I wrote the words *Dolph & Hil: No real alibi for Laddie's murd.* in the notebook. I had one more piece to fit into the puzzle, and didn't know how they'd take it.

"I apologize," I said, "but there is a question in some circles about a possible connection between the death of your son and that of Mrs. Benedict two days ago. Monday."

Dolph tried to cut in. "But that—"

I increased the volume and rode over him. "It's only a suspicion and may mean nothing. But some members of the investigative team think that Mrs. Benedict's accident might have been planned. And if so, it might have been planned by your son's murderer. I'm thinking we might be saving ourselves some time later on if you'll just give me your alibis for Monday afternoon. The official time of death was between four-thirty and five. Can you tell me where you were during that time?"

Dolph reddened. "This is really outrageous! I just—"

"Just tell the man, dear," Hilarie said coolly. "He's only doing his job." She turned to me. "As to my own whereabouts, Mr. Goldman, I was at the World Trade Center all day at an automotive services conference, under the aegis of the National Oil Jobbers Council. I was there till eight that night."

I noted it. "Did you see anyone you—"

"Anyone I knew?" Hilarie smiled coldly. "No, I'm afraid not."

We both turned to Dolph. "All right," he muttered. "You're right, hon, I suppose." He turned to me, his face still red, which puzzled me. "I sent Michele home early, about four. I was just in the office working. Worked till after nine."

"You didn't arrive home till nearly eleven," Hilarie said coldly.

"Okay, eleven. Anyway, I didn't see anyone. I was alone right here in the office."

Giving neither one of you an alibi worth spitting at, I thought. *For either murder.*

36

I TURNED DOWN Hilarie's offer to walk me to Di's office. "I'll have to talk to her sometime, Mrs. Compton, that's true. But I've got an appointment across town, thanks all the same." It was a golden opportunity, but I couldn't have her mother telling Di I was an insurance investigator when Di thought I was a cop. Oh what a tangled web we weave...

Instead, Hilarie walked me to the receptionist's desk. There she faced me and put a hand on my arm. "I hope we didn't bore you, Mr. Goldman. My husband and I aren't ourselves these days."

I assured her I wasn't bored at all, it'd been a most productive visit and, furthermore, I'd keep everything under my hat. She gave my arm a final pat. I headed for the elevators, still feeling the warmth of her hand on my arm. I turned a corner and nearly got run over by two attractive women just coming off the elevator.

"I'm sorry," I said, stepping aside. One of them was a striking brunette with glorious features. I glanced from her to her companion, a blond, and did a double-take. "Well, Ms. Compton! How nice to see you again!"

She studied me. "Oh. It's...Officer Goldman, isn't it?" I nodded. "Officer Goldman, Janine Mason."

So this was the redoubtable Janine. I gave her a closer inspection. I could see why Laddie'd been attracted to her. As to why his mother wasn't, it would take some time to find that out. Time I wouldn't mind spending if I got the chance. She was very small, very trim, with a very direct way of looking straight into your eyes. Her eyes were an astonishing blue, contrasting with a fine porcelain complexion and jet black hair. Right now those eyes were giving me a straight-on look.

"Please," I said. "It's Dave," and put out my hand. She entrusted cool fingertips to my grasp. I became aware that Diane was saying something. I tore my eyes from Janine.

"Excuse me," I said, turning to Di. "Did you say something?" Her eyes were cold. "I said, 'What are you doing here?' "

"Oh. I've been talking with your parents." I glanced at Janine, thinking fast. "But since I ran into the two of you, might I have just another fif—"

Diane's eyes glinted. "Another fifteen minutes of my time?" She glanced at Janine. "Fine with me. Okay, Janine? The officer's investigating Laddie's murder."

Janine shrugged. Beautiful shoulders. "Why not? We're not due at the Four Seasons till noon anyway, right?"

We turned and headed for the Midas Touch offices. I wondered how I was going to handle it if we ran into mommy or daddy. Well, I'd worry about that if and when. To make conversation in the meantime, I asked a question. "You two just come from the racquet club?"

That surprised them, especially Janine. "Yes," Di said. "Couple of sets of tennis. How'd you know?"

"Wild guess," I ventured, wondering how Di ever managed to find time to put carwashes into all those elegant locations when she spent every waking hour at the East Side Racquet Club. "Who won?"

"Oh," Janine said offhandedly, "we don't pay much attention to the score. We just have fun. And sweat off some pounds."

"*She* won," Di corrected, an edge in her voice. "As usual. Today it was four and two. Any calls, Viv?" The receptionist shook her head and gave me a suspicious look. I raised a supercilious eyebrow at her as the three of us swept past. (Take that, Ms. Kabulsky.)

"What more can I tell you?" Diane said, ensconced behind the desk in her office. The two women both batted blue eyes at me.

"Just a couple of things," I said, opening my notebook again. "First of all, a question for you, Ms. Mason. I imagine you've been all over this, but tell me again about the night Mr. Compton died. Starting about seven o'clock, up to the time you went to bed."

Janine frowned, and glanced at Di. "Okay. At seven I was at home. I live with my parents, Officer, just a couple of blocks from the Comptons. I was getting ready for the big party, though I wasn't looking forward to it. These big charity things are

such a bore. I was totally traumatized by the year I came out.
Well—"

I looked up. "The year you came out? Came out where?"

Janine's beautiful eyes twinkled. "I'm sorry. I meant the year
I was a deb. Such a drag, you have no idea."

I shrugged. "I'm sure I don't. Go ahead."

"Well, I wasn't looking forward to the affair. Then it was just
beastly when Laddie called and—"

"Sorry to keep interrupting, but when was that?"

"When Laddie called? Just after seven. Said he had something
he had to do, I should just go on to the party and he'd join me
there." She sniffed. "Well, you can imagine how much I liked
that! We had a bit of a spat right there on the phone. He finally
said maybe he wouldn't come at all if I was going to be that way
about it."

Janine turned to Di. "Oh, Di, I just feel so awful about it. That's
the last time I ever talked to Laddie. And I wasn't very nice to
him."

Diane nodded sympathetically. I was mentally comparing Janine with Ruthie, since Laddie had apparently been attracted to
both. Both beautiful, both charming; but Janine was as cultured
as Ruthie wasn't. She was Upper East Side from top to bottom,
Ruthie all Queens. I wondered if the Upper East Side could lie
as smoothly as Queens. Keeping that in mind, I interrupted Diane
in the midst of a sentence.

"I'm sorry, Ms. Mason, but could we get back to that evening?
What did you do after you talked to Mr. Compton?"

Janine smiled at Di and came back to me. "I'm sorry. When
Laddie called, I'd been just getting ready to go out the door;
Kamper, my driver, was waiting for me. I was planning to meet
Laddie at the party. Well, I just made Kamper wait. I sat and
thought about it. I finally decided that, for Di's sake, I should go
ahead and go. It was her evening, after all."

"Some evening," the lady in question muttered.

Janine nodded. "The grimmest."

I was consulting my notebook. "So you finally decided to go,
and got there—when?"

Janine said, "Just a few minutes after eight."

"Eight-fifteen," Diane corrected quietly.

"Maybe. Anyway, that's when I made the announcement that broke up the whole thing. That Laddie wasn't coming. I'm afraid I didn't do it very diplomatically. I wasn't happy with Lad—" Her voice caught.

Both women were perilously close to tears, and I needed to move the agenda along. "Just one or two more questions, Ms. Mason," I wheedled. "All I need from you now is where you went when you left the banquet. You left, I understand, about eight-forty-five?"

Janine cleared her throat and gave me the benefit of those gorgeous blue eyes again. "Eight-forty, I think. I just went home. And..." She was near tears again. "...was there till Dolph called and woke me up at ten-forty-five to tell me Laddie was— gone."

"Anyone see you at home from nine to ten-forty-five?"

Janine shrugged. "Kamper dropped me at a few minutes before nine. The other servants were all off. So I have no alibi."

I smiled at her, thinking *Join the club.* I looked at Di. "Any problem, either of you, telling me where you were Monday afternoon between four-thirty and five?"

They looked at each other. Di spoke for both of them. "Monday of this week?" I nodded. "Why do you want to know?"

I shrugged. "It may not be important. But that's when Ruthie Benedict died." I looked at Janine. "Did you know Mrs. Benedict?"

Di was getting mad. Her nostrils flared and her voice, when it came, was strained. "You can't—"

Janine interrupted. "Who's Ms. Benedict?"

"Mrs.," Di said through her teeth. "She's our butler's daughter. She was killed by a hit-and-run driver Monday afternoon." She took a breath and tried to calm down. "Mr. Goldman. I've tried to be patient with all your questions, despite their repetitive nature. But isn't it a bit far afield to start asking about Ruthie's horrible accident? That has nothing to do with us. Nothing."

I shrugged. "I'm sorry for putting you through this, Ms. Compton. And I do appreciate your taking the time. But I have to ask these questions. As to Mrs. Benedict's death, what difference does it make? If it has nothing to do with you, nothing's lost by telling me where you were for that brief half-hour Monday afternoon. Is it?"

She wasn't assuaged. I tried a different tack. "Look, Ms. Compton. If Eddie Goode really killed your brother, he ought to suffer for it. And I'll do everything in my power to help see that he does. But suppose, just suppose, he didn't. You don't want to see the person who did, get away with it, do you?" I looked at both of them. I seemed to be getting through. "Okay? Now talk to me. Where were you Monday afternoon?"

Janine gave a little shrug. "All right. I was at the U.N., giving a tour. I volunteer there, three days a week."

I nodded. "See, that wasn't so bad, was it?" I turned to Di to ask the same question, when something clicked. Back when Sally Castle and I were still on speaking terms, she'd introduced me to a woman who was involved with the U.N. in some way that involved volunteers. Recruiting them, training them, something . . . what was it? And what was her name? Oh, for a decent memory.

Both women were staring at me. Di spoke. "Do you—"

I raised a hand and smiled. "I'm sorry, something just crossed my mind. I . . . " Suddenly the name flashed in front of me. Vera . . . Vera what? Sampson! Vera Sampson! She was, something, coordinator of volunteers, something.

I beamed at Janine. You don't often get the chance to test a suspect's alibi right on the spot. "You volunteer at the U.N.?" She nodded warily. "You know Vera Sampson?"

Janine's face fell, almost literally. Her jaw dropped, her eyes flicked in both directions. For a second she looked like she had thoughts of jumping and running. At least she gave me that impression. She wasn't happy to find out I knew Vera.

She tried to smile. "Oh yes, Vera's in charge of the volunteers. She's wonderful!" Her eyes flicked both ways again. "Uh, do you know her very well?"

I shrugged. "Friend of a friend. But it's kind of convenient, me knowing her. When she verifies your story, I'll really know it's for real." I flashed another big smile. Very innocent.

Janine cleared her throat. She looked down. "Well, uh, that's great." Then she looked up with a wide-eyed look, one I'm very familiar with. The one I use whenever I tell a particularly big whopper. But with those blue eyes, she was much more effective at it.

"Oh!" she tittered. "My God, you were talking about *this* Monday, weren't you?" I nodded. "Well, don't call Vera, for God's sake, or she'll tell you I'm a liar! I forgot: I wasn't there Monday at all!"

I raised my eyebrows, still the soul of innocence. "No?"

"No! That's the day I called in sick. My God, I feel so stupid!" She looked at Di. "Remember, Di? You and I were going to see a movie that night, and I called you?"

Diane frowned, nodded.

"Well, I was just *so* sick. I called you and Vera, and cancelled everything."

"You seem fine now," I pointed out.

"Oh, it was just a twenty-four-hour bug. A little bed rest, and I was fine by Tuesday afternoon."

"Okay," I said, noting it in the notebook. "Anyone verify you were home in bed that afternoon? I mean Monday. Especially between four-thirty and five."

Janine shook her head and smiled. "Nope. Just me, myself and I. The servants leave at four, most days. And Mommy and Daddy are in Europe this week."

I smiled and nodded at her, giving her no clue to what I was really thinking: *You're lying through your teeth, lady.*

37

YOU CAN'T LET YOURSELF get too excited every time you catch somebody in a lie. A couple of things you learn fairly early in policework are, first of all, everyone lies, and second of all, being a liar isn't the same as being a murderer, or even a criminal. So I wasn't ready to start strapping Ms. Mason into the hot seat. But

I was intrigued, and intended to look into it the first chance I got.

But at the moment I had business with Diane. "Care to provide an alibi for yourself, Ms. Compton? Look at Ms. Mason: I just caught her in a whopper and she's none the worse for it." I smiled at Janine, who gave me an even brighter one of her own. But her eyes were watchful behind the smile.

Diane shrugged. "I suppose not. I was at the racquet club. But I'm afraid I didn't see anyone there I know. And they'd have no record of it, anyway. I didn't sign in. I never do when I'm just using the track and the Nautilus."

Well, at least she agreed with what Vosburg had told me. I jotted it down. "Thank you. Just one final question and I'm gone. I'm interested in your mother's jewels, Ms. Compton. And your brother's attitude toward them."

"What about them? They were stolen the night Laddie was killed. That man—Goode—took them." Her eyes widened. "*That's* why it's so ridiculous, you asking us all these questions! You've *got* the murderer in jail. He obviously stole them. You found them in his apartment! Didn't you?"

I shrugged. "Good point. But what I'm getting at is, were the jewels insured?"

She shrugged. "What's that have to do with anything?"

"Perhaps nothing. But were they?"

Diane tossed her head. "Of course they were. So what?"

"And didn't Laddie want to cash them in? I mean sell them and put the money into the company?"

"Oh," she said casually, "Laddie was such a ninny. Yes, he actually wanted Mother to sell them to pay down the bank loan. He was all nervous about the balloon. For no reason." She shook her head pityingly. "So stupid! Mother'd have had to take a huge loss on them; she'd never have gotten more than twenty-five or thirty cents on the dollar, just dumping them. And the business is perfectly capable of meeting the balloon payment. He was just—well, that was Laddie."

My next question was interrupted by a young woman standing in the doorway. Diane looked up, eyebrows raised.

"Excuse me, Ms. Compton, but Mr. Compton is on your line.

I told him you were tied up, but he wants you to pick up. He says it's important."

Diane nodded and grabbed the phone. "Yes, Daddy." As she listened, her brow furrowed. "But, Daddy, Janine and I were planning to have lunch!" She listened some more, her face becoming more distraught. "Oh dear. Yes, I suppose so. Hold on for just a minute, Dad. Let me ask Janine." Di held the phone against her chest and turned to her friend. "Daddy scheduled a lunch with the guy who's arranging to get us into California. But the manager of one of our units just walked off the job, and Daddy feels he ought to run out there to be sure everything's okay. So he's asking me if I'd mind taking the gentleman to lunch." She gave Janine a pleading look. "Can I give you a raincheck, Janine?"

Janine waved it away with a smile. "Tell your daddy I'm always willing to sacrifice for the cause. I've got some things at home I ought to be taking care of anyway. You go ahead."

Di looked relieved. "Are you sure?"

"Diane!" Janine said severely. "Don't worry about it! It's fine. Really."

Diane shook her head. "You're great, Janine. I'll make it up to you." She put the receiver back to her ear. "It's fine, Daddy. You go ahead, I'll take care of Joel Steinborn, don't worry . . . What? Sure, here she is."

She extended the receiver to Janine. "He wants to apologize personally."

"Oh, the silly!" Janine took the phone. "Hello, Dolph . . . Don't worry about it, for heaven's sake! I only see Di about seven times a day as it is!" She laughed. "Okay, Dolph, and don't worry about it. Di's promised me a raincheck . . . Bye."

She hung up. Di repeated her apology. "I'm so sorry, Janine."

"Will you shut up, Di! It's fine. Really." She got up and looked at me. "So if you have no more questions . . . "

I raised my hands. "I'm done. You two have been most patient, and I thank you. I'm leaving, too. Offer you a ride on the elevator, Miss Mason?"

She accepted my offer, so I got fifty-two floors of that perfume and those eyes. But not much conversation. Down in the lobby, I offered to share a cab and drop her.

"No no. I've got a little shopping to do anyway. You run along;

I'll be fine." She took my hand in another cool handshake.

I waved and headed toward Fifth Avenue, ostensibly to cross to the Plaza Hotel to catch a cab. That's what I wanted Janine to think. Something about her quickness to leave her friend's office, combined with her attempted lie about her activities Monday afternoon, had created an itch I just had to scratch. By tailing her and finding out where she was really going.

But I had a problem. Two, in fact. One, it's hard to tail someone who knows you; second, it's even harder when you've just said goodbye to them. You've got to turn your back on them and walk away. Turning around to look—at least more than once—is suspicious as hell.

I turned around the first time as I was just stepping out onto Fifth, and damned if she didn't catch me at it. I grinned and waved—a just-prolonging-the-goodbye wave. I'd now used up my quota of those. So out in the middle of Fifth I turned again, pretending to watch a passing pedestrian, and managed to catch Janine with her back to me, heading south. I made a sharp U-turn right in the middle of the avenue just as the light changed, dodged a taxi, and went after her.

For someone supposedly out for a little shopping, she sure wasn't doing much window-gazing. She marched straight ahead, like people do when they're heading for someplace definite. I stayed half a block back all the way to Fifty-third. There she turned the corner and disappeared.

I now regretted that half-block edge I'd spotted her and upped the speed. Or tried to. Trouble was, the sidewalk was filled with lots of slower-moving pedestrians, and it was a struggle getting through them. By the time I reached the corner Janine was nowhere to be seen.

I scanned both sides of the street carefully. No sign of her. I concluded that, unless my luck had really turned sour, or she'd made me somehow, she was still somewhere on the block—probably in one of the stores along the east side of Fifty-third.

As I headed east, checking out the stores, a sign caught my eye: LA FONTENELLE: CONTINENTAL CUISINE. I glanced at my watch: 11:32. Too early for lunch. But I had a feeling I should check it anyway—very carefully.

The restaurant was six steps below the sidewalk. I stood just out of view from anyone below and checked it out. Through the restaurant's wide window I could see a couple of lights burning over the two tables visible. The tables were unoccupied. But a sign on the door said Open.

I considered the situation. There was no way to get down those steps without running the risk of Janine seeing me—if that's where she was. If she wasn't, I shouldn't be wasting time on it. So: was she?

Sometimes you get lucky. I glanced back to the west and saw something that explained, in one blinding flash, a whole lot of things, maybe up to and including the murders of Laddie Compton and Ruthie Benedict. Walking toward me from the direction of Fifth—the same way Janine and I had come—was Dolph Compton. Spotting him was the least of my luck. The best part was: I saw him before he saw me.

Without pausing to think about it, I turned and walked east at a normal pedestrian's pace. As I walked I calculated, by the speed he'd been walking, when Compton would reach La Fontenelle. Precisely then, I turned and made like a window shopper. Out of the corner of my eye I saw Dolph descend the six steps to La Fontenelle.

38

I STOOD ON THE SIDEWALK outside La Fontenelle for a good two minutes, thinking. Partly about the implications of what I'd just seen. But mainly about whether I should follow Dolph down those six steps.

The temptation to catch them redhanded was strong. On the other hand, there was an advantage in knowing about them without them knowing that I knew. Could I achieve the best of both worlds: observe them and remain unobserved? I shook my head. Not possible except by sheer dumb luck. And I'd already exhausted my daily allotment of that.

I finally decided not to decide. Not with Regan in his office, available for a phone call. I found a pay phone at the corner, got him on the line and gave him a quick rundown of the situation.

"Are you sure the young woman is in there?"

"Oh, I'd say there's maybe one chance in ten thousand that she's not. Look: she turned the corner and then disappeared. I didn't see her in any of the other stores. And five minutes later, here comes Compton. You tell me."

Regan breathed for a couple of seconds. "Your estimate is probably conservative. Was it arranged well in advance, or was it an *ad hoc* assignation?"

"Don't know. The daddy called Di with what's turned out to be a lie: that he had to go visit one of their facilities. Then he told Di he wanted to talk to Janine—to apologize for breaking up their lunch date, he said. Ten minutes later he meets her. Obviously—at least it's obvious to me—he made the rendezvous over the phone."

Regan thought some more. Finally: "Come home. The advantages of our knowing without their knowing that we know outweigh any advantage you might gain by confronting them."

"I'll be right there," I agreed, and grabbed a cab.

Regan was waiting when I walked into his office ten minutes later. He was abrupt. I'm always glad to see that, because it generally indicates he's onto something.

"Well," he said. "Quite a morning you seem to have had. I want a full report."

"Oh, you have no idea. Amazing the stuff I'm able to learn, using no more than that one lousy suggestion you gave me."

He stared at me. "Yes, isn't it wonderful that you actually obtained some useful information in spite of my inadequacy. You must be very proud of yourself."

Once we got past the sarcasm I started the briefing. When Ernie came to announce lunch we moved the briefing into the dining room. Of course it was slow going with all his questions. My only surprise was that he had more questions about Dolph and Hilarie than about Di and Janine.

By the end of lunch he had the whole thing. So we headed back to the office and got onto alibis and opportunities. Using a legal-size pad, I jotted down times and alibis for both murders.

We figured the March 25 window of possibility for Laddie's murder was between 9:15, when Eddie left the mansion, and 10:00, when the Comptons arrived.

Ruthie's murder, Monday, April second—two days ago—was between 4:30 and 5:00.

We started with the first one. Using our memories and my notebook, we traced the movements of the suspects, in which category we were now placing the three Comptons; Jeremiah Healy; Janine Mason; and Gwen Jackson (a long shot). With his alibi, Vosburg was out of the running, unless as an accessory, but I included him just to justify all the hard work I'd done running it down. Also I made a strong pitch for including, even if he was another long shot, Junior Benedict.

"He's a known crook, a known killer, he might've had an in at the Comptons through Ruthie, he—"

"He had no reason to kill Mr. Compton, David, none whatsoever. And he certainly didn't kill Mrs. Benedict."

I stared. "Didn't kill—? *Certainly* didn't kill her? How can you be so sure?"

"What you overheard him say while he was trying to break into her apartment. You reported it to me."

I shook my head. What was he talking about? I pulled out my notebook.

"That's not going to help you. It's not in your notebook. You recited it from memory."

I squinted at him. "Okay, I remember. And I don't see how it shows he's innocent."

"Mr. Benedict is by no means an innocent. But one crime of which he is *not* guilty is the murder of his ex-wife. Tell me again what he said in the hallway."

"All he said was something like, 'She told me she signed it. So it's gotta be here.' That's all." I shrugged. "How does that—"

Regan was exasperated. "Think, David! Mrs. Benedict was killed before five o'clock, Monday afternoon. What sense would it make for him to murder her in the afternoon, then wait till the next day to retrieve an item he's after?"

"Well..." I tried to think of a reasonable explanation. Couldn't.

Regan leaned forward. "No. The only credible explanation of Mr. Benedict's actions yesterday is that he had just learned of her death and came straightway."

I scratched my head. "Okay, scratch Junior." A thought occurred to me. "Hey! We've now eliminated two of the three people she called Monday afternoon. The third was Healy. And she called him at four-twenty-eight, just minutes before she—Holy buckets! Oh man, it just hit me! That must've been the call he got while I was sitting in his office! The one that sent him running!"

Regan nodded. "Of course. It was obviously his daughter who called. That was clear from the moment you showed me the phone log Sergeant Parker obtained for you. I'd have said something but thought it was obvious." Ahead of me again. How long, O God? At least he was nice enough not to smirk. I mean Regan, not God.

"Which gives rise, of course, to speculation about Mr. Healy's possible culpability. Clearly he left you to go to her. And sometime during the next thirty-two minutes she was murdered. But it doesn't follow that he murdered her. Mrs. Benedict was his daughter, after all; and they were by most accounts affectionate. Before we start making assumptions, let us prepare a schematic of both deaths."

We spent the next hour working out a timetable for all known suspects for the two fatal evenings: a "Matrix of Opportunities," the Bishop called it. It gave me a couple of weeks' worth of alibi-checking, which I planned to do.

Here's what we finally arrived at:

FIRST MURDER: LADDIE COMPTON: SUNDAY, MARCH 25

Suspect	Time	Activity
Dolph	8:50	Left the Beauchamp; talked with friend on sidewalk outside. (DG: check this out.)
	9:05	Walked to GM Building.
	9:35	Arrived at office. (GM Building security people later confirmed this.)
	9:45	Took cab to pick up Hilarie; then home.
	10:05	Discovered body.

Hilarie	8:50	Went to lobby of Beauchamp, began phoning Dolph's office. (Checked later with hotel personnel; no one saw her.)
	9:40	Finally reached Dolph on phone.
	9:55	Picked up in cab by Dolph.
	10:05	Discovered body.
Diane	8:25	Left banquet in a huff. Drove halfway to Union Grove, turned around, returned to Manhattan. (No way to check.)
	9:52	Signed in at racquet club (checked with club, and they agreed. But murder probably committed before this, anyway.)
	10:58	Arrived home; learned brother had been killed.
Healy	8:50	Laddie comes to his sitting room.
	9:15	Laddie tells Healy he'll meet him at Red Lion; Healy goes there, spends next two hours. (No one at Red Lion able to verify exact time of arrival.)
	11:03	Returns to Comptons' to learn Laddie murdered.
Vosburg	All day	Sick in bed in Union Grove.
	11:07	Gets phone call from Diane. Leaves for Manhattan immediately.
	11:28	Arrives at Comptons' to comfort (and be comforted by) Diane, family.
Gwen	All day	At home in Harlem. (Never verified.)
Janine	8:45	Went home from Beauchamp (DG: check it.)

SECOND MURDER: MARY RUTH BENEDICT: MONDAY, APRIL 2

Dolph	In office from 4:00 P.M. till 10:30. No witnesses.
Hilarie	At meeting at World Trade Center all day till 8:00 P.M. No witnesses.
Diane	To racquet club at 3:30; picked up by Vosburg at GM building at 5:05; no witnesses.
Healy	Recd. ph. call from daughter at 4:28; ran out; returned home at 5:40; no witnesses.
Vosburg	Recd. ph. call from Ruthie at 3:10; stayed on phone till 3:21; says he was driving into Manhattan from 4:00 to 5:05; no witnesses.
Gwen	At the mansion cleaning till 5:30; verified.
Janine	At home in bed, sick. (DG: check it out.)

When we finished, Regan studied it, me looking over his shoulder. I could tell he was getting excited by the way his fingertip jerked from item to item. Finally he couldn't stand it anymore.

"David. Please sit down." He spun away from the desk before my fanny hit the chair. He spoke on the move. "A number of alibis need checking. The new information you picked up this morning—the assignation of Mr. Compton and Ms. Mason—points to four alibis that should be checked first: the whereabouts of those two during both murders. Only one of those alibis appears to be easily and immediately verifiable: Mr. Compton's of March twenty-fifth: his purported conversation with Mr. Stratford. Try to verify it. Now."

I looked at him and shrugged. Couldn't hurt. I headed for my office, thinking about an approach. Came up with one in a hurry. I liked it.

It worked like a dream. I found Stratford Tool & Die in the Manhattan directory, called the number, and soon had the man's secretary.

"May I tell him what this is regarding, sir?"

"You surely can," I said in my sincerest secretary-handling voice. "The Hotel Beauchamp is always concerned when a large number of guests leave a function early. This happened at the Easter Seals Banquet, March twenty-fifth. I'm calling because Mr. Stratford was among those who left. I just wondered if anything was wrong and whether there's anything the hotel could do to make things right."

"Ummm. Just a moment Mr., er . . . "

"Goldman."

"Just hold on, will you, please?"

I was on hold for about thirty seconds. Then an abrupt male voice came on the line. "Yes, Mr. Goldman. What's all this about?"

"Yes sir. The Hotel Beauchamp is concerned about possible dissatisfaction with our—"

"Oh yeah, that Easter Seals bash. No, no, everything was fine. What's the problem?"

"Well, sir, it's just that a number of guests left before the dinner was actually served. I believe you were among that number?"

A pause. Then a harsh laugh. "Well, I'll be damned. I thought

I was so careful to sneak out without anyone noticing. How'd you find out?"

I laughed politely. "I'm afraid your friend, Mr. Compton, gave you away."

He chuckled. "Can't even trust your friends anymore, can you? So Dolph ratted! I feel like a kid again, playing hooky and getting caught at it. No, Mr. Goldman, it had nothing to do with the hotel. I do appreciate your interest. My wife couldn't make it, I was bored and just wanted to get home, get out of the monkey suit and kick back. Don't worry about it."

"Well, I appreciate it, Mr. Stratford, but... I, uh, apologize for pushing it, but, are you sure? You aren't just being polite? I ask because Mr. Compton not only 'ratted' on you..." I tittered. "...but I also gathered from him that you might have been just a teeny bit upset with us."

"Upset? Me? Dolph Compton said that? Where the hell did he get that idea?"

"Oh, he said he had rather a long conversation with you as the two of you were leaving, and I believe he formed the impression you were upset. This was not the case?"

A long pause. "Well. Of course, that was the night his son— well. Mr. Goldman, I think Mr. Compton is mixed up—understandably so. You know what happened to his son that night?"

"Yes, sir. I am aware of the tragedy."

"Well, there you are. Actually, Dolph and I barely exchanged greetings. He was getting into a limo. I asked him for a lift, but he said it wasn't his car. That's really the whole conversation. He may have thought I was upset, but I wasn't."

"So you really had no conversation about—anything?"

"Not more than a couple of words. No sir."

"All right, sir. Thank you. I'm certainly glad you're not unhappy with the Beauchamp."

I went back into Regan's office thinking. Regan, at the south windows, reading, spun to face me. His eyes lighted up as I told him what Stratford had said. He put his face in his hands for a minute, thinking, then pushed back to his desk, frowning into space.

"So Mr. Compton lied. This is crucial information, David. The most important piece we still need is the truth about the Comptons' financial position."

He rubbed his chin and furrowed his brow. "And how can we go about discovering that? Nothing occurs to me. The company's bankers would surely not be willing to—" His mouth snapped shut and his eyes lit up. He looked at me. "I have it! I know precisely whom to ask!"

39

I STUDIED REGAN'S excited face. "Mind letting me in on what you're talking about?"

"David. The one matter in which our knowledge is still deficient is the Comptons' financial situation. According to the New York *Times*, a consortium of suburban banks made them a loan, a loan that is coming due. But the *Times* failed to name the banks." He squinted at the ceiling. "What would you think of calling Mr. Nathanson?"

So that was his inspiration. It would have been nice to poke fun at it, but I couldn't; I was too enthusiastic. Abe Nathanson's not only one of Regan's favorite people, he's one of mine. Regan introduced me to him in the McClain case, and Abe helped plenty on that one. His banking expertise filled in a couple of vital pieces.

Abe's in his seventies, has only one arm (he lost the other in World War II) and always wears a *yarmulke*. He's an observant orthodox Jew and one of the most astute and knowledgeable banking consultants in the city. His clients are mainly the smaller suburban banks, so he was the perfect guy to talk to about our current problem. In fact, I was a little irritated at myself for not thinking of it first.

Regan let me make the call, but grabbed the phone as soon as Nathanson came on. "*Shalom*, Abe! Frank Regan here!" He waved at me to go to my office and get on the line. As I got there Regan was saying, " . . . indeed! I'm surprised to hear that, Abe. Ah! I believe David is now on the line."

I mumbled a *Shalom* and heard Abe's high tenor: "Wonderful to speak to you! *Shalom*, David! How are you two fine gentlemen?" As usual, Abe pronounced my name the Hebrew way: *Da-veed*.

A round of cordialities ensued, including Abe's usual prodding of me to get to *schul* once in a while and start keeping kosher. Naturally the Bishop agreed with Abe, bemoaning my lackadaisical brand of Judaism. "But I shall continue to encourage him, Abe."

"Yes, I'm sure you will, Frank. Come the Messiah, your good works shall not go unrequited."

That obligatory minuet finished, Regan got into it. "Well, Abe, I did have a purpose in calling, pleasant as it always is to hear your voice. Are you familiar with the Compton family? Midas Touch Autocare?"

Nathanson's tone was guarded. "Yes, Frank."

"Yes. And the murder of young Mr. Compton last week?

"Yes. Tragic."

"Indeed." Regan rushed ahead. "David and I are looking into the matter on behalf of the defense. And it would help if I could learn more about the family's banking relations."

Abe paused, then said, "Well, Frank, it's public knowledge that the Mount Vernon Thrift Company is the lead bank in the credit."

Regan waited but Abe didn't elaborate. "Er, thank you, Abe. Could you perhaps give me a name? Someone at the bank with whom I might discuss the loan? Understanding, of course, that confidentiality would not be violated."

"All right. As it happens, Frank, I just spoke to the person, so I know he's in his office: Herb Crowe, senior vice-president. Here's his number." Abe rattled off a number with a 914 area code. He chuckled. "The examiners are in the bank and Herb's nervous. He called me because he wanted his hand held, I think. In any case," he said, sobering, "he's there and you may feel free to call him. Use my name. But don't expect him to violate any confidences."

"Of course not, Abe. But a final question, if I may. What quality lender is Mr. Crowe? Is he competent? I'd like you to be brutally frank. Naturally, Mr. Goldman and I will keep your reply in confidence."

"No need for secrecy, Frank. I'd be happy to let anyone know. Herb Crowe is one of the brightest young bankers in New York, in my humble opinion." Abe chuckled. "I'm showing my age, calling him young. Herb is probably in his forties, but I still think of him as a stripling.

"But he's good, very good. Astute, conservative, well-educated—Brown, I believe, or Dartmouth—and very hard working. He'll go far. Anything he tells you—and I fear it won't be much—you may rely on absolutely."

With a final flurry of *shaloms* we rang off. I went back into Regan's office. He looked up at me. "Well. I don't know how much we'll be able to learn, David. But I think we should try. Knowing the Comptons' true financial situation is crucial."

The Bishop frowned and turned his wheelchair away. "Whether you'll be able to learn anything useful is doubtful. But you must try."

"What's the minimum we need?" This was beginning to look to me like a washout.

Regan shrugged. "The size of the loan. The terms. Were any non-business assets put up as collateral? For instance, Mrs. Compton's jewelry?"

Regan looked at me significantly. "But most important is the question: how likely is the consortium to demand payment when the loan comes due next month? Their doing so could bring the business down. With disastrous effect on the whole family."

I was taking notes, not with a lot of enthusiasm. "I've talked to bankers before," I said. "What are my chances of getting any of this?"

Regan rubbed his face. "Perhaps small. But until I know the details of that loan I won't feel I understand the total picture. The loan and its implications may well have been what brought about Mr. Compton's death."

He sighed. "Well. You have the man's number. See what you can learn. It's worth a try." Regan pushed himself over to his desk and opened a personnel file. I was dismissed.

I went into my office shaking my head. I didn't like it. And I already knew I wasn't going to like Crowe. Not only was he a banker, he had a rotten last name.

But people can surprise you. As Crowe surprised me. He hadn't said more than two sentences when my attitude toward him changed. Some people you like right away; you can't explain it anymore than you can explain why some grate on you right away. Of course I hadn't assumed I'd dislike him just because he was a banker. I mean, I've got *lots* of banker friends. (Well, two.) Of course, the name was also against him. But Cabot Crowe was a lawyer, not a banker; no reason to blame good old Herb for bad old Cabot.

And *this* Crowe was friendly. "Yes, Mr. Goldman. Abe Nathanson just called to tell me I'd be hearing from you. He says you're *the* Dave Goldman: the man who caught the murderer in the Lombardi case, and in the McClain case, and plenty of others besides. I'm honored. What can I do for you?"

I didn't know how much of that was real and how much BS, but I liked it. "Yeah, well, being a co-religionist of mine, Abe does tend to pile it a little deep sometimes." Crowe laughed appreciatively, not a banker's laugh. A good, hearty laugh, from the belly. Something about his voice bugged me, but I liked the laugh. Of course, his regarding me as a hero didn't hurt.

"It's not Abe who convinced me," he said. "I've read about your cases myself. I'm impressed. Really. I hope I can be of some help."

I took a breath. "Well, I hope you can too. I'm looking into the Compton murder. I take it you know about it."

Crowe's voice turned serious. "Oh dear, yes. Horrible. Truly horrible. Yes, I knew Laddie a little. His parents better. They're very good customers of ours. Have been for years. I went to the funeral. Terribly sad."

"I'm sure it was. See, what I want to do—"

"But—excuse me, Mr. Goldman, sorry for interrupting, but don't the police have the fellow in hand? I've been reading about it, and this fellow—Goode, is it?—he's the one they're saying is guilty. Or has he been released?"

"No, he hasn't been released. But I don't think he's guilty. So I'm trying to find out who is."

A moment of silence. "Oh dear, oh dear," Crowe said. "Really? This must be very difficult on the family." Another silence. "You *really* don't think Goode did it?"

"No, I don't, Mr. Crowe. If you're willing to see me, I'll be glad to tell you why."

His voice sounded guarded. "How soon do you need to do this?"

"Yesterday."

He laughed. But when he spoke his voice was serious. "I'd be delighted to meet you, Mr. Goldman, but there are a couple of problems. Number one, today's not very good. The examiners are here..." He took a breath. The way it sounded, having the examiners there was something like having a root canal without the anesthetic. "...in addition to which, the CEO of our holding company is probably coming by at some point. So today's not too good. And frankly, because of customer confidentiality, there wouldn't be much I could tell you anyway."

He did a little humming exercise. I waited, sensing he was trying to figure out a way. I was right. "Okay, look. Why don't you come ahead? I'll work you in. I'm staying late because of the bank examiners anyway. We're *hoping* this is their last day. And I haven't even talked to them yet."

He sighed. "Look. I'm just brewing a fresh pot of coffee. Or are you one of those sissies who quits drinking coffee at noon?"

"You kidding? Real men drink coffee all day. And I like it black."

"Wonderful! Now I know we'll get along. Why don't you come straightaway?"

"I'll do just that." As soon as I hung up I realized why his voice had bugged me at first. It was a dead ringer for Cabot's.

I didn't waste time thinking about that. I told Regan and Ernie where I was going and headed for Fred's to pick up Regan's Caddy.

40

THAT WAS A LITTLE AFTER THREE; it was 4:35 by the time I reached the bank. The traffic was horrendous. A recent article in the *Dispatch* had talked about the recent increase in rush-hour traffic, but this was the first time I'd experienced it. By the time I got to Mount Vernon I'd come to a major conclusion: anyone who puts himself through this every day deserves everything he or she gets.

Tuning the radio to the traffic news didn't help a bit. Unless misery really does love company. I had plenty of both. Well, it *was* comforting to know the Major Deegan was just as bad as the Bronx River, the one I'd chosen. At one point, in a moment of temporary insanity, I even considered jumping on the Bronx-and-Pelham to head over for the Hutchinson River (the Parkway, not the waterway). Luckily, the announcer came in with a report on the Hutchinson River. Sounded like it was the worst of the worst. So I just kept trucking, and rolled into the bank parking lot at 4:35.

I found a slot marked Visitors and went to the glass front door of the bank. A uniformed guard inside waved me away, pointing at his watch to signal they were closed. Before I could start yelling at him that I had an appointment, behind him came a tall, handsome man in a dark suit who looked strangely familiar. He said something, and the burly guard nodded. They exchanged a couple of words, and the guard turned to me with an apologetic smile and a shrug. Using the key ring at his belt, he opened the door, muttering apologies. The tall banker stuck out his hand. As we shook, he said, "Mr. Goldman? Honored. Herb Crowe," and I realized who the banker was. He was Cabot Crowe. Except where Cabot's sneer should have been, there was a friendly smile.

I gawked at him. "You've *got* to be related to Cabot Crowe!"

The banker's smile widened. "Oh, you know Cab? My twin brother. Quite a resemblance, no? But there *are* differences." He

190

gestured me to follow. "Let's go to my office. How do you know Cab?"

Following him past desks staffed by eager-looking young bankers into a panelled office, I was thinking hard. How could Cabot Crowe's twin brother be so friendly when Cabot was such a jerk?

"Have a seat, Mr. Goldman," he said, waving in the direction of a chair. I saw a steaming mug of coffee on a table beside it. Why didn't it seem like an office? It looked too bare, but why? Four armchairs and a credenza against one wall equipped with a personal computer. Then I saw what was out of whack: where the desk should have been there was nothing. Crowe grabbed the chair nearest the computer and spun it around. He picked up his own coffee.

"No desk?" I said.

"Our new computerized work center," he explained, blowing steam from his coffee. "No desk, no papers. Just the Mac and a phone. All you need. At least that's what they tell me." He flashed the grin again and sipped coffee. "It's only our second month with it, so it still has bugs. But I think it's going to work out fine." He laughed. "I have to say that: the whole thing was my idea."

"You're Cabot Crowe's brother," I said, sipping the surprisingly good coffee and giving him a second look. Herb's face might have been a little thinner than Cabot's as I remembered it, the nose not quite as long, the hair a little thinner; otherwise it could have been the same guy.

"We often get mistaken for each other," Herb said, undisturbed by my scrutiny. "Always have. At Andover, the headmaster forbade us to wear the same clothes. Said it confused the profs." He laughed. "It's had its good points and its bad. When Cab went into law—he was in criminal law for a while—he warned me that he was going to give the perps my address. In case any of them wanted revenge!" He laughed again. "So how do you know Cab?"

I shook my head. "I'm afraid your brother and I didn't exactly hit it off. I was a cop at one time, and we worked on a case together. We had sort of a—well, disagreement's about as nice a word for it as any."

Herb frowned at me. "Let's see. Cab mentioned a run-in he

had with a sergeant once. Said the guy used poor procedures. Then, when Cab tried to correct him, the fellow threatened to beat him up." I shrugged, embarrassed. Herb burst out laughing. "That was you? God, Cab told me all about it! Said you threatened to thrash him within an inch of his life!"

"Aw, c'mon. It was just a friendly little invitation to duke it out. I was pissed."

The banker got serious. "Cab finally admitted to me that he wasn't very comfortable with criminal law. When he was at Brown—and even earlier, at Andover—he was fascinated by politics. He was student council president at Andover; and student body rep at Brown. He went to Harvard Law as a prelude to going into politics. So he was pleased as punch to get a job with the D.A.'s office right after graduation. But he soon found he had no talent for criminal law."

"So what's old Cab doing now?"

Herb grinned. "Practicing corporate law down on Wall Street, making a ton of money. And not getting his block knocked off by the likes of you."

I grinned back. "Or doing the knocking off. I doubt if either of you'd do too bad in the fisticuffs department. I mean, you look like you stay in shape."

He shook his head. "Yes, I run and all that. But I'm not ready to take on a cop. Neither was Cab." Crowe's face changed. "Well. I didn't know the famous Dave Goldman was the guy who challenged my brother to a fight. Glad you don't hold grudges. Cab notwithstanding, I'm delighted to meet you. Now. What can I do for you?"

I crossed my legs and gave him Regan's and my rationale for thinking Goode wasn't guilty of Laddie's murder. Crowe listened carefully.

"So your thought is that this could be some sort of family vendetta—that someone murdered Laddie for the insurance proceeds?" I nodded. Herb shuddered. "Dear God, that's—But I guess you have to consider it. At least coming at it from where you are."

The banker took a breath and looked me in the eye. "I know the Comptons. All of them. I know Dolph and Hilarie better than I know Diane or knew Laddie, but I know them all. And I refuse to believe they could have done this. They're a very close-knit family."

I nodded. "Do you know Jeremiah Healy? Or Larry Vosburg or Janine Mason; or Gwen Jackson, the Comptons' maid?"

Crowe frowned. "Know *of* them. Healy's the Comptons' butler, right? I may have seen him once. And Vosburg: he's the guy Di's engaged to, isn't he? Never met him."

"What about Healy's daughter? Mary Ruth. Just died."

Crowe raised his eyebrows at the last word but shook his head. "Nope. Never heard of her."

I flipped open the notebook and took a couple of notes. While doing that, I said, "So you don't think mister or missus could've done it. Or little sister. Let me ask you: if Goode *didn't* do it, who did?" I looked up from the notebook to check Crowe's reaction.

His face seemed honest and open. "Not a clue, Mr. Goldman. If this guy Goode didn't do it, I really don't have an inkling."

I turned to a blank page. "Okay. What can you tell me about the loan?"

Crowe winced. "That's what I'm sorry about. I'm afraid you wasted a trip. Frankly, there's nothing I can tell you. Nothing, that is, beyond what's been in the papers. And that's only what the Comptons have made known. Why don't you go to *them*? In my position, I'm not really at liberty to say anything. They could tell you everything you wanted to know. If they cared to."

I nodded, though rejecting the suggestion. If a Compton was the murderer, how much truth would I get from them? "Well, let me just ask you this, Herb. I think it's a fair question. Have you seen anything in any of the papers that's obviously false? In other words, can I rely on the newspaper accounts of the loan?"

Crowe hesitated. Then grinned. "They're not totally false—not *grossly* false." He got serious. "No, they're basically accurate. We bankers tend to be fussy, and there've been a few inaccuracies— errors in transmission. Dolph doesn't fully understand the ins and outs of banking terminology, so he may have given it to the reporter in garbled form. And these financial reporters are not always what they're cracked up to be. Even at the august New York *Times*. But no major errors. I'd say you won't go far wrong relying on what the *Times* has said."

I grinned at him. "But you ain't talkin'."

He grinned back. "Naw, copper. And you can't make me!"

I shrugged. "Okay. What do you think of the Mets' chances this year? Or do you prefer the Yankees?"

Crowe laughed. "Neither. I'm a Bosox fan. Have been ever since Andover. Used to love to go to Fenway and cheer on Yaz and the boys. And—I think this is *the* year!"

I shook my head pityingly. "Never happen. But dream on, you poor bastard." He laughed again. I liked his laugh. Even if he wasn't very helpful. "Well, thanks, Herb. I'd better get going. I know you've got things to do."

"Hey, don't rush off." He jumped up. "Oh! I'm sorry, your cup's empty. Let me get you some hot."

"No, I—" Too late. He was already out the door, both cups in hand. When he came back, the mugs were steaming again. As he handed me mine he said, "I like a guy who drinks it the way I do. Hot and black. Most of the wimps around here dose it down with sugar and cream. Ruins the taste." He grinned. "Also dilutes the caffeine."

I sipped appreciatively, wondering why I was staying. And why he wanted me to. "Actually, I *do* have things to do," he said, reading my mind again. "But I'm delighted to meet another baseball nut, who also happens to be a famous detective. And the guy who made Cabot Crowe back down. Something I was never able to do." He took another sip. "But mainly I'm postponing the inevitable. The dreaded bank examiner."

"Yeah, you mentioned you had to meet with him."

Crowe shook his head. "The guy heading the team this year is new and he's a real—well, being a non-banker, you might not understand the terminology, but, in technical terms, he's what we bankers call an asshole. You may not have heard the term in your line of work."

I grinned. "It's a little abstruse, but I think I get the picture. Not one of your favorite people?"

Crowe grinned back. "I can't really say that. I haven't met him." He made a face. "But I'm going to. Will Wilson's his name, and terrifying lowly bank personnel's his game. At least that's what the lowly bank personnel tell me. He's been tearing into our bank files like Jack the Ripper, leaving blood on the floor everywhere he goes. The last two days he's been trying to see me, and I've been ducking him like a madman."

The banker looked at the closed door. "He gets in about eight-thirty every morning and stays till six at night, so he's hard to duck." Herb took a deep breath. "Well, in a little while I'm just going to have to face the music. I've got to see him before he leaves. But as long as you're here, I'm safe. Say! Do you use a computer?"

"Me? Hell no, I'm barely literate in English, let alone computerese. My boss has one, but I stay away. If it can't be handled on the typewriter, I'm not interested."

"You're making a big mistake, my friend." The banker put his coffee down, spun around to the computer and pressed a button. "Come over here," he commanded, staring at the screen.

Figuring it was me he was talking to, not the computer, I got up and stood behind him. "Pull up a chair," he said, still studying the screen, which was coming alive with figures. "I just want you to see how simple this is."

It *was* surprisingly simple. Directing a pointer on the screen with a small box he called a "mouse," he soon had a blank spreadsheet before him. Punching out a few numbers, he displayed a balance sheet for some imaginary company. "Then," he said, moving the mouse around and punching a few more keys, "you can do projections. Let's say this company is building inventory . . . " He went on to spin out profits and cash flow for the next four imaginary quarters.

"See how it works, Dave?" He swept his hand around the room. "It's great. Anyone comes in, you can make them right at home, no desk in the way. No files—they're all in the computer. Hardly any furniture: a few chairs, the computer and a phone. Need to access any bank information, it's on the computer. Want any outside information, say from the Fed, there's the modem; just plug in the phone, you've got your information. Totally electronic, the bank of the future. Just too bad we can't substitute the computer for the examiners. At least for Will Wilson."

I found myself interested in spite of myself. I thought of something. "Well," I grinned. "Enough of these imaginary cases. How about let's plug into, say, Midas Touch Autocare. Might be interesting to see how *their* loan's doing."

Crowe laughed. "Hah! You'd like that, wouldn't you? Nope. Stuff's accessible only by password. Not even the examiners get that. Of course, they get the information, but we print it out for them. They don't mind. Examiners aren't comfortable around computers anyway—at least not this guy Wilson. In fact, I gather he's going to write us up for going totally electronic. Says we're jeopardizing our records by not having hard copy back-up. He hasn't got the foggiest notion of the kinds of back-up we have—electronic and non-. What guys like him—excuse me."

The phone had buzzed. He picked it up, said a word or two and listened. Then, "Yes sir, I'll be right there."

He jumped up. So did I. "No, no, Dave, stay put. I've got to run and talk to the prez. Won't take a second. I'll be right back. Your coffee okay? Sit here." He pushed me into his chair. "Fiddle around. You'll be computer literate before I get back!"

I shrugged. "Damn good idea, Herb. Being a private eye, I'll just deduce what the password is and access the Compton file. Should be a piece of cake for a pro like me."

Crowe laughed. "Good luck! If you figure *that* out, you're entitled to anything you get. Go ahead and work with it, Dave. I'll be right back." He went out, leaving the door open.

I'd been joking about accessing the Compton file, but I still gave it a shot. I punched both "Compton" and "Midas" into the program, but could only get the response, "Password?" with the question mark blinking at me. I tried "crowe," "secret," and "queens," but got back a sneering, "Incorrect password. Password?" with that same blinking question mark. I began to understand why people go berserk and smash their computers.

I plugged back into the spreadsheet program and was experimenting with a few numbers, wondering whether I ought to think about getting one of these things to keep my cases on, when Crowe returned. I said, without looking around, "Now I know the secret of this fine coffee. The ingredients are all right here in this secret computer program."

"I've got to see you."

It wasn't Crowe's voice. I swung around. A burly, beetle-browed man in rolled-up shirt sleeves glared down at me, tie askew, arms loaded with files. "I'm getting damn tired of being shunted off to underlings. You'll talk to me now, or I'm going over your head."

I blinked, then gave him a big smile. "Mr. Wilson?" He nodded abruptly, giving me no smile in return.

I was thinking fast. "Have a seat, Mr. Wilson. You're not going to believe this, but I'm absolutely delighted to see you. I really mean that." And I did.

41

WILSON STARED AT ME. He didn't accept my invitation to sit. "I'll just *bet* you're glad to see me. I suppose that's why you've been ducking me all week."

"I haven't been ducking you," I said truthfully. "And I really am delighted to see you."

I was thinking fast. Opportunities like this don't come along every day, and who knew when Crowe would be back? As long as Wilson thought I was Crowe I had a shot at learning something valuable. Fortunately, Wilson was also in a hurry.

"We want to get out of here tonight," he snapped. "And I've got to discuss our conclusions with you before we do. When can we meet?"

"What's wrong with right now?" Wilson looked relieved. "Pull up a chair, Will. May I call you Will? I was just pondering the Compton thing. Midas Touch, you know? I've been a little concerned about it. I assume it's one of the loans you want to talk about." I mentally crossed my fingers.

Looking even more disgusted, Wilson dragged an upright chair halfway across the room and plopped onto it. He stacked the files on the floor beside his chair. "Pondering it? I wish you'd thought to do that before you made it in the first place!"

I took a sip of coffee. "You don't *like* the loan, Will?"

Wilson snorted. "It's ridiculous. They've been ten to thirty days late on interest nearly every month the loan's been on the books.

And now you want to roll it! After letting them dividend themselves a million dollars to buy a house! From a company that's
virtually out of cash!"

He reached down and pulled one of the files out of the stack
and tapped its hard cover with an angry fingertip. "You say here
that any of the other four banks in the consortium would be glad
to take you out. I recommend you let them do just that." He
glared at me.

I glared back. I decided it was time to take the offensive. "Well,
I don't agree with *that*," I told him, hoping he wouldn't ask me
what exactly I didn't agree with.

Wilson looked triumphant and opened the file. "You say in
here..."

I held out my hand. "Let me see it."

Wilson looked at me. "I'm not giving you *my* copy! It's all right
there in your own computer!"

I shook my head wearily. "Mr. Wilson. I'm perfectly aware
what is and is not in my own computer. I don't need *you* to tell
me that." I paused. "But has it ever occurred to you that that file
might be in error?"

Wilson sneered. "It's the file your own people gave me. How
could it be wrong?"

I shook my head. "They're not *my* people, Will. And how can
I know whether it's wrong or not unless I *look* at it? *I* don't know
what the computer's liable to spit out on any given day! It wasn't
my idea to put the damn computers in here!".

Wilson looked at me suspiciously. "It wasn't? I heard you
spearheaded the whole thing."

I shook my head. "I had nothing to do with it, believe me. I'm
not comfortable with computers, Will."

Wilson seemed to view me with new respect. I held out my
hand. "Just give me the file, Will. Let me look at it. Please."

Wilson looked at the file, at me; finally, reluctantly, he put it
in my hand.

I opened it, trying to look as bored as possible, and immediately
started reading. Within thirty seconds I was wishing for a camera
or a Xerox machine—anything to help my feeble memory. But it
was memory or nothing. So, concentrating as hard as I could, I
read.

Fortunately, I wasn't a total novice in banking terminology. Thanks to the Bishop, Abe Nathanson and Lee Stubbs of Mid-City just the year before in the Penniston case, I had a beginner's knowledge.

My main problem was trying to absorb what I was reading while worrying about Crowe coming back, and at the same time trying not to let myself be distracted by Wilson's occasional nasty comment. Oh—and trying to make the kind of bankerly noises Crowe might make under the same circumstances.

"You act like you've never even *seen* that file!" came through into my consciousness as I turned the first page and started on the second. I was pleased at how much I was understanding.

I didn't even look up. "Don't be silly, Will. Who do you think wrote it in the first place?" (I'd seen an *HWC* on top of the first page. That had to be Crowe.) "I'm trying to see where it might have given you the wrong impression. Please keep still and let me find it." I started using my fingertip to help my comprehension. I've heard that helps.

Wilson stayed quiet a couple of minutes. Then he began to fidget. I was at the bottom of the rather abstruse third page, trying to memorize some meaningless numbers, when he erupted again. "Now see here! If you don't—"

I gave him an upraised hand. (How much longer could I carry on the charade?) "I think I'm finding where you went wrong, Will," I mumbled, following up with more mumbles, sufficiently incomprehensible, I hoped, to keep him quiet. It worked. He shifted in his chair, looked ostentatiously at his watch a couple of times, but let me go on reading.

I was on the fifth, the next-to-last page, gaining in understanding by the minute, when I got a double—and final—interruption.

First, from Wilson: "This is *absurd*! If you think I'm going to—!" Then, interrupting him from the doorway, Herb Crowe: "What the hell's going on here? Dave! What the—what in God's name is that you're reading?"

I looked up at Crowe just long enough to throw him a smile and see his reddening face. Never had he more resembled his twin brother. "Just seeing what this says," I mumbled and turned to the final page—half-page, actually. I tried to step up the pace.

My fingertip felt hot, though that may have been just my imagination.

I was vaguely aware of Wilson getting to his feet saying, "Dave? Who's Dave?" Crowe said something I didn't catch. Then both of them were standing over me. A hand—Crowe's, I guess, I was too busy reading to say for sure—grabbed the file and jerked it from me. I'd got to the third line from the end.

I looked up at the two angry faces and beamed. "I don't believe you two have met. Mr. Crowe, Will Wilson. Mr. Wilson, Herb Crowe!"

42

I CAN COUNT on the fingers of one hand the times I've heard Regan laugh out loud, and I remember every one. But the one I'll remember longest was when I described what happened right after I introduced Will Wilson to Herb Crowe. They were both ready to kill me, but both automatically started their hands for a shake. Then simultaneously, they pulled back, turned on me and roared in unison, as though they'd rehearsed it: "I *know* who he is!" Regan almost spewed coffee on the dining room table, and Ernie came rushing in, startled by the unaccustomed sound of his belly laugh.

The banker and the examiner immediately turned their anger on each other. First Crowe rounded on Wilson. "Did you give him this file?" No answer except a blush. "You *did*, didn't you! By what right did you—"

"He said he was *you*!" Wilson, enraged, loomed over me. "There are penalties for impersonating a bank officer, mister! I want your name!"

I shook my head at him. "If you don't even know my name, how can you say I was impersonating anyone, Will? I've never pretended to be anyone I'm not. People sometimes *think* I'm someone else, but that's their problem."

"But you—"

I cut him off with a sigh. "Look, Will. You march in here like you own the place and start yelling at me. Think back. Did you ever once identify yourself? Or ask me who I was?" Wilson opened his mouth, then closed it. "Nope. You just started blasting away. All I did was sit here. And that's no crime."

"You asked me for that file!"

"Also not a crime. But you may have committed one when you gave it to me."

Wilson was livid. "You—"

"I've heard enough of this!" Crowe to Wilson, through his teeth. "You, sir, are the guilty one. This man was a visitor in my office. He had just requested information of me..." Crowe tapped the file with his fingertip. "...about this loan. Which I refused, since it's confidential. I was then called out of the office. I return to find him reading the file on the very loan about which he'd requested information!" Wilson was wilting before the banker's anger. "Oh, I fault him too—" He threw me a glare, quickly returning it to Wilson. "—but you're far worse. A total stranger—"

Wilson's voice went up an octave. "He was at your *desk!*"

Crowe's voice overpowered Wilson's. "I don't *have* a desk, Wilson! This is a *deskless* office. It's what you've been *complaining* about all week!"

Crowe took a breath and brought his voice down. "But regardless of whether there was a desk or not, or whether he was sitting at it or not, you're at fault. Never assume, Mr. Wilson. Never assume. Didn't you learn that in credit school?" He shook his head. "Have a seat, Mr. Wilson. I'll have more to say to you after I see this gentleman out. I'll be right back."

Crowe handed the file to Wilson, got me firmly by the elbow and escorted me to the door. He stopped and turned back to Wilson. "Oh—and if some stranger comes wandering in, please don't give *him* any confidential information."

Wilson looked like he was about to explode but we didn't linger to see if he would. I didn't start laughing till we were twenty feet away and moving fast. It was contagious: in two seconds Crowe and I were both doubled over, almost unable to walk.

He recovered first. Wiping his eyes and clearing his throat, he said soberly, "Did you get everything you need?"

I took a breath. "Damn near." Then I did a double-take and studied his face. "Wait a minute! Did you arrange that?"

"No, no, no, no! Oh dear me, no! What I said about customer confidentiality? I meant it. And I really do feel terrible that I had some part in letting you find out what you found out. On the other hand..." He grinned. "...part of me is delighted to see the asshole—there's that technical jargon again!—make a fool of himself. And also delighted that you got something to help you find Laddie's killer—if you're right that the other fellow didn't do it."

He held my eye. "Since I can't do anything about it, I hope you can use it, Dave. But if it's possible, please use it in a way that won't come back to haunt us here at the bank."

We'd reached the front door. We shook hands. "Don't worry," I told him. "Nothing I've learned is going to be associated with you in any way, shape or form. Oh, one last thing."

"Yes?"

I kept a straight face. "Well, I've got some questions about that stuff I read. Would you mind explaining—"

Crowe laughed and threw a punch at me. I ducked. "Get out of here!" he chuckled, turned and headed for his office, no longer laughing. I wouldn't have cared to be in Will Wilson's shoes right about then.

I legged it to the car, anxious to get what was in my head into my notebook before it started to leak out. I scribbled shorthand for half an hour before putting the key into the ignition.

Arriving late for dinner was becoming a habit. Ernie just greeted me automatically and brought in the rewarmed casserole. Regan seized the opportunity to help himself to seconds.

"Well," he said, chewing. "Tell me what you learned."

I gave him the rundown on how I'd inveigled the information, including Crowe's unwillingness to tell me anything and Wilson's humiliation. By the time I finished that, we were both through eating and headed for his office. As soon as I sat down I opened the notebook with a dramatic flourish. "And right here in this little book is *everything* that was in that file!"

Regan smiled. "I hope it was worth the trouble."

"Me too. I'll say this: it's a lot of info. I just hope you can do something with it."

The boss closed his eyes. "We shall see. Proceed."

I did. The Comptons had *two* loans with the bank. The first had been made five years before, when they changed the name of their company from Compton Car Wash to Midas Touch Autocare. Crowe's memo backed up Hilarie's assertion that she'd put the entire $800,000 she'd inherited from her parents into the company. This, along with the nearly $200,000 the Comptons had been able to accumulate in the old car wash company, gave them what Crowe (in the memo) had called the leverage to borrow an additional million from Mount Vernon Thrift. Thus the newly named company started out with two million in capital.

Regan stopped me. "What were the terms of the loan?"

"Terms?"

He sighed. "Collateral. Maturity. Interest rate. Trivial things like that."

"That's coming up," I said, ignoring his sarcasm. "Umm, let's see. Yeah, here it is. Collateral: 'All Business Assets,' whatever that means. Maturity: five years with a fifty percent balloon, whatever that is. And interest rate floats at three over prime, whatever that is." Regan sighed again but made no comment.

The second loan, made three years later, Crowe called a "non-business loan." This was a mortgage for Dolph and Hilarie to buy the mansion on Eighty-seventh. Crowe again referred to "leverage." The Comptons had had Midas pay them a million-dollar dividend; then they borrowed another million and a half from Mount Vernon Thrift.

"But that's where," I told Regan, "Crowe had to bring more banks in. Something about 'legal limit.' "

"Yes," Regan murmured. "A bank is permitted to lend only a certain percentage of its capital to any one borrower. That's its legal limit."

"If you say so. Anyway, Mount Vernon's legal limit was two million, meaning the second loan was too big for them. So they brought in four other banks at one-fifth each. Then Mount Vernon loaned the Comptons the million and a half they needed to buy the mansion."

Regan frowned. "All right. Tell me about the business. I trust the memorandum included financial data on it."

"Did it include financial data on the business? Do bankers wear ties?" I shrugged. "More than plenty. And total gobbledegook, all of it. But if you want to know what I memorized, here goes."

I buried myself in the notebook and talked for what seemed like an hour but was really only fifteen or twenty minutes. While I talked, Regan took notes. And corrected my mistakes. Like "other debt." He was studying the page of my notebook where I'd written down the Midas Touch balance sheet as best I remembered it. He looked up and scowled.

"This is wrong. Wasn't there a line for 'Other Debt'?"

"Oh yeah, that's ri—how'd you know that?"

"Simple mathematics, David. The balance sheet doesn't foot: total assets exceed the sum of net worth and total liabilities. That's impossible; by definition the two are equal. You see, net worth is three million. Adding the bank loan gives three-point-six-million, but the company's real estate assets total over six million. One way it could balance would be if you left out 'Other Debt.' "

I shook my head. "Right again, oh Great One. Yeah, that's one I'd forgotten: 'Other Debt.' Let me think." I scratched my head and came up with a buried memory. "Yeah! A couple million and change. It said 'Mortgages.' "

Regan nodded. "They have outstripped internally generated cash flow and been forced to borrow. Encumbering some of their facilities with mortgages would be logical. No doubt the consortium permitted them to do so."

By the time I'd spun out all the financial figures I'd been able to get into my notebook, Regan had jotted a bunch of numbers onto some notepaper on his desk. "Is that all?" he said when I finished.

"Isn't it enough?"

Regan didn't answer for a while, just studied the figures. He made a couple of marks on the paper and looked up. "I think so," he said, and thought for a minute. "But we should try to— get Mr. Nathanson, David. And stay on the line, please."

I got up, shaking my head. Why call Abe? He'd already said he wouldn't tell us anything.

I went in my office and called Abe's home number, then buzzed the Bishop to pick up. He and Abe came on the line almost together, each with a *shalom*. Regan's deep baritone contrasted with Abe's reedy tenor.

"Bishop Frank!" Abe continued. "What can I do for you this time?"

"I won't keep you, Abe," Regan murmured. "But David and I have done a little spadework in the vineyards of the Lord, and would like you to tell us whether it's been productive."

"With you two working, I can tell you in advance: it's been productive!" Abe laughed. "But go ahead and tell me about it, Frank."

Regan paused. When he spoke, his voice had turned serious. "What I am asking is a bit delicate, Abe." He paused again. "What I want to do is ask a hypothetical question regarding the Compton family's financial situation."

Nathanson's voice was cautious. "Go on, Frank."

The Bishop did. "Through some brilliant detective work, David has extricated some of their company's financial information. Unfortunately, circumstances precluded his obtaining everything, and I have made a few leaps of logic in an attempt to fill in the missing pieces. Leading me to certain conclusions that point to the guilt of a particular person in the murder of young Mr. Compton . . . "

My eyes bugged. What was he saying? What *particular person*? But Regan didn't give me time to ponder. He continued:

" . . . and I don't want to go off half-cocked. You are the finest banking analyst I know, Abe. What I want to ask is that you listen to my analysis of the financial condition of Midas Touch and tell me if my conclusions are out of line."

Abe chuckled. "I'll try."

"Good. Let me describe the situation revealed by the financial figures. Net worth is roughly three million dollars; total debt slightly more than that; the debt load includes the six-hundred-thousand-dollar term loan coming due in less than thirty days. The remainder of the debt is in long-term mortgages against certain of its facilities, due fairly smoothly over the next fifteen years. Total assets come to just over six million."

Abe made a noise to show he was listening. Regan went on.

"The asset side of the balance sheet is heavily skewed toward long-term; nearly all is real estate, none of which is offered for sale. Cash is extremely slender for a company of its size: well under a hundred thousand dollars." Regan took a breath.

"The profit-and-loss statement reveals healthy and increasing profitability. Cash flow is strong, but the company is growing faster than its cash. Resulting in increasing reliance on borrowed funds. Now—"

Abe laughed. "Very well put, Frank. I am currently teaching a course at Columbia in money and banking. What you have just outlined would make an excellent case study for my students. But I have a question."

"Yes?"

"How hard are those real estate values? Have there been recent appraisals by qualified outside appraisers?"

"Oh yes. According to Mr. Goldman, all properties have MAI appraisals, all within the past year. Best of all, Herb Crowe is satisfied that the values are solid."

Abe apparently had no more questions. "Then may I," Regan said, "give you my conclusions? Perhaps you can tell me if I'm misguided. This is important, Abe. If I'm right, I think I know who's guilty of Ladd Compton's murder."

Abe was serious. "Go ahead, Frank."

"All right. This is it: given the solidity of the company's balance sheet evidenced by the financial information cited, and given the company's profitability and cash flow, there is no reason to believe Midas Touch is or ever was in any danger of losing its bank credit. That is, if the company's bank were to call its loan, the company would find another bank ready, willing and able to take over the loan. Given its substantial net worth, backed by real estate, a six-hundred-thousand-dollar loan would be attractive business to nine banks out of ten. This is my conclusion, Abe. Am I hopelessly confused?"

Abe chuckled his high, piping chuckle. "Hopelessly analytical is all, Frank. And hopelessly conservative. I'd say *ten* banks out of ten. My own conclusion is that your analysis is right on the mark. And just between us, if that fool examiner, Wilson, manages to convince Mount Vernon's board of directors to call the loan, I have a dozen clients who'd stand in line for the privilege of stepping into Mount Vernon's shoes."

Abe sobered. "But that won't happen, Frank. I know Mount Vernon's directors well enough to be certain of that."

Abe and Regan exchanged a few more pleasantries before ringing off. I headed back for Regan.

"Sit down, David." When my eyes got to his level, Regan sighed. "Amazing work, David. The financial figures you brought make it clear who killed Ladd Compton. And, by implication, Mrs. Benedict. Now our only problem is finding the evidence to prove it. And convincing Mr. Kessler that he's arrested the wrong man."

43

REGAN'S MADE SOME outrageous statements in the eight years I've worked for him, but this was the topper. Was he talking through his hat? I sneered, "Yeah, sure you know who did it. And you've also got a bridge you—"

He raised a hand. "This is not rodomontade, David. I know who the murderer is—to a near-certainty."

I stared at him. "Has it got anything to do with whatever's going on between Dolph and Janine?"

Regan's eyes were hooded. "Everything in this world is connected, David."

I rolled my eyes at that. "So where'd you get it? And don't try to tell me you got it from all that financial mishmash I brought from the bank."

"It's not mishmash. It supplied the missing piece I needed, the answer to the question, 'Is the Comptons' financial empire poised on the brink of disaster?' Answer: Not in the least. Though their business strategy has been overly ambitious, the company is sound, growing and well-capitalized. That leads us not to an overwhelming question but to an overwhelming answer. Think about it, David. I'm confident it will come to you."

"Well, it doesn't come to me. I don't see why you—"

Regan raised his voice. "I said think about it, David, not blurt out the first thing that pops into your mind." He sighed. "At the moment I also need to think. About the proper approach to Mr. Kessler. Let us both give the matter some thought. Perhaps we can come to some sound conclusions. I'm sure that after you think about what I've said, you'll come to the same conclusion as I."

He wheeled over to the window and pretended to ponder. The weasel. Want to know what he was really doing? Gloating over his triumph. Meanwhile I fumed. Like he knew I would.

Dammit, there was no way the smartass could've used that jumble of financial data to dope out who killed Compton. And Benedict. So Midas Touch was sound as a bell: so what?

Of course, that's what half of me was saying. The other half was chuckling *He did it to you again, Davey.* Happens all the time. That's what comes of working with a guy whose I.Q. is up there near the moon while yours is floundering around near sea level.

So I was fuming and excited at the same time. *He knew who did it.* And it wasn't Eddie Goode; the cops had the wrong guy. The real killer was out there somewhere, somebody I'd talked to sometime in the past three days. Somebody still on the loose.

Meanwhile Regan was over at the south window, staring out at Sally Mueller's garbage. Don't ask me what it is about her garbage he finds so fascinating. She's a widow living alone in the brownstone behind ours, facing Thirty-sixth. I've only met her once, and she seems like your typical ordinary little old lady. But I sometimes wonder if years ago Regan might not have worked out a deal with her whereby whenever he needs an answer, she arranges it on her garbage in some sort of code.

I got tired of watching him ratiocinate and decided to head for my own thinking spot. Maybe if I went through my notes one more time . . . I'd just got to my feet when he spoke.

Or was I hearing things? He was still hunched in his wheelchair, staring out the window. I waited.

"David."

"Uh, yeah?"

"I take it you still have the duplicate of the key you found in that envelope in Mrs. Benedict's nightstand?"

"You take it right."

"May I have it, please?"

"What for?"

He didn't answer. I stared at him. So it was that way. Game-playing time. He wanted me to beg. Well, to hell with that.

I went in my office, opened a drawer and grabbed the key. By the time I came back, Regan had wheeled back to his desk, put on his reading glasses and was riffling through his Rolodex. With a detective's sharp eye I saw that he was somewhere in the *K*'s or *L*'s.

I waited till he looked up at me over the glasses, his green eyes inquiring. "The key, David?" He didn't put out a hand. Or say please.

I stared back. "All right, I give. Who did it? And why do you want the key?"

He held the stare for another second, then went back to the Rolodex. He found the card he wanted—in the *K*'s, but he managed to shield which one it was—and redirected his eyes to me. "You're too impetuous, David. I think it best that you remain in ignorance. For only a little while. You'll soon see why. The key?"

I felt smoke starting to come out of my ears but knew better than to say anything. I slapped the key on his desk, turned on my heel to leave.

"David!" I stopped without turning around. "I have an assignment for you. If you please." His tone was somewhere between a command and a plea.

I turned. His face was impassive, eyes unreadable. "Oh? Want me to file some records or something? While you solve this puppy?"

He closed his eyes. "Sit down, David. Please." I thought about it. Decided it couldn't hurt to see what he had to say. Maybe he had something exciting for me to do. Like duplicate another key.

When he heard me hit the chair, he opened his eyes and spoke. "We need to pursue two lines of investigation simultaneously, David. The person we're after has killed twice and won't hesitate to kill again if threatened. So we need to move fast."

He sighed. "I've been thinking about how to approach Inspector Kessler with what we have. And that's a problem." He winced. "The problem is that all we have for the nonce is conjecture. While *I'm* convinced, he'd simply reject my reasoning as pure speculation. Your own failure to grasp what I see as the significance of the information you so adroitly unearthed tells me that. You're not a stupid man, David. Impetuous, yes, but certainly not stupid. If *you* can't see the significance of the Comptons' financial position, how can I expect the inspector to find it cogent?"

He looked at me. "David. I beg you. Curb your rancor and permit me to pursue a certain course of action without you while you pursue another. The murderer is devilishly clever and has spent considerable time and effort setting up the scheme. Exposing it will require pursuing two leads at the same time. Believe me, it's better that you not know the other line."

"Why should I believe you when you don't trust me?"

He smiled. "Oh, I trust you, David." He grew serious. "What I don't trust is your training. I fear you'd feel obliged to take action. And action of the type you'd feel obliged to undertake is precisely what must be avoided at the moment. That's as much as I dare to say."

We looked at each other for a few seconds. I finally shrugged. "Good," he said. "Now, may I tell you what I'd like you to do? I assure you it will be productive."

"Sure, why not? Maybe it'll keep me out of mischief."

44

NEXT MORNING, right after breakfast, I went to work on my assignment, which, it turned out, was really two assignments: go talk to the old lady across the street from the Comptons who saw Eddie come and go the night of the murder, and ask Jeremiah Healy a few more questions Regan had dreamed up.

Both assignments made sense, with the possible exception of a couple of the questions for Healy. What puzzled me was what was the other, the parallel track? The one I *wasn't* working on? And what was Regan planning to do with that key I'd found at Ruthie's? I was sure it must have something to do with Dolph and Janine, but he wouldn't say.

I tried a few probes the night before while cleaning up his office but got nowhere. For instance:

"I guess you think you know where that key goes." Regan didn't even lift his head from the book he was reading.

"You're not fooling me, though," I went on, ignoring his ignoring. "I figured out what you're doing. You're making two thousand copies of that key and sending one to every priest in the archdiocese. Then they'll run around and try them in the locks of every home in every parish till they find the one that fits. Then you'll have the murderer!"

Regan's reply was barely audible. "David. Badgering me will serve no purpose—yours or mine. Please desist and permit me to read. This book is difficult enough without distractions." End of discussion.

So I got up during the night and snuck a look at the *K*'s in his Rolodex. Got me nowhere. There were twelve of them, and not one could have had the slightest connection with the case. I later found out he'd suspected I'd do just that, and removed the card. Had I known one was missing I might have been able to deduce which one it was. But I didn't know.

I started on my double assignment Thursday morning by phoning Healy.

"Yeah, Comptons' residence."

"David Goldman, Mr. Healy. Terribly sorry to hear of your daughter's untimely death. My condolences." Healy muttered something. "I realize this may not be a very good time, Mr. Healy, but I wanted to come by and see you. We didn't get to finish last time I was there."

Healy sounded embarrassed. "Yeah, I had to run pick up Mr. Compton, didn't I? I'm really sorry. But what more do you need? I thought you—"

"Just one or two more questions, Mr. Healy. It won't take long, I promise. So if you—"

"But why are the Knights still worried about my daughter's divorce, now that she's dead? Why are you—"

"Oh, it has nothing to do with that. I have just a question or two on a different topic, if you don't mind. To complete our file. I can assure you, your membership in the Knights of St. Titus is not in doubt."

"Oh, good." He sounded relieved. "Well, now's okay."

I assured him I'd be there in a flash. I pressed the button to get a dial tone and called the Comptons' number. Healy again. "Comptons' residence." I changed my voice, lowering it about two octaves, and asked for "Randolph Compton." Healy put me through.

Compton was abrupt. "Yes?"

"It's Dave Goldman, Mr. Compton. Just making sure you'd called Ms. Lake. I want to see her."

"I sure did." He'd gone from abrupt to friendly in the blink of an eye. Amazing the respect people give you when they think you're the key to putting a million bucks in their pocket. I wondered what he was going to say—and do—to me when he found out who and what I really was. Maybe that'd be the time I should bring up Janine and La Fontenelle.

"I promised her you'd give her a call before you dropped in, Dave. But she's quite willing to see you. Oh, hold on."

He had a muttered conversation with someone away from the phone, I couldn't make out the words. Then he came back on the line. "Hilarie just reminded me the Lake sisters are coming to a luncheon we're throwing this afternoon for Di and Larry. So if you want to talk to them, better do it before twelve-thirty. You have their unlisted number?" I said I did and I would, and thanked him again.

I grabbed a cab to East Eighty-seventh and spent most of the ride worrying. First of all, about my identity crisis, which was developing into a major problem. I was now three different people besides myself: insurance investigator to Dolph and Hilarie; representative of the Knights of St. Titus to Jeremiah; and a cop to Diane and Janine. And Larry now knew who I really was. Sooner or later those five were going to get together and talk things over. At which time I'd better be ready to do some fancy tapdancing if I wanted to keep my health and freedom and good looks. In the meantime I didn't see any other option than just to play the hand(s) I'd dealt. Thank God, I hadn't used aliases.

After worrying about that awhile, I worried about why in the world the Knights of St. Titus would be asking Healy the questions Regan wanted me to ask. A movie I'd seen once, *The Exorcist*, gave me an idea. It was far out, but the best I could do on short notice. For it to work I was going to have to be awfully sincere. I spent the rest of the ride doing sincereness exercises.

At nine-thirty I was in Healy's sitting room, in the chair Laddie'd sat in just before he died; also the chair I'd sat in the day Ruthie died. Not a lucky chair.

Healy was subdued. "You had more questions."

"Just a couple, Mr. Healy. I, uh—have you ever studied diabolic phenomena, Mr. Healy?"

Healy stared at me. "Dia—what?"

"Diabolic phenomena. The works of Satan. That's always been a matter of concern to the Knights of St. Titus." Healy nodded. "Something you said Monday, Mr. Healy, about your visit with young Mr. Compton raises some questions in my mind. Do you have any idea whether he was involved in any Satanic cults?"

Healy's eyes widened. "Laddie? No! Why wouldja think that?"

"Well, I was struck by the way your phone kept ringing while he was here. And with one of the calls, you said, no one was on the line. That's sometimes evidence of a Satanic cult. May I have a look at your phone?"

"Sure!" Healy pointed a shaky finger at the table by the couch. It was a typical white business phone: five line buttons, plus one for Hold. Two of the line buttons were blank; the other three read *Compton, Compton # 2* and *Healy.*

I studied it. "So the daughter doesn't have her own line?"

"Well, she does have a private phone, but it's not hooked up to this one." Healy sounded resentful.

I relayed another of Regan's questions. "I noticed there's a phone in the bay window upstairs overlooking the front door. Anyone ever use that?"

Healy looked disgusted. "That damn—they call it the study, can you beat it? Naw, no one ever uses it."

I looked at him. "Back to that night: you said three calls came in. You're sure it was three?"

"Geez, I think so. Lemme see. Laddie got two." He thought for a minute. "And there was one more, where it quit ringing before I got it."

"And when were they?"

Jeremiah scratched his head. "Well, Laddie came, like I said, at ten to nine. Let's see, the first one came, oh, we'd been talkin' about five minutes. That's the one I tried to grab but no one was there. The next was about five minutes after that—or maybe ten. Laddie figured it was for him, so I let him take it. Just talked for a second."

"What did he say?"

"Hardly anything. Just somethin' like, 'Okay.' Or, 'I'll be here.' Somethin' like that. Just a word or two."

"And the third?"

"That was at nine-fifteen. It was another short one. Laddie said 'Okay,' or somethin'. I do remember the time a that one, 'cause he hung up and said, 'My buddy's not gonna leave me alone; let's get outa here,' and I noticed it was 9:15. That's when I went across to the Red Lion."

"And what lines did the calls come in on?"

Healy frowned again, more ferociously. "Geez, lemme think. The first one—I don't know." He scratched his head. "I know the next two were on my line, 'cause Laddie told me he'd given it to the guy. I think the first one was on the Comptons' line." Healy, thinking hard, squinted into space. "There was something about that first one, though. What was it?" He shrugged. "I don't know."

"Okay." I noted it in the notebook. "Now, thinking about the Satanic influence, did you hear any sound at all from upstairs that would have indicated anyone else was in the house? I mean, while Mr. Compton was with you."

"Naw. There was no one here. The alarm was on. Laddie told me he'd left it on when he came in. I asked him."

"So you're sure that you and Mr. Compton were alone in the house?"

Healy looked at me, something going on behind his eyes. "Wait a minute. You just said something that . . . what was it?" His eyes suddenly widened. "Wait! That first phone call! It only just hit me! There *was* someone else in the house!"

I opened my mouth but Healy raised a hand. " 'Cause that first call—the one where there was no one there—was on Dolph's line! And when I went to answer it, it'd quit ringing—but the light under the button was still on! Somebody somewhere else in the house had already picked up!"

45

THIS WAS SIGNIFICANT—if true. "How did you come to remember that now for the first time, Mr. Healy?"

"I don't know. I should of caught it before. Musta just had my mind on what Laddie was saying, that's all I can think of."

I wasn't surprised to learn someone else had been in the house while Laddie and Healy talked: I'd already figured the murderer probably had been. But why, I wondered, had he—or she—answered the phone? Had the murder been a conspiracy? Organized by phone? I wanted to consider the implications, but there wasn't time.

I changed the subject. "Did you resent that Laddie was seeing your daughter at the same time he had a regular girlfriend—what's her name?"

Healy's eyes turned sly. "Janine Mason. Naw, she was just—naw, I didn't mind. And neither did Mary Ruth."

I pretended to study my notebook while watching Healy. "I understand that Ms. Mason spent some time with Mr. Compton, Senior."

Healy looked surprised. "Where'd you hear that?"

I looked up from my notebook. "Just a rumor."

Healy gave me the most direct look he'd given me. "I don't know what you're gettin' at. But if you mean what I think you mean, forget it. Janine was Laddie's girlfriend. Period."

I didn't push it. I went back to an earlier subject. "Let's talk about your daughter and young Mr. Compton. You say you were talking to him, the night he died, about your daughter. What exactly were you talking about?"

Jeremiah's eyes didn't seem able to meet mine. "Uh, he just wanted to talk about, uh, Mary Ruth. He liked her and wanted me to let them..." Healy's voice faded.

Healy was lying again. I gave him a tough look. He shifted in his chair.

"What?" He met my eyes, looked away, came back. "What's the matter now?"

"You're lying, aren't you, Mr. Healy? Just as you lied the other day."

"What do you mean?" His eyes flicked wildly around the room.

"I mean you lied to me on Monday, and now you're lying again. Unless the Knights can trust each other, Mr. Healy, how can we call ourselves Christians?"

"I don't know what you're talkin' about!"

I sighed. "Let's talk about Monday's lie first. At the end of our conversation, you left in a big hurry. You got that phone call." Healy looked away. "That call wasn't from Mr. Compton, was it, Mr. Healy?" I gave him no respite from my gaze.

Healy finally met my eyes. "How'd you know? How do you know all this?"

I smiled. "I have my ways, Mr. Healy. Now. Will you please tell me who the call was from? And no more lies."

Healy was hoarse. "It was my daughter. Mary Ruth. She said she was going out to meet someone. About..."

He gulped and looked away. I added more shock treatment. "About the abortion she'd had? Was that where she was going, Mr. Healy?"

At first I thought I'd missed the boat. Healy's eyes were blank. Briefly. Then they changed. The blow had come so hard and so fast his reactions hadn't kept up. When they did, his face crumpled.

"Wha—what do you mean?"

"Where was your daughter headed Monday afternoon, Mr. Healy? Who was she going to meet?"

Healy looked at the floor. I could barely hear him. "She was going to the abortionist. Said since I wouldn't help with the money, she'd found another way to pay him. She was mad."

I thought about it, wondering if this was the truth. "She'd asked you for money before?"

Healy looked at me, red-faced. "Yeah. She'd had an—she'd killed her baby. She owed the doc a coupla thousand bucks. Said she couldn't pay it, wanted me to kick in. I told her I wasn't paying nothing to no child murderer. We had a—a fight over it."

"When?"

"The first time? Couple weeks ago. So she called me Monday to tell me I could take a flyin' leap, she'd figured a way. She was gonna go pay the guy. I didn't want her to. That's why I went tearin' outa here."

"To her apartment?"

"Right." Healy's eyes drooped. "But she wasn't there. I was too late." His voice quavered and he wiped his nose.

"About the abortion: was Ladd Compton the father, Mr. Healy? And was he responsible for her having the abortion?"

Healy grimaced. "Yeah, it was Laddie. Mary Ruth told me that. That's why he wanted to come see me that night—the night he died. I'd called 'im, yelled at 'im. He wanted to come and apologize. That's why he came. He wanted ... " Healy's words trailed off.

"And did he admit it? That he was the father?"

Healy shrugged. "Not in so many words. But he did say he felt responsible. So you tell me."

I waited till I had Healy's eyes. Then I hit him right between them. "Did you kill Laddie, Mr. Healy?"

The eyes didn't waver. "I never," he said firmly. "I swear it, Mr. Goldman. I never."

46

I'D GOT A LOT MORE than I'd counted on. I'd asked all Regan's questions and a few of my own. Now I just had one more, an easy one: "Can I borrow your phone?"

He didn't mind. I called the Lakes' unlisted number I'd gotten from Dolph. "Yes!" Harsh, female voice.

"Ms. Lake? I—"

"It's *Miss* Lake, sonny," she corrected me. "None of this 'Miz' nonsense for me. Now, who are you and what do you want? And how'd you get this number?"

"I'm David Goldman, the person Mr. Compton called you about, Miss Lake. And I'm at the Comptons' right now. Could you see me? I could come right over if it's convenient."

She had to think about that one. When her voice came again it was guarded. "Yes, all right, Mr. Goldman. Come right away. I'll go down and let you in."

I couldn't be sure whether the person who opened the door was the Lake sister I'd seen in the window. But she sure looked like her. Also like the Wicked Witch of the West. A tiny woman, all in black. Tight features, eyes severe. I didn't offer her my hand; I'm not sure she'd have taken it if I had.

The interior was configured like the Comptons'. Same huge rotunda, same wrap-around balcony. I was curious whether their alcove arrangement was the same. I tried to see it over my shoulder going up the stairs to the second floor, but she was moving too fast and it was too dark. She was in plenty good shape for her age, which I guessed to be around eighty.

Clipping along with birdlike steps, not looking back to see me puffing after, she led me down a short hall into a large room. The room contained plenty of furniture and another person: obviously the second Miss Lake.

The two looked nothing alike. The one sitting was about a

hundred pounds heavier and ten years younger than her sister. It didn't take a lot of detecting to detect that the blond hair wasn't hers. Not only did its color not match her dark eyebrows, it was about forty years younger.

"Crystal, this is Mr. Goldman," said the old one, winning me a nod and a friendly smile from the blond. If the blond was Crystal, the older one was Ruth, the witness who'd seen Goode coming and going. How's that for deduction? Ruth told me to sit and I did, in a chair on the other side of the coffee table from Crystal.

"Mr. Compton said we should be nice to you," Ruth said, sitting on the couch beside her sister. She tugged her skirt down and absentmindedly patted her sister's knee. "So we shall. He said you're trying to establish that none of the Comptons did— that—to Laddie. And of course they didn't. So we're delighted to help. What do you want to know?"

"Anything you can tell me about the night Ladd Compton was killed."

She looked at me severely. "I've already told this dozens of times to the police. Why can't you simply speak with them? I'd think that—"

"Sorry, ma'am, I *have* talked to them. But if you don't mind, I'd like to get it straight from you." I gave her my sweetest smile. "If you don't mind."

Ruth Lake gave me a long look. Crystal reached for a pack of cigarettes on the coffee table, muttering, "Oh, for sweet Jesus' sake, Ruth! Tell the man! You know you're dying to!"

Ruth transferred her severe gaze from me to Crystal—that is, to Crystal's cigarette. "I wish you wouldn't continue threatening your life, Crystal. And mine, too, you know."

Crystal just stared defiantly as she lit the cigarette, took a deep puff and leaned back. "Don't worry about it, Ruth. You'll live too long as it is. Now *tell* the man."

Ruth glared at her sister, returned her gaze to me. "All right, Mr. Goldman." She waved imaginary smoke away from her face. "I saw that man enter and leave the Comptons' house. He came at precisely nine-oh-four and left at nine-thirteen."

"Excuse me, Miss Lake. I hate to quibble, but—"

"Then why do it?"

I widened the smile. "Sorry. But I'm wondering. How do you know the time with such exactitude?"

" 'Such exactitude'!" Crystal said appreciatively through a cloud of smoke. "You're a very well-spoken young man. What did you say your name was?"

"You stay out of this, Crystal!" Ruth's tone was venomous. "He's *my* friend, and if you don't behave you can just go to the other room." She turned to me, her tone suddenly friendly. "We always note the time of all our calls, Mr. Goldman. We were playing Scrabble at that table right there." She pointed to a heavy oak card table in the center of the room. "And the phone rang at nine-oh-four. So I hurried. But I was too late. It's so exasperating not to have another phone in this house. But *she*—" She glared at her sister. "—won't permit it!"

"The calls are never for me," said the sister airily. "And they're boring, anyway. She spends half her life on the phone. So let her use her spy tower."

Ruth shook her head. "We have only one phone in this big house, Mr. Goldman. And then *she* refuses to answer it. And she *does* get calls, Mr. Goldman. But who has to run, run, run? Not her, oh no."

Crystal took a vicious puff. "Oh, you have it so hard, don't you, Ruth? The poor thing!" She got my eye. "Mother always gave her everything, Mr. Goldman. She likes to pretend she has it so hard. Well, *I'm* the one who's had it hard. She never—"

Ruth was opening her mouth to strike back when I cut them both off. "I'm sorry. I seem to have come at a bad time. Maybe I ought to talk to each of you separately. Is there—"

"I'm sorry, Mr. Goldman," Ruth said, looking like she meant it. "We'll be good. Won't we, Crystal?"

Crystal stubbed out her ciggie. "Yes, Mr. Goldman. Please stay. We won't fight, we promise."

I looked at them. They both looked at me, eyes wide. I gathered that I was the most exciting thing that'd happened to them in a while.

"Okay," I said, looking each of them in the eye. "But no more fighting, right?" They nodded in unison.

"Okay, go on, Miss Lake."

"So I went to the phone. It's in the bay window overlooking the street. They—"

"Her spy tower," put in Crystal. Her tone was contemptuous. Ruth ignored her.

"A bay window is what it is, Mr. Goldman. Anyhow, whoever it was didn't wait. It's funny, it only rang four times. Most people don't give up so soon. Well, I'd no more than hung up when I saw something suspicious across the street. A little hoodlum going up the steps to the Comptons'. Right away I could tell he was suspicious. I was thinking, 'That's the worst-looking salesman I ever saw! The Comptons'll never let him in the door,' when, land's sakes, he had a key and let himself right in! Didn't ring the bell or anything." She shook her head. "I thought, well, dear me, he must be a friend of Ladd's or Diane's. But he didn't even have his shoelaces tied! I never! I thought about calling the police, but what would they say? And he did have a key, I could see that. Didn't pick the lock or anything."

She looked at her sister. "I just hurried back to our Scrabble game. I was ahead. My sister asked who it was, as always. She refuses to have a phone in this room, it might distract her. But she's always eager enough to hear about it whenever a call comes in."

Crystal was outraged. "I am not! You are the most—"

"Please, please! Ladies, I'm going if you can't control yourselves!"

Ruth sniffed. "Oh, all right. I'll be good." She glanced at her sister. "We'd only been playing another five minutes when the phone rang again. I hurried even faster this time, but—late again. It rang right up to the moment I got there, then stopped. Just three rings, can you believe it? People can be so exasperating.

"I just happened to look out, and there was that man again— that shifty-eyed little rat—coming out the door of the Comptons'. Looking guilty as what-all. I should have called the police! I wish I had! But there again, you see, I didn't." Ruth shook her head. "I just couldn't make myself think anything might've happened to the Comptons. And it wasn't as if he'd been breaking and entering. He did have a key, you know."

"And you told all this to the police later?"

"Oh, yes." She threw another triumphant glance at her sister. Crystal responded by lighting another cigarette. "I told the police the whole thing the next day. Two of them came to the house and asked questions. When I told them what I'd seen they got interested. Came back later with pictures for me to look at. I recognized the man right away; it was that Eddie Goode fellow they've got in jail.

"Then two days after that, they sent a car for me. A patrol car!" Ruth threw Crystal another triumphant look and Crystal blew smoke in her face. "You quit that, Crystal!" She waved the smoke away and went on. "They took me to Headquarters and had me look at a 'line-up,' they call it. I picked Eddie Goode out of all those other men. So he's going to prison. I guess you know that, though."

"Yes. You're obviously a very perceptive lady, Ms. Lake. I—"

"*Miss!*" she sniffed. But she looked pleased.

"Excuse me. *Miss* Lake. So I—"

"Sure she wants to be called *Miss*," Crystal put in. "As if the likes of her could've ever got married. I was married, you know. But it didn't take."

"Of course it didn't take. It'd take a saint to live with this one, Mr. Goldman."

"Oh, it'd take a saint to live with me?" Crystal's voice was rising. "Well, I can tell you this, big sister. You're just about—"

"Hold it, ladies!" I got enough volume in it to shut them up. They both looked at me, red-faced and deprived.

"All right, Mr. Goldman," said Ruth. "Go ahead, please. I'll just be forbearing with Crystal. As always."

Crystal was opening her mouth to answer that one but I beat her to it. "Good! I only have a couple more questions anyway." Ruth's face fell. So did Crystal's. "Did you see anyone else at the Comptons' that evening."

Ruth sighed. "No. We played Scrabble right here till bedtime. And I didn't get any more calls. So I missed all the excitement. They say the police were all over the block, ambulances, everyone. We didn't even hear the sirens."

"She's just disappointed she didn't have anything to tell all her friends about," Crystal sniffed. "She just loves to—"

I cut in without apologizing, eyes on Ruth. "So neither of you were involved in anything that happened that night. Except for seeing that man."

"That's right. The police didn't come till the next morning. They told us they were going to every house on the block, asking the neighbors what they saw." Ruth sniffed. "I was the only one who saw a blessed thing."

"Any other phone calls that night? Ever find out who it was who kept calling and didn't wait for you to answer?"

Ruth gave an angry shake of the head. "It was a crank call. We get them sometimes. Though I'm the one who has to answer."

Crystal exhaled smoke. "It's just too bad about you."

I'd had enough bickering. "Could I see the phone?"

"Of course," Ruth said smugly, glancing at her sister. She jumped up and headed in her quick-stepping way for the door. I hurried to follow.

"Come again soon, Mr. Goldman," Crystal called after me. "It's been nice."

"Yes, indeed," I threw back over my shoulder. "It sure has!"

I followed Ruth around the balcony to the bay window. This balcony was shaped the same and had probably been identical to the one across the street when both were new. But the wood of this one was now dark, the walls covered with dust and cobwebs. Ruth seemed oblivious to it all.

The alcove was more spartan than the Comptons'. No bookshelf or anything else to block off the view from the rest of the house. Just a tiny, rickety desk and a straight-backed, uncomfortable-looking chair. No wonder Ruth had glared at me. Carrying on your social life in a chair like that all day would put anybody in a bad mood.

I looked across the street and into the Comptons' bay window. And caught a fleeting glimpse of Jeremiah Healy's back as he scuttled out of the alcove. He'd said no one used it. Then how come he was there?

47

I GOT BACK to the mansion at a quarter to eleven. I'd barely walked through the door of my office when the intercom buzzed. Stunned, I looked at my watch. Shook it. Held it to my ear and listened. Regan? In his office? Before eleven? He never leaves the chapel before eleven. What was going on?

I grabbed the phone. "What's wrong?"

A moment of silence. Then, "Nothing's wrong, David. If you mean why did I cut my prayers short, something came up. This is by no means the first time this has happened. Even during your tenure."

I felt like saying, "Like hell!" then remembered once in the Carney case where it'd happened. But that time he'd had an office full of people, including a murderer he was about to expose. I started to retort, but he cut me off.

"I have another assignment for you."

"Another one? What happened? Change your mind? Decide to move me up to the first team?"

Another long pause. "Yes, in a manner of speaking. It occurs to me that Mr. Vosburg might be willing to assist us. I take it you know how to reach him."

What was going on? "Sure I know how to reach him. Look, why are we talking on the phone? Why don't I come in and—"

"No, I—" He stopped and took a breath. "I can't take the time, David. I interrupted my prayers because of some urgent matters I must complete without delay. I must . . . get at them. Just pay attention. I'll tell you what I have in mind."

"Okay," I sighed. Geniuses. I pulled out the notebook and told him to fire away.

"Mr. Vosburg is the only member of the Compton ménage who knows your true identity. Also the only one with a trustworthy alibi. I want you to invite him here. And stay with him."

"What for?"

"I'm coming to that, David. Two reasons. First, I want to know where the three Comptons, Janine Mason and Jeremiah Healy are planning to spend the upcoming weekend. I may want to speak with one or more of them over the next forty-eight hours and would like to know where each is going to be at all times. Secondly, I have reason to believe Mr. Vosburg is in jeopardy."

Jeopardy? "You want me to be his bodyguard?"

"Yes." His tone was as calm as if this was the most normal thing in the world.

"How much should I tell him? He's probably not going to want to drive all the way into Manhattan just to talk to me. Also, he might not want to be pumped about the whereabouts of the Comptons. I mean, they are his future in-laws."

"Possibly. But you have great powers of persuasion. It may be he'll be coming into Manhattan anyway; he and Miss Compton may have plans. In any case, it won't hurt to ask him. But don't discuss any of this with him over the phone."

This was getting weird. "Look," I said, "I don't really understand. Why don't I come in there so we can talk it over?"

Silence. Then, "All right, we'll discuss it. In a moment. For now, I have an urgent letter to be typed. I wrote it by hand in your absence. It's on your typewriter. Take care of that first. Please." He hung up.

I stared at the phone a second before putting it back. Something was up. But what? I decided to take a peek, went to the door to his office, turned the knob. Locked.

Locked? That door was *never* locked! I glanced at the typewriter and saw a sheet of paper covered with Regan's tiny, precise writing. I went over, picked it up and read it. It was to a priest on the Upper West Side about a transfer the priest had requested. What the hell was so urgent about this? I'd just finished reading it when the intercom sounded again.

"David." Regan's voice was urgent. "I don't hear your typewriter. Is there some problem with the letter? It's important that it go out this morning."

"Don't worry! I'll walk it over to the post office in time for the noon pick-up. What's the big deal? Have I *ever* been late with one of your—"

"No," he said gruffly. "I just wanted to be sure you were aware of the urgency. I'll sign it as soon as it's ready." He was ready to hang up, but I stopped him.

"Why is the door locked?"

Silence. Then, "I locked it because I didn't want to be disturbed. Knock when you finish the letter." He hung up.

While typing the letter, I occupied my brain by wondering what was going on. Regan was up to something. But what?

This wasn't like him. I tried to look at it through his eyes, but that's hard. Well, no, looking at it through his eyes isn't hard. Thinking it through his brain—*that's* hard.

He claimed to know who the murderer was. Did he really? I couldn't think of any reason for him to lie about it, so I'd accept it.

He said he'd got it from that info about the bank loan. Was that possible? If what those numbers showed was that Midas Touch wasn't in financial danger, what did *that* have to do with any of our suspects? I mentally reviewed the list: Dolph, Hilarie, Diane, Healy. How was any one of them affected by that fact differently from the rest?

What about Junior? I still couldn't get him out of my head, for all of Regan's logic. I decided again, for about the fifth time, to drop Junior. Maybe this time for good.

What about Janine Mason? She'd had something going with both Laddie and Dolph. Was there a motive for murder in there? I wondered if Di knew about it . . . or Hilarie!

I finished the letter and pulled it, perfect as always, out of the typewriter. As I typed the envelope, I continued to think about Janine. Not that I could see any motive for her. As far as I could see, the fact that Midas Touch was in good financial shape gave her more of a motive to keep Laddie alive and healthy than to kill him.

I tapped at Regan's door. He told me to come in. *Fat chance,* I thought. *The door's locked.* I tried the knob—and it opened. He was slicker than I'd thought. Somehow he'd managed to unlock it while I was typing, without me hearing a thing. I didn't like that. Even typing, I like to think I keep my eyes and ears open.

As I put the letter in front of him and he signed it, I discovered something. Something buried in my memory. I *had* heard the click of the lock while I was typing, but was too busy thinking about the suspects to let it filter into my consciousness. And I'd heard something else, too. What? I dredged it out of my brain cells. The front door. I'd heard the front door open and close, very gently. *What was going on?*

Regan shoved the letter back at me and returned to the personnel file he was working on. When I didn't leave, he looked up at me. "Yes? Did you want something?"

I looked him in the eye. "Who was here this morning?"

"What makes you think—" His face reddened; he didn't look up. "It doesn't involve you, David," he muttered. "Please hurry and mail that letter."

I sighed. He pretended not to hear me, but he did. He turned a little redder. "Yeah," I said, letting the disgust come through. "I'll just do that."

"Good. When you return, you can phone Mr. Vosburg and make arrangements. After you've done that, I'd like a briefing on what you learned this morning from Mr. Healy and Ms. Lake."

"*Miss* Lake!" I hissed. He looked surprised, but I didn't explain. He went back to his file. I stood watching him for a while, shaking my head, but he didn't look up. Just blushed a little deeper.

What was going on?

48

I GOT BACK from the post office at eleven-thirty and called Vosburg. Got the answering machine and left a message for him to call me as soon as he got in.

Before checking in with Regan I decided to look in on Ernie in the kitchen. She was doing some sort of a casserole, and I told her it smelled great.

She didn't even smile. That was unusual. Was everyone in the house but me going off their rocker? Ernie looked at me, worried.

"He's waiting for you, Davey. Better go see what he wants."

"What's *with* him, Ern?" I said, coming over to try for a taste of the casserole and drawing the usual slap on the hand.

She shook her head. "He hasn't been normal all week, Davey." She looked up at me. "I think Mary Ruth's death has been harder on him than we realized."

I shrugged. "Could be. It was really a shocker for all of us, I guess."

She nodded and went back to work.

Regan, at his desk, file put away, looked up at me over his reading glasses. "Well. Tell me about your visit to East Eighty-seventh."

"What's *with* you?" I said. "Something's not right here. Either I'm going crazy or everyone else is."

He reddened. "Melodrama, David? Nonsense. I'm simply interested in resolving the case. Report, please."

"Okay. But someday I'm going to find out what the hell went on here today." I told him I'd missed Vosburg but left a message. Then I went to my office for my notebook.

By 12:30, when Ernie called us for lunch, I'd filled him in completely. It was while briefing him that I realized—we both realized—that my phone call to Vosburg was unnecessary. In fact, Regan was the one who caught it. As usual. It came when I was telling him about calling Dolph before going to the Comptons'.

"I guess," I was saying, "the Comptons are closer to the Lakes than I thought. They're having some kind of a do this afternoon for Di and Larry, and they've invited the two sisters. I didn't—"

"You say they're having a function for Ms. Compton and Mr. Vosburg?"

"Yeah, they—"

"Then Mr. Vosburg will be with them!"

"Oh, yeah. So he will. I guess that means I won't be—Hey! Is he in danger?" I glanced at my watch. "I can—"

Regan interrupted. He seemed calm. "Not at the moment. But what time is this luncheon, or whatever it is, being held?"

"Yeah, it's a lunch. And Dolph said the Lakes would be leaving for it at twelve-thirty. So I assume it's around twelve-thirty or one."

Regan glanced at his own watch and looked happy. I looked at my own. "Damn!" I said. "I wish I'd asked Compton where this party is. Should I try to find out? If you want me to get Vosburg over here, I—"

The Bishop shook his head. "That won't be necessary, David. Your assignment has been mooted by this circumstance. Continue, please."

"But shouldn't I—"

He waved it away. "No. Go on, please. You went to see Mr. Healy first?" He didn't interrupt me again. And he didn't lose that contented look, even while he concentrated on what I was telling him.

We sat down for lunch and I waited, as usual, while he offered his silent prayer. Knowing I don't believe in God, Regan's never insisted I pray with him. But I think he appreciates that I bow my head. Tell you the truth, with my upbringing, I sometimes feel a little twinge of something—maybe nostalgia, but probably guilt—for not wearing my *yarmulke* when he does that. He mentioned it once, and I said, "One *yarmulke* between us is enough."

"It's a *zucchetto*," he'd muttered. Then added, "But I suppose I should be grateful for small favors." He despises my calling his purple skullcap a "beanie," my usual name for it.

"So you're still not going to tell me who did it," I commented while piling a healthy mound of casserole on my plate. It smelled wonderful.

Regan took a mouthful and answered, talking around the food. "Soon, David. Quite soon. I'm still pursuing that parallel line of investigation."

He swallowed and apparently decided I deserved more. "The problem is the how, David. The financial information gives us the why. Actually *confirms* the why. Better yet, confirms *half* the why. What we need is the how. I think I know, but I require confirmation. With luck, we'll have that before the day is out. Then we can talk."

"Before the day is out? You mean today? Thursday?"

He nodded complacently. "Before dinnertime, with luck. If not, we'll have something *else* to talk about." He took another bite. "In any case, it's too early to talk about it at the moment. Let's enjoy our lunch." He looked up at the clock. "By two o'clock we should have our confirmation. Or know that no such confirmation exists. If it doesn't—" He shrugged. "Well, we'll see."

He didn't invite me to come into his office for coffee afterwards, which I guess made sense. He wasn't ready to tell me what he was up to. And until he was ready to tell me that, we didn't really have anything to talk about.

I was wondering how Vosburg fit into Regan's plans when the phone buzzed. Kessler. With an attitude.

"Well, Davey, you've screwed up again," were his opening words.

I grinned. "Hi, Inspector. Nice to hear your voice. I've screwed up again? Well, everyone's entitled to their own opinion. Now, if you want *my* opinion, I'll—"

"I'm not interested in your opinion, Davey. Not right now. I want to know something. Have you been running around town impersonating a police officer again?"

"Again? Hey, I've *never* impersonated an officer. Not since I left the force. It's a crime. Which is why I don't understand why you've never arrested Charlie Blake. I've caught him a number of times impersonating an officer—a lieutenant, yet. Talk about a lousy impersonation!"

But Kessler didn't want to talk about Blake. He wanted to talk about me. "I've just received a call," he said, "from T. Randolph Compton. I believe you've met him?"

"Sure. Talked to him several times. I know the whole family."

"You know the whole family. Well, chum, I've got a flash for you: the whole family doesn't want to know you. They'd like you behind bars. And if what they're telling me is true, they might get their wish. They say you've been finagling information out of them by pretending to be a whole lot of things you're not. They're mad as hell and they're not going to take it anymore."

Kessler's tone became mock-regretful. "And unfortunately for you, Davey, they've got lots of clout. Mr. Compton knows the mayor. The only reason he hasn't already called him to complain about you is that the good mayor's in Bermuda, vacationing. When he gets back you better believe he's going to be getting an earful."

I yawned. Audibly. Into the phone. Kessler hit the ceiling. "Dammit, Davey, you can't *do* this! I'll have your license! It's unethical, it's against the law and I'll not have it! If you—"

"Hey! Do I get to say a word or two in my own defense?" Kessler muttered something. "Look, Inspector, you've known me a lot of years. When I was on the force—and since—I played fast and loose, I'm not about to deny that. But I've never lied to anyone. *Never*. And I've never told anyone I'm someone I'm not. I—"

"Don't give me that, Davey! I know damn well you—"

I rode over him. "You know damn well I've *hoodwinked* a lot of people. But not by *lying*. I always let them fool themselves. If Dolph Compton tells you I told him I was a representative of Mid-Atlantic Insurance, he's either lying or misremembering what I said. I can tell you exactly what I said, and—"

"All right, never mind Mr. Compton. You told Diane, his daughter, you were a *cop*! And that's a felony, Davey."

"Yes and no."

"What?"

"Yes, it's a felony, and no, I didn't tell her that. Do I look stupid? Don't answer that. Look, Inspector, I'm working for Eddie Goode. I think you know how I feel about Eddie Goode. Am I getting paid? Not a penny. Think about it! Am I going to get myself thrown into prison for a *freebie*? For a guy I despise? Why the hell would I do that?"

Suddenly I knew what was going on. "Hey! They're all together, aren't they, Inspector?" The whole family was at their luncheon. The family and Larry Vosburg, prospective son-in-law. Somehow the name *Dave Goldman* had come up. And up. And up.

"You're damn right they're together, Davey. They're having some kind of bash at the Carlyle. And they've been talking. They've realized that you've been impersonating a whole bunch of different people, changing your story every hour depending on who you're talking to at any given moment. They're furious about it, and I don't blame them. Here their son gets murdered, we have the perp in custody and you're running around trying to get him loose. *And* apparently using all kinds of underhanded means to do it. Can you blame them?"

"I only blame one of them, Inspector. The one that killed Laddie—and Ruthie Benedict."

"Yeah, yeah." He was disgusted. "Parker told me all about your suspicions. Parker and I have the same thought on that: bullshit. We've got Goode dead to rights. And this time we're putting him away. The case is airtight."

"Well, I've got to tell you something, Inspector. The Bishop thinks your case has some holes in it. He's got someone else tabbed."

Silence. Kessler knows Regan. Doesn't always like him but respects him. A lot. When his voice came next it was cautious. "Regan's working this one with you?"

"Damn straight. And he knows who did it, and it ain't Goode." Kessler started to say something but I cut him off. "No, he hasn't told me who it is, so don't bother asking. But when was the last time Regan was wrong on one of these?"

"When was he *wrong*?" Kessler blustered. "He's only *worked* on a couple."

"He was right on Lombardi, he was right on McClain, he was—"

"All right, all right," Kessler said wearily. He thought it over. "And he's convinced Goode didn't do this?"

"That's right."

"Hmm." Kessler thought some more. "I suppose I should talk to him. Is he there?"

"Yeah, he's here, but he can't pick up on this line."

"I'll call him on his. What's that number again?"

I told him and hung up. The phone rang—the Bishop's line this time—a few seconds later. I grabbed it. Instead of hello, I answered with, "What makes you think *he* wants to talk to *you*?"

"You'll clown at your own funeral, Davey," Kessler growled. "Put him on."

"Give me a minute." I went into Regan's office and explained the situation. His eye movements told me there was a lot of brain activity going on.

"All right," he said, and picked up the phone. "Hello, Inspector." The Bishop gestured at me to listen in. I hurried back to my office and picked up. Kessler was talking: "... demand to know what you base your judgment on. You know I respect you. And you've been right more than you've been wrong..." I grinned. Regan hadn't been wrong once. Not yet. With the possible exception of his decision to hire me.

"...but I can't have you going off like a loose cannon. Why can't you work *with* me instead of *against* me for once?"

"There's nothing I'd rather do, Inspector. In fact, I have a suggestion—if I may." He paused. Kessler waited for the suggestion.

"Why don't you come over, Inspector? I apologize for not coming to you, but my disability makes that difficult."

"Quite all right, Bishop. I'd be delighted to come over. If Sister Ernestine doesn't mind providing me with a cup or two of her excellent coffee."

"She'll be delighted to, Inspector. But I have a further suggestion." Kessler muttered something. "Why not invite the entire Compton ménage to join us? I'll be glad to extend the invitation personally, if—"

"Not necessary. I told Mr. Compton I'd call him back after I had a chat with Davey. I'll suggest they join us. I think they'll come if I promise them an apology—from Davey."

I snorted, but Regan overrode me. "He'll be happy to, Inspector. In fact, I will join them in insisting that he do so. Good. Oh— my invitation also includes Mr. Healy, Mr. Vosburg and Ms. Mason. I assume they're all together."

Kessler thought about it. "I recognize Vosburg's name. He's the guy going to marry the daughter, right? Who're the others?"

"Healy is the Comptons' butler," Regan murmured. "And the father of the murdered Mary Ruth Benedict. Ms. Mason was a friend of the late Mr. Compton and also, I gather, of the rest of the Compton family."

"I'll give it a shot," Kessler said. "Though I don't know what you're trying to accomplish."

"Very simple. I know who the murderer is. I need to prove it to you. With the help of those six people, I mean to do so."

49

THE FIRST GUY TO SHOW, at 2:40, hadn't even been invited: Sgt. Joe Parker. I wasn't surprised to see him, especially with Kessler right behind him. I mean, it was Joe's case. Once, Kessler brought Blake along for the same reason and I wouldn't let him in the door. Kessler won't make that mistake again. Of course I'd never do that to Parker.

Regan's eyes lighted up when Kessler walked in. "Inspector! It's been too long. And Sergeant Parker! Nice to see you, sir." He waved vaguely at a couple of the six chairs I'd arranged in front of his desk, four of which I'd brought in from the dining room.

"Coffee, gentlemen?" Unusual hospitality for Regan. Before either one could answer, he turned to me. "Please, David, go see if Sister is adequately prepared for our guests. Coffee, tea, other postprandials. If you please. Perhaps you could assist her with it."

I didn't say anything, but I did shake my head. I'd never seen him like this. Ernie doesn't need my help, for God's sake. The thought even crossed my mind: is he looking for a private word with the boys in blue? But about what? To work out a pre-trial sentencing arrangement for me so I wouldn't have to do the full term when they threw me in the slammer for impersonating an officer? I grinned at the thought. Naw, Regan was just a little loonier than usual.

As expected, Ernie had everything under control: full coffee urn, already perking; plenty of hot water for tea; soft drinks on a tray. As for *postprandials,* Regan's word for booze, Ernie had four half-full bottles of different kinds of cordials. The whole thing was on the rolling table so Ernie needed me like she needed a second head. We took a couple of minutes to commiserate with each other for having to live with such an eccentric boss.

My eyes and ears were working overtime when I returned to the office, but if Regan had got rid of me so he could have a private word with the cops, he'd already had it. No furtive glances or interrupted dialog. Kessler had grabbed the best chair, of course, the way he always does.

As soon as I sat down, he drilled me with his gimlet eyes. "I've got to tell you, Davey, you're in hot water. You say you didn't impersonate an officer, but the Comptons disagree. Vociferously. So I'm going to—"

"Please, Inspector." Regan was placid. "Surely you know Mr. Goldman better than that. I'm not a lawyer, but I have a fair understanding of legal matters, and aside from a possible assault and battery on Mr. Benedict—a charge I doubt that either Mr. Benedict or you will be likely to pursue—Mr. Goldman has broken no laws. He had a right to interview these people. He's been retained by Davis Baker, an officer of the court, as an investigator."

Kessler shook his head. "Never mind that nonsense with Junior. That's not what I'm talking about. Davey can beat up on the Junior Benedicts of this world all he wants and get nothing but cheers from me. No, I'm talking about going around and telling people he's a cop! That's a felony!"

Regan looked at me. "Did you do that, David?"

I shook my head. "Absolutely not. Who says I've been telling them I'm a cop, Inspector?"

Kessler looked at me. I realized for the first time that his goatee was now nearly white. It was totally dark when I first met and went to work for him. Over the years it had progressed through various shades of salt and pepper, the salt slowly but surely gaining the upper hand. Now it was in total control. Only a few streaks of brown marred the white. By contrast, the hair on his head was still youthful and thick, the only white being distinguished streaks at the temples.

"You want to know who says you've been claiming to be a cop, Davey? They'll be here any minute." He looked at his watch. "In fact, they—" The doorbell chimed.

I jumped up. "Speak of the devil! I'll go let them in. And I promise not to flash my junior G-man badge at anyone."

Kessler reddened. He was starting a retort when I left.

It was all six of them. The stretch limo at the curb explained how they'd come. Not a very friendly group. Dolph, prizefighter jaw jutting, was in the lead. Without offering a hand, he looked me in the eye and stated, "I believe we're expected."

I gave him a grin and swung the door wide. "You sure are. Go right down the hall to the office. Sister Ernestine will take your drink orders."

Hilarie followed close behind her husband, not even giving me the courtesy of a glance. Her face was pinker than usual. Di and Janine came after her, also with nothing to say. Janine threw me a beautiful smile before she remembered I was the enemy and wiped it off. Healy's face was red, but that was normal. He gave me an angry look and hurried by.

Only Vosburg was semi-friendly. He hung back after the others trooped down the hall. "I'm afraid you've got your tit in a wringer this time," he smiled, sounding regretful. "And I'm afraid I didn't help matters much, telling them who you really were. Sorry."

"Hey, you told the truth. Don't worry about it. I don't."

Larry grinned. "Yeah, your life's an open book, right?" The grin faded. "I've got to tell you, Dolph's really got the bit between his teeth. He's planning to ream you good."

I shrugged. "He can try. Who knows? Maybe he'll succeed. Shall we go in?"

People had sort of arranged themselves by the time Vosburg and I came through the door. Everyone was sitting down except Hilarie and Kessler, who were conferring about something over in a corner, and Ernie, who was taking coffee orders. Dolph had copped Kessler's chair and was saving another one for his wife, leaving Vosburg nowhere to sit but on the couch next to Parker. I introduced Larry to him, mentioning what Larry did for a living. Parker's eyes widened. He was asking for golf tips almost before I'd finished the introductions.

Ernie was glum. She'd enticed only three drink orders: coffee for Di, Janine and Kessler. I knew Parker wanted some but was afraid to say so. He's intimidated by nuns. So I grabbed her as she headed for the kitchen. "Bring the sergeant some coffee too, Ernie," I muttered in her ear. "Lots of sugar and cream." Her face brightened. Her customer list had just expanded by thirty-three percent.

"Come *on*, Hilarie!" Dolph barked. Kessler turned in surprise and looked at him. Hilarie reddened and hurried to her seat.

Dolph patted her hand. "Sorry, dear. But let's get this over with. You can talk to the inspector later."

Kessler, looking grumpy at having had his seat stolen right out from under him, headed for the couch, that being all the seating left. Dolph waited for Kessler to sit down and Vosburg to wind up his golf tip to Parker, then said, "Shall I tell the Bishop why we're here, Inspector?"

Kessler opened his mouth, but Regan beat him to it. "No need, Mr. Compton. The inspector has told me of your pique. Since Mr. Goldman works for me, I find it appropriate that we discuss his behavior together. He has given me a detailed description of his activities and, with one exception, I can find nothing reprehensible in them. Please tell me your version."

Dolph looked at him. "Nothing reprehensible? Then he obviously didn't tell you that he lied to me and my wife. And my daughter. You're a Catholic bishop. I take it you disapprove of lying."

"You take it correctly." Regan was emphatic. "And believe me, if Mr. Goldman has been lying, he'll have more than you to face." Regan transferred his gaze to me. "You didn't tell me you lied to these people, Mr. Goldman."

"I told no lie." That brought some dissenting noises from our guests. They quieted down as Ernie arrived with the coffee. Murmured thanks from the four recipients. Parker looked pleasantly surprised when she put his mug on the table at his elbow. "Thank you, 'ster," he mumbled.

When she left, Diane grabbed the floor.

"You're lying right now!" She looked me in the eye. "You told Larry and me you were a cop—I mean, a policeman!" She threw an apologetic glance in the direction of the two cops—I mean, policemen—flanking her fiancé on the couch.

I shook my head. "Not so." She snorted. "Oh, come on, Diane. When did I tell you that?"

"When Larry and I first met you. You said you were a cop!"

"Did I say *cop* or *policeman*?"

Diane hesitated. "You said you were a—policeman." She frowned. "Officer! That's what you said! You said you were an officer!"

I opened up my notebook. "Nope. What I said was, 'You're

probably wondering who I am and what I'm doing.' " Diane
frowned, remembering.

"Then I said, 'I have just a few more questions. If you don't
mind, ma'am.' "

Diane nodded. It was coming back. I turned a page. "Then I
said, 'I have some questions I need to have answered. We can
do it here or, if you'd prefer, downtown.' " I looked at her. "That's
as close as I came to saying I was a cop."

Diane stared at me. "I think you're right. I guess I had such a
strong impression you were a cop, I just imagined you'd said you
were."

I looked at Vosburg. "Right, Larry?"

He nodded. "Right. But it *was* kind of unfair. You knew what
we'd think and did everything you could to encourage it."

That steamed Diane all over again. "That's right! You did
everything you could to make us think you were—an officer."

"But I didn't lie. I never told you I *was* one." She shrugged,
sullen. I looked at Dolph. He wasn't assuaged. I also heard a snort
from Kessler.

"All right," Compton said. "But I remember our phone conversation *very* well. I've got my *own* notes on it. And you definitely claimed you were representing Mid-Atlantic. Maybe you'd
be interested to know that I just called my insurance agent. The
company hasn't hired a P.I. and has no intentions of doing so.
They're satisfied with the police investigation, they know none
of us is under suspicion, and they're preparing the paperwork
to disburse the funds for Laddie's death benefits. Those go to the
company, by the way, not to any of us personally. So that stuff
about having to investigate the beneficiaries was pure hogwash.
Wasn't it?"

I smiled into his glare and raised my hands. "I guess. But I
never told you I represented Mid-Atlantic."

"The hell you didn't! I've got—"

"Please. Listen to this." I turned to the page. "I said, 'The
company hasn't notified you about me?' You said, 'What company?' I said, 'Mid-Atlantic Mutual Life. They haven't called?'
You mentioned your agent, and I said you'd go on working with
him. Then I said, 'Insurance companies often retain outside investigators in cases like this. I'd like to come talk to you.' You

said, 'Oh. You're an investigator.' " I looked at Compton. "Then you said, 'For Mid-Atlantic Mutual Life?' "

I held his eye. "Tough question. If I'd said yes to that, you'd have me dead to rights. But I didn't. I just said, 'So when could I stop by?' And you said, 'Why not right away?' You let me off the hook."

Dolph's face reddened. "Maybe so. But that wasn't the only thing you said. Later on in my office you told Hilarie and me that you'd expedite the payout if we'd give you our alibis. That was a lie. You got us to spill our guts. All under false pretenses."

I turned pages. "I never said I'd expedite the payout." I found the page. "Here it is: 'The laws governing disbursement of proceeds of a life policy in cases of murder are somewhat complicated. The law requires that the company pay out *only* after a judicial finding.' "

"That's hogwash!" Kessler blurted. "In New York—"

I stopped him. "Hey, did I say in New York? I said, 'The law requires.' I didn't say in what state."

Kessler cursed under his breath but gestured for me to continue. I looked at Compton. "Then you said, 'You mean, you won't pay till Goode is found guilty?' I said, '*Can't* pay.' And that's the truest statement I've ever made. If you don't believe *that*, Mr. Compton, I'll show you my bank statement. I haven't got a million dollars. Or anything close to it."

Compton was outraged. "That's the weaseliest, grubbiest piece of—"

Hilarie patted his hand. "Never mind, dear. I think he's got us. Or rather, we *haven't* got him. He tiptoed around the truth so delicately there's nothing we can get him on." She gave me a smile, not a pleasant one.

"Good." Regan looked around. "Now that we've resolved the matter of Mr. Goldman's alleged duplicity, let's get down to more serious matters."

Dolph, now on his feet, was abrupt. "Get down to anything you like, Bishop. But you'll do it without us. We're leaving. Come on, Hil. You too, Di."

"Just a moment, Mr. Compton." Regan looked up at him. "I'd like a word with you privately. Then if you still want to go, I—"

"Forget it, Bishop. No offense, but I've heard about you. The inspector's told me how you like to involve yourself in murder cases. Now you're trying to get into Laddie's. Well, we're not playing. As far as I'm concerned, Laddie's murderer's in jail. We're going. Let's go, Hil."

"Not quite yet, Mr. Compton." Something in Regan's voice made Dolph stop. "Someone told me something yesterday that surprised me. On a subject of which you have some knowledge. A minute of your time? Privately? After that you can decide whether to go or stay."

Compton was decisive. "I told you, Bishop, I—"

Regan held his eye. "Please, sir. I simply want to tell you what he told me. Oh—did I mention? It was just outside La Fontenelle late yesterday morning that he garnered his information. Two minutes of your time—I beg you."

50

AS THE NAME of the restaurant rolled off Regan's tongue Compton turned white. He leaned heavily on the back of his chair. Hilarie seemed to sense something and looked up at him.

Dolph swallowed and cleared his throat. "Oh. Well, all right, Bishop, uh . . . Surely. Where?"

Regan nodded at the door. "We can use Mr. Goldman's office. It will take only a moment." He looked around at mystified faces. "Please excuse us, ladies and gentlemen. We'll be brief." Kessler started to say something, then changed his mind. He didn't look happy.

Regan pushed away from the desk and rolled toward the door, Dolph trailing behind. The Bishop stopped. "Please join us, David. And . . . " I knew what was coming.

" . . . on a separate matter, I'd also like a word with you, Ms. Mason. Join us also, please. I promise to be brief."

Janine, almost as white as Dolph, looked up at me. Her beautiful blue eyes looked like a rabbit's when it's caught in the headlights of a car. I smiled and offered her a hand. She took it with a cold, shaking grip.

I gave everyone else a big smile. "We'll be right back, I promise," I assured them. I looked at Joe. "Why don't you tell Sister Ernestine she might be able to sell some more coffee, Joe?" Parker, looking as puzzled as everyone else, nodded abruptly, got up and headed for the kitchen.

Regan had wedged his wheelchair between my desk and the wall. Maybe he'd learn from this impromptu meeting that I had a point when I complained about my office being too small. Dolph was on the leather couch, pale as before. As Janine and I entered, he heaved himself up.

"Close the door, David," Regan muttered. I did, eyes on Dolph and Janine. They looked terrible.

"Please sit down," Regan growled. When we all did, he spoke. "Mr. Compton and Ms. Mason. You now know that I know your secret—part of it, anyway. I'm not going to prolong this, but I have a question and an invitation.

"The invitation, first. Frankly, I did not invite you and your family and friends here, sir, in order to provide Mr. Goldman a forum wherein he might defend himself against your charges. I had an ulterior motive. I now invite the two of you—and insofar as you have the power to affect their decisions, everyone else in your party—to stay while I attempt to show Inspector Kessler that Mr. Goode did not murder your son."

Dolph threw up his hands. "I think you're nuts, Bishop, but you've got me. And a few minutes of my time's a small price to pay." He raised his eyebrows. "I take it, if I do this, neither Janine nor I will ever hear about La Fontenelle again?"

Regan sighed. "I assure you, Mr. Compton, my failings, many as they are, do not fall under the rubric of extortion. I am not enjoying this experience any more than you are. I have no intention of repeating it."

"Then you got a deal." Dolph's head turned. "Janine?"

She gulped. "Sure."

"Good," said Regan. "Now, the question. In addition to knowing about your tryst at La Fontenelle, I am also aware that both of you lied about where you were during the late afternoon hours on Monday, three days ago. I refer to the interval of time wherein Mrs. Benedict was murdered. I want you to tell me where you were. If you tell the truth, you have my assurance that this secret will not leave this room. But it must be the truth."

Both guilty parties looked at each other, shocked; but they weren't any more shocked than I was. Not about Janine: her attempt at a lie about having been at the U.N. suggested that her alternate story—home in bed alone—was probably also fabricated. But what made Regan think Dolph's alibi was a lie? He'd said he'd been alone in his office from four till nine. And Hilarie had said he'd arrived home at "nearly eleven." Was Regan's parallel track checking Dolph's alibi?

Dolph glanced at Janine and chuckled bitterly. "How *can* we lie? You obviously already know where we were. La Fontenelle." His eyes narrowed. "You did know that, didn't you?"

"I do now," Regan said, and sighed. "As you may imagine, I do not approve of such assignations. I think—"

"It's *not* what you think!" Janine blurted.

"No?"

"No! We—tell them, Dolph."

Compton had a hard time meeting Regan's eyes, but he managed it. "I know it looks bad, Bishop, but I swear, there's nothing going on between Janine and me. The night Laddie died, Hilarie went a little—crazy for a while. Janine had come right over when I called her and told her what happened. I'm afraid Hilarie yelled at her, said it was all her fault. It got to Janine."

Janine spoke up. "Dolph felt bad about it, so he asked me to have an early dinner with him on Monday at La Fontenelle. To talk it out. Hilarie had an all-day meeting down on Wall Street. Anyway, we got to talking and stayed till ten. I—"

"Excuse me, Madame," Regan said. "I apologize for interrupting, but it would not be advisable for you to be here too long. I have one more question for you, and then you'd better return to the other room." She bit her lip and nodded. "You and the senior Mr. Compton were also together, were you not, following the banquet the night your fiancé died. From approximately eight-forty-five to nine-thirty? In your limousine?"

They were both shocked. So, again, was I.

"How did you know?" Dolph said, taking the words right out of my mouth.

Regan looked at Janine's face, then at his watch. "That's sufficient answer for now. You'd better return, Ms. Mason. If anyone asks why you were in here, you may tell them I was curious about Ladd Compton's state of mind the night he was murdered. And tell them we'll be just another moment."

"Thank you, Bishop." She got up. "Thanks for understanding." Regan, blushing, waved it away. She left.

Regan turned to Compton. "In answer to your question, sir, I didn't know that you and Ms. Mason were together, but it seemed possible. From the outset I didn't believe your accounting of your movements between eight-forty-five and nine-thirty-five that night. You claimed to have walked from the Beauchamp to your office. The banquet was black tie. Thirty-two short and six long blocks in a tuxedo and evening pumps? That seemed unlikely.

"My skepticism was confirmed when Mr. Stratford reported first that you had engaged in no conversation with him—contrary to what you'd told Mr. Goldman, and that he'd seen you enter a limousine, also contrary to your ridiculous story about walking over two miles in patent leather slippers."

Compton stared. "Then you must have suspected me of—murdering Laddie!"

Regan nodded. "The thought did cross my mind, loath as I was to believe a father would murder his son. But my subsequent analysis of your company's financial condition persuaded me otherwise. So I looked elsewhere for an explanation for your lies. It appears that I found it."

Regan sighed. "When I was advised that you were seen yesterday morning, meeting Ms. Mason in La Fontenelle, I guessed that all your lies were in the service of your assignations with her."

He held Compton's eye. "I have one or two more questions." The businessman nodded. "If you and Ms. Mason are not sexually involved, what were you doing in her limousine—in secret—that Sunday night at the Beauchamp? The *contretemps* with your wife had not yet occurred."

Dolph shrugged. "Not the major one, but you should have seen the daggers Hil looked at Janine when Di walked out of the banquet. I wanted to apologize. I felt Hilarie was treating her badly. So had Laddie, for that matter. I wanted to tell her she was still part of the family as far as I was concerned. But knowing how Hil felt, I wanted to do it secretly. I got in the limo with her, and she had Kamper take us to the GM building. We sat in the car talking for twenty minutes with the motor running. Kamper can tell you that nothing happened."

Regan nodded. "And why yesterday's meeting?"

Compton shook his head. "I was scared. Goldman was asking about Ruthie's death. He was checking alibis. When Viv—our receptionist—buzzed me and told me he and Janine were with Di in her office, I felt I had to warn Janine to be careful of what she said. That's why I went through that whole phone routine." He shook his head. "Such a lot of intrigue for something so innocent."

Regan nodded. "It certainly was. I don't want to belabor the point, but you are playing with fire, Mr. Compton. Ms. Mason is a beautiful woman and you're a married man. I cannot—"

The door chime interrupted him. I jumped up and breathed a silent sigh of relief. I'd heard this lecture before—directed at me. But before going, I had something to say. "Without disrespect, Mr. Compton..." I turned to Regan. "...shouldn't I check these alibis out? Talk to people at La Fontenelle and this guy, Kamper?"

Regan looked smug. "That has already been done, David." I stared. The doorbell chimed again.

"Please get that, David. It should be Mr. Kelley. It is he who has already verified Mr. Compton's story."

My stare became a goggle. "*Dennis Kelley?*" Regan nodded. The way a cat might nod when it's just polished off a very tasty canary.

Dennis Kelley. Golfing buddy, fellow P.I., job offerer. And owner of one of the largest and most successful investigative agencies in the city.

It was him all right—beefy face, big grin and all. "Look, Dennis," I said, as I opened the door and let him in, "you want my job, you got it. But the Bishop goes with it. So I'd think about it, buddy."

"Hell," he said, puffing from the eight steps he'd just climbed. (He's in lousy shape.) "I wouldn't *have* your damn job. You gotta be Jewish to put up with a bishop."

"Shhh, he'll hear you. What the hell's going on?"

Kelley looked uncomfortable. "I'd better tell him."

Regan's voice floated down the hall. "If that's Mr. Kelley, David, bring him. To my office, please." Regan was heading back.

The sound of Regan's voice triggered an idea. "In a second," I answered loudly, then lowered my voice. "That was you in Regan's office this morning, wasn't it? When I came back at a quarter to eleven."

Unable to meet my eyes, Dennis shrugged. "He wanted it that way, Davey. He didn't want you to know. Uh, shouldn't we go to the office? I've got stuff to tell him."

Confused and a little mad, I followed Kelley down the hall and into the office. Regan was behind his desk, Dolph and Janine back in their same chairs. Every eye in the room was on us— make that on Kelley.

Regan's especially. The detective caught his look, gave him a nod and a thumbs-up. Regan nodded back and permitted himself a smile so small I'm sure no one saw it but me. Tiny as it was, for him it was a crow of delight. Whatever he'd sent Kelley for had been important—and Kelley'd come through for him. I felt a pang of jealousy.

I've never resented—not much, anyway—Kelley's making more money than I do. Frankly, I find his kind of investigating intensely boring. A lot of marital crap, some industrial. Crap I don't understand or want to understand. I say if he can get rich off of it, more power to him.

But I did resent his taking over my job. Regan had talked about parallel tracks. Obviously Kelley had been assigned the other one. What—besides checking up on Dolph and Janine—was it? And why him and not me? Something I couldn't handle? Makes a body insecure.

"David," the Bishop said, waving a hand. "A chair for Mr. Kelley." I headed for the dining room while Regan did introductions.

When I'd brought it and Dennis and I were sitting down, Regan leaned forward and got the eye of all.

"Mr. Compton has agreed to stay awhile. I hope everyone else will also. We have some work to do."

Kessler growled, "What kind of work, Bishop?"

Regan looked at him. "Establishing to your satisfaction who murdered Ladd Compton. And Mary Ruth Healy Benedict. The murderer is in the room at this very moment."

51

THAT RESULTED in a fairly long moment of silence, then a hubbub. Dolph said, "Oh, great!" Hilarie, looking equally disgusted, said something like, "That'll be the day!" Diane came through with the old standard, "You mean—" I couldn't tell if Janine said anything; her eyes were fixed on Dolph. Healy's comment was unprintable. So was Parker's—not the same as Healy's but equally objectionable. Vosburg, eyes circling the room, muttered something. In the jumble one thing was clear: if Regan's idea had been to create pandemonium, he'd succeeded.

He raised a hand. "Please. Ladies and gentlemen, if we may proceed. I—"

Hilarie interrupted. "This is ridiculous, Bishop. The murderer's in jail." She turned around to look at Kessler. "Isn't that true, Inspector?"

Kessler nodded, stroking his beard nervously. He looked at the Bishop.

Regan met his eye. "Shall I give you my exposition of the matter, Inspector?"

Kessler blinked twice. "Okay, let's hear it."

"Thank you, sir." Regan leaned back and took a deep breath. "Let me describe my own thought processes once I satisfied myself that Eddie Goode was not the killer."

His mouth turned down. "Let me say at the outset, I am not proud of my performance in the matter. I apologize to all of you—and you in particular, Mr. Healy—for my many mistakes. Without them, your daughter might still be alive. I say that to my shame."

Healy gawked at Regan. I didn't think anyone could tell it—I certainly hoped not—but inside I was gawking right along with him. What was the Bishop talking about?

"I sometimes suffer," he went on, "from the same disability as Mr. Goldman, my associate: overhasty decision-making." Regan looked at Kessler. "As in this instance. I was precipitate in accepting Mr. Goode's story about his role—rather, his lack of a role—in the murder. Instead of considering it carefully, I asked Mr. Goldman to bring Mrs. Benedict to me posthaste. As is his wont, he complied without delay. Before I had any leverage to use on her; worse, before I had certitude that Mr. Goode's story was true; worst of all, before I had an inkling of a motive for the murder."

"And I suppose you have now," Kessler said.

"Oh yes, Inspector. Indubitably." Regan shook his head. "But when I spoke with Mrs. Benedict I had neither an inkling of a motive nor any leverage to employ. She lied to me with impunity and walked away. To her death. I will not soon forgive myself for my careless and inadequate preparation for my interview with her."

He looked down. "Then I compounded matters. When I learned of her death I was not so much saddened by it as enraged. The murderer had struck again in despite of me—in defiance of me. As the secular adage has it: having lost my way, I redoubled my speed. Learning that her first phone call upon leaving me was to Mr. Vosburg, I seized upon him as the most likely suspect and sent Mr. Goldman on his trail—again, without a clue as to what motive might have impelled him."

"I *thought* you suspected me!" Vosburg burst out. "It was weird, all those questions Davey was asking!"

Regan nodded and looked at him. "Yes I did, Mr. Vosburg. Only when that brigate foundered on the shoals of your unassailable alibi did I remember St. Augustine's dictum: 'Original sin came about when Adam and Eve forgot to contemplate.' Too

late—at least for Mrs. Benedict—I betook myself to contemplation: contemplation of the case as a whole, with the emphasis
on motive."

Regan looked around the room. "As I considered possible motives, two presented themselves. The more likely of these appeared to be financial and tied in with the Compton family."

Regan looked at Dolph. "You, Mr. Compton, and..." He
switched his gaze to Hilarie and Di. "...the members of your
family—all had motive. At least, potential motive. Newspaper
articles called attention to the death benefits from the life insurance policy on Ladd's life. Giving rise to the question: Did his
death mean life for Midas Touch?"

"That's ridiculous and insulting!" Di burst out. "You can't
believe everything you read in the newspapers!"

"That's true, Madame. But let's look at it in some depth." Regan
surveyed the room. "Let's start with some background. A family
owns and operates a car wash company. Business is good, the
company is growing—too fast for its own good. For every dollar
it makes, it spends two in new facilities. Cash is—"

"That's not true!" Diane interrupted. "Mom and Dad had
everything planned. Those financial reporters didn't know what
they were talking about!"

Regan eyed her. "Perhaps. And you may have had a plan,
Madame, but your company's growth unquestionably outstripped your resources. You have built or acquired new facilities
at the rate of five or six a year since you recapitalized five years
ago. Each of those represents approximately a quarter-million-
dollar investment. Until last year your cash flow never reached
a half-million. Furthermore, two years ago you paid out a one-
million-dollar dividend. This meant—"

"Where'd you come up with those figures?" Dolph growled.
"Those are private numbers. There's obviously been a leak, and
I—"

"Please, Mr. Compton. If laws have been violated, that can be
pursued later. At the moment we're trying to find a murderer. I
was about to ask you to confirm those figures, but your outrage
is confirmation enough. Besides, you yourself—and you, Mrs.
Compton—told Mr. Goldman that you have been short of cash
for years."

"I suppose we did, Bishop," Hilarie said. "I'd note for the record that Mr. Goldman was there under false pretenses."

Regan nodded. "So noted. But I suggest, Madame, that that is of far less importance than uncovering the identity of the person who murdered your son. If we—"

"That's it." Kessler stood up. "You've been making some big statements, Bishop, but you're taking your sweet time getting to specifics. It's time to put up or shut up. Parker's already told Davey how much we've got that points to Eddie Goode. Goode's in jail. He's going before the grand jury next week, and the D.A. tells me a true bill is a foregone conclusion. So either tell me why you think anyone besides Eddie Goode did it, or Parker and I are leaving."

"All right, Inspector. Sit down, if you will, while I explain." Kessler slowly sat down and Regan went into Baker's theory: that Eddie, a streetwise jailhouse lawyer, could easily have come up with a better story than the one he handed out.

Kessler glanced past Vosburg at Parker on the other end of the couch. "Joe? What do you think? Make any sense?" Parker, without taking his eyes off the Bishop, shook his head. Kessler turned back to Regan and shrugged. "There you are, Bishop. Us dumb cops just don't appreciate logic."

"Hardly dumb," Regan murmured. "Nor unintelligent, either. If you'll give me just another ten minutes, Inspector, I think you'll be glad you stayed." Kessler nodded glumly and crossed his arms.

Regan turned his eyes back to Dolph. "I was speaking of the financial motive. To forestall any more outbursts, Mr. Compton, let me say it eventuated in nothing. The company, I discovered, was strong, with no need for the million-dollar injection of insurance proceeds to continue a highly successful and profitable existence."

Dolph stared. "That's right! But you were just saying—"

"I was just saying that I had suspicions, Mr. Compton. Suspicions that, as it developed, were unfounded."

"So where did that leave you?"

Regan nodded. "It left me with the second motive. A motive related to the most baffling part of this whole affair: the strange case of Mary Ruth Healy Benedict."

52

THE BISHOP GAVE HEALY a slight bow of the head. "My condolences, Mr. Healy. Before she died, your daughter told Mr. Goldman and me about your happy family life."

I gave Healy a sharp glance. His face was impassive, not acknowledging the Bishop's condolence with even a nod.

Vosburg had perked up at the name of Mary Ruth. "What about her?" he demanded. "What do you mean by strange case?"

Regan studied him. After a second he said, "Well, let's look at it, Mr. Vosburg. She grew up with you, didn't she? Along with Ms. Compton..." He looked at Diane. "...and the late Ladd Compton." Vosburg gave a slight nod.

"Indeed," Regan went on, "she kept company with both you and Ladd Compton from time to time, did she not?"

Vosburg shrugged. "We both dated her, yeah. What's that got to do with motive?"

"Everything, Mr. Vosburg, as it turns out. Everything. And now they are both dead. And you are alive."

Vosburg flushed. "Well, that's not my fault. No one's sorrier than I am for what happened to them."

"Oh?" Regan turned to Diane. "How close were you and Mrs. Benedict, Ms. Compton?"

It was Di's turn to blush. "I wouldn't say...but yes, we were friends. I liked her. I cried when I heard she died."

"I'm sure. Was she a close friend of your brother?"

Janine erupted, face pink, eyes flashing. "Laddie and I were going to be married! I resent what you're implying!"

"Indeed?" Regan was calm. "And what is that, Madame?"

"That they—you know. That they had an affair. He was my fiancé! We were going to be married."

"You were never engaged!" Hilarie, red-faced, eyes narrowing. "Laddie would never have—"

"Please, Madame." Regan's voice was soothing. "The relationship between your son and Ms. Mason is peripheral." Hilarie subsided, but not without a bitter glance in Janine's direction.

"That aside," Regan went on, "my question about a possible friendship between Mr. Compton and Mrs. Benedict was not intended to imply any impropriety on the part of either of them. My question for Ms. Compton referred to their spiritual relationship. Did Ladd confide in Ruth? And she in him?"

Diane glanced at Janine and frowned. "Yes," she said slowly. "Yes, they *were* close in that way. He loved Janine, but I think he sincerely liked and trusted Ruthie."

"Thank you, Madame." Regan turned his eyes to Ruthie's dad. "Mr. Healy. I don't want to breach confidentiality, but as I suggested, the second motive—the true motive—is closely tied to your daughter and her recent—problem. I think you know to what I refer."

Healy reddened. "Yeah, I know to what you refer. And I gotta tell you, Bishop, if Goldman didn't lie to Dolph or the others, he damn sure—excuse me, Bishop—he sure lied to me, and that's the God's truth. He told me he represented the Knights of St. Titus! And that's the only reason I told him what I told him!"

Regan nodded. "I apologize for Mr. Goldman's equivocation, Mr. Healy. I know that membership in that society means a great deal to you. I do not approve of Mr. Goldman's conduct as regards you and your dedication to that organization. It was highly insensitive of him."

Healy studied Regan's face and gave a slight nod. "Thank you, Bishop."

Regan returned the nod. "I'd like your permission, Mr. Healy, to reveal your daughter's secret at this time. It's highly relevant to Ladd Compton's death. And your daughter's as well."

Healy frowned, then nodded abruptly. "Go ahead," he growled.

"Thank you." Regan turned back to Diane. "Were you aware, Ms. Compton, that Mrs. Benedict recently had an abortion?"

Di's eyes widened. "When?" Janine opened her mouth and immediately closed it.

Regan answered, "Five weeks ago."

"No! An abortion? Did she—no, she didn't tell me. I didn't see her much after she got married. But Ladd stayed in touch with her."

"Indeed. My question: Would it have been in character for her to have confided in your brother about the abortion?"

Di frowned. "I don't know. Well, yes, I do. I think she'd have told him." She thought about it and nodded. "Yes, she'd have told him. I'm sure she would. They were close that way."

Hilarie, with a glance at Janine, spoke up, her voice shaky. "I hope you don't mean what I think you do, Diane. That Laddie got Ruthie pregnant."

"No, Mother! Laddie and Ruthie didn't have that kind of a relationship! No, I meant what I said: Ruthie would've confided in Ladd. She told him everything."

"And he her?" Regan said. Diane nodded.

"And what does all this have to do with the price of tea in China?" Kessler. "So she had an abortion! So what?"

"So this, Inspector." Regan wasn't going to let any cop make him lose his cool. "So she told Ladd Compton of her condition. And of her decision to abort. And, most importantly of all, who had sired the child whose life she was terminating."

Dolph spoke up. "I agree with the Inspector. I don't see where you're going with this. Can't you get to the point?"

Regan looked at him. "I'm almost there, Mr. Compton." He looked at Larry. "I'd like Mr. Vosburg—and only Mr. Vosburg—to see this." He pulled a sheet of paper from his desk drawer. "Would you come over here and read it, Mr. Vosburg?"

Larry stared at him. I stared at the paper. I recognized the Kelly green ink: it was the letter Ruthie had started to Regan and never finished. Larry got up. "Sure. What is it?"

He went to Regan's desk to read it. He was nearly finished before my mind started catching up. Regan didn't *have* the letter—Parker did. All Regan had was a Xerox. So . . .

I glanced at Parker on the couch. He glanced back, his eyes expressionless. He wasn't giving away a thing. But he had to have brought the original with him and given it to Regan. *That* was why Regan had banished me to the kitchen. So Parker could give him the letter without me knowing. But what for? The letter didn't really say anything.

Or did it? Vosburg seemed to have a different opinion, judging by the look on his face. He'd turned pale and was looking at Regan like the Bishop was his executioner. Regan held out his hand for the letter. Vosburg looked at him and back at the letter . . .

"That's not the only copy, Mr. Vosburg," Regan murmured. "Let me have it, please." Vosburg, looking like he was in shock, handed it over. Regan slipped it back into his desk drawer.

Larry licked his lips. "So you got a letter from Ruthie," he said in a quavery voice. "What do you think that proves? That Ruthie and I were lovers? We weren't!" He glanced at Di, whose eyes were burning holes in him.

"Why don't you return to your seat, Mr. Vosburg?" Regan said. "We need to talk about this, and I dislike craning my neck." He waited for Larry to return to the couch. Diane's suspicious eyes went back and forth between the two men.

"Whether you," Regan said, "and Mrs. Benedict were lovers may be a question of semantics. But you were the father of her aborted fetus. This seems to make that clear, don't you agree?" Larry stared, and then gave a tiny nod. I looked at Parker. He appeared interested, not puzzled.

At that moment I mentally started writing my letter of resignation. Reason for quitting: total incompetence and stupidity. At least four people in the room had seen the unfinished letter. And I was the only one who didn't get it. And I'd read it four times. I shook my head. *How* did it show Larry was Ruthie's lover? And father of her aborted child?

I tried to remember exactly what it said. Ruthie had apologized for lying. And that was all of it—wasn't it? It didn't even mention Larry, I was sure of that. What did Regan—and Larry and Parker— see in it that I couldn't see? I was obviously a total incompetent fool, and had no business being a detective.

Meanwhile, my feeble mind was also absorbing what was going on around me. Di was glaring at her fiancé (now ex-fiancé?) and saying, "This is despicable, Larry! You got Ruthie pregnant while you were engaged to me?"

Larry didn't know what to do with his eyes. He seemed to be trying to look everywhere but at Diane. He bowed his head and said, in a low voice, "All right."

Finally he looked up and turned his eyes to her. He blanched when he saw the look she gave him. "Diane, you know Ruthie and I were friends. It happened *once! One time!* Rotten luck it got her pregnant. God! We couldn't believe it! Naturally, we didn't want it. So we talked and we both agreed to just—terminate it. The pregnancy, I mean."

His voice got very sincere. "It had nothing to do with you and me, Di. Nothing. It was just something that happened one night when—"

"You son of a bitch!" Healy jumped to his feet and headed for him. I started to get up, but Parker was already handling it. Joe's big and he can move, especially when he's had some warning. He was on his feet a split second after Healy, got his own chest against Healy's, muttered "No, you don't," moved Healy back across the room and forced him into his chair. Then gave him a friendly smile. "You don't want to do this. No fighting in the Bishop's house, okay? Wouldn't be proper."

Healy glared past him at the golf pro, who was as pale as the father was red-faced. "I thought it was *Laddie*, you chicken-livered piece a—"

"Mr. Healy!" Regan's voice cut through. "Please let us finish. We are very close to identifying the murderer of your daughter. Surely that's more important than bloodying Mr. Vosburg's nose. If you'll be seated, Mr. Parker? Thank you for your intervention. I have a few more things to say to Mr. Vosburg, and I'd prefer that everyone sit down."

Healy didn't shift his blazing eyes from Larry. Joe went back to the couch and sat.

"So you *were* Mrs. Benedict's lover, Mr. Vosburg," Regan resumed. "You acknowledge that."

"Not if you mean—"

Regan showed him a palm. "I'm not implying a long relationship, sir. But you fathered a child with her. Or, if you prefer, a fetus, a fetus who was never given the opportunity to become a child. You do acknowledge that?"

Vosburg gulped. "It was a mistake. It just happened." He gave Regan a bitter look. "I don't see why you have to bring it up here." He looked tenderly at Diane, but she ignored him. She was keeping her eyes on Regan.

"I had to bring it up, sir, because it's crucial to my understanding of the case. It was an essential part of your motivation in killing your friend, Ladd Compton. And your other friend, Mary Ruth Healy."

53

FUNNY HOW YOUR MIND works in times of stress. Mine, for instance. I'd been listening and watching while Regan talked. When things moved in Vosburg's direction, I'd started focusing on him. I'd got sidetracked for a few seconds on my resignation letter, but soon went back to planning what to do if and when the pro got nailed for it.

Now with Regan almost literally pointing at Larry, I started planning what to do if Larry tried something. And realized Regan was ahead of me again. Larry was wedged in between Kessler and Parker. Another thing Regan had obviously talked over with them when he sent me to the kitchen. *Nice move, fellas.* Parker had everything under control. His eyes were glued on Vosburg and both hands were ready if needed.

And a good thing too. Beyond being a little pale, the pro didn't look a bit nervous. And his voice was firm as he answered the Bishop. "Oh, so that's it! You think *I* killed them. Well, I didn't."

Regan nodded. "Oh yes, you did, Mr. Vosburg." Without taking his eyes off the suspect, the Bishop threw his next question at Kessler. "Shouldn't you advise him of his rights, Inspector?"

"I was just about to make the same observation, Bishop," Kessler grumbled. "You're not making my job any easier."

"I'm sorry," Regan said. "How can I help?"

"You can't. You're sitting here accusing a man of murder. And I'm present. *Two* policemen are present. The law says he's got certain rights—and if I arrest him, I've got to notify him of those rights. But I don't have a damn thing beyond your accusations

to arrest him on. It would have been nice if you'd seen fit to talk
this over with me before you got started."

"I'm sorry," Regan said, not sounding like it. "What do you
suggest?"

Kessler scowled. "Oh, go ahead. Get on with it. But we're going
to advise him of his rights." He looked past Vosburg at Parker.
"Go ahead, Sergeant. Mirandize him."

Parker was already turned toward Larry, who must have been
feeling pretty hemmed in. "It is my duty to inform you, sir, you
are now a suspect in a case or cases of homicide..." He went
on with the standard warning. It sounded like he'd been rehears-
ing it ever since I got back from the kitchen.

"You have the right to remain silent. If you choose not to
remain silent, anything you say can and will..."

Vosburg waited through it patiently, not interrupting, a small
smile on his lips. He looked more at ease than any murderer I'd
ever seen. I threw Regan a nervous glance, but he was as calm
as Larry.

When Parker finished, with the standard offer to furnish Larry
an attorney if he didn't have one, Larry, smile still in place, shook
his head. "I don't need an attorney, Sergeant." He looked at
Regan. "Though before we're done, the Bishop may."

His chin jutted forward. "You obviously don't know much
about the case, Bishop. Aside from the fact that Laddie was my
closest friend in the world, Goldman has met people in my apartment building who'll swear that I was at home before, during
and after the time Laddie was killed. Or do you think I *ordered*
it done?"

Regan shook his head. "No, you did it yourself. And very
cleverly. You went to great lengths to establish what you thought
was an impregnable alibi. As you'll see, it was much more preg-
nable than you imagined."

He took a breath. "But at the moment we're discussing motive.
You admit that it was you who impregnated Mrs. Benedict. Yes?"

"I'm admitting nothing."

"Come, come, Mr. Vosburg. You have just told your fiancée
and eight other witnesses that you were the father."

Vosburg was beginning to look trapped. "All right. You forced
that out of me." He was no longer looking at Di. He seemed to

have realized he had a deeper hole to dig himself out of.

"And," Regan went on, relentless now, "it was you who advised Mrs. Benedict to have an abortion."

Vosburg gave that some thought. "Well, it was really her idea. I only—"

"You're a liar!" Ruthie's dad was on his feet again but this time not moving in Larry's direction. "Ruthie wouldn't never of killed her own baby. Never!"

Larry looked at him. "It was hard, Mr. Healy. On both of us. But we agreed it was the right thing to do. She was as much in favor of it as I was. I only—"

Healy blurted something and Larry raised his voice, but Regan cut them both off. "Please! Gentlemen! This is not *ad rem*." They couldn't argue with *that*. He looked at Healy. "I'm inclined to agree with your opinion about your daughter, Mr. Healy, having met her. But only she and Mr. Vosburg knew the truth and, since he did away with her, only he knows. So let it pass. The self-serving assertions of a murderer will not harm your daughter's reputation."

His eyes returned to Larry. "You admit, Mr. Vosburg, you did at least share in the decision to abort." Larry, sullen now, shrugged.

"But you had a problem, didn't you, sir? Because Mrs. Benedict had told someone else. Hadn't she, Mr. Vosburg?" Larry just looked at him, defiant. Regan sighed.

"Mr. Healy. You knew about the abortion, didn't you?" The big man nodded. "Who else knew, sir?"

Healy stared at him. "What do you mean, Bishop? Who else knew, you mean, besides me and Mary Ruth?" Regan nodded. Healy scratched his head. "I dunno."

"Of course you do, Mr. Healy. You told Mr. Goldman you knew who the father was. And who advised your daughter to abort. And it wasn't Mr. Vosburg."

"No. You're right. I thought it was Laddie."

"Ladd Compton." Regan said the name and paused. The words seemed to resound through the big office. "And he hadn't learned it from you, had he, Mr. Healy?" Healy shook his head. "He learned from his confidante, Mrs. Benedict. And, of course, she also told him who the father was. Isn't that right, Mr. Vosburg?"

Larry's face twitched. He had a big problem. Parker now had a notebook out. (He'd warned Larry he might "take down" his words, and by gum, he was doing it.) And Larry'd waived his right to a lawyer's advice. He was trying to wing it, but the noose was getting tighter. And the question Regan had just asked was nearly impossible to answer. If he said, "No, Laddie didn't know," he was facing the follow-up question, "How do you *know* that he didn't?" But if he admitted that Laddie *had* known, he was granting Regan's thesis. Which was—what? I still didn't see the motive.

Larry finally handled it the best way he could. "I don't know," he said. "How would *I* know what Ruthie might or might not have told Laddie? All I can tell you is he never talked about it with *me*."

He was lying, I knew. And with the realization that he was lying, I saw the motive. As Regan immediately confirmed.

"Oh, but he did, Mr. Vosburg. He did. To his—and now your—great misfortune. He was outraged, wasn't he? He forced you to cancel your wedding plans with Ms. Compton. As the protective older brother, he threatened to expose you to his sister unless you cancelled the wedding."

Diane's eyes were wide. Her head swiveled from Larry to Regan. "But he *didn't* cancel. We were still engaged when Laddie died!"

"Oh? When is the wedding scheduled?"

Diane frowned. "It was originally scheduled for this May. Then Larry wanted to postpone. We finally agreed to stay engaged and get married sometime next year."

She turned to her mother. "Mom, when did we start talking about a fall wedding?"

Hilarie closed her eyes, opened them. She answered her daughter's question but addressed it to the Bishop. "It was last week," she told him with a positive nod. "The day after Ladd's funeral. Larry said Laddie's death had made him realize how much he needed my daughter. He wanted to have a fall wedding."

Regan turned back to Di. "So. Till late February, the wedding was scheduled for May. In February, Mr. Vosburg became apprehensive. From that moment till your brother's death, on March twenty-fifth, there was no definite date. And then a day or two after your brother's death, Mr. Vosburg was suddenly willing to make the date definite again. Is that right?"

Di's voice was wondering. "That's right."

Regan's eyes found Kessler. "*That* was his motive, Inspector. Mr. Vosburg wanted to be rich. Every day at the Williamsport Golf & Country Club he came into contact with men of wealth, position, power—none of which he had and all of which he wanted. So he made a decision. He 'made a play,' as they say, for Ms. Compton. His plan was working beautifully until he—"

"Couldn't keep his hand out of the cookie jar!" Healy turned in his chair to glare at Vosburg. "I warned Mary Ruth about him. He was always the best athlete, most popular, everybody's buddy. Had to have everything his way."

Dolph suddenly jumped to his feet and faced Vosburg. Parker started to get up, probably thinking he was going to have to protect his prisoner from yet another angry father. But Compton didn't move. Just looked Larry in the eye. "Is all this true, Larry? I wish to God you'd tell me it's not! I wish you'd tell me you didn't kill our son." His voice broke on the word *son* and he put his hand on his wife's shoulder. Hilarie, head bowed, reached up for her husband's arm.

Larry struggled to get up, but Parker held him down with a firm hand on his shoulder. Larry didn't take his eyes off Dolph, but he stopped struggling.

"I didn't, Dolph, I swear!" he said. He threw Regan a venomous look. "I don't know what this guy's trying to pull, but I don't know anything about this! God! I was home all that evening! You can talk to my neighbors. *All* of them!"

Compton sat down and faced Regan. "I've got to tell you, Bishop, I've known this boy a lot longer than you have. And I'm telling you, I think you're wrong. I believe him. A gangster named Goode killed my son, and Jerry's daughter died in an accident." He swung around. "Isn't that right, Inspector?"

Kessler looked from Regan to Compton, nervously stroking his beard. I knew what he was thinking: *I wish I had my pipe.* "Umm, yes, the evidence shows, and I'm personally convinced, that Eddie Goode killed your son, Mr. Compton. As I've said before. But let's let the Bishop have his head a while longer. If, as I suspect, this turns out to be nothing, we'll—"

"Then I'm leaving!" Larry said, slithering from under Parker's paw and making it to his feet. He headed for the door. Parker and I looked at each other, then at our respective employers, both thinking the same thing. *What do I do now, boss?*

54

BUT PARKER AND I—and our bosses, for that matter—turned out to be irrelevant, immaterial and unnecessary. What stopped our major guest from being a party pooper was Diane. "Larry!" She didn't say it loud, but she got results.

The pro, already in the doorway, stopped dead in his tracks. She waited for him to face her. "You walk out of here and we're through!" He stopped. "Look at me!" He faced her. "Did you kill my brother? Did you?"

Larry, pale and shaking, looked her straight in the eye. "Diane, I absolutely did not. It's all a lie."

Diane met his gaze. "Then *stay*, Larry. Don't run away."

Larry's eyes flicked around the room. Very briefly. I had a pretty good idea what was going through his head. First: stay or go? He resolved that one quickly: stay. Then: where to sit? Back on the couch, between two cops? Not good, but what alternative did he have? "I wasn't running away, Diane," he muttered, moving back to the couch.

Seated again, he looked Regan in the eye. "The Pope may be infallible, but you're not. You're dead wrong. If you really think I did this, you're dreaming."

He switched back to his fiancée. "Okay, Di, I was out of line with Ruthie. But it was a one-time thing. Remember, Ruthie and I go back a lot of years. And I—I let it get out of hand, okay? Then I just couldn't tell you. I'll always be sorry for that." Her eyes softened.

Back to Regan. "But to say that I killed Laddie, well, that's ludicrous. I *loved* Laddie! He was my closest friend!" He looked around. "You all know that!"

"Your closest friend?" said Healy with a murderous look. "He protected you, you scumbag! By letting me think he was Ruthie's lover. And then you killed him!"

"No!" It was a shout. "No! I didn't kill him! How many ways do I have to say it!" He turned to Regan. "Look, Bishop. Be reasonable. You still haven't explained how I could have done— that—when every one of my neighbors knows I was in my apartment when it happened. My God, my *cough* kept them awake if nothing else! They even complained about it!"

"Indeed they did." Without taking his eyes off Vosburg, Regan said, "Mr. Kelley. Tell Mr. Vosburg and the others what you learned today."

Kelley nodded. His cold, shrewd eyes, out of place in that round, friendly face, surveyed the audience. "The Bishop hired me this morning. He sent me to the Grove Apartments in Union Grove. He said he suspected a man named Larry Vosburg of having murdered Mr. Compton but that the guy had an airtight alibi. I was to find some holes in it."

"Inelegant but accurate," Regan murmured. "Go on."

Kelley blushed. "I contacted a guy in the building named Keith Price. A friend of Vosburg's."

Kelley glanced my way. "You needed someone besides Davey to talk to the guy, since Davey was already known to him. You figured he might talk more freely to a stranger."

Regan's eyes were closed. "And did he?"

"Oh, yeah. I told him I was interested in electronics and gadgetry. Told him I'd heard Vosburg had a fantastic stereo system, that I'd tried buzzing Larry but he wasn't home. We got friendly real quick."

"He offer you a beer?" I asked.

Kelley grinned at me. "A couple. I practically had to pull a gun on him to stop him from bringing more." He dropped the grin and turned back to Regan. "Anyway, Bishop, I got him talking and, like you suspected, Vosburg's got all the toys he needed for his alibi."

Vosburg interrupted again. "This is so much balon—"

But Kessler was getting interested. "Just let him talk, sir. You'll get your innings soon enough." He turned back to Kelley. "What toys?"

Kelley began ticking them off on his fingers. "First of all, his phone has call forwarding. That can be verified with the phone company, but Price was positive. Second, he's got a top-notch tape-to-tape sound system. Third, he's got a VCR with a timer. Fourth, he's got at least two other digital timers, expensive ones, accurate to the second."

"Big deal," Vosburg muttered. "I like gadgets. So sue me."

Kessler, puzzled and irritated, seemed to agree. "Yeah. What the hell does all this have to do with anything? You can't—"

"Let me explain, Inspector," Regan murmured. "Mr. Goldman visited Mr. Vosburg's apartment two days ago. I was struck by what Mr. Goldman called his 'entertainment center.' Especially the audiotape equipment. I was also struck by the fact that none of his neighbors actually *saw* Mr. Vosburg that evening till after nine-thirty. They heard his television; they heard him cough; they spoke to him on the phone; but no one saw him. As the second motive surfaced, I was led to wonder whether he could have arranged for all of those contacts beforehand and been elsewhere during the time he was 'heard.' "

In the silence that followed I could almost hear the wheels turning in Vosburg's skull. His eyes flicked from Regan to Kessler and back to Regan. "I suggest, Inspector," Regan said, "that you obtain a search warrant for Mr. Vosburg's apartment. Unless he's erased it, you should find a tape containing the sound of coughing."

Larry exploded and pointed a finger at Kelley. "You're a liar!" He looked at Regan. "And you too!" Back to Dennis. "You broke into my apartment, didn't you?"

"Mr. Kelley," snapped Regan. "Did you force your way into Mr. Vosburg's apartment?"

"No, sir." Kelley was positive. "I understand he's got deadbolts on the door. You couldn't get in there without a key."

Larry turned to Kessler. "Okay, yes, there's a tape like that. I was transferring some CDs onto tape the other night and forgot and let the tape run. I later discovered it'd picked up my coughing. But these guys are lying; the only way the Bishop could know I've got a tape with coughing on it is if his man broke in. And that's illegal. You can't use the tape."

Kelley shrugged. "If I broke in, there'd be plenty of evidence of it. I—"

Vosburg waved it away. "It doesn't even matter. I never went anywhere that night. The neighbors'll all tell you my car stayed put."

Regan was calm. "So they will, Mr. Vosburg. So they already have. Your Chevrolet did not move from its appointed slot while you were murdering Mr. Compton. You used another mode of transportation. I didn't expect to discover what it was, but Mr. Kelley proved equal to the task. Mr. Kelley?"

"Yeah. After leaving the Prices I made some calls. I checked the major car rental agencies, both at the airport and in the city. Through a couple of contacts I have, I got lucky." He smiled lazily. "National Rent-A-Car at LaGuardia..." As Dennis named the agency Larry's eyes shut tight. All the blood seemed to run out of his face.

Dennis was watching Vosburg too, so he saw his reaction, but he went right on. "...shows a subcompact Fiesta rented to a Laurence A. Vosburg on Sunday, March twenty-fifth, at seven-twelve P.M., returned Monday at twelve-twenty-nine P.M. Ran up fifty-one miles. Party declined the extra insurance coverage. Charge was twenty-eight dollars and sixty-seven cents for one day at the weekend rate. Paid with Visa. Gold card."

The Bishop took over, eyes on Kessler. "The crime itself was deftly done, Inspector. Mr. Vosburg had observed the Comptons' second-floor alcove in the bay window over the front door, as well as the matching one across the street. Here's the sequence as I envision it." He glanced at Vosburg. "I invite you to correct me, sir, if I err in any detail." Vosburg didn't return the look. His eyes were on the door—longingly.

Regan leaned back. "When Mrs. Benedict told Ladd Compton of her dalliance with Mr. Vosburg and the resulting pregnancy, Ladd Compton was undoubtedly horrified. He went to Mr. Vosburg, insisting he call off the wedding. A spirited discussion no doubt ensued, but Mr. Compton was adamant: friend or no, Vosburg was not to marry Ms. Compton and that was final. At least not without confessing to her the entire sordid affair."

Regan looked around. "I suspect Mr. Vosburg agreed to terminate the relationship with Ms. Compton, but begged for time to 'break it' to her. He then effectively broke it off by postponing it indefinitely. I have no doubt he told Ladd this was the kinder, gentler way to do it. But while telling him this, he set in motion plans to destroy Ladd Compton."

Regan sighed. With his usual pacing lanes blocked by all the visitors, he must have felt hemmed in. But he jerked his chair to the side, looked at Vosburg and continued. "You first asked Mrs. Benedict for names of her underworld connections, didn't you? You needed a known criminal for a sacrificial lamb. All unknowing, Mrs. Benedict delivered over to you petty thief Eddie Goode. At your urging, Mrs. Benedict then staged a phony suicide attempt, the entire purpose of which was to get Mr. Goode's fingerprints onto the prospective murder weapon. I suspect Mrs. Benedict, with her underworld connections, also provided the gun—unaware of its ultimate purpose.

"You then masterminded the plot to steal Mrs. Compton's jewels. You started by convincing Ladd that it was the only way to save the family business. You then gave him Goode's name and address, and the plot was set in motion.

"All was in readiness. You met your victim that fatal evening and accompanied him to his parents' home. You knew that Mr. Healy would be home. Ladd's assignment was to occupy him while the robbery took place. Meanwhile, you had set the necessary timers in your apartment to mislead your neighbors. And forwarded your calls to the Comptons' residence.

"Once there, you established a command post in the second-floor alcove overlooking the street where you could own the high ground: able to observe all around you while remaining yourself invisible."

Vosburg shook his head. "Neat story, Bishop."

"Tragic," Regan corrected. He took a breath. "You had told Mr. Compton you'd call him on Mr. Healy's private line upon Eddie Goode's arrival and departure. You also received at least one forwarded call during your time in the alcove, that being the wake-up call from Mr. Price.

"During the interval from nine o'clock to nine-fifteen it was essential that Mr. Healy be preoccupied with—"

Kessler interrupted. "Wait a minute! Something just hit me."
He glared at Healy. "Is all this true what he's saying about Ladd
Compton being in your room while the robbery was going on? I
thought you were in that bar across the street all evening."

Healy couldn't meet his eyes. "I—uh, yeah, it's true."

Kessler was outraged. "Why didn't you come forward? You
were the last one to see the man alive."

Healy shook his head helplessly and looked away.

Kessler looked at Regan. "How long have you known this,
Bishop? Why wasn't I told?"

I spoke up. "Hey, Inspector, I talked to Healy, he told me, I
told the Bish. What's the big deal? You'd already interviewed
the guy, and he assured me he hadn't lied to you. How was I to
know you'd asked all the wrong questions?"

Kessler refused to look at me. "Go ahead, Bishop," he said.
"Talk! Anything to shut Davey up."

Regan went on. "But the telephone at his elbow was too valuable a resource to use merely to notify his confederate of Goode's
arrival and departure times. And to take forwarded calls. He had
noticed, when visiting the Comptons, the idiosyncrasies of the
two sisters across the street, the Misses Lake. Obtaining their
unlisted phone number, known as it was by the Comptons, was
child's play.

"He knew that one of the Lake sisters took great interest in
the comings and goings of the neighbors. He had also discovered that the only phone in that house was in the bay window,
with its unobstructed view of the street and the Comptons'
front door.

"So the moment he saw Goode approaching the house, he
called the Lake residence, letting it ring till a sister was at the
window and thus ensuring that she would see Eddie Goode.

"As Goode departed with the jewels, Mr. Vosburg, in perfect
position to see but not be seen, phoned Miss Lake and Ladd
Compton again. And—"

Dolph spoke up. "But Goode would've heard him! Sound carries all through that hallway. That's why that phone's so im-
practical and we hardly ever use it—the acoustics in the mansion
won't let you have a private conversation there."

Regan met his eyes and shook his head. "He didn't say a word,

Mr. Compton—not while Mr. Goode was in the house. All he needed do was place a call. How much noise is required to tap out a number on a push-button phone?"

Dolph shrugged and nodded. "So," Regan went on, "he was in perfect position not only to signal his partner but to ensure that a witness could identify Mr. Goode."

Regan looked at Kessler. "Mr. Goode departed, duly observed by the designated witness. Mr. Vosburg's co-conspirator and his victim sent away the house's only other occupant: Mr. Healy. The stage was set. Mr. Vosburg no doubt suggested to Mr. Compton that the two of them go to the bedroom, perhaps to be sure that Eddie Goode had done his job correctly. While Mr. Compton opened the safe, his friend put the gun to the back of his head. And eliminated forever what he saw as the one obstacle to his marrying into wealth.

"He had but one more self-appointed task to perform before fleeing in the rental car back to Union Grove. He made one more call, a final support for his alibi: to Mr. Price in Union Grove. Excuse for calling: faulty television reception; could Mr. Price suggest a remedy? Mr. Price could and did."

Regan shrugged. "All that remained was to get out of the house, into his rental car, and drive as quickly as possible back to the suburbs. He hurried to his apartment and had no sooner released the call-forwarding than the phone rang. It was Ms. Porterfield next door, complaining about his coughing. He apologized and told her he had left the phone turned off a few minutes. He then called Mr. Price and asked him to come check the television— the oral instructions hadn't solved the problem. While his neighbor made his way down, Mr. Vosburg quickly changed into pajamas, turned off the sound system and returned the apartment to its proper appearance. He had perpetrated the perf—watch out!"

His warning was a split second late. Vosburg was quicker than Regan or I—or, most importantly, Parker—had given him credit for.

As Regan approached the end of his speech, Vosburg must have been gathering his feet under him and making plans. He waited for a time when no one—especially Parker—was paying attention. When that happened, he made his move.

On the words, "had perpetrated," Larry sucker-punched Parker right below the left ear and was on his feet running for the front door. He was in the hall before anyone moved. Parker was semiconscious and Kessler's no spring chicken, which left Kelley and me. We went on the jump, hard as we could, but Vosburg would have been gone—except for Ernie. I burst into the hallway, Kelley breathing down my neck, to see Vosburg at the front door, struggling with the knob.

The door, as I soon discovered, was deadbolted, the key safe in the kitchen in Ernie's hot little hand. Whose idea it was, I'm still not clear on. Ernie says Regan told her to deadbolt it as soon as Kelley arrived and everyone was in the office. The Bishop denies it. I don't know who to believe. They're both tricky and underhanded. Typical Catholics.

Anyway, Larry was through fighting. We held him till Parker arrived, cursing himself and Vosburg in that order, and slapped the cuffs on him. Kessler phoned for back-up. Five minutes later a squad car arrived with a pair of uniforms. Vosburg, now attached via the cuffs to Parker, went quietly. He did have a final request: "Could I have just a minute with Diane?"

The Inspector started to stroke his beard, but Di took him off the hook. "No way," she said. "Get him out of here." I couldn't detect a glimmer of regret in her voice.

55

THE PARTY DIDN'T BREAK UP for nearly an hour after they hauled Vosburg away. Janine and Di huddled together for a while, comforting each other. Hilarie and Dolph soon joined them. After all four shed a few tears, they came at Regan with some questions, which he fielded graciously.

Healy accepted my peace offering: a cup of Irish coffee (heavy on the Irish). My impersonating an officer of the Knighthood was forgiven, if not the fact that I was a Jew.

At some point I managed to herd Dennis into my office for a chat. "I've got a question for you, buddy."

Kelley grinned at me, his eyes sly. "Go ahead and ask. I'm not saying I'll answer."

I nodded. "You know the question. Regan gave you a key, didn't he? And it was Vosburg's, wasn't it? You used it to get into Larry's apartment and found that tape."

Kelley's eyes narrowed. "How'd you know? Am I that easy to read?"

I shook my head. "Your story made sense to everyone but me. I'm the only one that knew the Bishop wanted Vosburg quarantined. I just realized why: so he wouldn't be there while you searched his apartment, right?" Kelley just shrugged, but I had my answer.

We finally managed to disperse the Compton entourage, but that still left Kessler and Kelley to contend with. Dennis preempted the couch and the Inspector plopped onto the chair in front of Regan's desk like he owned it. He looked Regan in the eye. "You still owe me something, Bishop."

Regan raised his eyebrows. "Oh?"

"Yeah, *oh*. The *letter*, Bishop. I want it. Hand it over." Regan looked puzzled. Kessler's voice took on some bite. "The one from Mrs. Benedict. Sorry if you've got a sentimental attachment to it, but—"

"No."

"No, you won't give it to me, or no, you're not sentimentally attached?"

"Neither. It's not evidence, it's not a letter and it's of no value to you."

Kessler exploded. "No value? I'll be the judge of that! If you think—" He took a breath and calmed down. "Look, Bishop. I'm not spoiling for a fight. But I'm not going to be shilly-shallied around with, either. Just hand it over, I'll give you a receipt and you can have it back after the trial. Or after Vosburg cops a plea. But I need that letter, and I'm not leaving without it."

"I'm afraid you have no choice, Inspector. You see, I have no letter from Mrs. Benedict." I blinked. What the hell was Regan pulling? Okay, so technically maybe it wasn't a letter, it was only half a letter. But he'd obviously got it from Parker at some point—presumably when I was in the kitchen with Ernie—so how could he think he didn't have to give it back?

Kessler's jaw was set. "Look, Bishop. You showed Vosburg *something*. And he immediately caved in. So I'm not going to argue with you. You give it to me, whatever it is, or you're coming downtown, wheelchair and all. I don't care if you are a bishop. You don't fool around with evidence."

Regan rubbed his face. Finally he sighed, reached into his desk drawer, and handed Kessler the paper. Kessler spent the next minute or two studying it, not seeming to mind Kelley reading over his shoulder. I'd have joined them but didn't have to; I had the photocopy I'd retrieved from my office when they took Larry away. So while Kessler and Kelley read, I did too:

Deer Biship.

You were darn nice to me & I lied to you & I want to apolagize. I was wrong not to trust you & I shouldn't of lied like that. Specially talking about my mothers grave. If Id of had the least idea that gun was the one that killed Laddie Id of never gone along with it. Im thru lying now

When the three of us finished reading, Kessler, jaw clenched, slapped the letter with his hand. "This isn't a letter from Mrs. Benedict? Isn't evidence? You nuts, Bishop? Hell, this nails Vosburg's hide to the wall! At least on the abortion. And the abortion's crucial!" Kelley gave a slight nod of agreement. I gawked at them. Dammit, why could everybody see it but me?

"It would indeed be evidence," Regan said calmly, "if Mrs. Benedict had written it. But she didn't."

I couldn't let that pass. "Didn't write it! The hell she didn't! The handwriting's exactly the same as—"

"Excuse me, David. I see you have the photocopy. You'd better see what the Inspector has. And let him see yours."

I stared at Regan for a second, then looked at Kessler. He didn't want to trade but finally agreed when I gave him my word of honor I wouldn't swallow or burn it. He and Kelley read the copy while I read the original.

Except it wasn't the original. The Kelly green ink was the same, and the swirly penmanship, and the spelling. But the contents were totally different:

Deer Biship.

I was wrong not to trust you. Larry first told me hed marry me but then he had excuses. Then he told me hed pay the doctors bill for the abortion but he didnt. But I still trusted him. (I know you think thats stupid but I still did.) Well I just talked to him and he said hed pay the bill. Were going to see the doctor. Ill tell you what happened tomorow.

> your friend Mary Ruth

I looked at Regan, stunned. "Where'd you get this?"
Regan shrugged. "From my imagination. I wrote it."
Kessler's eyes bugged. "You wrote—you *what*?"
Regan nodded. "I wrote it. I had no proof whatsoever that Mr. Vosburg was responsible for the abortion. But I was certain he was, so I—"
Kelley struggled to hold in a laugh. Lucky for him he succeeded; the Inspector was in no mood.
"It was a trick! You—" Kessler took a breath. He narrowed his eyes at Regan. "So this isn't evidence of a damn thing, is it? You know, this may destroy our case. You lied to Vosburg and—"
"Come, come, Inspector Kessler!" Regan's eyes twinkled. "A bishop lie? Never!" He got serious. "I told no lie, Inspector. I simply handed the paper to Mr. Vosburg and suggested he read it. I made no claims for it."
Kessler was still mad. "But it's a fake! What if he'd asked you some question about it? Like when did you get it? Or did Ruthie really write it?"
Regan was calm. "I wouldn't have lied."
Kessler nodded and suddenly let out a chuckle. Kelley started to chuckle with him but choked it back when Kessler quit as suddenly as he started. He'd thought of another question. "What would you have done if Vosburg'd seen through it?"
Regan winced. "That would have made it difficult, but the

hoped-for outcome justified the risk. I took great pains with it. Mrs. Benedict's penmanship was far more difficult to duplicate than I'd have imagined. All those flourishes! Spelling and style were child's play by comparison. As to its contents, I did some guessing. I agonized over whether Mr. Vosburg might have promised to pay for the abortion. I concluded that it was sufficiently likely. The event seems to have justified the decision."

Kessler and Kelley left together, the Inspector insisting that Dennis come downtown and give his statement before the day was over. Kelley wisely agreed.

As I held the door for Kessler, he grabbed my hand in a prolonged grip. But his look was threatening. "One of these days, Davey," he growled.

"Yeah? What's going to happen one of these days?"

He opened his mouth and closed it. He shook his head. "One of these days." He turned on his heel, walked down the steps, gave a small wave to Kelley, got in his Chevy and drove away. I don't suppose I'll ever know what he meant. At least till one of these days comes along.

EPILOG

YOU'VE GOT QUESTIONS, of course, and I'm happy to be able to answer them for you.

First of all, you're undoubtedly wondering whether Junior Benedict ever came after me with a knife or any other deadly weapon. I'm sure he would've, if circumstances had permitted, readiness to forgive and forget never having been one of Junior's outstanding characteristics. Luckily, circumstances didn't permit. A big intra-family squabble resulted from his uncle's death, Junior being among the chief squabblers, and he expired rather suddenly one day when a stick of dynamite someone had carelessly attached to his car engine exploded while he was in the car. The careless individual was never identified. Don't look at me; I had nothing to do with it beyond breathing a sigh of relief when I got the word.

More importantly, I'm sure you're dying to know whether the Vosburg Grip led to my resurrection as a golfer and subsequent emergence as one of the top stars on the pro tour. For a couple of months it looked like I had a shot. In one glorious round during the Memorial Day weekend—the only time I've ever broken ninety—I even took some dough off Rozanski. That had never happened before and probably never will again. Immediately following that round I went to Kirschbaum's, bought one of their fine angel-food cakes and took it straight to Larry on Riker's Island. No, I didn't, but the thought did cross my mind.

After the verdict came down—life for killing Ladd, ten to twenty for Ruthie—and Larry went to prison, my golf game promptly reverted to its old, rotten ways. A valuable lesson there: golf tips from a murderer don't hold up. Something to keep in mind.

The final surprise in the Compton case didn't come for a couple of years, by which time, as far as I was concerned, it was strictly ancient history. One day, just the same way it started, Davis Baker showed up at the mansion, wanting to see both the Bishop and me. Only this time Eddie Goode was with him.

I opened the door, greeted Dave and looked at Eddie. It took me a couple of seconds to recognize him. His hair was nearly white. And he'd decided to grow back the mustache.

Baker was embarrassed. "I, uh—Eddie and I have something to say to the Bishop. And you."

I let them in. Goode couldn't look me in the eye. He started a smile and a sentence, but something in my expression stopped him. Baker made some nervous conversation, something about our last golf game, at which he and I had both had our pockets picked by Rozanski. The lawyer looked pale, even paler than Eddie with his prison pallor, which I found strange.

I went into Regan's office and announced our visitors; he told me to bring them in. As they walked in, he looked up over the reading glasses, studied Baker, then Goode. "Have a seat, gentlemen," he murmured, flipping his glasses onto the desk.

After everyone sat, an uncomfortable silence settled in. Baker finally spoke. "Eddie and I have something to tell you, Bishop." He looked at the ex-con.

Goode cleared his throat. He wasn't finding Regan's eyes any easier to meet than mine. "Uh, right." He cleared his throat again. "Uh, I just got sprung yesterday, Bishop. I was doing a six-to-ten for stealing the jewels, but I got credit for time served in jail on that murder thing, and then time off for good behavior. And the parole board, uh... Anyway, I'm out. And I'm gonna stay straight this time, Bishop." He finally met the Bishop's frosty eyes.

"If you're here to express your gratitude," Regan answered, "it's quite unnecessary, sir."

Eddie flushed and Baker jumped in. "No, Bishop. That's not why we're here. Our letter of thanks—the one we wrote back when it all happened—said that as well as either of us could say it. Umm. No, what it is, we both have a confession to make. And an apology." The lawyer threw a glance my way. "To both of you. We... " He looked down. The silence grew. Eddie broke it.

"It's hard for him to say it, Bishop. It's not so hard for me." He grinned. "Since I'm a born liar, confessin' to tellin' a lie's easy for me."

I was interested. Confess to lying? I flashed back to the Compton case; if Baker and Goode had lied, what about? Vosburg had maintained his innocence right up to the day of the verdict. Could he have been innocent all along?

Baker read my mind. "No, it's not what you're thinking, Davey. You nailed the right guy."

Regan's tone was glacial. "We didn't 'nail' anyone, Mr. Baker. We pointed out certain facts to Inspector Kessler. Those facts led him to Mr. Vosburg. If you are now saying that Mr. Goode was an accessory to that crime, I certainly need not point out to you, an attorney, that there is no statute of limitations on murder. What you're—"

"No," Baker cut in. "That wasn't the lie." His face turned even redder. "It was that hypnosis thing."

I stared at him. "What—"

"Let me," Eddie interrupted. "See, Bishop, we figured—or at least Mr. Baker figured—you were the only guy that could dope out how my prints got on the gun. And we knew you hated me for what I—"

"Please, Eddie!" Baker was now doubly embarrassed. "The Bishop doesn't hate you." He glanced at the Bishop. "It was just that you had no *reason* to help, Bishop. And I was convinced you were our only hope. I needed someone to figure out how Eddie's prints could have gotten onto that automatic. So—"

"So that entire rigmarole with the hypnotist was faked." Regan's tone was flat, his eyes unreadable.

Baker nodded, looking at his shoes. "Oh, we tried hypnosis, all right, hoping to get Eddie to remember when he'd touched the gun. With a real hypnotist. Eddie turned out to be a lousy subject. Some people just can't be hypnotized. But seeing the way the hypnotist worked gave me the idea for what we did.

"I wrote the script myself. 'Maurice Highland' was just an out-of-work actor who needed the bread. He and Eddie did three run-throughs for me, then I taped it. I was only hoping you might—"

"You were hoping I might be fooled by it and help? I wasn't fooled in the least." Regan looked smug.

Baker stared. So did Goode. In fact, so did I. Baker asked the question all three of us had to be thinking. "You knew? How?"

"You should have done a better job of homework, Mr. Baker," Regan murmured. "The introductory comments by the 'hypnotist' were authentic as far as they went. But no hypnotist would have permitted himself to be taped without a disclaimer regarding the value—rather the lack of value—of what he was doing. Hypnosis is useful for one purpose only: to dredge from the unconscious that which the conscious mind has suppressed. Though amused by the man's performance, I was struck by the lack of any disclaimer."

Regan sighed. "To confirm my suspicions I asked you about the hypnotist's credentials. You flubbed the answer, claiming you neither knew nor cared. Hardly the performance of an experienced and accomplished trial lawyer."

Goode blurted, "But if you knew, why did you help? Weren't you pissed that we lied to you?"

"Why should I be, Mr. Goode? You were fighting for your freedom in the only way you knew—underhandedly. And your lawyer was assisting with all the resources at his command. I respected that."

"But why?" said Baker. "Why would you help him if you knew it was all a scam?"

Regan sighed. "You may find it difficult to understand, Mr. Baker, but I wanted revenge. And I got it."

"You got it?" Eddie was startled. "How?"

Regan studied him. "You now owe me, Mr. Goode. Believe me, I know what it is to owe. Eight years ago, when you shot me, I'd have died had a police officer not intervened and saved my life. I can never forget it. I must endure his many piques, character flaws and personal idiosyncrasies."

(Later, Regan and I had a long heart-to-heart about that comment. He ended the discussion thusly: "Now you know what it is to be a constant target of a fusillade of persiflage." I'm not in the habit of responding to that kind of scurrilous attack, at least till I find out what it means. By the time I looked up *fusillade* and *persiflage*, I'd lost my edge.)

Meanwhile the Bishop continued, eyes on Eddie. "When Mr. Baker came, appealing for assistance in your defense, I refused. Why should I help you regain your freedom when you had cost me mine? But as I sat watching that trumped-up hypnotic 'trance,' I was touched by a flash of inspiration. My hatred could never touch you—only forgiveness could."

The Bishop looked down. "The only way I could avenge what you did to me was to help you. If I could somehow rescue you from your predicament, perhaps I could touch you, make you feel the agony you had put me through. And I did."

Goode started to say something, but Regan wasn't finished. "I take some satisfaction, Mr. Goode, in knowing that you know. You owe me, do you not? Your very freedom. That's a debt you'll never be able to repay.

"Oh, you may not acknowledge it. It doesn't matter. Acknowledge it or not, I know it and you know it. It's a debt you'll carry to your grave."

Regan continued to hold him with his eyes. "How does it feel, sir, to have burning coals poured out upon your head?"

Eddie looked at Baker, at me, back at the Bishop. He was totally confused. His scalp was on fire and he didn't even know it.